MW01223913

frozenassets

by
George E Skelton

authorHOUSE®

AuthorHouse™
1663 Liberty Drive, Suite 200
Bloomington, IN 47403
www.authorhouse.com
Phone: 1-800-839-8640

First published by AuthorHouse   12/26/2007

ISBN: 978-1-4343-2173-2 (sc)

Library of Congress Control Number: 2007906775

Printed in the United States of America
Bloomington, Indiana

This book is printed on acid-free paper.

By the end of the 24th century, human rule by incompetence had been replaced by a humane Cyber governance.
It was a start.

But it was six centuries after that, three 21st century 'survivors' came to learn that longevity had become a final triumph over all mankinds' frailties and inadequacies.

With thanks for the inspiration and imaginative genius of Arthur C. Clarke.
This conception of a distant future is dedicated to some of those
who will contribute to the beginning of that future;
grandchildren, Quinn, Emily, Paul.

Preface

The state of humanity, now and beyond

Aristocrats exert power over the lives of ordinary people leaving infinitesimally little of earth's riches to share with a global majority. Result... Futility. Dissention. Hopelessness.

Power bloated politicians persist in offering up constituents as fodder to genocide and poverty, condoning life's imbalances where the wealthy garner more – the poor accept less.

Evangelical demagoguery, predicated on ancient parables, false icons and inherent fears, limits faith in oneself, just as does equally, self-deprecating religious or militancy dogmas.

When governing powers lack the courage to yield up their privileged positions to impose hard decisions to save earth from *eco extinction,* common mans' futures are sacrificed.

* * *

Back in the 21ˢᵗ century, one deep thinker, Sir Jeffery Cairns, had foreseen a means whereby our species could be convinced to co-exist with all other societies on earth.

Recovered from the Atlantic in 3132 AD, at Reykjavik, Cairn's 1000 year old spheroid is breached by an advanced humanity who will rejoice in solutions for a new age renaissance.

From the frigid corridors of an orbicular tomb, renowned scientists are staggered by the miracles of functioning remains of *preserved* citizens from a long gone era.

Enlightened by evidence of the species' resiliency, 32nd century citizens are in awe of a phenomenal exhibition of human durability...inherent in the marvel that is man.

frozenassets chronology

Addendum; Reunion

"We have been here a little too long at this depth."

MAURICE BENNIE BENNAUVILLE self-admonishes both his penchant for detail and for paying less heed to the time it takes. But now, he is satisfied with the job done at the concrete-filled drill stem at dry hole 22-64-B well head. It was intended to serve as an immoveable anchor to the spherical vault he had hoped would, some day, be found by his descendents. The pain in his stomach and lower lung area is becoming something more than tolerable. Twisting backward, he stretches the flexible joints of his roll-cushioned diving suit, to look up through one of the helmet's triple-windowed face plate. Through icy cold and colorless water, he can now just barely see his diving partner kicking up towards the steel holding platform, lowered to the 250-meter level. This conveyance will take them both to the surface. With a grimace, he too kicks off out of the silt fog. Now, he speaks into his helmet phone.

"Bonjour skipper – we're finished here. All is ready for the next team with their welding kit equipment. And the rest of your crew can unwrap the sphere's anchor chain now. Have them start to play it out as we clear the area coming up. See you in a couple hours, mon amie."

Bennie made sure that his groan of discomfort was not heard through the mike, by the time he had to clamber onto the platform. The weight of his dive helmet seemed extra heavy. This sign of weakness was now mentally bothersome. He just hoped that what might be an indication of embolism, would hold off until he reached the tugboat on top. "Without treatment", he thought, "this could be my last dive – into anything more than a hot bath!"

Some men, like Bennie, seem to know more about their mortality than they let on.

Ten Centuries of Rebirthing Pains

Chapter 1

Generations Apart Schoolboys Plan
Centuries Apart Get Together!

2034/21ST Century – Oxford, England

MARCH 31, 2034 -. Now into his second university year, Physical Engineering Sciences, sophomore Lorne Harris Jr. hunches over open textbooks. But he does not digest the text. From time to time, his mind is taking a holiday from study, to reflect on other reflections. It is just after 9pm. Under a green-shielded table lamp in Oxford's University study hall B3, he mindlessly scribbles exercise equations into his reference note pad. Next to him, also prepping for pre-holiday, three quarter term exams, sit three other students, one of whom is Harris's roommate from their dormitory. Back home, in his first university year at Ryerson, he had learned the priorities of 'exam cram'. For him, it was not the dry mouth, sweaty palms, frosh experience it once was. Still, he mused, studying for the "big leagues" seemed an over taxing exercise. Moreover, having come this far, he was determined to make this special educational opportunity pay off. He had pulled every string to gain entrance to Oxford, the English flagship of practical academia. His entrance qualifications to Oxford were aided by his grandmother's British heritage and the status of his father's senatorial position in the 'red chamber' of Canada's national capitol.

He was not alone in his quest to break out of the brain strain of intensive cramming. Harris's study table buddies, one by one, had momentarily digressed from their own study course texts.

Amid their somewhat restrained horseplay in a library environment, some are leafing through a stack of books left out on their table by previous readers. They take particular interest in university student annuals from thirty to forty years ago. They giggle and ridicule the photos and articles citing many much earlier campus fraternities and sororities. Excitedly, the students recognize the names of some now well-known people. Leaning over the shoulders of his classmate Charles 'Chuck' Orwell, face buried in a past Oxford university annual, was Lorne's residence roomy, Gerald Bagshaw from Little Glasgow Head. One article caught Bagshaw's eye. Quick handed, the burly Bagshaw swiped the book from under the nose of Orwell, and then whispered loudly across the table.

"Lorne! Hey Lorney!"

With a crooked finger, Bagshaw pointed to an open page of his 'stolen' volume.

"Would you believe this? This photograph. It's *Momsy!* She was a student right here back in …What's the date on this thing? Apparently she was into Fundamental Market Accountancy - ah - there it is – class of 2000!"

The foreign student, American Orwell, from whom Bagshaw has snatched the thick yearbook, jumped to his feet, his face red with fury and shouted in forced semi-whisper.

"Hey Baggie, you cheeky bastard! Who the hell do you think you are? I was into that stupid book… damn it! Come on, you bag of shit! Bring it back here!"

At this point, the hall librarian tapped his pen sharply on his oaken desk, scowling at the two students.

"Gentlemen – please!" He rebuked in a controlled but stern volume.

He had both forefingers plugged into his ears.

12

"Take your hooligan behavior outside if you must, but *not* in here. This is a *library* – not a soccer pitch! Please conduct yourselves accordingly."

Bagshaw turned to the librarian, raised his eyebrows submissively, and drew his finger across his mouth to designate a zipper. Then, with the annual clutched tight in thick fingers, he leaned over where Lorne Harris Jr. sat – still at his books and holding a finger to mark the page Bagshaw wanted him to see. He had been interrupted by the Orwell Bagshaw argument.

Now, Bagshaw was at his shoulder. He whispered in the ear of his roomy.

"See Lorney? Check this out. That's her there. *That's* momsy. See chaps? She's one to the left of the statue."

"Oh yeah" said Lorne.

He paused until he could think of a smart comeback, yet pretend to admire Mrs. Bagshaw's published image.

"Right Gerr – I can see now where you get your face full of ugly. You must have got your looks from your old man's side of the family. But, hey – your Mom's a bit of a looker!" Just then, Lorne had spotted something else of interest a few pages from the back of the book. He started flipping pages.

From across the table, Chuck Orwell spoke under his breath, "Don't you mean – hooker?"

"I *heard that*, asshole!" swore Bagshaw.

"You'd be wise to keep your head up for the next few days, Orwell. You arrogant Yankee prick – don't say I didn't warn you!"

Protectively, Gerald slipped the annual back from his Canadian confidant.

Still angry over the insult of his 'momsy' he said,

"Don't get too deep into this stuff, *Mister* Harris. After all, you're still only a bloody colonial around here! Beside, you couldn't *possibly* have any relatives in *these* year books – so what's this annual to you?"

"I thought I saw something in here – but where? What with all that squabbling – And by the way, *Mister* Bagshaw, *we 'colonials'* have long since been weaned off the royal tit. Just the same, – as part of the *commonwealth* – *ever* heard of *that?* We colonials *still* came over to help you beat back those dastardly jerries – not once but twice! So back off that *colonial* bullshit!"

Orwell and his fellow American around the table burst into soft scattered applause.

Harris nodded and went back to flipping pages in the annual from 2002.

Now ... lemme find that article again."

"Hey! Waaait a minute. Here it is. Have a look at this, fellow judges!"

Lorne rapped his knuckles on the open book's page. "*Here* it is! *This* article! - Something about a super, big time capsule project being designed – right here, on this campus. Isn't that a kick in the knackers?"

He started scanning the graphic drawings pages.

Orwell spoke up again

"So what's the *big* deal?"

Lorne is deep into studying reproductions of architectural drawings. He mutters,

"Fascinating – these colored ball sketches! Look at the ant-like man beside it. Gripping stuff!"

He looks up at his table companions.

"Y'know, back home, I used be into this kind of thing –

He flipped over a page, interrupted himself and exclaimed.

"Yeah! Look at the photo of this guy on the next page – He's the one who designed this glitter ball! And listen. Here's the headline – 'freshman configures plan for a thousand year Time Capsule'. See? There's his architectural rough renderings, calculations, sketches...side notes – everything."

American student body member, Chuck Orwell glanced at the annual in front of Lorne and remarked,

"Must have been a dead news day that year. If this guy were designing mobile bordellos, I might get interested – but time capsules. Phew! Like, who cares?"

Ignoring Orwell and the others now back at their textbooks, Harris returned to the annual's story.

"Seems this one particular geek – that guy right there, in the thick specs – some cat by the name of Jeffrey Cairns. Seems he is asked *why* he messes around reinventing a fifth wheel. He is quoted as saying, like, 'I know. A time capsule. It's been done before – an over-done gimmick if there ever was one. It might look like a waste of energy.' He admits it's been all been done before but 'not this way – and for *this* reason' he says..

"Not many capsules this size are ever dug up for posterity."

Lorne continued to read the quote aloud.

'BUT – there *is* a much bigger picture he says right here...

'...and furthermore, I have a jolly good reason to want to structure up this size of time capsule at this time. Believe it or not. I am bound and determined to confess all our sins and non-achievements to our descendents in a few centuries or so. And with *all* the mistakes humans have made on this planet, it's going to take a pretty big storage chamber!!

Then this guy is asked who is going to want to pry it open in a few hundreds or so? What's going to be in it that anybody would want to look into it?' Then Geekie Cairns answers. He says, 'other people, for one thing.'

Orwell looked up and sneered,

"Won't those *other people* have something to say about that? What a crock of crap, that is!"

"Not crap, my good man, but a history-making monument to improving our species." Lorne Harris reads on, determined to make Cairns' point if not his own.

"Apparently, our resident genius, inventor Jeff Cairns, maintains… 'Our capsule would be loaded with scientific and historical data plus articles of everyday humans of *this* age – not just National Geographic museum artifacts!' Hey – now *that's* the kind of off-beat project *I'd* love to get involved in."

Suddenly, Lorne Harris Jr. scoops up the book, snaps it shut and tucks it under his arm.

"I'm going to check this one out and read it over – tonight in the dorm."

"You can't." whispered Gerald Bagshaw. "It's a limited print edition – archival piece. Not to leave the library."

"It's just a *student annual*, y'turkey! Its part of the historical enrollment record of this institute – So *if* I have to bloody well pay a couple of bob for *copying* a few pages from this article, I'll do that…"

Then Lorne realized he didn't have a Euro on him. He clapped a hand on Bagshaw's shoulder.

"So spot me a few coins, Geraldine".

Bagshaw checked his pocket change, coming up with a few pence and a fiver.

"Sorry all's I got is bigger stuff. Damned if I gonna give you that. As it is, I won't be holding my breath waiting for your pay-back for a measly Euro or three".

"It'll do. Thanks partner!"

Lorne leaned in, took Bagshaw's fiver, his annual book, and sprinted for the night librarian's desk.

* * *

April, 1. Just after 02.55 a.m., Greenwich Mean Time. Lorne Jr. had spent the last few hours reading, rereading and studying the architectural drawings of Jeffrey Cairns time capsule venture. He used the dorm hallway landline to put in a carded collect call to Senator Lorne Harris' office, just down the granite-pillared corridor, adjacent to the Red Chamber on Parliament Hill in Canada's capital.

It was a very frosty Thursday in March. Ottawa was closed for business. The House of Commons had prorogued for Easter holiday. Most politicians and bureaucrats who had not left for homes across the country would be seeking solace in the arms of their mistresses before picking up their tickets for travel back to their home constituencies.

It would be the same laxity for the old unelected senators – sometimes anointed and *always* appointed friends of the prime minister and his party. The Senate was often referred to as, 'God's Waiting Room'…an elderly group of seldom seen, low volume legislators, all too frequently not seated for the Speaker's roll call.

Young Lorne Harris he knew one guy and his middle aged secretary, Janet Armstrong who *would* be at their desks already, even on this pre-holiday occasion.

"Good morning, Mrs. Armstrong. Is the Senator still pondering his position on which bills he will send back for revision? Or will he talk to his favorite son?"

He paused for her response – he could guess which one was coming. She would likely say - and did, "He doesn't *have a* favorite son"

"No kiddin? He doesn't? Oh. OK then… how about his *only* son? (He smothered a chuckle)…Fair enough…Oh, *I'm* very well, thanks Mrs. A… how about you? Is Mr. Armstrong up and around after his operation? Oh good… Tell him hello from Jolly old – and all that. Great…Sure. I'll wait…Thanks Mrs. A."

The phone clicked as a receiver was lifted. Now the dialogue was less predictable.

"Happy Easter, Pop!

"More like April fool, isn't it? Lorne! Why aren't you getting your night's rest?"

"Yowie, Pop! *That* sounded just like old home week! Hey – listen to this coincidence! 'Bout thirty years or so ago, Mom was attending Oxford too, right? And you'd still be there too, right? Anyway, I found her class picture in the Oxford student annual for that year. Tell her I'll send her a copy in with my belated Easter basket. But there's something else I wanted to talk to you about."

"Yeah. I didn't figure to get off *that* easy." replied the Senator "How much do you need this time?"

"No. No. Nothing like that. I just want your *thinking* – not bucks!"

"Uhuh. Well, that's cheap enough – by the by, Lorne, this connection is lousy. For God's sake. After thirty-five years, why hasn't residency updated that dormitory's land line? Anyway... so now, what's the 'something else,' son?"

"When you and Mom were here - back in those nostalgic days of Elton John's syncopated elevator music, times were –"

"Watch it, Junior" The Senator interrupted. The younger Harris ignored his father's mock warning.

"While you were at Oxford, do you recall getting involved on any House projects relating to time capsules? Maybe you'd heard of a campus creep enrolled as Cairns? Jeffrey Cairns? Even though you graduated 8 years ahead of him, would you have heard of an engineering or political sciences student working on a time capsule? He'd probably have been a frosh while you were in your final year?"

"You're calling me for that?" the Senator admonished. "Sounds like you're planning a campus prank at the expense of the old man?"

"I wouldn't do that to you –"

"Oh *yes* you would. But to your question, the answers are - no and no. Why do you ask?"

"Pop, this guy Cairns was a special kind of 'Home Alone' kid. Despite being a bit of a loner he *was* an on and off again, participating member of Gamma House. Kept mostly to himself with both his personal life and his studies. But, according the item I read in the 2000 engineering class section of the annual... he actually *did* propose a *monumentally* sized time capsule project, in very precise detail."

"So what's the object of that hair brained scheme?"

"This guy claimed the contents of his capsule would depict our way of life, both positive and negative, in *this* century to humans about a thousand *years* from now! The article I read seems to imply that his objective is to leave some kind of educational legacy. I'd love to find out – and I will"

"Well – don't get your hopes up. Look at it this way. By now, Oxford Campus must be a small city, made up of mostly enrollment; probably about 40 to 50 thou in residence – I would guess – plus a similar number of bodies in off-campus enrollment - plus staff. And it wasn't all that much smaller, when we were there. So in view of the numbers, it's quite understandable that these auspicious of halls of learning would likely attract its share of weirdoes doing their outlandish nocturnal stunts – especially engineering students!"

"Hey, Pop." interjected Lorne junior, "Go easy. You're talking about your one and only, off-the-wall *engineering son* here!"

The politician ignored the admonition and carried on,

"You see, the mentality of those long gone days was that the world was so uncomfortable, that the lunatic fringe figured space capsule planning was as good an escape from reality as any. Anyway, in answer to your questions Lorne, *these* days, neither your Mom nor I can remember the names of our next-door neighbors let alone people we didn't really know twenty years ago or so...There's little chance we would recall *any* Jeffrey whatzizname. Moreover, like you say, I was way ahead of his time at Oxford. So what's this Jeffrey Cairns to you?"

"Just so we're clear, Pop...his plan has *nothing* to do with escaping into *space*. Cairns *was* working on an unusual time capsule conveyance, one that doesn't involve an astral environment of any kind."

"Umhmm. So you say. Sounds to me like the '*dream zone*' crowd we knew and loved, back then. Nice to know those mindless zombies are still alive and well in fraternities out there. This history buff – what was his name? Cairns? *Sounds* vaguely familiar; more latterly from somewhere other than university. And no – I don't remember our frat house having anything to do with any time machine project – Hey, weren't you into all that time capsule stuff as a kid?"

"I guess that's really why I'm calling, Pop! Like every kid. I've always had this interest in time capsules."

Lorne Junior was beginning to sound excited.

"Hey! Do you remember that old hot water heater that you and I dragged off the old basement furnace? 'Member how Morley Anderson and I set it up in a dugout in back of our property? It was going to be the first time capsule in Canada! Remember?"

"Oh yes. Indeed. I *do* remember. As I recall, that hot water tank was destined for our Summer cottage, before you and wotzizname had trouble convincing your 'limited pool of investors' - like old moneybags – your uncle Harry. So your only real prospects for your hot water tank venture were an Uncle rancher out west near Regina – one over-solicited science teacher and - oh yeah - *me* – to finance the idea that the project would indeed, *somehow - someday* get off the ground."

"Pop. Listen. If I was to enlist a group of qualified engineers, *including* Jeffery Cairns – wherever he is – to reopen what Cairns had started back in '07 or '08, do you think I might find and convince enough money men – each with a wish to be remembered long after their demise, if not immortalized *for centuries* – to *invest* in such a project? Don't know about here in England, but at home we'd find ways of using it as an investor tax write off."

"This is pretty heady stuff, Lornesome! Isn't there *enough* challenging class work ahead of you, just to get out of there with a certificate to prove your sanity? Do you really need to go looking for more?"

"Yeah, I read you, Pop" Lorne responded impatiently "but you know, I'm only using 11 hours of a twenty four hour day – so that leaves me with thirteen hours with *nothing* to do...Seriously Father, if I proceed with all the authenticated data I need, can I count on *your* influence to back me up on it – again, this time?"

The PR wise politician snickered and said "Anytime you address me as 'Father', I know I'm due for no less than a commitment written in blood. Mine! Still, (sigh), I've never pooped out on any of your ideas yet – But, and this is a *big But* – you know the drill of our own 'contracts' - we've been into all of this before! Make sure everything you gather on this one is straight up, undeniable and monetarily viable or keep it to yourself, until it is verifiable. Dig?"

"I hear you loud and clear, sir," Lorne promised.

"OK Lorne. Now, go get one or two of those hours you're not using to get some sleep. We'll talk again soon. Goodnight son, Love you."

"Bye for now, Pop. Love you too. Tell Mom I'll call her Sunday -- collect, of course."

"Of course." sighed the Senator.

* * *

 Acting for student council, young Harris was off to an interview with Oxford alumnus, Jeffrey Cairns. For newsworthy reasons, the timing could not have been better. The ex-Oxford graduate was soon to become a member of the House of Lords. He was to be knighted for encouraging and sponsoring youth all over Europe to further their science projects.

Lorne took a morning train to Manchester for the opportunity to visit Lord Cairns at the offices of his recently acquired mortuary.

Naturally, in discussing the charitable work and successes of this famous Oxford alumnus, interviewer Lorne Harris would lead up lead up to another subject - the one he really came to get the 'scoop" on – for his *own* purposes of course

'What *was* Cairns early Oxford work in sphere capsule containers'?

The answer was not an expected one. But as Cairns talked to the younger Oxford student, he recited a simile of his capsule concept to one from Greek literature – an Ovid myth... True to his intent, Lorne Harris Jr. sought approval of the editorial boards of the European astrological and historic media. He knew he had to dress up his pitch so he employed the classic best reason of all - the annuls of the history of man. The soon to be *Sir* Jeffrey Cairns was in no way associated with romantic or literary proclivity. He had the lived up to the general impression of a humorless mortician.

But he became recognized for the parallel of his character and the oceanic version of the Greek mythical seed husk, Cypsela. Ovid had described that fragile marine-going 'vessel' – that had "carried Cygnus, an exiled King of Liguria, first to sea, then to the stars." Both Jeffrey and young Harris laughed at the seemingly disjointed correlation, emulating *the purpose* and action of the sphere story to the 'mythic' sea voyage by Cygnus. By now, both men also found themselves enjoying each other's company, having much dialogue on their common interests in the mechanics and purposes of time capsules.

* * *

Weeks later, back in the Oxford University library, third year legal-engineering scholar, Marvin Klieneman, whispered what was on his mind to others gathered around one end of a twenty foot long British, dark oak library table. It was strewn with both their course texts and Cairn's most recent sheet drawings of his 'Cygnus' sea capsule. These were an enhanced version of the very engineered drawings Cairns had drafted a decade or so before.

Somehow – and though he wasn't saying how - Lorne Harris had secured most of the time capsule's *original* schematic sketches and drafts from 2007.

They were spread out under green-lamped, desktop lights, at every meter, along both sides of the library table. Klieneman looked up at his three friends leaning over one of the schematics.

"Why does this thing require that inverted cone aperture, some 25 meters *beneath* its attachment to the big sphere? Could its cone point be some kind of mechanism for a sea anchor chain?"

Since Harris had studied the drawings for a couple of days prior to this gathering, Marvin's questions were directed at him.

"At first, I thought it was to serve only as ballast. Sort of like an extra deep keel to keep the sphere upright under any condition – and yes – it could also be a fixture by which to store and secure an anchor chain. But now I'm not so sure that the scrooge-like mind of my mentor would allow for that kind of ancillary space without a specific purpose for it in mind. Frankly I didn't question him on the reason for this configuration. I *just knew* he had one."

Sliding the very print he had been looking at up the table to be right under the lamp, Marvin Klieneman put an index finger on a particular spot.

"Yeah, you're probably right, Chum, But something doesn't ring right here. Cairns' *drafts* show floors and compartments all through the *main* sphere but in this massive *cone section* space there's no levels or walkway configurations to indicate as to what other cargo he had in mind for it – if anything. Y'think this is *supposed* to be empty? Pretty expensive ballast space, if you ask me – or just as a place to hook up and store an anchor chain. Hey! Maybe it's a big bin to store feed for the armadillos and giraffes aboard!"

Orwell scowled querulously at his schoolmate.

"Oh fun-*ny*, Klieneman– For your information, Jeffrey Cairns is not in this for the same reason Noah was. But I don't expect you to see that. Just remember. An Ark, this isn't. Get with the tour"!

Lorne interjected over the byplay.

"Yeah. At first, I thought that cone section was an oddity to begin with. But then I figured – this guy Cairns doesn't go to these lengths for no good reason.

He's got to have something else in his mind for that cone. I'll find out when the time comes."

Marvin Klieneman plunked down his pencil and turned to face his Alpha House colleagues.

Nodding his crew cut head, Eddie Johnson said,

"Yeah. Right now we've got other fish to fry."

"Ok Mr. legal beagle. We're all ears." Chuck Orwell challenged.

Never one to pass up a straight-line opportunity, Marvin retorted with a smirk,

"In your case, Chuck," said Marvin, "that's not just a figure of speech!"

Waiting for the giggles to subside, Klieneman went on.

"Granted that this project, to our knowledge, is not yet copyrighted nor registered for world patents. Just remember, ethically or lawfully, it is not ours to act on. It *is* the proprietary work of one of one of our own alumni members. And since it we don't see signs of embossed patents or copyright certifications, protected property it probably isn't. So we could be subject to whatever infringement charges they have for that in England, if we progressed from here without creator permission.""

Orwell chided, "Now, what loony would want to infringe on *this* kind of fantasy anyway?"

Pretending a sudden reminder, he exclaimed,

"Oh. Wait a minute! That's *us*, isn't it?"

Without waiting for confirmation, Lorne asked,

"So. What's your point Marv?" asked Lorne.

"I'm just trying to get a fix on where *we* fit into this hair brained scheme. As you guys know, after Lorne's interview with the mortician, we now know one thing. By law, in *any* country, these designs are still the property of his forthcoming Lordship – revised or not." said Klieneman. "And apparently that was so, even then, in 2007 or 2008, or whenever Cairns graduated. What I can't figure is how Lorney talked this stuff out of Cairns archives!"

Orwell piped up.

"And another thing! How the hell did Cairns and his original band of collaborators ever figure to get enough bread to finance this monstrosity?"

Never afraid to openly show how little he knew, Athlete Eddie offered more input.

"Y'know guys, we had a middle linebacker buddy on the Owls – that was our North East, Big 10 football team at State – he told me one time, there was a whole third year class at State working on a limited college grant to research and develop a space vehicle that would serve as a time capsule for future finders. So – when design application pushing came to shoving for development money, that very same question came up with them too. Maybe we should be getting into bed with *that* bunch. Y'know, working jointly? With them, we wouldn't have to get entangled in legal tape like what I was talking about. They've already faced that. Apparently, this college group got a U.S. Federal starter grant and may already have some answers to what we're dealing with here, y'know?"

Lorne explained to his group that he had already conceded that he knew of that University group working on an analogous but much smaller vehicle for a much costlier *space* journey. He lied even further. He told his fellow students around the library table that Conn. U's proposed time vault was limited in capacity. By comparison, the Cairns proposal was centered around a structure whereby space for *contents* like cars, boats and church bells would be almost unlimited.

Up to now Lorne Harris had never grappled with the total monetary cost of this kind of endeavor. That would be the deciding factor when it came time to go after to approachable investors.

"We touched on money matters during my recent visit with the *originating designer* of *this* venture, Mister – soon to be 'Lord' -Jeffrey Cairns," said

Harris, "and the prospect of a future working alliance with him and his close associates. On the matter of financial support, Jeffrey Cairns assured me that when the time came to proceed, funds would be readily available."

Bagshaw put in his four pence worth. "If you can't trust the word of a Lord, who *can* you trust?"

Ignoring Gerald's attempt at humor, Lorne Harris the second, thought it less complicated if he were not to mention further funding possibilities to his study buddies. They needn't know that Cairns himself might eventually be able to jump start the whole damned sphere capsule financing out of his own, and other big shooters' corporate resources. If that were an option, the schoolboy initiative would be quite academic. He mused that in withholding privileged information from his schoolmates they would ultimately figure it out. Double cross!

Wasn't it the uncle of Francis Drake who was organizing a pirate and pillage voyage to the edge of the earth – until his younger relative actually beat him to it? Sorry – but that's the way businesses bounce.

Lorne figured, "Right now, there's no sense breaking up that old school gang of mine until I can make sure we've got whatever worthwhile ideas they might come up with. I'll give them the bad news later – maybe.

"Now anybody else got something to think about?"

The library discussion went on. Yorkshire man Dickie Rafferty lifted his chin from his hand to open his mouth. He asked skeptically,

"Ok guys, so much for financing. Now let's get down to some *technical* nitty gritty." Until now, he'd been pretty laid back on previous sphere capsule discussions but now it was his turn to lead a problem solving expedition. "How would one propose to have a 'package' like ours, floating a few leagues under an ocean surface make its debut *when* we figure it's time to be found?

"There's ways, Dickie," responded Undergrad Eddie, the Yank with a big raised Green E badge sewn on his sweater. He thumped his stubby forefinger on one of the schematic drawings of the sphere.

"In my opinion…." led off the American – only to be greeted with groans of ridicule from the other students. Undiscouraged he prattled on.

"This big ball concept, which is to be buried *at sea, right?* Ha! fat chance! Look! At a hundred yards diameter, this Cairns ball is already too freakin' unwieldy to have to figure how to make it pop up like a balloon on a given day a thousands years or so from now. Get real!"

Now, Eddie Johnson stood up, leaned over the table and with felt pen, scribbled a diagram on two side by side sheets of his note pad. Other boys stood to look at the quickie sketch. The whole scenario resembled and sounded like a storied Knut Rockne locker room pep talk.

"Instead, how about… First, you sell people on the idea of being remembered by future populations. While you're collecting their checks, you cram a whole bunch of smaller, bullet-shaped cartridges full of all the personal stuff they give you to include in your *underground* capsule. Then you negotiate working rights to an Oklahoma petroleum producer, like ah….American Standard, BP, Exxon…whichever has a capped dry oil or gas hole they're not using. There are hundreds of them around. Too little crude or gas left, even at today's high per-barrel prices, to send to the refinery You ring these guys in with profit commitments to whatever charitable causes. They donate rights to the hole to take advantage of the huge tax deduction on the lost drilling costs. Now you sink a time capsule canister with all these canisters, down into that hole. Like I say, the canisters are loaded with 21st century stuff…everything from a girl's love letters, marriage certificates, family photos, a couple of sealed test tubes with a person's DNA skin samples or blood samples, everything from a families pet's dog collar to a kid's album of drawings, done at five years of age. Whatever it takes at ten bucks per item. Figure it out. A ten spot for every item times 50,000 items into one hole. There's your first half million to cover your costs to promote the next one and so on and so on and so on. Then you open up another hole, and do the thing all over again.

Lorne raised his eyebrows and turning his head, interjected.

"You're *thinking* laterally, – and that's *good* Eddie, but now, let's deal with the one unanswered question that came up before and we have to find a solution for before we take people's money!"

"If nobody in the future knows it's there…how – when you program a time for your capsule to be opened – how the hell is something like that going to become visible at the designated time?"

Marvin Klieneman jumped up again.

"Ha! Elementary, Lorney old chap!"

He did his Sherlock Holmes act puffing on a non-existent pipe.

"If we're talking land based capsules sunk down in capped, dry holes – fixed with a timer and an explosive… Set to go off at – ah, let's see, let's say we'd set it during the year 2028…So pick a date, like a Saturday morning – lots of available spectators, kids and weekenders. Springtime. May 21st in the year 3000. The canister with its extra hardened steel nose cone and contents is blown up and out of the well hole. Canisters full of junk come firing out of there! More noise than firecrackers at a Chinese New Year's blow out! Gung Hay Fat Choy!"

He giggled when he added the Chinese New Year greeting for emphasis to his suggestion.

"Ok. OK. Fair enough but let's forecast a scenario." Lorne agrees, "Let's say that a few centuries earlier, before the canister's 'coming out' party, a Synagogue has been built over that *same* dry hole. When the time for the capsule explosion to go off – say possibly during Marv's great, great, great, great *grandson's bar mitzvah*. Here's the scenario. The rabbi shits his pants, the Torah scrolls are torn to shreds and all the kosher cookies for the reception have to be used to repair the hole in the roof!"

"Aw – laych lazozayl!" swore Marvin in Hebrew, half laughing himself as he envisioned the chaos just described.

"Or – if you can imagine!" added Harris, "*Another* capsule explosion is planted in a banana plantation for instance in what was once a 20th century

Venezuelan oil field. Such an eruption of capsule goodies could produce an otherwise very marketable, if not gigantic, messy, banana *cream* custard!"

"Or – or, or – and maybe..." chided Chuck, "Maybe another would blow the manhole covers off storm sewer drains in the middle of Emblem Court or Piccadilly Circus. You'd prob'ly catch shit for *that* too!"

Belly laughter at the table drew a disapproving pencil tapping from the librarian's desk.

Lorne loudly whispered his next remarks,

"All right, guys. Give ole Marv a break. You know, Marv. You might have unwittingly passed over a great thought.

Looking bewildered, the Jewish kid sat slowly down in a library chair and asked,

"I did?"

"Think of it, Marv. "

Now Harris stood up and looked down at the object of his address.

"The possibility of cloning! We take samples off you and shove yours into a down hole canister. Can you imagine? Another Marvin Klieneman being duplicated for life in the 32nd century – simply by including his ass wipe containing DNA on tissue samples – stinking up the whole time capsule? What an intriguing thought.

One of guys groaned again.

"*Intriguing???* More like *disgusting* – eeuuuck!!"

"So it's not a total loss; if it were worth it we'd think of a way to bring all that stuff out of an *underground* canister at an appointed time – If we *had* to."

Addressing himself to Dickie Rafferty, Lorne Harris continued.

"Seriously though, Dickie, what d'you think?"

"Well. Every dog buries his bone where he thinks it won't be found – and sure as hell *not* intended to be dug up right away. Same thing with underground petroleum holes, not a bad idea But instead of dumping a time capsule down an inactive well hole *on land*, why not attach a capsule to one or two of those many non-producing oil or gas well caps – the ones they install at *sea?* Let's *add* to our thinking. How about actually *anchoring* a submersible sphere so that it's out of the way – tethered but floating a few hundred fathoms beneath the surface!"

Harris paused a second or two.

"Not bad thinking Dickie. But from an engineering standpoint, wouldn't that be a touch *too* loosey goosey to guarantee discovery. Given unknown turbulent factors off a sea floor with massive currents and unpredictable quake tremors to jar it loose it might never be found."

Rafferty persisted.

"But suppose, in a marine environment the thing *could* be preprogrammed, somehow, to pop up when it's *engineered* to do so?"

Harris opens a giant National Geographic Atlas.

"Yeah but there's no known method to ensure an enduring technical means or device that I know of, anyway, that can be counted on to react to electronic signals after 500 hundred years or so...and even *that's* too early to break open a message from one civilization to another... The only thing that could do it *might* be..."

His cohorts were quiet, waiting for Lorne Harris to explain, He flopped open an Atlas page, thumbed to a chart of the North Atlantic slapping his hand down an area of the Arctic Ocean. The page featured the Russian north coast. Now he carries on.

"Soooo," he mumbled about as though he were stalling for his next brain wave.

"Why not let the ocean's salt water be the firing pin on an anchor chain? All it would take would be *a chain link* or two that would be of a composite metal formed to be subject to *total* erosion *within* a certain time period.

As he talks, Harris is scanning chain-link tether specs in the margins of the drawings. Then by securing our floatable sphere with chain to the sea floor apparatus of a dry well – one that's been drilled and capped in Russia's North Sea waters for instance."

True to his upbringing, the American athlete objected. "Ok "But then – why Russian waters? There are lots *of* dry holes, closer by. And in less trafficked seas. Just east off the Scottish coast is one."

Chuck Orwell signals his concurrence by nodding his head.

"Sounds like a bit of logic." murmurs Dickey.

"*Sounds* alright. But we still haven't got a sure fire answer to the question … How can we really *be sure* that a giant capsule is released when it's scheduled to come up? Seems to me it would be a metallurgical matter… Now, *I* figure all it takes is simple, mathematical engineering configurations, based on known, conventional salt-water deterioration charts and known effects on certain tensile strengths in composite alloys. OK Marv! You're the real engineer here. *You* figure it out. Once we have a proven means of raising a sphere to the surface we'd have solved that resurrection!"

"Hey!" spoke up Dickie, historian of the *group*.

"You know what? That makes all this technical crap analogous to Ovid's ancient Greek mythical sea voyage of Cygnus, king of the Liguarians. *But* gentlemen, does the romance of ancient Greek mythology really have any real influence on our engineering calculations?

Putting on his wind jacket and scarf, Marvin Klieneman offered his parting shot, "Not bloody likely. Outside of you – and maybe Harris here, who the hell really gives a purple piss about mythical sea shanties and half buried balls in ocean waters Goodnight nurse!"

After Marvin passed through the library's swinging doors, dozing Bagshaw's head jerked up spun around the room and asked,

"Who left?"

Somebody said, 'Nobody. Just Klieneman."

Chapter 2

Astrology And Other Love Signs

2035AD/21st century – London England

NEW YEAR'S EVE 1999. The 20th Century had passed on its troubles to what had been referred to then as the "new" millennium.

Ecstatic manufacturers of computers and software technology had been neck deep in a rocketing consumer movement - "kitchen table" computers, lap top applications and operating systems and peripherals. Burgeoning market demands for government, home and *business* applications were almost endless. Skirmishes and quickie take-over of boom or bust, dot com companies were rampant.

As a result of their blithe shortsightedness, most producers of up to 30 year old computer hardware and software, established commercial users were left with incurable headaches when the millennium changed from 1999 to 2000 but dates and times on cyber equipment *didn't*.

It was like that hairy old joke between the long married couple who finally had to take 'Mother' who had lived with them for thirty years, to the geriatric ward in the local hospital. "*My* mother! I thought she was *your* mother." Incredibly, a 'laissez faire'" attitude prevailed based on the 'pass the buck' theory. "Gee we thought *you* had looked after that, already."

"Us? No we figured that you people were working on that and that *you* would let *us* know when to include two more digits to date lines."

Ensuing global apprehension became known as the dreaded *Y2K crisis*.

So wildly speculative were the ensuing doom and gloom warnings that hundreds of airliners in mid flight would be 'plunging to earth'; hydroelectric systems might well 'turn the world cold and dark'; the lights would go out on all satellites, including the vitally necessary CPS craft; industries 'could collapse' at midnight Dec 31, 1999; multi-billion dollar space projects could be voided; every country's monetary system might go uncontrolled, thereby rendering any form of exchange useless at best. While infinitesimally little of this actually happened, the chilling prospect of any of these possibilities seemed almost as perilous as the predicted events themselves.

* * *

At about the same time, those younger generations of that era were becoming increasingly concerned as to whether their grand plans for life would ever materialize, in any form. Today that same group would ashamedly admit, 'We were so damn naïve. We day-dreamt, mused, imagined and speculated about our future, our world and our place in it.'

For a very young Jeffrey Cairns, the penalty for daydreaming and being inattentive in grammar school had cost him more than one detention and at least 3 trips to the master's office. His parents, school and junior college professors as well as his classroom peers all knew him to be obsessed with what he perceived to be *a future need for a time capsule*. They just could not figure out why he thought this was so all-fired important. And worse, neither could he. He just knew there was material and social justification for one sided communication with his ancestors. As he entered young adulthood with all its inherent responsibilities, more and more he began seriously questioning his motives for that rationale. How would a crypt full of tokens of *his* era's lifestyle edify the life of future inhabitants? In *that* frame of mind, now Cairns was full of self incriminations.

He pondered. Who of them of them would really give a rap? Medical people? Legal minds? Sculptors of industrial advancement? For that matter, why would *anyone* of *this* era find anything of use in a centuries old capsule full of already known data and trinketry that one might find under any torn down building's cornerstone?

In the Fall of October, 2002, at his parents' summer home in Sussex, Cairns was packing his possessions for his first term at Oxford. Supplementary to toothbrush and dormitory essentials much of his bag contained two three-ringed binders for hundreds of double spaced notes and hand scribed diagrams of time capsule structures he had envisioned.

He was still cross-examining himself as to his 'venture' when his mother's dinner bell chimed its call to the table. 'Ok. Should a capsule-filled depository exposing incidents of man's social *shortcomings* impress any future body to know that this era's people are truly repentant for the mess we left for our descendents? Of course no one would bother turning the page.'

He plunked himself down in his bedroom desk chair.

"But isn't the message to our great, great and greater descendants so much more meaningful than an apology for not evolving fast enough for those that followed? Look what we had to work with. Elvis Presley. Adolph Hitler. Idi Amin. Juan Peron. George Formby. Leona Helmsley.

Wait a minute. Gad! This has all been *done* before! Hasn't many a worthy civilization left their cultural ways all over the sandy, tiled floors of Luxor and Giza? And not just of Easter Island societies or Chinese dynasties! Other time period's creations were equally significant!

'In early America's remnants, pre-Spanish existence, Mayans too, left evidence of their existence. Every aboriginal on earth has left their sacred-ground messages on cave interiors all over the world. Did the ancient Persians and Greeks create art and scientific inscriptions strictly for *their own* entertainment value? Multi thousand-year-old crypts and pyramidal structures were designed for and aimed at future folk.'

'Where is all this now? It's in every museum in every country of the world. And will be for many, many millenniums from now. So why duplicate it in digest form? There must be a better way to reveal deities of human triumphs and transgressions. I will find them. Human habitation to the 22nd century was right *here* … *I can prove it* and this is what it was like….!'

His bedroom door opened. Mother Cairns stood in the doorway, arms folded, her thin lips and scowling eyes reprimanding him for not joining others already gathered at the supper bell.

Perhaps humans *do* have an *instinctual* drive to communicate with upcoming communities." As he forked up a banger in a pastry blanket, he thought

"Not so off the wall, after all – eh, Jeffrey old boy?"

Still, he felt in an upbeat mood as he proceeded to his chair at the dinner table.

Later, well into his coffee and dessert, Jeffrey could still almost hear himself debating with himself.

'How about if our descendents were to be shown what we did not achieve and what it cost us. Surely, they'd be just as interested in what we could not get done. How important was it that Cabot *did not find* a Northern trade route to China? What differences would it have made to the future of aviation, if disregard for the signs of disasters of inevitable metal fatigue *were* known prior to the eight crashes of the Comet, world's first commercial jet liners? Are today's *surgical* medics that much more enlightened, now *aware* of the unknown shortcomings that beset Dr. Christian Bernard's first *unsuccessful* human *heart transplant* operations of the mid 20th century?

So the one pound and six pence question remains. Will time capsules containing this and past centuries' key historic archives, arts, medical and technical data, shed any sprinkling of value on the lifestyles of distant generations? In actual fact, outside of plain, dirty old curiosity, would any of our message matter at all to people a few hundred years from now?'

Jeffrey had to admit the obvious. Trying to rationalize purpose to an irrational concept is like having to dig for treasure *you know* is there – but the maps and signs continue to elude you.

He even *imagined* himself at the lectern, addressing scientists of a later world.

"We, of the 21st century, do herewith tender a legacy to our children of the future, justifying our message of concern for their world. We take pride that *at this stage* in the development of humankind, at the very least, *we* had the foresight to *show* ourselves as a useful template for generations ahead, blah, blah blah."

Cairns thought about it for a quiet minute. Then he shook his head back to reality.

'Who am I trying to fool? *Useful? Template?* How utterly arrogant – taking credit for development of man! Like trying to breed a horny Corgi to a footstool!'

He scolded his mixed up mind.

'Where do I get off? I can't even *dream up* a good reason for *creating* my message to my audience.'

More morosely, he thought, 'That kind of conclusion would spell "forget it" to any monument citing glory for a concept of *any* kind."

* * *

The night before he finished packing for his first semester in his first year at Oxford, a dejected Jeffrey Cairns spent an hour in his mother's garden hammock looking up at the stars. Notwithstanding the horoscope chart of ready-made shapes and signs, every stargazing one of us has imagined our own forms from the way in which the stars are aligned. In fact, in one group of stars, Jeffrey imaged that very same Greek figure on the horoscope, standing spread eagled in the center of the chart of astrologic signs.

He dozed. Starlight seemed to meld together in his sleeplike state,

Then – *there it was!* A sign he never imagined could exist – existed!

Right then, he *knew* he had a clearly enunciated answer to all his self-doubts. It seemed to be written across the night sky…where one thousand years is but a momentary flash in the universal scheme of things. The universe holds the secret to the miracles of *preservation*.

* * *

While attending Oxford, from 2004 to graduation 2008, Jeffery Cairns was enrolled in Physical Engineering Sciences. In his fourth year of study, his curriculum called for postgraduate studies in Mathematical Applications, Electrical and Fluid Dynamics, as well as Thermal calculations and Applied Business Technology. In the final analysis, such courses were not exactly essential for his on-the-side time capsule project. Still, it was part of his overall strategy to one basic objective; a master's degree. Also, if he was going anywhere towards engineering an agenda for time capsule production he was going to have to be able to comprehend the precise precepts of those professionals who could get it done.

By mid term of his final year, Cairns was on his way to attaining a degree with honors. Nevertheless, by then, he was accelerating detailed development planning of the sphere capsule project. He had developed hundreds of renderings and schematic drawings for his 300 foot (91.44 meters) diameter marine sphere.

Then, while still completing his final year of engineering, he had enrolled in a *mortuary* curriculum. Cairns added eighteen months to his existing curriculum with night study at another kind of institution.

His few friends would never understand Cairns' rationale for determining a mortician's practice. Typically, it was based on sound logic. He took notice of shifting world animosities, particularly the continuing turmoil within Islamic ideologies and Moslem led states. They were again threatening to engulf the dubious stability of Middle East, Arab, and Asian perimeters. Escalating armed conflict was a certainty. Casualties would be accelerated. Undertakings would be a requirement. Cairns knew that as part of warring, involved governments had to build in sizable budgets to cover cadaver and other waste disposals. How else could he contribute to the realization and fulfillment of his multi billion pound, sphere-capsule project?

Good fortune and dogged hard work - this route was to ultimately take him into a partnership-owned chain of funeral emporiums and crematoriums all over Europe and even one in south East Asia. In a matter of a few years, Jeffery Cairns eventually bought out major partners. With a controlling interest, he became the business's sole decision maker. He bought in on still *another* funeral home. This time, an established mortuary venture in Manchester. By the time he had passed his fortieth birthday, he had accumulated a string of eleven European mortuaries with four more scheduled to open from Johannesburg to New Delhi.

As a sideline, workaholic Cairns dedicated himself to still another interest. He nurtured and inspired scholarships for youths' science projects everywhere; that is, Britain and parts of the commonwealth – as well as on mainland Europe.

Aside of his string of annual Youth Engineering Exhibits, many of his imaginative, structural concepts were now an accepted part of every British grade school curriculum. Without fees, without fanfare, he gave classroom lectures, contributory to advanced studies in every major school and junior educational institution in Britain. Fifteen years of voluntary service to the educational process eventually attracted feature news stories in major media. According to principals of honorific Orders, his appointment to a Knight of the Bath was a certain eventuality. Introverted though he was, Jeffrey Cairns accepted the sword-to-shoulder ceremony, with an aging King Charles XXII of England officiating.

As for his visionary time capsule obsession, the distinguished but taciturn businessman kept that interest much to himself. By virtue of his flourishing mortuary businesses competently administered by a board of directors, Sir Jeffrey made time for his youth sciences projects and his pursuit of capsule development. He readily attended *every* convention and gathering in the British Isles, having anything, even remotely, to do with engineering of time capsules.

*   *   *

One day in 2036, his receptionist came into the fifty-year-old mortician's lavish Manchester office to announce a visitor. The business card she had left led him to believe that this chap was the same with whom he had been interviewed for an Oxford campus paper a dozen years ago. Apparently, his caller was now a junior partner in a Norwegian based, marine salvage firm with an office in London.

As stood waiting on the deep pile carpet of the reception lobby to reintroduce himself to the renowned executive, the 32-year-old Lorne Harris Jr. rehearsed his opening statements. Striding toward the familiar younger man, Cairns recalled his affinity for Harris as a young Oxford student. Jeffrey remembered that he had liked him. He was to recall that they had spent many hours discussing his favorite subject, time capsules. As they would again, many, many times over the next five or six years.

Sir Jeffrey would spend many a fascinating hour with the young marine engineer. It was as though Cairns had assumed Harris to be the one to rejuvenate development in the capsule project. So much so, that Cairns shared his latest, very detailed data and renderings with his new associate in the many meetings and planning sessions that followed.

For now, young Lorne's sessions with Sir Jeffrey were between him and his mentor.

At the initiation of Sir Jeffrey Cairns, a lesser-known Lorne Harris Jr. would become the registered and patented domain name of the 'Cypsela Concept' as his Lordship had tagged the project. Now, it would be Harris who would reapply for all associated patents, copyrights of logos and titles and all related registry activity

* * *

Now, the 'Castle Cairns' study clock had chimed out eleven hours.

Though Lorne Harris Jr. and Jeffrey Cairns had spent the evening in earnest discussion, they were in fact, relaxing. They shared drinks across the coffee table.

"That was one busy day, Jeff."

"For me too, I had *very private* discussions with a Cryogenics treatment committee today. Both their cardio-thoracic surgeons and infectious diseases staff tell me they can foresee over two hundred cryogenically treated and thermally prepared subjects added to preservation storage within a ten-month period if need be. Of these, at least a dozen so treated will have 'recognized' names. Anyway, they tell me transport of most of them for designated delivery will be within a fortnight of orders to ship to disembarkation. Ancillary arrangements will be provided closer to launch."

"By the by, Jeffrey, some of those special mechanical exhibits we wish to put aboard? Rolls Royce will make their antique Shadow – the limo model, available to us right after Auto Expo. Believe it or not, we may yet have an expendable Harrier Jet in the cargo. It could shake loose with the help of our friends at the Imperial War Museum. And that Sportsman Yacht, Cruise-liner we wanted? That's the one that got totaled by a rogue wave in the Biscayne, so that's out – but I've got a lead on a refurbished, old German E-boat we could take aboard...Mind you, this stuff has to go aboard *before* those complicated outer capsule shells are fabricated to – "

Cairns waved a dismissive hand and spoke softly,

"I know. I know, Lorne. Which comes first, the chicken or the yacht? Just another timing factor we must contend with..."

Cairns let this thought run out as something else occurred to him.

41

"Did I understand you to say there seems to be some problem from some University labs to meet their commitment to organ specimens? If that's still because of next of kin changing their minds... then, even with signed agreements in place, we have to let it slide for fear of creating a noisy public fuss."

"But – but if that's the case, Jeff, and some of those Brazilian Cryobiology labs come through, hopefully, as a result, we can have any resulting shortfall resolved within a couple of weeks."

His older partner slanted his head downward, looked up and said,

"It must be soon though. It occurs to me there is still so much errand boy work to do – and the worst part is we have so *few secretive* ways to process them all - which just puts that much more critical time on your shoulders and additional deadlines for me, Lorne.

Draining the last of his single malt scotch, the mortician moved to get up out of his chair to return the empty to his French provincial sideboard. Before he could raise himself from his easy chair, Lorne took his glass. As he refilled it, he said,

"Meanwhile I had telephone discussions with refrigeration programmers and installers. They're almost finished preparing the electrical diagrams for installation *and* power system components for our installer in Brest. So since I had the time in Brussels, I scheduled a meeting with our contracted tugboat firm. I toured the industrial craft that will 'plant' the sphere. Even talked to their Senior Captain, one Jorgen Johansen who will himself direct the actual 'deposit' in the North Sea..."

He tailed off and was quiet. He stared off into space for almost 30 seconds or so.

Lorne Harris Jr. looked across at his colleague, who was staring down absent-mindedly and fingering the rim of his own almost empty old-fashioned glass.

"Hey Jeff!"

The younger man pretended to put a microphone to his mouth and a hand to his ear.

"Lorne calling Jeffrey!" In his most jocular form, he added,

"Was it something I haven't said yet?"

Cairns looked up, smiling wryly. He remained quiet for another couple of moments. He sipped his scotch, leaned forward with his glass in both hands. Then he asked,

"Lorne. Do you think anyone has any idea – about us?"

"Right now? No – but yes, I think they probably *will* get around to it"

"Who?"

"No one – *specifically*. But judging from what media reporters are *not* asking, I suspect that *someone* – maybe from an exposé media form, will dig deep enough to find out. There's enough to...well, like – both of us are bachelors for instance. And whenever we *do* show together up at any business meetings or societies' cocktail functions, – which is rare – we can start getting used to that "I wonder if" kind of look."

"As I've often said to you, Lorne, it's not in our better interests to be labeled gay – not at *this* point in time anyway – with respect to the credibility of our capsule project. Homosexuality may be government approved but it'll take another few generations to dispel the unfortunate physical imagery. I'm afraid, genuine, emotional love between gay people is still not an accepted general impression."

Lorne took both empty glasses to the bar. He tipped them both another scotch.

"That's for sure, Jeff. We will have to be *especially* cautious during the public preliminaries of the most spectacular venture ever staged... Still, discovery is a risk we ran when we decided, four years ago, that this was to be our life *together*. For the best part of a couple of years now, we've probably appeared to be a 'conjugal 'item.' So I guess it's bound to come out - *sometime*."

Lorne paused,

"What made you *think* of that just now?"

The older man again took his glass in both hands, gazed unseeing over the top of it, took a large gulp, then said,

"Oh. I don't know. It is just that our relationship wasn't supposed to go *this* way. Outside of my mother, you are the only person, my dear Lorne, that I've ever let into my life - either professionally or intimately - and I guess I don't want it to end – especially now, anyway. And besides, if it were really known far and wide right now, that would be the end of the Cypsela project."

With a glass in his hand, Lorne Harris stood behind Jeffrey's chair. He put his free arm around his lover's shoulders and said,

"Don't worry, dear. We're both closed mouthed people. And both of us have always kept our homes separate - away from the maddening crowd, so to speak. So nobody should bother digging."

Putting Cairns' neat scotch in front of him, Lorne walked around to his chair. He took a sip and a swig from his own glass and then continued...

"As far as I'm personally concerned ... frankly, I don't give a damn about anybody *knowing* about us – well, except for my father. Though I suspect Dad's probably always wondered. He'd be so devastated to *have* to accept that his only son wasn't straight. Mom – had she lived, would be accepting – but disappointed, I know. But, for me – and you know this - if it weren't for falling in love with your creative genius, Jeff, I'd probably be running a flower shop right now – or maybe have become an interior decorator or doing something not as gender fixated as engineering".

Sir Jeffrey, held his glass up in a quiet 'toast' towards Lorne smiled wryly and said,

'With realities like that, I guess that's what our pretended reaction will, at worst, *appear* to be - a sort of unrequited love. Anyway, it's late. Let's go to bed"

Chapter 3

Messages in A Spherical Bottle

2051-54/21st Century - Port of Brest/Barents Sea

At the earlier request of Lorne Harris Junior, Canadian Senator Lorne Harris Senior had indeed ceded to his son's request that he use whatever influence he had with affluent private and public commonwealth friends to make possible finance and construction of Cairns 'Cypsela time capsule project'. Already set up were international bank accounts, to received interest bearing funds from a multitude of 'investors.' Each institution had a determination that their personal legacies to the future of humankind would occupy secure archive space aboard the 1000-year capsule project.

With that outcome already in place, the actual construction was formally assigned to a French marine engineering contractor, UDS Undersea Dive & Salvage Ltee.

The capsule project did not lack for global publicity. Its creator, business tycoon Sir Jeffrey Cairns, was a respected visionary, entrepreneur and imagineer of the 'Cypsela Sphere' Time Capsule. He had been twice featured on the front page of Time Movement Magazine; a four part serial in the Euro/Business Intermittant edition of the London Times; the half billion circulated, Interplanetary Quarterly. Such attention was justified. Cairns' project was probably the most unusual man-created structure since the sculpting and erection of the Colossus of Rhodes.

* * *

Five business-suited passengers debarked from their private chartered jet, Gatwick to Brest, at 0700 hours Wednesday June 5, 2049.

The now retired and aging Canadian Senator, Lorne Harris Senior was assisted off the aircraft by his 41 year old son, Lorne. By now, the younger Harris was a practicing engineer and Junior partner with a Norse company, Sløghtmassen Technology Corporation with facilities in London, Oslo, Antwerp, Buenos Aires and Boston.

Britain's House of Lords member Sir Jeffery Cairns and two senior executives from another prominent associate engineering firm, DBD on Thames, accompanied them off the aircraft. Their appointment had been scheduled since January. They were met by research engineers and experimental teams, all with the executive staff of UDS Undersea Dive & Salvage Ltee. – Suite 5749, #.8, Le Parc Marin nord-ouest, Brest, France.

Groundwork for the meeting involved hastily devised, taped televised interviews, preparatory to face-to-face encounters between relevant British government officials and their senior engineering advisors at Dunham, Braxton and Dunham on Thames. The initial meeting, with the constructors' four Special Projects vice presidents of UDS, was to be conducted, en anglais, in the elegant Brest offices on the La Tour de Parc de marina.

Also scheduled to be in attendance were two Paris senior bureaucrats, members of Le Conseil Terre/Spatial de France (Earth/Space Council of France), an agency of the government. It was their assignment to monitor the exchange of views by all parties as they pertained to international trade agreements and conformity to the Council's mandated objectives.

Following the protocol of introductions, the eleven functionaries gathered around a smaller conference table for preliminary discussion.

The Senior VP of UDS smiled his greeting.

"Bonjour, accueillir, les messieurs... our distinguished guests.

"Merci, monsieur Minister," said the contractor's Senior VP, UDS Undersea and Salvage Ltee. In lieu of the large volume of details to be dealt with during your stay here, allow us to initiate a fast start to our discussions."

Everyone around the table nodded in concurrence.

"From the exchange of materials data we have had so far," started the UDS executive, "we are all aware that the primary casements are made of the special composition metals on the exterior shells to withstand every possible corrosive and destructive sea elements – salt deposit erosion, iceberg collisions, salvage pirates and quakes. As you leave the conference hall later today, you will be issued with a cardboard DVD folder containing our sphere's overall statistics. It is to enable concerned parties, at their leisure, to more arduously review UDS recommendations in this regard. But we are –"

One of the French government officials stood and raised a hand to speak.

"Pardon, Monsieur. Since we in Le Conseil Terre/Spatial de France, and were *not* part of earlier discussions with UDS, may I address the right honorable Sir Jeffrey Cairns? May we be apprised of the initial motivating reason behind the intent to provide a capsulated record of man's life on earth in the 21st century, addressed, as we understand it will be, to a future people we will never know? S'il vous plait, what motivates this intent? More importantly sir, why a time capsule? Why not simply, a taped or disc message buried in a crypt somewhere?"

Cairns thought 'Trust a government official to interrupt the flow of a good beginning to the conference with a trivial question on personal motivation! Inappropriately timed too." Just as he was about to reply, he noticed that the 78 year old Canadian ex-Senator stood – probably to detract Cairns' irritation from showing. "With respect, Sir Jeffrey, let me first offer a political reply as to why visionary people like you act on their revelations."

The old man walked to the back of the chair occupied by his son.

"When my son Lorne relayed this time capsule concept to me – well over twenty years ago now – I knew what motivated *him* – even then. I explained to Lorne, that sometimes, works in our lifetime are *really* intended to affect *future* lifetimes. Otherwise, what other value could Tolstoy have had for writing that long, long, long and very boring, century old, history novel, War and Peace? I happen to believe that The Torah, The Qur'an and the Bible were scripted for the same reasons. Just as pyramid and temple builders did *not* inscribe hieroglyphic inscriptions in stone just for *their* generations, but for *future* ones! In the year 1481, artist, prophet, visionary and inventor, Leonardo de Vinci did not draw pictures of bicycles, flying apertures and other such inventions to come, just for the shock effect on his peers of the day. Those were *meant for us*, right here – right now."

He took a moment to clear his wavering voice before proceeding.

The senior Harris seemed to lose his voice to phlegm in his throat. He finished hoarsely,

"Forgive me, Sir Jeffrey. It was not my intention to usurp your response."

Lorne Harris Jr. thought, 'Smooth, Pop, smooth. When all logic seems a waste of time, go for the big emotional picture!'

"Quite all right, Senator. Thank you, sir.

"Now, messieurs, gentlemen…On the matter of security, we are all *signatories* to non-disclosure agreements. As agreed, all work is to be expeditiously performed, executed to our satisfaction, delivered to our principal shareholders as specified and contracted at the figures shown on your charts in order to meet our original mutual agreements. Of course the usual guarantees are in effect. Mind you, somehow I suspect that when this capsule is found several centuries hence, guarantees will be quite academic, wouldn't you agree?"

Knowing smiles and chuckles at the humor of that statement from such a normally somber man as Sir Jeffrey…He looked up, smiled and returned to his meetings documents.

"While all this has been discussed and resolved here as specified in our letters of intent based on previous correspondence, allow me to résumé general specifications in a condensed version, for the time being..."

Cairns paused in his opening statements, opened the top file in his brief case. He took out a bottle of Perrier water, sipped and set it on the table. Dimming house the lights, he began by projecting specs on a circular screen.

"This outer shell of the time capsule sphere, which we have named Cypsela, for reasons which will be detailed for you, is 91.44 meters diameter, outside dimensions. We will deal with the specifications on the cone aperture later. Viewed from an aerial or seaward craft at a distance of 4 to 5 km, the exterior is to *appear* as luminous, multi-colored strands of glass, criss-crossing its surface. Specialty engineers have assured us that this effect will be produced by a series of channels in the steel hull with 24 cm wide, sealed transparent coverings containing *colored*, light oil. Rolling about, as it would in a beam sea, produces an in-motion effect – bands of color against a darkened sea to attract attention. Therefore when the submerged sphere, after one thousand years, mind, is let loose to the surface it will bring intelligent life to investigate. If not – well, that too, makes this whole thing quite academic."

The Cypsela sea sphere project with colored channels engineered across its surface.

A British Government engineer interjected

"At the risk of repeating specifications known to most of us, would you give us a quick run down on structural basics relating to supporting the sphere's longevity?"

Sir Jeffrey appeared momentarily confused. He had forgotten that some of the delegations were not up to speed on assembly particulars. He recovered "Quite right. Of course. I do apologize. Just so we're *all* on the same page let me introduce you to Monsieur Marcel Guilliame, UDS Project Engineering Director who can deliver a generalization on sphere structure. Monsieur?"

Merci, Sir Cairns. Let me first reiterate that which most of us already know. Since centuries of built up salt water *encrustation* eroding the sphere's exterior surface is a certainty, special repellants, embedded in the composite metal shell will act as self-sterilization instrumentation to the semi-pressurized hull. Inside, simply put, precise refrigeration control to protect interior contents calls for a three-layered shell part of the sphere's 11,400 metric tonnes, to withstand sea pressure of more than 273.7 psi under a submerged displacement of 6800 tonnes. The sphere shell alloy will also have to be as light as aluminum, as smooth and as hard as a diamond surface, not unlike titanium. Once sealed, riveted outer seams will be almost impossible to detect even with the latest radiation techniques known and forecast. There will be three hidden entry ports, enabling passage in and out of the sphere's interior.

The half meter thick husk or outer shell is to be crafted in three layers. One hollow, flotation, layer will be penetration proofed with a kind of explosive substance between the first and second layer. Hopefully, this will act to discourage sea salvage "pirates" who might attempt access. To that end, the device is a sensitive detonation mechanism that, when exposed to certain instrumentation such as acetylene torches, causes an ensuing detonation to explode outward.

In the matter of the exterior channels with their neon-like, phosphorescent color criss crossing facility, this is to attract attention when the capsule is on sea surface, UDS labs have already concocted an oil and an alcohol content, to prevent freezing.

The actual sphere will be tethered to a stable seabed object, such as one at about 300 meter depth, with special composite 30 cm thick, steel link chain from the cone extension to the sea floor anchor position. This will stabilize and secure the sphere some ten fathoms below the sea surface. As to the interior profile and contents, I must prevail upon his lordship, Sir Jeffrey, to detail that for you."

The capsule creator stood again, shifted his stance, pausing to flip his own notes and to turn the projector carousel to its designated position.

"Merci, Monsieur Guilliame. As the rendering projected in front of you indicates, content will include canisters and large artifacts, libraried in compartments on the five levels you see here. The main hall of the sphere will be divided into compartments over five 'floors' with extra high ceilings to accommodate some exhibits. One whole floor will contain compressed data in archived encyclopedic events, DNA, personal records, video and pictorial data of every person and most creatures on earth dating back to the beginning of the Gregorian calendar. Additional, yet to be established contents, within the attached *cone* compartment that is below the main body of the sphere, will be known only to a select group of fourteen agricultural people and their porters before transport of the entire combination sphere and cone structure for deposit at a specified latitude and longitude in the very North Atlantic.

By self sustaining nuclear energy, the *cone* will be insulated, partly to retain an exact "*deep freeze*" –196° Celsius. This will ensure a lasting quality to an extensive, special cargo of hibernating hybernating forest products, domestic root edibles such as Polish potatoes, radishes, beets and parsnips..."

"M'excuser pour l'interruption, monsieur," a French government engineer rose to speak.

"Is not the English word 'hybernating,' in reference to a bear's winter cave?"

"Non, Non monsieur! You are referring to h i b e r n a t i n g. Hybernating is our term for a relatively unknown preservation process by which living protoplasm in plant dries life and the seed of hydrogen molecules render the product inactive for any extended period of time. They can be – " Cairns hesitated. He looked skyward for a moment as though searching for a comparative example. He found one and continued.

"Monsieur. Have we not all seen dried out acorns on the forest floor? These are uncontrolled examples of what has become a phonologically new agricultural term. "hybernate" – h Y b instead of h I b, referring to the winter long sleep of hibernating bears! You see, some vegetation seeds, like the acorn, can lie in a dormant state for literally hundreds of years – hybernating, *not* hibernating,. When given an enriched soil/moisture supply, they can grow later into a forest of full grown aging oaks, or pines or – you get the idea, oui?"

Returning to his notes, the speaker continued.

"It is the consensus of present day prognosticators that our earth will be sorely in need of seed stocks within multi millenniums. Therefore, it is our hope that future generations will find our seed gift, an opportunity to regenerate the earth with food stocks from our sphere's massive storage bins of grains and green feed. As well, there would be other farm produce, which could be rejuvenated, restored and replanted – after controlled thawing, *anytime* after centuries of such storage. As specified, and in order to preserve the sanitary conditions required for agro product, our own cargo installers for the cone section will be the *very last crew* aboard the 'Cypsela sphere', to arrange all seed cargos before the cone hatches are sealed forever for the long journey into time.

While Cairns talked, Senator Lorne Harris thought to himself, 'Where did JC get all that crap about the capsule being a root cellar for plants and grains? Considering the volumes of 21st century lifestyle items that we *could* have taken on as sphere cone cargo, it might seem ok, but there's something that doesn't ring right somehow...the way Cairns announced it, anyway. The senior Lorne decided he *had* to secure answers later, right from the designer's mouth."

Meanwhile the knighted lecturer continued with his sphere profile description to the boardroom audience.

"The capsule's 40 meters of chain link tether are to be anchored deep, attached to the equipment capping a known but abandoned well hole in North Sea floor. The location is above the Arctic Circle in a deepened trough some 100 kilometers off the west coast of Russia's Zamlya Island. When located, the *submerged* sphere will "float" above the trench sea floor to a height of no less than 21 fathoms, beneath a mean average tidal surface. The sunken sphere will be well out of the way of heavily trafficked sea lanes, though, as winter drilling platforms move out of the area, marine traffic is minimal. It will be submerged away from all current *major* shipping routes and to the extreme depths of iceberg and pan thicknesses allowing it to be totally undisturbed. Moreover, the capsule must be easily recoverable. With the programmed deterioration of a specially contrived link, the anchor chain releases our intact sphere; our jobs will have been accomplished."

* * *

Another of the French government's Public Relations officers, who had been furiously taking notes during Cairns' presentation, looked up to ask.

"S'il vous plaît, les Cairns de Monsieur, we assume there is some special significance in the terms of reference for the sphere's motif and the name Cypsela. May we be apprised of the meaning of Cypsela and the promotion materials' references to Cygnus, Liguria, and etcetera?

"I believe I will let my colleague, Mr. Harris *Junior*, speak to that. It was he who first drew the analogy of a mythical venture to the one we are addressing today.

As Jeffrey Cairns gestured towards his young Oxford friend, Lorne Harris responded by opening a leather art case and posting the contents up on easels behind him... graphics and schematic renderings of *designs* for metal sculptures that were to be formed *into* the shell surface of the sphere capsule. One set of drawings duplicated the design in ceramic tile.

"Thank you, Sir Jeffrey. Messieurs, There *are* those of our critics who are of the opinion that our project may just be a borderline *fairy tale* – *and* they are *not entirely* wrong!"

Lorne paused to allow for the amused reactions to his statement.

"They don't know how close they have come to relating to our time capsule similarity to a variation of one of Ovid's many Greek mythological epics. Call us romantics but I'm afraid that we may be guilty of actually *pilfering* the poetic beauty of a particular Greek myth. We've also turned its story line somewhat to our own analogous publicity purposes. According to Ovid, King Cygnus *was* the mythical beloved and benevolent ruler over a Ligurian kingdom – a region somewhere about where Genoa is now,

Sometime during his reign, he is fabled to have been was lost at sea. His vessel was a *hollow sphere*. This hollow Cypsela was described by Ovid as an achene. In Greek terms, an achene is a small dry one-seeded fruit, thus an inferior and under developed ovary."

Harris took up his pointer and pointed out parts of the Greek styled drawings as he described their relevancy.

"Imaginary though it may have been, there were similarities to our concept. The outer covering, or pericarp, does not burst open as does some Mediterranean fruit were it to become laden or over-ripe. It stays closed. Here's where the myth becomes hazy...almost pointless. "No one", states Ovid "believes this dried up seed husk has anything more to offer". So for reasons known only unto villains in the myth, while inside the Cypsela, the revered monarch Cygnus was changed into a swan, to assuage the sorrow of losing his best friend, Phaeton, the son of the sun god, Apollo. So out of Cypsela, Cygnus is resurrected as a star fish and placed among the stars.

Anyway, in another mythical version, Metamorphoses (XII 581), Ovid follows a different course, suggesting that the seed carried was the fallen body of Cygnus's best friend, Phaeton. And what does Phaeton have to do with all of this? I haven't the foggiest idea!' But according to the dreamers who created this unlikely story, it was really Phaeton who was turned into a swan and sent to live among the stars. Confusing? Remember, ancient Myths are not *supposed* to make sense to anyone but ancient Greeks!

But – if it seems to you that, to suit *our* purposes, we are shaping a 'knock-off' ' – pardon the American colloquialism - our claim to the analogy is justified. In a sense, we are sending *our* spherical time capsule to sea and it too shall remain mythical, until found. We do so, in the fervent hope of its *resurrection* from a sea society, by a race of our species, well into the future of this planet. Gentlemen, Messieurs, let me be more specific ...One *thousand years* into the future!"

Harris waited for that punch line to create an effect. It did. In looking at each other with open mouths, the French people at the table murmured their astonishment. The young engineer went on.

"This shouldn't surprise you. For what *other* kind of *impossible mission* might we spend these valuable hours with you to achieve a less prolific objective than this?"

He turned to his graphic cards.

"If you will oblige us, please direct your attention to these renderings of the insignia that will be sculptured into the hull of Cypsela. It is the head of a *swan*, representing Cygnus not yet in the stars but among the star*fish* depicted by this relief image of a large starfish, and the Greek inscription, Cypsela, 2054. This design will also be applied in ceramic tile in the floor of one of the key control compartments inside the cone section"

With an impish smile, he put down his pointer, saying,

"With apologies for excessive and necessary detail – but Messieurs, but you *did* ask! …and many thanks for your patience. Merci".

*   *   *

UDS's Senior VP rose at his seat and directed his gaze to Sir Jeffery. "Your lordship, you chose Undersea Diving and Salvage, not only for its expertise in design and structure of unusual marine vehicles, but for its contracting, innovative capability in submersible vessels. As you were speaking of the need for seamless hull shells with everlasting quality, I am reminded that you should know that for well over 50 years, UDS fabricators have been working closely with the Air Bus Industries manufacturers and engineering facilities at Toulouse, Hamburg and their far East facilities. An attached marine forensics division, through Air Bus parent shareholding corporations EAD and BAE systems has also been involved in UDS's underwater product development. Their revolutionary work in composite metal fuselage and hull creation is renowned for meeting the quality requisites of a select group of clients including NASA. We are another such client. That, Sir Jeffery, is how and why we can guarantee, with complete certainty, your stipulations for a three layered shell of space age specifications.

All facets will be engineered precisely as are needed to meet the structure's intended purpose. They will be proven by both our sea trials and extreme pressure tests.

In order to meet our appointed completion dates, some parts of the project have already moved past the drawing boards to actual fabrication and the vessel is expected to be ready for thorough evaluation by early February. Meanwhile, the cone's drawings have been modified as directed and will be integrated into the sphere just before the initial assembly.

*   *   *

Three days later, when all meetings and committee sessions had been concluded, a gourmet banquet of French cuisine and champagne was hosted by the UDS Corporation in honor of its clients. During the pre-dinner cocktail hour, Lorne Harris Senior took the opportunity to seek out Sir Jeffrey Cairns for a *private* discussion and a quiet walk through the company's treed garden pathways.

The Senator chose his words carefully

"Jeffrey. I am aware that there are aspects to this project to which I am not privy."

I also know that even as a *patron* of the concept, it is *not* essential that *I* be given an accounting of every nut, bolt and cargo package, but there is one thing, I believe I am *entitled* to learn."

Cairns stopped. He looked up at a clear night sky, already so full of stars.

"Yes, I know, Senator. You are about to ask me about the little white lie that I implied at the inception meeting, two days ago. Your intuition serves you well. *And yes.* There *is no* intention of using the sphere's cargo cone to carry agricultural products, is there? But with respect sir, I must *decline* to reveal more information than what I have already given."

The politician replied.

"My younger brother, Harold Harris is a mixed grain/beef farmer on the prairies of Western Canada. He knows agriculture backwards. Whatever I know, I learned from him by osmosis. And I can tell you, face to face, that both of us know as well as *you* do that there is *no such thing* as a 'hibernated' – hyber Y – and especially in the feed and grain business."

As both men stopped on the path, looking intently at one another, stern and unsmiling,

"In fact, Sir Jeff, I'd lay even money that the *true* description of that cone's cargo is a *much more* questionable subject than mere plant life."

The Senator opened his mouth to debate further but Cairns hurried to speak on, now in low tones towards the older man.

"What *is* still *true*, Senator, is that we British are still helpless to conduct ourselves other than as the covey of people we have sculpted ourselves to be over many centuries. Overly conservative, typically evasive, hopelessly indirect, and often given to 'bafflegab' consisting of 'pony poop' rather than, as you might say, straight goods. Happily, you North Americans are almost direct opposites. Straight talk or nothing"

He paused for a moment as though to consider the best way to frame his answer..

"OK. Then it's *nothing*. The fact of the matter is, Mister Harris, I confess that the subject of the real cone *cargo*, is *much too delicate* to discuss – particularly at a time when *ethical* conduct is supposedly to be the watchword of people of science. It isn't always. But it must be *now*. I can only ask your forgiveness, Senator, that I choose to keep that part of the project a secret reserved for the scientists of the 31st century."

As Sir Cairns moved away to continue their walk, he said....

"I have revealed it to *no one* – with *one exception*." He paused again. His voice turned softer.

"*Your son* is cognizant of the hidden cargo slated for the Cypsela 'ballast' cone section. Besides me, only the junior Lorne knows what we are really sending into the future. And while he understands *why*, we can not inform others of this in this 21st century, we both concur that that, if expectations are met, the contents in the hold of the cone will be the most meaningful *content* we can send to people of future centuries"

Some people with less wisdom than Senator Harris would have taken umbrage with Cairns' refusal to divulge the secret. The language difference in the 'hybernating' agricultural plant life story was given to cover why the cone's climatically controlled hold was so necessary. The true answer would never have been accepted.

The Senator slowed his step, and then stopped his strolling shuffle.

"There's something else that's bothering you, Senator?"

"I didn't plan to bring this up Jeff. – But it is Lorne Junior's intense and long-standing interest in the project – but since you have... "

The Canadian politician was fidgeting. He was now glad that their face-to-face discussion was cloaked in evening shadow. Gathering his courage, he spoke.

"It is apparent that you have a compatible working relationship with Lorne. Everyone can see that. Obviously, you have placed great professional faith in my son's contribution. Not so apparent to others perhaps, is the degree of intimacy I detect between you. As a father, I cautiously broach this matter – simply because I *am* a devoted father. Quite naturally, I may be disappointed that my own son favors uni–sex relationships.

"Not *relationships*, senator – *one* relationship – and I speak for both of us. I am in no position to comprehend how a father might judge an offspring's involvement with anyone of the same sex but I *can* assure you neither he nor I harbour *any* remorse, guilt nor even regret at what might seem to you – and others – like an untenable if not clandestine association. It's just that both of us safeguard our privacy and the closeness that has captured us – almost by accident. Perhaps if you were aware of the *respect* we carry for each other, both professionally and as fellow human beings, you might feel less distressed."

The older man, looked away, dabbed an eye and murmured, "Perhaps"

Then as if to sign off that line of conversation, Lorne Harris Sr. raised his voice to emphasize that this most recent topic was a closed matter.

"*Your* vision sparked and devised this floating time capsule project to fruition, Sir Jeffrey. Your supporters, contractors and investors are fully cognizant of that. Therefore, it is *your* prerogative to divulge – or not, both the method of delivery of sphere and content to *whomever* the hell you want. But is vitally important that *all* parties involved have been up front and forthright as to the full reasons *for* and the methodology *of* installation of your Cypsela project."

After a few moments of reflective thought, he added,

"However, to my chagrin, I note there were no details made as to the *ancillary cargos* in the sphere and cone ballast sections....

With a drawn out sigh of resignation, he went on,

"But, aware of those who would oppose our aims for whatever reasons, I accede to your desire for confidentiality."

Cairns nodded gratefully, extended his hand and said quietly,

"Shall we go back in and drink to that, Senator?"

*   *   *

By early February, two icebreaker class tugs, sailed out of the Westerschelde Inlet away from the Belgium fleet at their Antwerp pen. As the lowest bidder to the Cairns combine, they had contracted for harbor work at Brest on the northwest tip of France and for a towing assignment to an unspecified vector in the North Sea.

In that regard, the task had been doubly difficult to configure, considering the deep draft underneath the cone. Sphere roll movement in shallower water complicated a functioning ballast application.

Like two behemoths struggling against a leash, the oversized tugs positioned themselves ahead of the twenty story high, UDS dock crane. On this immense arm, the 91.44 meter, (300 ft). OD ball was lowered, with the cone protruding some 20 meters downward beneath the underside of the sphere. This was the deepest part of the bay port of Pointe de St. Mathieu. At low tide, the draft was not that far off the ocean floor on the bay. With the top of the inverted cone, inset about 10 meters into the sphere, the entire package was afloat so that the sphere's top curvature was a mere 25 to 30 feet above water surface. Submerged, the entire craft could be compared to the proverbial iceberg. Most of its bulk laden with cargo is unseen from above. Viewed from the middle deck of the five floors on the inside, the voluminous space would have been like an empty 16 story circular-sided warehouse with 50' foot high steel ceilings. Standing against the interior wall on one side, one human might make out a human figure on the other side of the sphere – but too far away to know *who* it might be.

Intended as a form of ballast and to act as a tether by which to secure the sphere at its final undersea location, an enormous chain led from the sphere's subsurface, cone point to a multi leveled, steel platform in one of the tug's storage holds just below and annexing the tug's capstan extension below deck. In the event of a wallowing, high sea, some chain was allowed to drag off the tug's stern, allowing it to act as a stabling sea anchor. Each platinum-sheathed chain link was 1.82 meters (6') long, 53.43 centimeters (21") thick. In order to disguise their unusually shaped 'barge' as it sailed past the heavily trafficked shipping lanes, mill hands at UDS in Brest covered the top of the sphere with a fold away Quonset hut shaped roof, from the water line up. In this disguise, this huge profile might be perceived by whatever passing traffic hove into view, as a huge wooden granary vessel, or perhaps as a massive ship's repair shop being relocated.

* * *

After making fast both steel-corded towlines from the tugs' rear capstans to exterior cleats on the now-sealed and stowed sphere, both nuclear powered tugs, sailed from Brest on May 21st 2051. Their headings would eventually take one of the tugs hauling the sphere to the 'summer' waters east-northeast of the Russian port city of Murman'sk. After rolling over some foothill-like swells coming off the Biscay and on towards the mouth of the English

Channel, the smaller companion tug cast off its towlines and headed east to its home base in Belgium. Meanwhile, super tug would chug past Iceland to port and the Faeroe Islands Group on their starboard side – much too far off the horizon to catch sight of those still snow patched lands. On a northeasterly course, their headings would eventually take them to a final destination over the top of the Arctic world on into Russian waters, over 1000 kilometers northeast of the port city of Murman'sk.

Commanding the tug was Danish Captain Jorgen Johansen. It was he who had had plotted the most expeditious route; an arc-like course past Northernmost Norway into a sea of cork-screw twisting – conflicting winds , inconsistent currents and drifting ice pan. This and their unwieldy cartage slowed course speed, never exceeding 13 knots.

* * *

Just before leaving Brest, Sir Jeffrey had had a confidential meeting with Captain Johansen. As a result and unknown to his crew, the Captain was committed to make a clandestine nighttime stop enroute. They were instructed to position themselves close aboard a harbor buoy at Bear Island's inlet entrance some 500 kilometers south-southwest of Spitzbergen. At an appointed time, still moderately light at 2300 hours, a low frequency marine radio contact directed a terse message to the tugs' bridge to watch for a visual Morse code signal coming from the direction of Bear Island. Only Johansen knew that it would come from a small, unmarked, unflagged and probably unregistered freighter emerging from the drift ice and half-fogged shadow of the island's silhouette.

By the time they closed sufficiently, Johansen gestured to the freighter's on-board derrick operator to indicate that the floating Quonset had to be shifted aside. Now close aboard the tug and the freighter the working boat's crane was now poised to swing over the sphere. At the end of the derrick arm, its magnetic claws and clamps picked up the huge, now uncovered orb, so that it cleared the surface, exposing the top of the cone extension. The freighter's bow tilted precariously downward under the added weight of the sphere and cone at the end of the derrick's steel lines.

At that very moment, the freighter slipped close aboard the tug and the gently swinging ball. Parka-clad and wearing ski masks to protect them against the frigid night, a crew of 10 men in a Zodiak craft were disgorged from a midships hatch of the freighter, They were followed out by a 2 meter (6 ft) wide sheet of flexible material, trailing like canvas or carpet. Clamped to the bottom ledge of the hatch opening, the material wound out from the roll in the Zodiac as they paddled a very short way to the still partly submerged cone section, below the towering metal ball. The Zodiac crew broke out illuminated light sticks. They sought to find the cone's upper hatch door mechanism just where it joined the underside of the sphere. As the hatch swung open, they trundled their end of the roll into the hatch door. In the dim flickering light, it became apparent that the 'highway' of material from ship to cone, was really a flexible steel mesh of. chain mail. This is linked steel of immense strength and overall flexibility.

From within the cone, nine of the men shouted echoing commands just as the first of a string of huge 'packages' began slide down a long trough of pliable chain mail; a sort of ramp towards the cone door. Norwegian accents were the only human sounds heard in the dusky darkness and calm leeside waters of the inlet.

Instructed to stay below, both vessels' non-functioning crew was nowhere to be seen. Those that were functioning were working with frantic ferocity and speed in the misty darkness of a hidden bay and an overcast midnight sun.

Large black shadows of weighty crates, 3 meters in length, less than a meter high and wide; emerged one by one from the freighter to begin their almost continuous slide downward on the chain mail ramp right through the cones one open hatch.

No one thought to count, but well over 100 such pieces came down the slide in a surprisingly quiet stream of rolling stock. Three times larger than the now cone stored packages, one additional and final elongated crate came out, just as the freighter's hatch was closing. It barely fit through the cone's entryway hatch. Shrouded in canvas, a part of it caught on an inside hinge and was ripped. A sharp eye would have spotted it, the surface showing through the ripped cover. It was not a carton, but more like a cage.

In less than forty-five minutes from the opening to the closing of hatches, one last Zodiac crewmember withdrew a twistable strip of what looked like moldable metal. With that and a portable weld kit, he sealed the cone hatchway as though it had never existed. The cone and sphere were lowered back into the bay's waters. The operation was done. Men on the water scrambled up their freighter's icy net ladder. As the freighter got underway and slipped the bay, the Zodiac was being winched up on its deck.

Now Captain Johansen's tug with its nuclear power house clatters into life. They were reheating the tug interior after a freezing 35 minutes of scurried, numbing cold of the last hour. A ship's bell sounded and the tugs crews materialized. They were put at re-installing the Quonset hut disguise over the above sea surface part of the sphere. Then into the wardroom for hot coffee. Without running or steamer lights, the small freighter had long since moved out.

* * *

Back on course after Bear Island and while chugging onward to a destination, in relatively calm, 'neutral' Norwegian waters, Captain's Jorgen Jorgenson studied his manifest and shipper's directions. These instructed him that he slow to five knots. He was to stand by for a drop deck landing by a helicopter from Spitzbergen. That was to facilitate the landing of five UDS French diving specialists and their equipment. Five pressure resistant dive suits with composite steel helmets and 19 kg weighted 'shoes', that were also equipped with closed circuit, mixed gas rebreathers, (CGR) recycling used air into breathable air. It was these adventuring deep seas specialists who had the dubious challenge of doing a visual discovery of Dry Hole 22-64 B, some 250 meters down, on the silt covered ocean floor.

Once arrived at the Barents Sea quadrants, latitude 073°004m N, longitude 052°002m E, the Captain's manifest had directed that he secure the massive geo domed sphere from its towlines. To avoid passersby detection of activity on deck, even at a time when sea traffic was virtually nil at this remote bearing, they were to stand at that position for no more than twenty four hours, to enable performance of a cursory underwater survey.

Aft, two divers finished suiting. Now, UDS Diving Chief, Maurice Bennauville and his welder associate were ensconced in self-sustaining, bulbous-like, 'deep sea jump suits' with built-in lead weighted belts and heavy helmets. Weighted boots and bulky, multi-direction helmet portals were also vision and motion restricting.

One is reminded of the cartoonish Michelin Tire Man commercials of forty years ago. So much more advanced were deep dive suits and accoutrements now, that UDS chief diver Bennauville could assure himself of hazardless underwater function at deeper depths. It was not so long ago, he thought, that the narcotic effects of mixed gas breathing at minus *300 feet* could be responsible for oversights of function, *let* alone at 300 *meters*!

Exactly at 1120 hours, July 2nd, positioned at the tug's wheel house railing, Captain Jorgensen watched as the Assistant Chief Dive Chief of UDS and his associate, were hoisted off the transom platform and down into the forbidding black ice water. Following a precautionary slow descent to 249 meters (816 ft) to this very western edge of the Barents Sea, thirty seven minutes later, the divers were at search depth.

Just off the stern of the oversized tug, a surface the crew was readying the submersible sphere, cone and chain for installation. Meter plus long, steel chain links, leading from the cone's pointed bottom 43 meters were let out 43 meters downward toward the anchor position on dry hole, 22-64B. Welding the bottom chain link to a well head would complete the official planting of Lord Cairn's sphere, where it would be securely immersed and hopefully, unfound for 1000 years plus.

At an appointed time, to be determined by Johansen, they were to maneuver their special 'weight scales house' over the exact position, given to them by the divers ready for winching the sphere into the depths.

The Captain strode to a deck table teaming with charts and drawings. As he did, he issued a beep signal into his head set.

"Maurice. Maurice?"

Into his earphone, came the response.

"Vous avec appele´mon Capitaine? Over!"

"Oui Bennie! I have some guys here recounting the sphere's chain lengths. When you find our anchor spot, would you be sure to have your people recheck that depth again to make sure our chain lengths meet the specs. Oh yeah – and that capped well head *is at exactly* one hundred and thirty seven fathoms; you should be right under where we calculate you to be right now. Report when your metal detectors pick up the 'Christmas Tree' or whatever is sitting on the wellhead. Over"

Judging from the heavy panting into his radio, Maurice Bennauville was busy on station. In a pensive mood though, he said to Johansen,

"You know, it may be the middle of midnight sun up this way, Capitaine, but even with a couple of those high shine halogens, we're still in the dark down here'"

Then he added,

"Oh…and with these cheap 'Made in Lower Slobovian-type metal detectors', we keep getting distracted by debris, from a couple kilometers away, so *they're* not much help. Right now, at our depth, we're practically going by Braille to find *any* item bigger than a Citroen sedan – especially with the 'silt clouds' we're kicking up, And those robot detector crawlers keep stirring up even more of this silt bottom. More metal down here than we expected. Our bouncing detector needles are making us look in ten directions at once – "

Bennauville paused for a full ten to twenty seconds. Only his heavy breathing filled the earphones for what seemed like an intermission at the palladium.

Captain Jorgensen cut in.

"Bennie?! Where'd you go? With all the problems we got, we sure as hell don't need a phone failure right now. Come back. Come back. Over."

Then Maurice's voice filled his phone.

"Hey Boss. We just had a strong sonic ping from a 'biggy' to the ten o'clock position of where target should be… Could be a world-war-two transport, loaded with hardware. Wouldn't mind coming back up this way some day. Love to check it out... Meanwhile – the search goes on. We *should* be looking for any indication of a string stem in capped well hole, shouldn't we? Right? Over."

"You're asking *that* – *now*? Over"

"Je comprend! Je comprend! This is damn confounding! C'est - like looking for passion in the red light district!' A dry hole is filled with cement, oui. It had better be a *dry* hole, mon Capitaine – else we're going to have to use it anyway. It has to be close by! Over! I guess"

"Bennie, we've only got less than seven hours left to anchor this ball." Jorgen Johansen rattled his set,

"Figure we can do? Over?"

No reply.

"Oh great!" the UDS dive Director exclaimed into his radio set..

"That's all we need. More pressure. Still, we should be – Oh – Attendre – une second, Jorgen - have to leave you – une momente, - we might have a have a lead here. Over."

Now the tug's Danish captain turned to UDS techies at the table console.

"Ghislain?"

He addressed one of them.

"Find me a Tectonic plate chart with co-ordinates of our position from the nearest point of the Nansen Ridge plate."

"Got it right here, Monsieur. Regardez? 1480 nautical miles – due north."

"For Satan!" swore the captain, in a mild Danish curse.

"Don't think *I'd* want to leave *anything* that close to a spreading plate, Ghislain. Under sea ice or not, that's could be like a zipper on a fat man's pants! *If the*

Ridge were to bust loose, that big ball may not be here *when* it's supposed to be."

"Non m'sieur...*us* neither!'"

* * *

The crackle of the diver's phone "Jorgen! We got it"

Then he gave the exact position of the well head.

"So lower that cone chain. And we're ready for the power winch down here. What do you say? Twenty minutes to lower? Start letting the chain out at the same time, Comprenez vous? But by that time we're going be part way up. So send down the chain gang! Oh - Skip. If we're to finish this job within your time frame, our other three divers should be on their way down within ten minutes. On our way up, we will be spending about seven extra minutes stringing our winch wire connectors leading up to the lowest chain link. So tell Kurt and the next crew – do not forget to grab the winch wire on their way down. OK Jorgen, old boy… ready or not, we're coming up - Over and out."

Captain Jorgen had had his second dive team of three in the mess room going over details.

Just before sealing space helmets with their three mesh steel ports, the ship's commander gave them a final word.

He said "Kurt, just remember, after you have powered up your winch in readiness and when the sphere is ready to swim, give us the *high* sign on the phone and we'll give you the *pull* sign, OK?. OK? Over"

"Kurt, what *is* your Celsius read reading? Over"

"Aye, Skipper. We read minus 11° Celsius. For the North Sea, that's a like balmy summer day. Over."

"OK. Keep calm. We're ready when you are....Give us your high sign when you guys are hooked on and coming up. Over."

Jorgen was calmed. The finish line was in sight. Now he gave diver Kurt his final word.

"Don't forget to hook up the platform so we can bring up the winch. Oh – and don't forget to turn out the lights. See you shortly. Out."

A relieved Jorgen Johansen blew out a big breath of air through pursed lips. He felt like that thinker guy - Rodan's statue of a man with the globe on his back. He felt a great weight had been taken off his shoulders too.

After steel welding the cone's downward links onto the well head's 'Christmas tree,' Lord Cairn's 1000 year Cypsela sphere was officially planted. Thank Thor – or whoever!

Captain Jorgen turned to a "fire crew" ready to go and sitting in a tender to be lowered from the tug.

"OK. You guys know the drill. The sphere is down and secured. When the second dive team is aboard, fire and sink the fake Quonset Hut! And guys! *No smoke!* We don't need an audience, got it?'

Bennie and his very tired first team finally dumped their equipment on the after deck of the tug for the deck hands to stow. Joining them below for a coffee and sandwich, Jorgen wasn't as elated with fulfilling his job as he should have been. An uneasy feeling suddenly came over him. Everything, since Brest, had gone almost too smoothly. .

He was right. On the voyage home to Antwerp, his good friend and world-renowned deep-water diver, fifty-five year old Maurice Bennie Bennauville died. For two days, Maurice was committed to his bunk experiencing a high fever, headaches and respiratory difficulties. The on-board medic tended to him and administering controlled doses of pure oxygen. What was at first diagnosed as a flawed decompression problem was later pegged as a cerebral air embolism possibly caused by unforecast and extended tenure underwater. It wasn't the first time, but now there was Bennauville's advancing age. And there was the stress, anxiety and exertion of the whole exercise. As the coroners later report was to determine, a somewhat rare pulmonary anteriovenous malfunction (PAMV) was the cause of his sudden illness. Anyway, to his friends, diagnosis was not their concern, Bennie has passed on, never to come this way again – never to 'ping' out discovery of sunken wartime sightings he wanted so badly to explore on his return trip.

* * *

Fifteen days earlier, on the way to the sphere deposit site - at the time of taking on the diving personnel and equipment, another person, also garbed in winter fur trimmed parka, scurried unnoticed across the chopper landing platform to below deck quarters, going directly to a reassigned compartment. He rarely ventured out thereafter, except to converse with Johansen in his cabin and to check on deck crew duties, preparatory to launching activity.

 Now while the tug's crew was at work make preparations to depart from the sphere's anchoring position for the return voyage to home port, the mystery passenger stood in the shadows of the tug's wheel house as the ship pulled away from the downloading site. Bundled in a Nordic sweater, the tall, middle-aged man, flapped his arms around himself, in an effort to shake the penetrating cold of this most ungodly place on the top of the world.

Sir Jeffrey Cairns muttered to himself in the vapor of his breath in such cold air,

"There's your dream, Jeffrey, old man. After thirty something years... it's hard to believe, it is actually happening... Bon Voyage Cygnus, Old boy. May the husk of Cypsela bring you safely to those future shores."

Chapter 4

Seeping Celestial Gas Silences Human Voice – Forever

2360-2370/24TH CENTURY – AUSZEALAND/ ARIZONA/FINLAND/MYANMAR

THE WORLD'S LONGEST *over-seawater* bridge had been under construction for just over 8 years. Here was another structural world wonder that would enable endless caravans of highway ore carriers to deliver tungsten to mainland deep water ports with automated handling facilities. Shipping traffic embarkation advantages at Dunedin's deep port, Port Chambers Inlet and Timaru docks insured delivery commitments.

Five way bridge traffic lanes ensured continuous lorry flow unimpeded by incoming, deadheading traffic and that which brought day to day requirements for the more than 25,000 company employees and residents of the mining complex.

In terms of size and economic benefit to this mega mining and industrial project, the bridge itself would permit the mining complex to guarantee transport for multi-million tons of ore volume and mine site waste products, night and day. The whole endeavor heralded a bounty of export trade possibilities over the next two or three centuries. Spiraling monetary benefits would accrue, raising gross national production figures and resulting in increases in the standard of living of every citizen of AusZealand. For all of that, structured and operational procedures were in accordance with all International Environmental Pacts, which would minimize atmospheric pollution. For 104 kilometers along the southern hemisphere's longitude of E166°55', this steel *anaconda* would snake its way in an arching curve against the heavy currants of the far end of Foveaux Strait. It was a high arch structure straddling the deepest part of the channel, allowing for the world fleets' largest vessels to pass under it. The 86km stretch of tempest-plagued sea would now be connected to the mainland at the most northerly of the farthest eastern isle of the Solander Island Group. There, a massively, gargantuan complex of mixed metal mining and production factory was being constructed to extract raw ores and produce byproducts from tungsten and titanium source deposits to produce steel structural implements, thereby operating some manufacturing processes with its own raw minerals, right on top of it's own underground facility.

The north end of the bridge met the first stretch of plastic/rock composite, simulating a *cement* roadway on the peninsula some 20 meters west of the bottom end of the Fiord's National Parkland.

It traversed alongside dense foliage, threading its way through a green and jade colored mosaic of multi jungle-like rivers and lakes. It took on steep alpine grades and tunnels on its way to meet up with the existing east coast highway settlement at Clinton.

Zealand's Public Works were as delighted as the mining conglomerate of Solander's Great Bear Island Group. Even though the public works administration's capital investment had contributed billions of Aussie bucks, they were fully aware of the higher eternal value of this stretch of highway widening and reinforcing. Without such cooperation, they knew that the cement- ribboned highway up into Dunedin and part of the new route 150km further north into Timaru, would never have been completed.

* * *

Attentive to his inspection of touch-up welds on the very top of the centre bridge section, Weld Inspector Art Devonshire looked up momentarily to see his working partner Reginald Ahikaata struggling to bring his trolley cart to a stop on the other side of the Solander Island Bridge's tower rail track. Without yet clipping his safety strap to the bridge cleat, Reggie waves, then swings one leg over his cable cart by way of getting out to step onto a work platform at the top of the tower. Art turns away for a couple of seconds. When he turns back to greet his aboriginal co-working rigger, he sees the man, standing up, clutching his neck and swaying outward.

Art yells, "Reggie! Grab – grab a joiner bolt or...! Ooh m'god – NOoooo. Fer Krisake – Reggie –"

Looking back at the welder, toppling Reginald Ahikaata's normally narrowed eyes were wide, before rolling over to big whites, looking almost as though pleading with his friend to stop what was about to happen. Reginald seemed to hesitate in mid air – pausing, sputtering one muffled throaty sound and then, spread-eagled backwards and outward, he almost sailed like a professional acrobat– downward. Eerily, there was absolutely no sound except the usual screeching whistle of wind through cables. Not even a sound of what would have been a squelching thud of Ahikaata's mid section hitting the guard rail of the emergency pull off lane below. When the body finally *did* hit water, the barely discernible white splash quickly dissipated in the azure sea.

With numbness initiated by the eight seconds of surrealism which he has just witnessed, Devonshire mindlessly mounts his own cable cart, disengages his automatic security belt from a tower bracket and starts the mini motor to wind down the infernally slow descent to the bridge surface. Halfway down to road level, he flips his collar lapel button, to open the emergency remote channel. He had been so shocked he had almost forgotten to call in the accident care team. In the few minutes it takes the medic group to reach him from one of their multi-stationed medical bridge bunkers, just a half kilometer away along the bridge, Art Devonshire reaches the road deck. Now he half shuffles and half runs the half kilometer back to where the rigger had hit the guardrail. By now he was well into shock mode.

An hour later, he is sitting on the tailgate of a crew vehicle, sipping coffee from the emergency-care team's catering surrey and apothecary, trying to accept the reality of what he has just seen. Art's hands still shook from the mental images he mentally processed over and over again.

Notwithstanding his choked up and broken voice, Arts words were being recorded by two hard helmeted men in suits.

"I never really – saw him ...whole thing... too fast." Art stuttered, then sighed, "One sec... he's there – in – in his cart, the next he's off the side – smack up against the blue sky – in mid air! *Geezzus.* He had his mouth wide open ...like he was trying to holler out...and then he just dropped away. Aw jeez..." he utters, "I don't want to think about this any more..."

One of the hard hatted men in suits, obviously a company safety officer, asks him "Did Ahikaata seem to trip getting off the cart – or did it appear like a piece of his harness gave way?"

Art shakes his head. "No way. Reggie was always special careful – even though he loved his steeple jack job. He took *no risks!* Ever!"

The safety officer had another query

"There was virtually no wind at water surface – maybe ten, eleven kilometers. At the tower top -- were there intermittent, on again wind gusts making it difficult to — could he have been blown off –"

The company investigator didn't finish as Devonshire shivers and shakes his head violently. "There's always a gale up that high but I've seen worse up there!"

In the hope of settling himself, Devonshire lit up his third straight filter-tipped Players.

"Did Ahikaata yell out *anything?*" he was asked.

"Not a word, mate."

The bridge welder appeared to stare into space but he was remembering the sequence of events.

"Though – for few second there, Reggie sure looked like – it seemed... like he *tried* to scream something but – n n noth nothing came out – not even a squeal. But it all happened – so bloody fast." The rigger inspector pauses and reflects...I think he might have coughed or tried to gasp coupla times – but no other sound from him that I could hear – I only heard *myself!* I was yelling something at him. Other'n that, - nothin', I don't know what..."

One of the safety officers picked up on Art's cough remark.

"Mr. Devonshire, did you say earlier that your friend coughed – instead of yelled?"

"Yeah – in a choking kind of way. Funny, I thought about that coming down. But y'see, Reggie had a bit of an asthma condition and I figured – he sometimes got all stuffed up... Hey look mate...Can we talk about this a little later? Sorry – right now, I don't feel so good... Nauseated...Think I gotta..."

Later when factory big shots convened to share the disappointment of the company's first bridge fatality, the coroner's report came as a shocker. Recovered from the fast moving tidal currants of the strait they *found no sea water* in Ahikaata's *lungs.* They reported the cause of Reginald Ahikaata's death, suffered about the same time as he reached to top of the bridge, was apparent *suffocation.* A severe asthma attack could have hit him just as he docked his cart at the top of the tower. *Something* had panicked him, such as becoming unable to breathe all of a sudden. In their autopsy, forensics discovered an unusual anomaly. Nasal passages and larynx tissue had become coated with an adhering coating of faintly, yellowish particles. Composition of this light throat canal dusting was inconclusive, though initial chemical breakdowns *did* reveal a chemical akin to sulphuric acid with minute traces of a nitric oxide.

* * *

Within two weeks of the coroner's inquest, Arthur Devonshire is admitted to Invercargill Hospital with what is first diagnosed as a severe bronchitis condition bordering on emphysema. Speech was limited to a few desultory grunts. Just when attending specialists were preparing to evacuate Art to the Respiratory Ward and research center at St. Marie Hospital in Melbourne, too late they conceded, to consider a more serious malady than first diagnosed, suddenly, in a cardio care cubicle, Art gurgles his last breath, and expires. Though his mind had ceased to control bodily function, the muscles of his heart continued to contract, convulsing his carotid artery for a full minute, before it too became motionless. A slight trickle of yellowish fluid trailed out of a twisted mouth. Like his deceased friend Reginald Ahikaata, an autopsy certificate noted that barely visible, yellowish, strands of phlegm cluttered his mouth and throat. On later and closer inspection, the vocal cartilage within the vertebral structure at the top of the trachea seemed to be somewhat misshapen from normal tissue in the vertebral cord package. Again, respiratory failure was speculated. However since cause was unknown, this was not entered as relevant on the death certificate of Mr. Arthur Milton Devonshire.

* * *

Catching on with the under 30s crowd is the new daredevil sport of *Stratobatics*. Since the early part of this 24th century, the object of the game is to take a 30 minute or so ride in individual helium filled, plastic bubbles, rising from earth's surface to the outer edge of the troposphere 10 to 12 km up. The object of the sport is the free fall ride down. It is to be made *as slow* as the competitor can make it. Fit only for the well-conditioned, medically approved athlete, the sport beckoned those daring young '*immortals*' to test their metal against the forces of gravity.

Some compare the sport of *Stratobatics* to be a combination of the late 20th century's sports of hang gliding off a mountain cliff and Hawaiian surfing on Oahu's north shore.

Just the very extreme rush of lifting to varying layers of stratosphere attracts carefree thrill seekers from all over the western Americas.

The game's challenges are to utilize lift assisted rockets and a disposable, bubble carrier to achieve as much height as updraft and natural flotation would take one rider. Naturally, participants are outfitted in Safety Standard Approved, pressure-controlled, thermal suits and self-contained oxygen helmet. The transparent safety engineered bubble is a double bubble. The inside filter compartment containing ground based air, is a clear paper-thin cover enfolding the pilot. When the outer bubble disintegrates, the filter cover comes away, freeing the competitor to soar from at whatever elevation is achievable. The higher it takes it's human cargo, the better the chance for longest and *slowest* descent) the rider begins a "body surfing" maneuver to earth – not unlike the parachuting or bungee jumping sports of two centuries past. Competitive 'scare devils' then endeavor to defy the streaming downward drag of gravity, by slowing descent as long as possible. That can be achieved by skillful use of "cup brakes", (hard polyethylene shapes, like suction cups perforated with holes, strapped on knee caps, back of elbows, palms of hands) hand gliding but no other slowing device permitted. For instance, under the watchful eye of telescope-equipped referees, using retro-rockets to lower the rate of the free fall disqualifies the entrant.

The length of 'drop-flight' is registered when the suit's inflatable "ParaBrella" canopy and back-up, mini-retro-jets system used for braking just prior to landing, is employed at 600 feet above ground elevation. A soft and controlled landing to ground surface is assured. Wrist meters record individual altitude and elapsed time, during the "slow-surf" descent. Here is the *unique* sports rarity. *Slowest* time wins!

* * *

To promote various tournaments, *Stratobatics* members and friends from all over North America are advised with mailers of impending events. This one was sent out in late September 2362.

"Sun Country STRATOBATICS Championships"

November 17, 18, 2362

Near the southwest corner of Arizona, the desert town of Quartzsite, 20 km east of the California state line on Route 10 into Phoenix. (Check signs for site turn off)

Ideal Site!! Flat, orange brown desert, visually fair to all competitors.
Away from primary scheduled carriers' flight paths and limited air traffic space.
Ground level at just 234.70 m (770 feet) above sea level.
First 100 registered qualify. Quality lift off equipment.
First 10 lift offs commence November 17 at 0615 hours
Top 3 winners get certificates to finals.

Free Camp Ground.

Free Fly Party Nov.18. (just east of Lizard Creek)

Another fun filled day of unobstructed sunshine flights.

Fly Master, Gordon McFadden

* * *

Riding two Hover Cycles, four "sky surfing" regulars from up north pull into Quartzsite's camp and launch grounds. University of Oregon seniors, Beryl Jamison, Raymond Tragg, Lee Chown and Mary Edmondson, had left Eugene very early, two days before, and headed southwest 120 degrees on overland back routes. Considering somewhat indirect, major interstate expressway routes to their destination, they had decided on rental specials of two Harley Hover Cycles. Low cost transportation – their best choice where few full speed routes exist to their target location. These vehicles had the capacity for the stowage of sports equipment on board, thereby maximizing shortcuts and minimizing expenses.

Immediately on arrival, they work out knee cramps from sitting astride their passenger saddles. They busy themselves with preparation and staking of tent accommodation, ancillary equipment. They hung out thermal suits to dry.

As he helps Lee Chown with a tent tarp, Ray Tragg says,

"Seems to me.. This place is so far off the beaten path, there isn't even a path. What's so much better about this place than – say, up Canada way – like at Swift Current's Grasslands Park, where we had the last spring's 'Batics competition? Or better still, how about in the Nebraska prairie? Isolated. Good visibility. Wouldn't it have been a little *closer* for us, too?"

"Nebraska?! Are you kidding me? That's a minimum three day trip *plus*, driving all day 'n all night. And Swift Current!? Get level! This is November going on *December*...unless *you* prefer to freeze your ass off landing in snow banks. Remember it's winter up there right now. Hell no. This place is better by a short shot"

"Yeah Ray. You're going to have trouble as it is, without making an obstacle course race out of it."

That was Lee Chown, preparing to inflate a sleep mattress with a pneumatic inflation unit.

"Do something useful, except complain. Grab that tent corner and stake it up, will you? And besides," he continues. "This semi desert is ideal for lift – and most important, highest hill here is 'bout 500 feet, so no one is going to get pranged on any sharp craggy peak. Know what I mean? Coming down here on thick air will be slicker than oysters in heat. And... *And...*" he hurried to make this point.

"For our purposes, this area has way more predictable air currents than most other southern areas at this time of year."

Standing back to survey his erected tent, Lee said, "There. All the comforts of home. All ready for sleeping – and other things, if we get lucky."

He stopped.

"Hey Ray. You got your mailer with you? What times do they want us to be on the pad tomorrow? Whoap! Never mind. I found *my* mailer."

He pulled his helmet over his head, ostensibly to check out the eternal clock, altimeter and speedometer graphic readings superimposed on the inside of the glassine windowed face plate "Wonder if that time is right...Hey! Jamie!" He yells at Beryl, putting out her ground sheet. "Hope you've attached your suit cups by now if we're going to make the initial lift off times, at sun up, shouldn't we attach our braking cups tonight? What time *you* got now?"

Beryl yells back "O six fifty! No sweat! Did mine already. We'll make first lifts ok. But a hundred other guys here have the same idea. If we were that smart we'd sleep in our thermals tonight so's to be first on the pad tomorrow."

Then she adds, to no one in particular,

"And, we better hope the lift-off crews have our *reserved* bubbles ready for *immediate* helium injection." She adds. "Otherwise we probably won't get off until noon."

"Women are such worry warts..." said Lee, under his breath.

But everyone knew it was Tragg who was the real worrier of the bunch. As fearless as he is, he is gaining a reputation for his natural soaring skills, not to mention his almost bird-like maneuverability. Sometimes he almost seems like he is backing up. But as in his previous flights at Swift Current last spring, he always seems overly picky and tentative just before a competition. Maybe his nervousness was his lack of trust for his oxy-helmet equipment. Ray would always say,

"This sealed off bowling ball always seems to be *closing* in on me!"

It wasn't that he was claustrophobic, by definition, but being enclosed in that helmet just didn't feel totally comfortable to him.

Another group of tow-headed male contestants walk by. One hunk asks, "Anybody here got a closure periods schedule?"

Mary Edmondson hollers out, "Yeah Doll, Wait a sec." Rummaging into one her snakeskin saddlebags..."Anything for you, sweetie! Got a sked right here... for the morning – first closures are ...in two separate one hour periods first from 0948 and ...and then from 1131 hours. For those of us who survive, that is – that gives you guys time to buy me lunch."

"God. I hate the sound of horny-assed women in the morning!" Lee Chown mumbled under his breath. He struggles as he tests the overly snug leggings on his thermal flight suit. He curses, "Who invited that Edmondson nympho this time anyway?"

Having just four completed falls to his credit, Ray Tragg is still considered a novice 'batic. Ever eager to learn, he is never shy about asking stupid questions. Now he asks one,

"By the way, Lee, who is it that stipulates those closure periods these other guys were talking about?"

Since Lee is still busy talking to himself, Mary Edmondson responds, "It means we're all grounded during heavy scheduled atmospheric air traffic and other programmed flight vehicles – like NASA's outgoing rocketry ...that sort of thing. Each sponsoring Stratobatics committee clears all that stuff with federal air traffic control and in this case, you don't have to worry about getting a rocket up your back end. They actually –"

"Last one to the fireside Chili has to sing solo tonight," shrills Beryl Jamison and away she runs with Ray Tragg in hot pursuit.

* * *

Day One. 0720 hours Desert chill is still on at 38° F. Clear for heat. Six of the ten Flight one combatants are having their plastic balloons filled with helium-mix injections. When completed, they are all released at one time, forty feet apart – or eighty, equi-distant.

0812 hours. Ray Tragg's automatic breaking devise device works, just as it should have, lowering his body gently to the surface. Still ground crew sensed there was something not right. Ray lay where he fell, inert. Something is definitely amiss. The first field man to reach the fallen Stratobatics surfer unscrews Tragg's helmet. His face is blue. His eyes are wide open. He had to be dead while still aloft. Ground crews and paramedic attendants conclude that at some lower elevation point, between 5000 and 4000 thousand feet, this Stratobatics competitor had shut down his oxyhelmet and opened a side portal to allow him to breathe atmospheric oxygen levels rather than the controlled oxygen mix in the helmet – even though at that altitude, earth's oxygen *is* breathable for most people. They offer no speculation as to why Tragg came down dead. All his landing procedures had occurred just as they should have – automatically. Gentle ground braking procedure *before* the 500m level still resulted in this dead man in the final descent process.

0835 hours. By the time the second lift of 12 surfers is ready in their almost filled balloons, the next following flight lifts are lined up hoping to be let up when all four are down and in time enough to be ahead of the first closure. According to the observers watching by binoculars, they learn that the latter four of the group of seventeen previous sky surfers from the first lift are down. All are in their tents – each experiencing some breathing difficulties. Paramedics have been summoned. Therefore, the lined up contestants are in a state of silent trepidation. The usual line-up chatter is weirdly non-existent.

0955 hours. Paramedics are loading Tragg's bagged remains into an airborne red cross marked AirBulance, when a camp organizer reports two other jumpers are still in serious condition in their tents needing immediate attention and transport to medical facilities. One of those is Beryl Jamison. Young Miss Jamison lapses into coma. To everyone's disbelief, she fails to respond to resuscitation.

Before death, neither victim could speak much above a croaked whisper. A macro substance was also found in the throats and esophagus areas of both deceased Ray Tragg and Beryl Jamison and three other *surviving* competitors.

Respiratory examinations were performed on the remaining fifteen Stratobatics survivors who went up and down, before the main body of competitors arrived at the launch pads. In the light of the unusual happenings, all next programmed flights were cancelled. This was not an auspicious start for promoting the sport.

* * *

February 2363. Making its usual Sunday morning run, Holiday Charters, Fin Euro Fun Cruiser, flight #FN5577 departs Helsinki. Loads factor: 703 tonnes. All 4 decks were loaded with over 2250 winter-weary vacationers and aircrew. Ultimate destination for Flight FN5577 was Myanmar's Lanbi Kyun group of Resort Isles, S.010°48' lat. (just above the equator) on the eastern edge of the Andaman Sea. Three and a half air-conditioned hours later, evading unseasonable turbulence on the last leg of the flight, the air cruiser passes over the eastern coast of India at 25.4 km altitude, Chief Officer Miikka Rakenen issues an order to the program control officer in front of a bank of computer equipment in the cruiser's computer control offices. (Nee flight deck)

"Peter. Confirm our course heading, rate of descent and ETA Myeik, Myanmar. Advise Myeik control tower. Let them know we're standing by for their control's ground-level conditions report and final landing instructions. When you're ready, feed that into our auto guidance system. I have – ah – twenty seven minutes scheduled to touch down."

Now Captain Rakenen swings around in his command seat to address his flight deck staff.

"As I was saying, folks, Myeik 'Port is a *brand new* facility expanded and designed by the Myanmar government to handle the size of our aircraft – and the expected future volume of their incoming tourist trade. So, on landing, as instructed, we'll have to taxi to the west end of the field, - and remember, shut down *all* solid fuel compartments on the way over. Where the Sea Skimmer fleets are parked, is where *we* connect with our load's ongoing charter vehicles over to the Lanbi Kyun resort destinations".

Chief Rakenen switched on the cabin station phones and buzzed the stews.

"With your unrecorded 'spiels' for landing, also inform our guests that uniformed hosts persons will be available at the bottom of all debarkation escalators to escort passengers to their respective connector Sea Skimmer craft – they are all marked with one of the three satellite resort hotels - Clara, Daung and Sagantht. Please be sure that all passengers are clear on their destination and that their name cards are visible with their island marked on each. No need to tell you how important it is that guests *and their* baggage and arrive at the *same* time on the *same* carrier. OK? Also, in order to make our return flight with full load factor of returning vacationers, please supervise cabin maintenance crews, so that we get out of here on time. OK? We don't want to have to bring this old bird back in, to sort out any foul-ups. Thanks for your help, people. That is all."

Chief Rakenen punched in some codes to ensure landing procedures were normal. Air carriers in this day and age truly flew themselves and needed no pilots, just engineers to take care of technical trivialities, (large and small) and an occasional computer genius to maintain the engineering status quo in flight.

Meanwhile at a window table on senior deck A, Norwegian passenger Torolf Ipson mentally tallies his next 14 weeks in the equatorial splendor of the Clara Kyun. He pictures himself on the rented skiff he intends to sail around the south cays of the resort complex. According to his tour promotional material, all the islands were swept by cooling sea breezes to fill sails; transparent water amid shallow lagoons with a Technicolor world of fish to distract a sailor's concentration. Ideal for a weekend sailor like him.

A Swedish father and son finish their card game in the Sports Lounge, just as this giant Airbus platform tilts itself downward to begin gradual descent onto that tiny dot, the former Burmese city of Myeik at southerly end of the Myanmar peninsula.

"Haken," said his father, "I can see you have played this game before. But I warn you, by the time your *next* birthday trip comes around – that will make you – what? – 13 or 14? – I shall see you never win another as easily as you have today! You've been warned, my man!"

In the next compartment from them, an elderly gentleman leans over his dozing wife, hoping that her intermittent guttural throat sound might be lessened by adjusting her seat space air button, pushing repurified oxygen into an already cool fuselage interior. He turns to dial in his own comfort level on his own armrest. Suddenly the woman jerks to her feet, extends her face to the ceiling, clutches her neck with both hands, and rasps out the words,

"Ach Horst…vas ist – Caoo! Caooaakkkk!"

Before her handicapped husband can stand to intervene, her long purple-coated nails tear away tissue chunks of her own lips and cheeks in a frantic attempt to jam her entire hand down into her throat. She is desperately attempting to clear *whatever* has become an *impediment* to her breathing. Her eye sockets show all white, as her eyes roll back. Dentures are spit out in broken sections. Streams of bloody saliva jet from her mouth all over the forward two rows of passengers now turned to face her. Suffocation is a pitiful and painful depiction of death in its most frightening and insane form. No less so in an aging person. Her husband now screams, in Deutsche.

"Mutter des Gottes! (Mother of God!) Marianna! Don't – Bitte sterben Sie, Marianna nicht, Bitte atmen Sie, meiner Liebe!

But she was already in her death throes. She hears nothing. Her thrashing body spasms diminish as she struggles against the fear and pain of air starvation..

By the time Chief Engineer Rakenen and his medical officer arrive at the old woman's side, she is gone... they were far too late, and she was too aged to endure the 72 seconds it took to bring the pure oxygen canister from the medical closet. Far too fragile a heart to wait for the medical officer's frantic search of his bag for his scalpel – his intention being to perform a quick tracheotomy. He ended up doing it anyway, just in case there was a reflex breath left in her. There was not.

Now the chief is on the lapel radio with his first officer.

"Peter – ETA gate time, now is (pause) fourteen minutes? OK. Have an ambulance and Myeik port police meet us on the west end taxi apron– and Peter – report to corporate – passenger death, female, late seventies, suspected choking. Note the time, please."

Bringing calm to a shocked gathering of 200 people in this one section of the carrier was unnecessary. Other than an occasional whimper of sorrow and a soft crying and sobbing, this cabin section was silent.

* * *

Within five minutes of Marianna's last breath, a perspiring flight engineer grapples with a flat nylon cord, securing all luggage compartment bindings. It is overly warm in this cargo hold number 33 of Cruiser flight FN316. He has found a loose connection. He secures a tripped flip lock on the binding on a baggage pallet. Perspiring in the stuffy air of the overly warm pit of the aircraft's under belly, He checks a nearby altimeter and descent gauge. In hopes of getting a quick cool off, he spins opens a tiny air cock in fuselage wall. In seconds, he is on his hands and knees gasping violently. His lapel remote is open. He squawks a Finnish phrase into it.

"Peter! Peter!! Call Miikka! Get him down here on the double –"

He breaks into a more rasping air intake with each attempt to draw another deep breath. Then a horrible thought hits the unfortunate crewmember.

"No - No! Peter! Belay that order. Don't let *anybody* down here!"

As the hold's walls begin to fade in his out of focus view, the dying engineer gives the first and only clue to a planetary "invasion", such as had never been heard before. Between fits of futile gasps, he even gives a name for the source of his tortured struggle for air.

"Peter – tell Miikka... air tainted – I can see – it's a mist. A yellowish haze. Misty –- like dust...a dusty gas - some kind of toxic poison ...from outside..."

Whatever legacy he might have left of his life, this courageous flight-deck crewmember had saved his colleague from attending to him in the last 60 seconds before passing into oblivion.

Amid this distress – the sudden death of one passenger and now, one crewmember... high altitude Fin Euro Cruiser Flight #FN5577, lands itself, without further incident.

* * *

Meteorologists, geophysicists and physicists stationed on Antarctic's Larsen Island in the year 2367 issued reports involving sites of increasing and unexplainable respiratory fatalities in AusZealand, ArizAmeria, Myanmar, Tibet, Afghanistan-Pakistan highlands, Bolivia, Peru and unspecified African states. Even the Swiss Académie of Astral Sciences elected to issue a statement to confirming sporadic atmospheric penetration of a chemical gas mix seeping though the ozone cover. There have always been recorded instances of minute amounts of alien gaseous clouds "floating" in and out of *every* galaxy. However, no recorded data in man's tenure on earth have reported anything like a 'yellow-tinged, dusty gas cloud' *ever* penetrating our ozone cover. A chemical cause and effect assessment of the yellow death mist was anticipated sometime within the next 20 days. That proved overly optimistic.

* * *

Almost four years after the last known occurrence of Dusty Gas, the Larsen Island Antarctica research team is finally able to declare, unequivocally, that the hazardous dusty gas had *now passed* out of the orbit of earth. Suspended remnants and pockets of remaining gas have been dissipated. According to most scientific monitoring devices, the earth's orbit spun through this vaporous "cloud" and now any future incursion is over. However, the lasting effect on all of earth's living things, because of that four-year experience, is yet to be seen.

Humankind was not to be struck dumb all at once by Dusty Gas. There were those bio-medical science people who maintained that time and the 'bodies own healing mechanism would arrest residual regressive effects on the specific tissue cells' – or at least, return them to normal, within in a subsequent generation or two. However, as it turned out, *it didn't and it wouldn't.*

Medical evaluations were depressing. It was deduced that oral voice box capability in the human being would *cease almost entirely, within 50 to 90 years.* Who and what groups and over what time period would be first to cease use of voice would depend on many factors. A community's elevation was one. Reporting suffocation fatalities, Tibet's scientific people in Lhasa, Tibet would be one of the first to note vocal loss on the general population. Sadly, it was also true in medical prognosis emanating from alpine counties like Bolivia and Peru. Remaining traces of Dusty Gas remained more dominant in those regions than in human settlements on the 'shores' of the Dead Sea or in the deserts of Death Valley.

*   *   *

The world's most ingenious people were unable to offer a ready-made alternative. No wonder. Voice communications, that took thousands of years to evolve will gradually cease – for all time. So now what?

Animal world techniques and ESP guessing games? Do those mental midgets who actually believe in the practice of extra sensory perception still abound? Would the existing digital language of the deaf be of any use to implementing full-blown communication, as we know it? How about, if and when some lawyer-engineer tries to reintroduce an abbreviated form of the courtroom recording method? Maybe the introduction of the now extinct African tribal tongue clicking to spell out messages could be done by clicking out oral messages using that old, reliable but learnable and workable Morse code.

Awareness that most of the backward countries of this world have never ever known what the now outdated email system was like, might tend to exclude this as any kind of universal communications answer. But then even new 24th century technical gadgetry would appear to be too consuming and too artificially contrived to facilitate meaningful interplanetary 'dialogue', one individual to and from another.

Considering the multitude of different tongues, variable expressions and scribed *interaction* would *have* to be implemented – an inexorable, worldwide methodology that has yet to be conceived.

* * *

Meanwhile, cattle would cease to low and bawl. Only a deep down stomach rumble would 'call' her calf to her teat. Whales, dolphins, sea mammals and some fowl species will carry on by whatever instinctive senses they possess. Therefore, in time, man too would *have to overcome* a very essential dialogue deficiency...by whatever means possible. Somehow contact would have to be *restarted*.

Until then, squawking speech would be reduced to raspy and gravelly utterances to convey a thought, resorting more to body language as emphasis to their 'message. '

By 2369, as ensuing events are recounted and exposed in all print media, Dusty Gas dispirit follows one mind-chilling misfortune after another. The arid 'chemical' that assaults the throat, invades all respiratory bellows – the lungs. In most cases of chronic bronchitis, emphysema, severe asthma, particularly of the elderly, deep penetration of this insidious gas would eventually lead to an indescribable death by suffocation. The indomitable will of the most optimistic to carry on, no matter what, erodes with each passing day.

Expectedly, general depression starts to set in. Loneliness in a silent world will do that to the human psyche. Prior to this attack, not many would ever have guessed that the greatest loss would be the association with others of the same species. Unfortunately, misery truly does love company. An "all is lost" mentality begins to inundate the human psyche. As a result, mass suicide becomes commonplace in many societies.

* * *

Man had experienced this overall state of mass despair at least once before. For the second time in less than ten centuries, an equally horrendous pandemic threat to humankind showed its lethal effects. More recently and for a second time, an avian flu virus was a recent cause of a worldwide pandemic. In poorer countries, similar results emanated as a result of the deadly Ebola virus, strains of E. coli, Bubonic and Black Plagues which snuffed out million of lives every year not to mention the human flotsam of survivors' disabilities. The Americas' epidemics of smallpox, attacks of poliomyelitis and scarlet fever took out vast populations in their time. Surviving loved ones of those who succumbed experienced broken hearted despondency, grief and severe self degradation in the gloomy aftermaths of personal losses.

While the remnants of Dusty Gas lay in invisible 'pools,' upon the lowlands of the earth, very few blessings were still countable. Salty oceans dissipated the gaseous fall-out more readily than did fresh water lakes and streams. Nevertheless, uninfected fresh water for all living things depended on glacial run off over long distances; still nature's way is best at replenishing potable water reservoirs.

* * *

Dusty Gas left the world without the companionship of the human voice. – the absence of the comfort and joy of experiencing vocal arts, – the laughter of a child, – the companionship of a friend – a lover's professed devotion, , – the shouts for encores at stage presentations – the ground swell of human cheer at sports events,– the contact and bonds one establishes with another human like dinner table conversations, – the family jabber of jungle or desert peoples around a campfire – the interaction of school room lessons teaching mankind the value of brain power. Dusty Gas left all people with little solace to cope with the effect of *loneliness* on the human spirit. Such a *lonely* vigil brought many souls to outright cessation of life by their own hand as a final solution to unbearable silence in a *now inhuman* world.

Official medical analysis reports were concise. Normal functioning voice organ areas were contagiously bound and protected by a lid-like epiglottis below the trachea. It has a complex cartilaginous or bony skeleton capable of limited motion through the action of associated muscles. In most forms of mammals – a set of *elastic* vocal cords that play a major role in sound production and speech emanating emanate out of this called *voice box*. Broken oral sound is caused by that stretching that *elasticity* in now affected muscle and cartilage.

Cases of impaired and deteriorating human speech are one thing but now, deceleration of *human propagation rates* appears to be final nails in the coffins of a few remaining positive thinkers.

One group of anthropologists, a collection of academics that often combines hard research with soft theory, produced some shocking conclusions that clearly demonstrated an even more dreadful physical fact. In the testicular apparatus of the human, *there is a similar elastic tissue* activated when males climax euphoric, orgasmic convulsion. They reasoned that the gas affected Pubocoygeus (PC) muscle, part of the muscle group at the base of the penis. Elasticity controls genital reactions. Involuntaryitis contracts nerve ends at orgasm. However 'dry orgasms' occur when there is virtually no expulsion of semen, constituting 5% of effective ejaculate volume.

With a conviction borne of fear of someday being proven wrong, a speculative body of bio researchers advises that no documented studies exist to indicate that voice box components are, in any way, *organically related* to male reproductive tissue or organs initiating emission of spermatozoa. However, proponents suggest that elasticity in humans' reproductive parts and vocal chord components effected by Dusty Gas has been documented to indicate that there is indeed a relevance; a connection when referring to male regenerative capability in the same topic.

On the other hand, there are those other groups of medical scientists, who speculate that an ion of the mysterious gas composite in the blood stream *could* cause a negative genital function. One anthropologic research clinic submitted a very recent paper to the Lancet, a medical news publication, reporting a study of the sample residual astral gas showing traces of an *Endocrine* activating substance in the space cloud of yellow tinted gas. Endocrine, indexed for its disruption of hormones, can impose *gender-bending* repercussions. Therefore, that could be interpreted to imply that the presence Endocrine influent, with still unknown gaseous components, *could* be responsible for a now suspected neuron affect causing male impotency.

Chapter 5

Image Invention Restores Dialogue In A Lonesome World

<u>2478/25TH CENTURY – SCOTBRITIRE, INDIASTAN, SINGAPORE</u>

DESPITE EVIDENCE TO the contrary, a few folks believed they could create direct image transference in sleep mode but very few human minds are actually capable of *receiving* mental messages directed their way. Some of these august bodies of show-offs flaunt their 'advanced ESP' skills as a superior mental status facility. *If* it really *was* an accomplishment, one in a few hundred thousand people might become semi-accomplished in perceiving another's meanings and intentions without having to resort to any other primitive means of articulation. The unlikelihood of those few folks to possess that neuron-advanced level of mental power, prompted one prominent and caustic media wag to state in a syndicated newspaper column;

'Conversation by thought transference alone – ESP, is like concentrating on your hand, persuading it to grow another thumb. But accepting such a premise, caused by the fervent need to communicate – is a hell of a lot less likely than the need to acquire a better digital grip!'

However, there were few workable alternatives, so that adolescents could be schooled to understand dialogue instruction. Three of them were:

1. Learn the known methods and limited accuracy of ESP (extra sensory perception) the added 5th mental dimension, presently in use by animals, dolphins, insects and such. (a tall order and a tough sell!)

2, Become proficient in the art of digital body language, such as that used when asked for route direction (In most experiences, that's only useful if the unknown destination is right across the street!).

3. Exercise the 'throating' of a grunt and coded, tongue-clicking language, used centuries ago by Kalahari Bushmen. (But then, how *does* one communicate an expression for 'coke bottle' in Kalaharian?)

* * *

Though rebuilt many times over, there is a new version of 2470 Raffles Plaza Club, a historically famous landmark, revived from that elegant old Singapore hotel and nightclub, so called after Sir Thomas Raffles who founded this special area of Singapore in 1819.

On this particular late evening, Edward Greig's, "Spring Thaw." wafted up from the lobby. This melancholy classic by the Singapore Chamber String Quartette was a pleasant musical background to the hotel's sophisticated lounge patrons 'night-capping' on the mezzanine. The library bar was about to close up for the rest of the very early morning. The waiter leaned forward to receive some indication of the drink orders of five customers who had just sat down. While they could have chosen to pencil check marks beside photos of drink orders on the menu tabs, none of the five people made a move to do so. They just looked back at the liveried waiter and at each other, sometimes smiling as though they were putting something over on him.

Following a moment of awkward silence, the waiter finally caught on. With the aid from, his TransPinder, (a recently introduced new image transference system) and a rudimentary grasp of ESP communication, the Raffles waiter received the telepathic thoughts of their order. He nodded as each order was given him, nodded and mouthed a thank you, concluding with an audible tongue click - then went off to fill the orders.

"That's easy for him to say,"

Grant's thought was directed at all them collectively. All five gurgled their laughter for what by now was an oldest joke in captivity but still applicable in this *now semi-silent* world of ESP and intuitive communication.

"It's hard to believe that we all live longer lives these days… Especially since we all are still affected by the ravages that that damned noxious, dusty gas infestation put upon us."

For which, lady guest Rhazia's observation was received and agreed to by them, as indicated by four nodding heads.

Other late night – and/or early morning patrons – in the lounge were using notes, body language and other coded means of discussions amongst themselves. At the same time, judging from furtive glances, they must have been marveling at how well practiced the five at a neighboring table all seemed to be at their *mental* dialogue. While they looked directly at each other, and conducted their facial expressions as they would for any oral conversation – not a sound was uttered.

Meanwhile, Grant Emerson continued his thought.

"I'm not so sure that the outcome of the dusty gas effect, as it pertains to *our* telepathic skills, could be termed 'ravaging.'"

He turned to Chen Sui, "Would you not think so too, Chen?"

The Viet Asian glanced at his watch as he thoughtfully responded.

"The way I see it is, if this gaseous permutation had *not* affected the human race, forcing us all to reach the communications level where we now – that is, all of *us* reading each other's thoughts instead of engaging in oral dialogue, as did our late ancestors – I would probably still be communicating with an oriental accent."

As the group throat chuckled at his self-depreciation, Chen turned his head direction of the waiter's station, in hope of attracting quicker service for his order of Armagnac. Meanwhile Rhazia emitted her image comment.

"Extra Sensory Perception *has* really been a wonderful advance in so many ways for what few of us there are. For one thing, in the scant hundred years since its inception here, imaging by ESP has actually *forced* our intelligentsia to be proficient in thought transference.. So, it can't be all that bad."

Bolstered by some still bubbling martinis from a previous club stop, Ralph Truscott expostulated,

"For the educated and the upper crust of society, exclusive use of ESP or 5th dimensional dialogue, as some professors call it, at least tends to clearly designate our academic capability and even our social status. Others, like our waiter, who have to emphasize mind wave conversation with lower class clickery and hand waving would have to concede that *they* will never inherit the earth at that level."

"I'm not so sure *we* will either, if the majority of people never bother to tune in!"

Natasha countered Truscott's thought as she leaned forward, trying to keep her 'remarks' confined to the group.

"But Ralph, doesn't that line of thinking bother you – smacking as it does of discrimination?"

There was lull in further exchange of thought. Therefore, Natasha went on.

"And how about mental interpretation by an eavesdropping waitress, a cabbie, a repairman, a hairdresser or – a waiter? When you refer to them as people of *lower* class... does that not concern you that, one day, you might have your nose rearranged by some husky, lower class warehouseman who just might have understood as he 'eavesdropped?"

Natasha turned a swift glance to their waiter picking up their order at the bar.

Conceded Ralph,

"Maybe, but that's like being condemned for using the *right* fork. It's an unlikely supposition. Most of the time, most of '*them* that clicks' wouldn't know the difference."

"Meanwhile, as the hour is almost two AM, my capability to think of anything but sleep is taxing. I really *am* ready for my beauty nap," announced Rhazia.

"You know, if I don't get my four hours...Ah here we are..."

The waiter had arrived. He placed the drinks in front of each as ordered. He extended his thought with a patronizing click, a check of his watch and a hand gesture or two in addressing all five guests that the lounge would be closing within 30 minutes. He wished them a pleasant goodnight.

When the waiter left, Grant Emerson interjected with thoughts of his own. Waxing philosophical, he conveyed his musing to the four others.

"I know we've all been through this before, but really – can you imagine what our species would have turned out like *if* an image sound system by which to exchange thoughts and ideas *had never* have been invented? What would it have been like?"

"Like guppies in a fish bowl! But hey - I'm sure we would have found other ways to mess up our *civilized* way of communicating." Grant predicted ironically.

Somewhat irritated by Grant's state of inebriation, Natasha faced him with,

"Well, maybe we have already. We have actually proved it – and as few as we are right now, *we* have perfected *our* conversational art, without the need for technical trinkets. How long have we been working together now? Eighteen - nineteen years? Has it really been over twenty? This simply verifies that, given the time, the integrated association in which we've spent generations of practice, had made *direct thought* a possibility for us. Just as it possibly could for thousands of common folk in future. N'est pas?"

Chen mentalized a thought.

'I see your point, Natasha. It took the animal world a few hundred thousand years to work out *their* communication methods – but *they* did it too, with the help of their other developed senses and several other instincts."

They all sat in semi reflection. This kind of a speech at this time of night, seemed to justify the 'we're more clever than you are' attitude that all five of Grant's fellow party members had shown off to others during the entire evening. Each of them wallowed in their collective ESP accomplishment and they seem to lord it over everyone they met. His eyes half closed, Ralph had his head resting on the high backed armchair, extending his muse. He continued to project his thought.

"It would be like the miracle of those deep, deep ocean creatures existing without eyes. Those fish managed to flourish by their own regeneration – getting around and using other environmental senses instead of vision..."

Getting his second wind, Ralph implied,

"Thinking of ancestral survival, as we were – in the aftermath of dusty gas, I think ---

Chen's secretary Rhazia stifled a yawn, as though to emphasize her sleepy impatience.

"Ralph! Put your brain to bed and allow us to do the same! After all, who really cares about how clever we all are? I didn't get any kudos tonight, how about you, Nat?"

Natasha shook her head..

More 'going nowhere' mental banter went on for another five minutes. Finally, Chen Sui stood too, gulped the last of his snifter of Armagnac, looked at his watch and offered his final thought for the night.

"I don't know about you, my friends, but I'm much too weary to challenge any form of logic this morning...but like Ralph, I *do* wonder if that human attitude has made any real difference, considering the way our species are back at it, once again putting pressure on the earth's limited yield. I for one, will sleep on it. Wouldn't you agree, my friends?"

Natasha gestured with flipping fingers to push out her thought, "Well it really is a toss up. Who really knows what our population numbers would have been today without interchange with others – especially of the opposite sex....", "And *that* "...mouthed Grant, as he rose to his feet,

"...is another, hermetically sealed can of 'roaches', which, considering the lateness of the hour and the emptiness of our glasses, we'll not get into."

"As I was saying," intimated Chen,

"This means of mental communicating is exhausting especially when one is as mentally bushed as I am. I just wish someone would invent an *easy grade school* means of transporting my thoughts, without me having to work so damn hard to deliver it."

Ralph Truscott turned to Chen, emptied his glass, flopped some bills on the low lounge table, stood and strained to tease Chen Sui with his ESP thought.

"Someone *did*, old chap... How *you* missed getting a TransPinder injection, *I'll* never know."

Chen responded,

"Well, *I* know. Nobody fools with *my* brain. I can do that *by myself*."

Never one to leave the last word to anyone else, Grant rejoined,

"You really *are* fearful of a TransPinder vaccination aren't you, Chen?

* * *

for the less intellectually competent early indications of fast spreading frustration from such wide spread crippling voice-box dysfunction was obvious. It was as though every person had a mild but persistent case of laryngitis. An oral raspiness gave way to traffic-cop-type waving and semaphored signals. These were accompanied by varying elevations of grunts, mouthing semblances of words, breathless crying and choking chuckles.

To send and receive a transmitted mental message by retraining human senses for ESP was *not* a realistic option. The only other alternative was to resurrect and train every human being in Morse code or to 'write symbols in the sand!

As conversational inadequacy of any kind grew and hopelessness pervaded, it became evident that the most painful suffering of all in a voiceless society, would be *loneliness*. For humanity, loneliness is as fatal as starvation.

Then, along came Jones – Kamaljit Gupta Jones!

* * *

Within one brain in the *same* body, one part of a lobotomy communicates with the other side of the brain so that feet and toes, which really balance the body above them, are vital. Without that nerve 'cooperation', the body topples over! Not since earth traded in its excess carbon dioxide for breathable oxygen, have living things been in such dire need of a lost human faculty. Without communication between them, human beings have very little to justify the effort to commune with each other.

Trite though it might be to quote 'dire necessity' as being the mother of invention, no greater truism would ever be more apropos in the wake of the Dusty Gas scourge.

One professional woman doctor in New Delhi goes deep into her brain cells to conjure a physical working method of *interpretative* electronic dialogue. *Muriel Mae Jones* had come to be in India as a vice-president for the New Delhi office of a 1400 year old, multi-national British based franchising corporation, Beltone Electronic Corporation. If and when she was to be successful in her intent, she was partly convinced that she would have to consider a procedure that might restore oral *regeneration* – hopefully in time to keep the species of man from becoming extinct.

The real advance of the TransPinder, as she named it, was the result of the humane initiative and the miracle of genius that was Madame Jones Gupta, honorably invocated, as *Doctor* Kamaljit Indri, Muriel-Mae, Jones-Gupta at the University of New Delhi.

Afterwards she frequently extended credit for TransPinder development to the fidelity and commitment of her multi linguistic husband, Dr. Ranjit Gupta.

Following perfecting of product technicalities, through repetitious testing, surveys, redesigns, and adaptations, it was he who attended to the contractual matters of production and distribution to medical clinics and hospitals worldwide. Beltone was the natural option for this launch. It could be speculated that an expenditure of several 'oxcarts full of rupees' was theirs for starting up a massive marketing endeavor.

Following her marriage to linguist Dr. Ranjit Singh Gupta, of the capitol city's Technical Institute, England's East Middleton born Muriel Mae had assumed part of the Hindu faith of her mate. Even though oral language was literally extinct as an application, she had learned to think and work in the linguistic mindset of Dravidian, the officially registered 'language' of Hindi and one of the thirteen dialects in the region.

In her adopted country, she was commonly addressed as Kamaljit Indri. For international practice reasons, she kept her British surname, Muriel Mae Jones. Her experience and marriage contacts had also led her to become head of computer sciences for the speech and hearing impaired at a major college laboratory.

Following 100 hours of intensive study of the molecular restructure of the intricate human larynx to finally reject that remedial recourse as complicatedly impractical at the masses level, it now became her objective to seek alternatives to *deficiencies* in oral communication. Muriel Jones firmly believed that in order for the human mind to be able to effectively focus on created mental images – and so that others could *'see'* them, a combination bio/technical simulation in some transmittable form had to be the most likely resolution.

But in *what* form?

One day, leaving her laboratory offices in New Delhi, she hurried to catch a passing transit car at its next street stop. The antique tourist trolley was clanging it's noisy old bell to warn all on-track pedestrians to get clear of the rails. Crossing the rails without looking, one of the deaf trainees at her

Beltone offices was bumped. Rolling under the lead wheels of the trolley the young female was practically decapitated. Aghast, the lady Jones Gupta was witness.

Later, it occurred to her how ironic it was, that one person out of millions, who actually *could* communicate in sign language, was destroyed for lack of an audio capability to warn her. In Jones *mind's eye*, she would always see the senselessness of the accident. At the same time, a bright light of realization came upon her. Now all she needed for transference of a mind's eye image was some kind of simple implement. At that very moment, she had only an inkling of what that implement might be.

In a continuing depression for this needless loss of young life, Muriel thought,

'It's not right. This child lost her life as much by chance and circumstance as it was by her handicap – yet, out of it, I think I can actually see the specter of a concept – a solution for an image component by which we might all benefit.'

* * *

Thus began a fervent quest for ways and means to advance her concept. The prospect of her inventive reality brought Muriel Mae, Madame Kamaljit Indri Gupta, to the laboratories of several highly regarded neuroscientists all over the western hemisphere. What she took from them, she melded with relevant information she gleaned from discussions with friendships she had established with Beltone's electronic technicians at head offices in the UK.

The germ of her idea began early one morning when Madam Gupta was suddenly awakened from a deep sleep by the clashing and banging of a street cleaner's handling of refuse receptacles. With eyes still closed, she 'saw' very clearly, a repetition of the trolley accident. Her eyes popped open. She realized then that even by semi-conscious concentration or recall, a practical application of neurological images, thought out in sequential order, within in a 'sender's' mind, could electronically flash pictorial descriptions through to a receiver's mind. Of course the receiver would have to be alert to the thoughts of the person who is transmitting the message. But an implement would have to be conceived to both transfer and pick up on the thought.

At this point, Muriel deduced that given the techniques to exchange a thought, a sequence of image, originating in the mind's eye *could* duplicate itself *if both parties* had a similar implement, connected to the image center of *both brains*.

She reasoned further,

'*That* would necessitate that both the speaker and audience would have to have duplicate, implanted transponders and receivers.'

What evolved over the next seven-year period was to be a multi-purpose *microscopic pin*, less than the width of the smallest sewing needle and *half the length* of just the *stem* of a thumbtack. *Injected at birth* - or later – into the base of the back of the skull, the pin would be activated by the human brain and perpetually powered by the rhythmic energy of the human heart, annexing a specific blood vessel in the neck of the recipient!

At a medical convention of over 15,000 neurological surgeons in New York's World National Congress auditorium, this remarkable woman, Kamaljit Muriel Mae Jones Gupta, in the company of an entourage of her colleagues, 'addressed" this world body so. . .

Her thoughts were electronically delivered, as were those of all convention speakers, by a software program that 'reads' a typed message in the English language. These were amplified over giant projectors and spotted around the around the convention hall.

In order to be understood by all, her message was peppered with simple image analogies. Very adroitly, she imaged basic communicating in this fashion. She reasoned,

"If ever there was a need for mind control and mental discipline, this is it! Precise Communication must first be organized in one's mind, before delivering it."

In introduction announcements to the public, she often imaged examples to her audience aided by pictorial exhibit. Her line of logic would involve a simple analogy.

"Since shish kebobs look the same the world over, ordering one in any restaurant anywhere in the world would simply be a mental image – without the impedance of specifying a specific with a language - or accent. At first, diners ordering meals in a small café in Marrakech, for example, would have to *improvise* their minds' pictures should exact images became too difficult to conjure up or to understand. On the other hand, one could probably get a shish kebab, if one could point to a printed menu of that plate. If not – for the benefit of tourists abroad, one such customer might try to place an order for shish kebab by envisioning in his or her mind, a picture of a beef cow image – with a wooden spear through it! I *didn't* say the images would all be that tasteful, did I?"

Bowing apologetically, with palms pressed together and pointed upward, before imaging a corrected version, a waiter dismissed the customer's imaged order by picturing the cow with the spear sticking out it and shaking his head violently! Then he would probably smile patronizingly at her and rethink his shish kebab icon as a skewer image, steaming hot and being served with accoutrements on a dinner plate.

When the patron beams approvingly, she might look might look up at him inquiringly and with the waiter's shish kebab picture in her mind, picture *his* image of the shish kebab and in another image, a picture a beef quarter, or a pig or a sheep. That *could* be enough to get her a shish kebab – but with anybody's guess as to meat content. However, in short order, it would not be too long before one could order a ten course meal in Bangkok, Cincinnati, or Lima.

If applied from infancy, a *child's* image of a desired food; say the image of a milk container, cup, or breast from which a little one is fed, would be understood by infants from Lithuania to Luxembourg.

Allowing for future reference picture publications, Madame Jones Gupta also implied that with use, *common connectors* to designate timing, like the implications of *'now'*, 'going' 'want' and even some human expressions – words like 'tolerance,' ' fun,' 'patience', 'fairness,' 'loving,' and so on – would, in time, evolve into universal images of their own just by variable and repeated use, common to all.

The TransPinder became the most advanced and ingenious communications method ever conceived. It would render all post TransPinder devices, totally redundant.

* * *

It took a group of NorAmeric public relations professionals with graphic arts skills to first conceive an interpretive manual that would be an reference manual of mind pictures. It was to be an expandable sort of dictionary – a thesaurus, to aid people in the use of *commonly* recognized mind images, for use in common ESP dialogue. For example, one person's idea of a house might be a castle, to others it would be an igloo, a tent, a dog house, An apartment or a chateau. A reference book would portray the house as an *actual* picture of a castle or an igloo or a tent, or whatever to be imagined when conveying the exact meaning and be received precisely as was meant by the person transmitting the thought.

Common 'joiner' expressions like, is, want, out, like, from, into, and, before, would be symbols. Arrows would express *direction*. *Want* - could be a hand formed as though grabbing. An image of clouds would symbolize *outside*. Two symbols drawn exactly the same would indicate like or *likeness* or *twin* or *pair*. Many such universal symbols already exist such a cupid with bow is symbol for romance.

Such a pictorial edition could soon become the world's best seller – a must-have directory for all schools, libraries, institutions and in every home on earth - a sort of "Visual Aid Manual" for new TransPinder users.

Meanwhile, to cover the costs of manufacturers' and distribution of millions of the Beltone patented – *TransPinders,* Health and Welfare systems would have be responsible.

For those not hospital born and humans of varying ages, born after the innovation, a two minute skull inoculation by any licensed medical practitioner or pharmacist, would be available at minimal or no cost to the recipient at anytime, to everyone on earth, regardless of location.

* * *

Everywhere on earth, this electronic marvel was to become the means of pictorial telepathy for electronic media broadcasting of events. In some applications, even live stage performances and plays could be received by an 'in-house' audience. Forecasts for TransPinders future development was indicated by unbridled enthusiasm of world impresarios who felt confident that Operetta and musical productions, involving human voice artistry, would be forthcoming, thanks to the TransPinder participants of the future. Others saw a new horizon for the education of children; and forensic training; still others would laud a now open gateway to understand the mental workings of mentally disturbed patients.

More exacting than a 'lie detector', the TransPinder could more easily evoke confessions of guilt for law enforcement and judiciary purposes; it would enable victims of pain to pin point their feelings of pain; and newborns to identify their immediate discomforts and needs; news broadcasters would became a 'voice' again to be received en masse by 'brain tuned' audiences.

TransPinder Accessories came shortly after the TransPinder product had been introduced and was in use. For example, one U.S. company developed the "TransPinder Alert' device. These were mini pliable orbs, powered again by the heartbeat energy of one's body. Like the old cell phone concept, they were mass-made. They could be produced as jewelry in all kind of shapes to be worn as rings, medallions, broaches or discs inserted into electronic devices, or stored in an ear chamber, like a hearing aid. Like the emergence of the cell phone. For 2000 populations it was the opening up of a new life of one-on-one personal communication, anytime, anywhere. The TransPinders and Alert medallions purposes were to be able to 'dial' the object of a transmission so that the receiver or group of receivers would 'feel the faint buzz" to *alert* them to a incoming image contact. From that point on, no image communication distance would be too far from an incoming image dialogue.

* * *

A World Body for Controlled Certification and Implementation approved the Jones TransPinder as effective and totally safe for application in humans. Thereafter it was as much a part of evolution as were feet, with ten toes – and no thumbs!

After 2520, the Beltone people invented an add-on innovation in honor of the memory of Doctor Kamaljit Muriel Mae Jones Gupta. This advance to the Jones TransPinder helped to bring back the 'sound' of human song lyrics. It was short of the hopes of opera lovers who required the true timber and resonance of tenors, altos and bass voices for full appreciation of musical delivery. Respectable instrumental renditions of worldwide contemporary, country, jazz, folk material *was* achieved. That, in turn, eventually brought back the entertainment industry to a semblance of its earlier centuries past prominence. By now, the *real* universal thought-transference of image and simulated sound as a communicative technique was the elixir that helped to dispel mankind's bleak outlook and his renewed vision of the future. The 'Jones TransPinder' became a part of the human entity for a lifetime. Man would *never* have to *be lonely again.*

Footnote: Kamaljit Indri Muriel Mae Jones-Gupta retired shortly thereafter, bequeathing most of her TransPinder royalties to global poverty care agencies but catering mainly to the poor of her adopted India and the people of African, Asian and SouAmeric nations. Following her passing at the age of 96, her legacy was ever remembered by a created cenotaph in a quiet corner of Dr. Snow's Soho Square in London, with a sculptured likeness in her honor.

Chapter 6

North Sea Yields 21st Century Cargo.

3129/32ND CENTURY – SKAGERRAK SEA

SISIMIUT, ROYAL GRŒNLAND Corporation's major fish-processing harbor was conveniently situated about 400 statute miles up the west coast of Greenland, the world's largest non-continental Island. Shrimp fleets from every port in the western hemisphere unloaded here where facilities were on par with Greenland's capital, the port city of Nuuk, originally Gothåb, under Danish administration.

For centuries back, fishers of this band of adventurous ancient mariners out of Nuuk set off on voyages into the west Greenland current of Davis Strait. All too often, these were frequently stormy seas, between their own coast and Canada's Baffin Island. Hundreds of years of over-fishing of the island's traditional home grounds by multi-nations fleets, compelled Greenland fleets to go farther a field for worthwhile Arctic water catches. They had to exploit the more often unpredictable coasts and shelves of other lands.

Again, for centuries, Greenland assigned its health department's circuit doctors and dentists to travel to all community corners of this massive 'ice cake' tending to the needs of its population. This is why, following 24th century Dusty Gas attacks, most of Greenland's eighty thousand inhabitants had been administered the semi-surgical TransPinder vaccinations. Thus to secure their livelihoods, they could carry on remote ship-to-ship and ship-to-shore communications via electronically transmitted images.

So it was in these early Summer days of 3124, when Aurora Borealis was putting on one of its most dazzling northern lights shows, that that many of Greenland's fleets of co-op independents headed southeast to more distant, ultra depths of the North Atlantic between England and Norway proper. They were most often in pursuit of halibut or crab – depending on their trap line scheme and scoop equipment. Improbable as it might have been normally, one trawler, "The Tunv", positioned itself south of the towers of the Viking Bank and on a southern heading along the Meridian of Greenwich. The plan was to fish along a predetermined 'fishhook shaped course', altering direction southwesterly past Devil's Hole depression. Depending on catch prospects, they would make the swing back in a northwesterly direction, completing the bottom of the planned fishhook route that would take them into the chop of the Skagerrak Sea and hopefully fill all six icy holds full of ocean bounty.

Ten to twelve clicks south of Norway's Kristiansen City, the ship's ear-shattering auto klaxon sounded, the net-wheel whirred and screamed in protest. Had he any voice box left, the skipper's curse might have been heard from the helm position to the school for the deaf in Oslo.

Above the equipment and engine commotion, the rest of the voiceless crew too would have been yelling. But they *did* receive a desperate image order from the Tunv's skipper.

At the very same moment, the line master was transmitting his own screeching message.

The deck master was able to get off a jumbled image message,

"We've hooked onto an under surface something! Submersed vehicle or – Cut the winch!

Turning his head toward the bridge, he imaged again.

"Wheelhouse! Captain! All engines st –! "

He never got to finish his flashing thought. Both orders came split seconds too late.

Seconds later, the man was lassoed by a loop in the brake line, dragging him at top speed across the slippery deck and through an open hatched hold At the very spot where he had stood on deck split seconds before, he left a rubber boot with half a bloodied leg, where it had been ripped off at the knee.

The boat had taken a taken a corkscrew turn. For what seemed like minutes, the stern dipped precariously below the water line as though a huge unseen hand was about to bat the steel craft from the surface. Cutting loose their gear lines, the Tunv's idling twin Volvo diesels roared into loud life, powering up to a remarkable 22 knots, pushing water in the Skagerrak high and heavy chop. Agitated and frightened for their severely injured deck master, whose system was even now approaching shock, they imaged by TransPinder, an 'All ships' message calling for medical aid craft to meet them from their present position setting a course and speed of 23 knots for Norway's port of Kristiansen.

* * *

Unknown to the rest of the world –nor would the world, at that time, care much, one way or the other – a massive, semi-submerged sphere would ultimately surface years later in that same unfortunate accident site. However, the Tunv's sudden pull on the sphere's special titanium chain and steel and cement anchor might well have been what jarred loose the still submerged object to ensure its eventual dislodging a few hundred years from then.

* * *

Due to the enormous area, over 2500 miles long, precise records of the great Nansen Ridge Earth and Ice Shift of 2919 would best be described as sketchy. At one time there were detailed geographic charts and volcanologists assessments in the archives of Moscow's Hall of Volcanic Studies to reveal that some unknown sonic sea markers had been implanted in their North Sea. Rumored sightings of giant steel spheres planted some 850 to 1000 years earlier in the quake-ravaged, Barents Sea were not *officially* confirmed by any archived documents. It wasn't a factor anyway. An unimaginable,

111

planetary force – the longest, undersea quake of tectonic proportions since the formation of the Alps, had carried any and all scientific experiments to extinction. Nature's violent reshaping of the top of that icy world caused all scientific platforms and measuring devices, moored in and around 075° N latitude, 045° E longitude in Russia's east Barents Sea, to be ripped away and sunk before the mighty movement of water and bergs.

What *was* later calculated and recorded was that until the 400 metric tonne orb was discovered and recovered, the object was torn from its original anchorage at the well head in a whirling turbulence of icebergs and jagged fragments of marine wreckage somewhere in the reforming Barents Sea.

As a result the sphere and cone had been pounded as evidenced by deep dents and crumpling on its steel surface. Dragging its massive titanium chain and fifteen meters of half meter diameter, cement-filled pipe stem, it had to have been swept over thousands of kilometers of sea floor trenches, chasms and mountainous undersea ranges from one extreme depth to another. As it ground its subsurface way along in a constantly raging, northwesterly current, continually bumped and battered, it finally lodged itself in 200 fathoms of sea between Norway and Denmark... the Skagerrak.

It was that location when the Sphere's 'weak' chain link had sufficiently corroded to release the sphere's to the ocean's surface.

Viewing the earth's surface through their implanted eye cams, stratosphere travelers in high flying Magnipods, spotted the top of the now surfaced sphere bobbing on the surface. The 300 foot diameter 'titanium-stainless steel composite ball was double crane lifted from the Skagerrak. It was hoisted aboard the extra wide beamed Japanese jet barge, *Akamaru*. This 'island-sized', bulk cargo carrier had been contracted while it was wait-listed at the Stockholm dock for a cargo of Beachwood bound for Israel.

South of Norway's Kristiansen, the gargantuan globe was loaded on to the Akamaru's recessed deck by two giant cranes, then sailed for Iceland. Accompanied by a flotilla of Universal Navy and scientific research vessels, the Akamaru docked at Iceland's military pier.

Thirty days later, at Reykjavik, teams of marine investigators were examining what was believed to be one of the most important finds in since the 1974 underground discovery of 10,000 full sized figures of China's ancient terracotta army.

* * *

The imposing "multi-colored" sphere, sadly soiled and streaked by its centuries-long time at sea, *now* sat in its specially constructed and braced 'saddle' on the floor of the Reykjavik Navy's Dirigible Hanger.

Until recently, the expansive dome canopy covering downtown metro Melbourne, victimized in 2906 by its second human-killing hail fall, was the world's largest horizontal structure. Now, with it's 27 foot high ceiling and three square kilometer interior space, this Icelandic hanger was the world's largest all purpose craft enclosure. It was so spacious it could, and sometimes did, contain 132 navy reconnaissance blimps at any one time.

Within two days of its arrival the sphere was surrounded by a web of specially constructed scaffolding and catwalks. On day thirteen, the entire scientific assembly of the visiting Multi-National Authority personnel stood on the grey cement floor looking upward 300 feet to marvel at the battered hull of the sphere. Still, its hundred plus colors reflecting off the mirrored surface of the hull was intriguing intact. All personnel had been gathered on the hanger's elevated mezzanine, for an on-site examination of the work in progress.

Expressing his enthusiasm his one young assistant electric arc welder imaged to another, "Luminicious!" from their precarious positions atop the scaffold.

"...but how the hell could this simulated plastic-metal and whatever kind of alloy this thing is formed of, be melded to form these kinds of sculpted channels?"

"It's one of those 'hows' we'll eventually learn." responded his partner.

"Looks like this ball broke away from another galaxy. Some kind of ore structure made to look and act like moving light and strands of metallic glass on a thing *that size*? Anyways, it's about as spooky as my wife's intuition."

His helper rapped at the nape of his neck to adapt his TransPinder and imaged his reply.

"Yeah. S'kinda similar to the effect of that old neon gas they used to use for commercial signing"

"I know we don't know what kind of power driver is *inside* this package yet but it occurs to me the light show it was supposed to have been seen at a hundred thousand feet is not all that bright up close!. Thing is, not *how* but *why* – why would it be lit up like that from afar by dullsville in here?"

"Maybe to *attract attention* from way out there – not from in here?" imaged a white coated woman on a nearby scaffold level. She was busy with stylus equipment probing the 'invisible' seams of the sphere's hull.

"Attention of whom?"

"Well, *who* would you think – dummy! Those moneyed high flyers! First class tourists! They're used to seeing things from afar!"

* * *

Senior directors of three pertinent groups of Hall Of Academic Sciences investigators of 'alien objects' had been called to attend a newly discovered, ten century ago creation now in possession in the Northern Forces lecture hall in Iceland's capitol of *Reykjavik*. Twenty-eight men and women in all, representing the Interplanetary Transport Safety Commission, Academy of Terra Researchers and Curators of the Hall of Academic Sciences were gathered for a cursory introduction to the project if not to themselves.

Under first-time circumstances, it was an upper level decision to have the chosen these few to engage in a face to face, one on one, with thought-processed "dialogue" concerning discovery of the time Capsule. Not only was it the most effective way to put everyone on the same page as to what was ahead of them, but also a more secure way to keep the inner workings of this project as secret as it can be for the time being without being hacked into by electronic zealots of a teleconferenced meeting. Already the news hounds had sniffed down the story...

"Mysterious Sphere Found Near Scand-Euro Countries! Public Catastrophe Mooted!. It was only a matter of time before some whistle blowing bureaucrat leaked word and the paparazzi would be pulling up to the docks in Reykjavik in their 'long boats'.

* * *

Most people of the 32nd century were experienced and rarely surprised at events and innovations in *their* ever-changing world. Highly educated and aware of their professional and family social standing in community they took the advancement in their lives, without subterfuge and pretense. A special committee, almost a cross section of 'new age' humans, was standing by today, waiting for the first official meeting of project principals who would be assigned to investigate the arrival of the 'big ball'.

* * *

Sophisticated though the group may have been, to an audience not of the year 3100 plus, they would be perceived as a representative cross section of the better educated demographics of regions of this updated world. Their manner of dressing and apparel and styles for instance, were well advanced beyond the passé clothing of centuries past. Notwithstanding that these people were from all over the world, the evolution of human garb in 'civilized' cultures at least, had in the last couple hundred years or so, gone with the flow of both fashion and utility!

The objective in the art of covering one's body had been to present a trim, simple look in 'miracle fabrics'. As comfortable as being naked, 32nd century apparel allowed for individualism in color, cut and "fabrication of fabrics" as the stylists put it. What really evolved was a very fine, net like, draped or form-fitting garment, be it suit, dress, skirt, shorts or pants. This was referred to as the *undergarment* for the way in which it was *fitted to the form of the wearer.* The over-garment might be a simple full-length cape or coat of light weight or woolen textured material, depending on climate, occasion or workplace. As always, sexual attraction was still primary motivator for style chosen.

It was always not so much *what* women wore, but *how* they wore it. For example, shapely-breasted women of 3140AD chose imaginative accessories, accentuating trappings of jewelry or loose scarves in appropriate body positions. Men's apparel too, was a fitted body covering of pliable fine net, in a huge choice of composition coverings in either jump suit fashion of formal two pieces – with built in, bulge-resistant 'restraints'!

All such styles, even in office work wear, were being worn to this meeting hall today. But it was the *ways* in which these accoutrements were *applied* to human forms that were just a much a miracle in fashion and haberdashery. What would have amazed clothiers of earlier centuries was that *every* home had a *shower style appliance*, an upright tunnel-like device from which bare bodies "dialed up" their apparel choice for the day. It then sprayed those bodies below the neck, with its preset gauge of simulated "material, style and shade combinations" for cool or warm weather conditions. A limited selection of preferred colors, patterns and cuts of garment were available. Even comfortable and/or medical *footwear* excluding spikes, could be coded and programmed to match and dialed in as chosen *for the day's wear*. Should one wish to wear the resulting combo more than once, every apparel 'shower' imprinted a coded number on an inside arm, read only by ultra-violet light built into every other 'fabric-shower appliance'. At the end of the period of 'garment' use, the same shower washed a person off for sleep. It could also be peeled off with 'still in vogue' finger tips, for medical attention, spur of the moment sex or just another dress-up for another occasion on the same day.

In a mixed group of young and older people, gathered today for the Reykjavik meeting, the mode of dress was optional, if not casual. Now three members of group leadership filed in to be seated at the podium. And the assembled 'fashion plates' went to their amphitheatre seating with table counters in front of them.

After the last three and a half centuries of cyber-created wear, haberdashery life in most civilized countries was progressing well. By the 32nd century, The Selectronics Committee had made it possible for independent innovators and aggressive world corporations to confer upon consumers of earth, exciting product advantages and expectations in life such as man had never before envisioned.

Since the last century, personal appliance products were distributed and marketed by a world wide consortium of personal franchise owners. Such were two million retail outlets around the globe, operated under 'YouNique Lifestyles' labels.

A personal body groomer *appliance* was typical of 32nd century life style endowments. This bathroom/bedroom companion could perform almost any cosmetic function. At the discretion – or not - of almost any individual, one acquired a haircut or hair elimination, style or trim, hair coloring, face shave, beard shaping, preferred make-up and application of eye and skin care treatment, wrinkle diminishment, teeth cleaning and mouth conditioner, eye and eyebrow grooming. Body groomer-devices could be preset to whatever function was specified by the user. Some low-powered portables could be worn while the user was attending to other matters like reading, preparing meals - but excluding making love – for obvious reasons.

Body massage and medical attendance was still a matter for outside servers. Nevertheless, even medical appliances were now consumerized, with what was professionally termed, MediCastPaks. These were an assortment of polyethylene body part shells shaped to individuals by air-filled surfaces. Optional was the digital massage cast. Used just as casts, or back and neck braces, they could cover, protect, reshape and render prescribed treatment to limbs, torso, feet and hands. One MediCastPak being marketed was a warm-water filled, full body suit, with an internal whirlpool action to treat and sooth athletes' aches and injuries as well as to relieve body discomfort in the elderly. Again, such treatments could be applied with ongoing functions and duties being specified by the user.

Corporate innovators offered personal and household appliances and instrumentation at most *YouNique Lifestyle* outlets. Another example of upscale 32nd century living would be a household's exterior equipment. When given the GPS location and exact metric dimensions of any lawn or field, grain and grass were automatically harvested, cut, aerated and trimmed to prescription on a regular schedule. In winter, drives and walkways could be similarly cleaned, blown clear of snow, by automatic lowering of built-in, fold-down conversion tools in the same robotic device.

To the 21st century *visitor to a 3150 world*... here was the best part! Cars and traffic jams were things of a distant past – because smog-makers like fume exhausting vehicles had long since been recycled into protective devices for humans. Traffic lights were only found in museums. Today's human consumers, going anywhere, went on cushions of air currents without ugly, blacktopped lanes of bumper-to-bumper aggravation so familiar to the 21st century primate.

Taken for granted, in this day and age, was the option where anyone traveling anywhere within close proximity, had only to slip into a climate controlled, light weight, chain-mail-like *'vehicle-suit'* called a *SAR* - (Shuttle Air Rider). One hung in every hall closet for every family member in every western industrialized nation. For those preferring to travel with others, 'bundled couplings' were a feature option. Having donned one's 'liquid' metal mesh net 'suit' one simply 'walked it' out the door. Once there, 'pup trailers' for carrying items to or from a destination, could be clipped to this 31st century innovation.

The occupant to the SAR then folded down the sun visor's control panel in the helmet. A commuter configured the task agenda and time itinerary, selected one's lift-off point and destinations utilizing GPS (global positioning system), also setting an acceptable rate of speed. Then one stepped onto the 'suit-vehicle's' built-in start platform for magnetic levitation to rise gently to a predetermined above surface level, joining thousands of other SARs' transients being propelled forward on a cushioned airflow in the direction calibrated on the task dial destination code. Such currents were centrally controlled, just as were trains and planes of hundreds of years ago.

A SAR wearer could travel in a sitting, stand up or prone position. The itinerary could include stops at the hair dresser, flower shop or even to a rooftop café for lunch. The universal driver, controlling a hydro electric power cell, did all the rest. No unpredicted stops. No messy fuel stops. No more parking lot hassles.

* * *

The attention of assembled persons was drawn by two taps on the podium. A strong 'thought projection' brought the meeting to order.

"Gentlemen. Gentle women. Kindly take your places at the table seats and come to order... Please. Thank you."

TransPinders being adjusted rattled in the minds of assembled audience.

Occasional light coughing, and scraping chairs being brought to the board table ceased, to enable the opening thoughts by the 'speaker' to continue without distractions.

In the expression of image dialogue involving sustaining communication by transmission of mental pictorial focus, the tall, steel-grey haired man at the dais, put his thumbs in his net vest pockets, wrinkled his brow to imply concentration, looked out over his audience and began a series of normal facial appearances, just as one would, had his voice been employed. His eyes and mouth features were moved slightly accompanying his thoughts as he conveyed his introduction. While his TransPinder did most of the image transmissions, his hands and arms were also used to help convey the images of his address.

"Good day all. For those of you, who have not read a good science novel lately, let me introduce you to one, – in the flesh and as it happens. Unlike my orally endowed ancestors of five hundred year ago, it is indeed a pleasure not to have to strain vocal cords I no longer have, just to get our first meeting of otherwise *noisy academics* underway in our lecture hall today. Forgive my weak attempt at levity - a state of nervous apprehension will do that to you.

For those of you whose linguistic telepathies and thought processes are not up to speed - or others who might have difficulty with my *mental accent,* you may have to be a little more adroit with your use of your TransPinder. And please feel free to use the automatic image/speech translations of transponders in your chair arms should you feel the need. Don't concern yourself with how *you* look with those trappings on – I'm sure I'll look worse than you because I'll also be using my lips, hands, arms, legs and *body English* to make a point. So – Just plug in, close your eyes and suck up the info!! Let's begin."

"My name is Prentice and my first moniker is *Anson*. I have the pleasure and responsibility to head up NTSC's Terra Academy's Investigative sector as senior research grand poobah... (Oops. That shows my years, doesn't it? Tough translation too! – I'll try to limit those...) Anyway, I welcome you all to this rather clandestine meeting of scientific rebels.'

'Let me welcome first-time visitors to Iceland. This *is* a unique and fascinating place. This is earth's last remaining mass energy source – of economic viability anyway.

The locals' will brag to you that if you stick a straw through Iceland's icy surface you'll get volcanic steam heat. Don't bother trying it. But for eight hundred thousand Iceland inhabitants here, core heat is harnessed as cheap power for everything. Anyway, all that has little or no bearing on why you've been invited to Reykjavík".

Prentice paused, as though thinking how to image what he wanted to express, without upsetting some of his audience.

"Secrecy and terms like, 'your eyes only', are expressions you will run into a lot right now, at least on the grounds of this compound. That's mainly because we haven't the foggiest what we have to be *open* about just yet.

So far, cursory examination has yielded us little in the way of hard data except that from a protection standpoint, we have made sure the device we have discovered is *in no way, nuclear*."

FN;* Dr. Anson Norman Prentice* BSE;
Credentials: Former NorAmeric High Commissioner (now retired) to the Hague For Contaminant Disease Control; NorAmeric Medical Academy Fellow, Guest Lecturer in Macrobiotic Sciences at London and Zurich Senior Studies Universities; Intermittent Resident Professor, U. Of. California, Pacific Region - Consultant to Philippines Disease Control Research and affiliated medical university departments and similar institutions of South East Asia. He is presented authorized and contracted by World Council, to conduct and co ordinate scientific studies of unidentified sea-salvageable objects and landed persons thereto.

A hand went up from one of the white coated staffers around the table. Spotting the hand, Anson Prentice looked in that person's direction and held up his forefinger.

'Assumedly, you have a query – right? Can you hold it for a moment? But if you can't hold it – just go out these doors to your left and take the first door across the hall…you won't need a key!"

The restrained and grunted chuckles subsided as he went on, still directing his images to the white coated audience member.

"Seriously – please remember your thought. We will deal with that and others shortly. That's a promise. Meanwhile, and in order to get a better grip on how we intend to involve you all in our initial research, I will introduce you now to someone who has been working under the auspices of the Investigative Branch of the Multi-National Security Authority.

As such he will inform you that *his* initial objective is to ensure we don't open up a can of worms – or worse – in our zeal to twist this thing open. In other words, he will approach our investigation with an archeologist's brush and toothpick technique, so that, (a) we do not inflict damage on the sphere in *any* way. And (b) that the sphere does not infect *us* in any way!

Doctor Bochelli here is currently in residence at the Space Vehicular Recovery Projects Centre in California. When he is not co-directing recovery process teams with responsibility for security, he resides at his hillside villa home in Italy…in the famous Chianti producing region – that's located down about the *middle* of the boot, isn't it Elio? – I *should* know. I've been there as the Bochelli family's guest. Anyway, it's in the famed Monte Casino district… which might explain his off-the-vine demeanor - Doctor Bochelli?"

"Good day Anson and folks. I'm afraid that the Prentice family's visits with us at our Casino vineyards have left our chief of staff here not knowing *where* he's been, from time to time. Like me, he's accumulated lots of mental mileage, which accounts in part for both of us running out of power once in while. But you know, there *is* something to be said for *older* guys like our Doctor Prentice – what is he now??... over 120 years old? I recall that he used to start off his lecture-hall addresses with…'nobody is born with a sharp wisdom tooth.

121

Smart is honed by knowledge, acquired mostly from just *getting* to maturity.' That's got to be true. I find *I'm* getting more mature in just my sleep! Anyway, thanks for the intro, Doc."

The heavy set Italian scientist with the boxer's build grins and forms up his next images.

"With your patience, I continue to *practice* my image processing cells for TransPinder dialogue – so forgive me for thoughtless slip ups. I've got a perfect excuse. I'm Italian! …And by the way, folks, my doctorate does *not* specify that I can engage in mental communication, only when addressed as "Doctor". Fact of the matter is that I've never understood why it is that the title, 'doctor' gets a better table at a restaurant. If I signal the maitre d' that as 'Sewer Engineer Bochelli', I am entitled my usual table down front, you know he's likely to explain to me where I can stick my table!? So please…unless you're a visiting maitre d', my name is *Elio*. I'll accept nothing more? Capice?"

He waves his forefinger at the staffer in the audience who had held up his hand,

"Now sir. Do you still remember what you were going to ask?

The white coated person grinned and nodded his head up and down.

Bochelli responded.

"Great! Just remember – because I'll be asking *you* questions when I'm finished.

Folks. What we have here is a bit of a puzzle. We've got hearsay evidence that lets us know *why* this junior sized planet is in our hanger space right now. But not much else. It was literally fished out of the Skagerrak less than a couple of weeks ago. It is spherical in shape with an inverted dunce cap shape cone beneath it. Looks like a disproportioned ice cream cone.

The alloy shell is old as hell and when our metallurgic tests get through with it, we'll have a fabrication date. Right now, it's circa 2000 plus. It is one hundred *meters* in diameter and seemingly – impenetrable. With all its colored exterior channels, up close, it's kind of an ugly crate. When compared to the size of an

American football stadium, this ball takes up the entire 100 yards, and part of the end zones seating space. From what the crane engineers are showing us this baby should weight in at about 10,000 metric tonnes plus, including whatever heavy cargo is in its holds."

Bochelli nodded to a small group of people in white lab coats in the audience.

"Our metallurgist colleagues over there will be checking out material composites, alloys, etc. of the outside shell. Pardon the alliteration - but it seems as if there's 'no seams' on the outside shell! We know there *has to be* sectional joints. But right this minute, that's about all we know for sure. So the order of the day is, we continue to go slow and confirm as we go. We do not intend to rush to our next big mistake. Looks like we're no where near to being ready for most of you other specialists just yet."

Bochelli paused, took a drink of water - thought a moment, eyes turned upward, toward his frontal lobe, then went on.

"If I were to guess - and risk egg on my face – which, on previous occasions, I've actually had to eat – *after* removing my foot – I *can* tell you. . ."

Bochelli paused to allow his 'wait for it' brand of humor to set in *and* to collect his next thought to be sure of clarity.

"This one *is* definitely man-made – but not during the Great Napoleonic Wars! Still, it *was* assembled in what we now refer to as *our* middle ages – but only because the sphere's outer surface has an odd ball inscription.

It's quite artistic, really. Could only have been devised by skilled artisans. I tend to support the two thousand year old guestimate of some of my colleagues! Some materials and hieroglyphics *appear* to be not of this world, but I can categorically state, that by comparison, this *is* in fact *man's* handiwork. After sand and emery blasting, we'll have uncovered a sculptured insignia embedded in the hull, giving us some indication of its source. Possibly Greek in origin.

With a playful yet scurrilous, twisted grin on his face, Elio Bochelli images,

Did I imply Greece? Hell, I wouldn't understand Greek hieroglyphics anymore than I would, inscriptions on the walls of a Shanghai men's room!"

The space vehicular recovery specialist gave a wry smile at own admission and went on.

"However, in noting the graphic insignia, you can see on the mini screens in front of you the reason for our assessment. Our combined guesswork is that in ancient Greek antiquities?, the inscribed glyph has connotations of Liguria age and region. The graphic shape like a starfish with a swan's head in its center reminds some people here of a Greek Myth. If I recall anything of the boring social studies courses I that I had to take in high school, I'd say it was meant to refer to a mythological king of Liguria, today an Italian province up about where the city of Genoa is now. According the legend, this early king was pure wop like me – some gaucho by the name of Cygnus, loved and respected by his subjects. He was committed to the sea in some sort of "ovary seed pod,' called Cypsela. Apparently this cat was to be reborn to live among the stars. None of us can figure out what the hell the swan's head is all about, unless it is related to this character's complexion. The starfish is obviously a connection to his destiny to 'live among the stars'. Bochelli shakes his curly mane to emphasis his skepticism.

"I'm always baffled by those artsy fartsy folk who quote from ancient Greek fairy tales as though they were trying to make a moral out them. They never seem to have an answer to the question "*why*" and when they do what they profess to do, none of their stuff ever relates to the human experience. Anyway, so much for old Greek myths translation. Real interpretation of whatever meaning it has to the sphere will be the job of our team of linguists and ciphers. OK. You've got what *we* think we've got so far."

Elio Bochelli swung on his heel, back to the table's dais, looked askance at Anson Prentice and added an imaged,

"Wait a sec. One more thing, Anson"

He pointed to the white coat who wanted to pose the question earlier.

"Now that we have brought you up to date about what we *don't* know, what is it that we can tell you which you really *want* to know? "

The young man stood up and grinned. Then he imaged,

"Thank you for remembering, sir. My field is structural engineering. From what has been seen of the structure of the sphere, what has convinced you that it has been built by our forefathers instead of a allowing for the possibility of an off-earth construction source?"

Bochelli images back.

"There are *several* clues but the obvious ones are three antique welds that would never hold in a celestial journey. Two. *Man* welded seals around two cleats – the ones used to load and unload the sphere aboard the Akamuru. The other weld, less obvious, done for *whatever reason* after the assembly of the ball itself, is where a seal weld has been done well around a non-existent hatch– possibly just to mislead us. These are things we all recognize – not extra terrestrial!

While I'm on the subject I should add that, judging from its tonnage, we speculate that its hull *may be* some kind of equipment warehouse-type container from so many centuries back. That's *my own* first impression, mind. So, you can safely ignore my unsubstantiated remarks! See? I'm doing it *again* – I'm now in the process of preparing my lunch – raw crow with foot in the mouth for desert! You and your teams are obviously not here to listen to these kinds of assumptions. So I'll quit while I still have some credibility left."

The audience grunted out laughter and clucked as Anson Prentice walked to the front of the group. He was smiling ear to ear as he anticipated the opportunity to pay back Elio's kibitz for the age remark.

"Thank you, *Doctor* Bochelli...and for *your* information – I *am* proud to admit to a bubbling *97 years of age!* To you all, admittedly, that's almost middle age.

To be perfectly honest, I must admit I *know* I'm getting on. For instance, my daily *grooming* and taking care of my body is now *a full time job!* As I recall, it was a 20th century writer, Alcott Steven Kerr who once suggested, 'By the time one has lived long enough to know everything one wants, it's too damn late and not enough time to use it anyway.' I *can* testify to the truth of *that* too."

A meter by meter schematic drawing of the sphere hung on the wall behind him. He turned to it and pointed to the print.

"On your electronic image pads, you'll find a transmission regarding your agenda to examine this monstrosity, over the next 8 to 24 hours. Ladies and gentlemen, following our initial tour of the Cypsela sphere this afternoon, you could probably guess and be right to believe that you will be at liberty to leave the 'Reyk' for a month or so until your particular science is required. We'll keep you in the loop at all times. Naturally this entire investigation from engineering to living matter analysis is all under the direction of – and to whom we'll be reporting – the Selectronics Committee's Science Interpreters at The Hague who have asked for electronic confidentiality certificates from all of us."

* * *

Anson Prentice reflected a moment, then looked up and imaged,

"Would you indulge me in an introspective appraisal of human brain power for the next few minutes? That which has, this day, has positioned us together in this setting is all relevant, I assure you."

There is a patient silence, an expectant anticipation for what Anson is about to image to them.

"For all his scientific and social awareness, even in the face of adversity such as we have endured over the last few centuries, our species appears self-satisfied – even smugly oblivious to the achievements of a few deep thinkers ahead of their time. Trouble is, we rarely see the *direct* evidence of their outside-the-box thinking, then or at a future time. Such were people of the ilk of Archimedes, Newton, Da Vinci... As late as the 28th century our civilization was the benefactor of Johannesburg's De Wet brothers, Christiaan and Luther, harnessing the earth's magnetic energy field for the eventual benefit of earthly travel, among many things. Ah. But now, in this 32nd century – now – we get lucky. We are delivered a 22nd century gift package from that period's one

126

visionary, Sir Jeffrey Cairns. Its *value* is to enable us to *evaluate* a present day version of our species on the basis of an earlier civilization".

Returning to his lectern, Anson Prentice looked out over his reflecting audience.

"Ok. Relax. My philosophical history lesson is over. But if you *can* believe that we can rise above our disdain for those space cadets from another century – like the Sir Cairns group who created and assembled their sphere, we might still advance the cause of our own citizens. Who knows, we may be given even more proof that humanity of any era really *as not* as smart as we thought they should be!"

* * *

One Summer's day, (December, 3112) in AusZealand, couple Don and Yvette Richardson had occasion to welcome and billet an excited aboriginal teenager, student artist, Gubor 'Teddy' Bassett, from neighboring Pitt Island. The boy was visiting the 'mainland' for his first time ever. *His* island home was part of the Chatham Island group, roughly 300 km directly east of the Richardson home in the city of Wellington on the North Island.

By choice, rural Pitt residents have remained unchanged and unfazed by fellow inhabitants in a 32nd century world. Beyond administering compulsory medical injections of what was centuries ago, futuristically new 23rd century TransPinders, little had changed to bring its island members into an updated civilization. Leaving TransPinder application methods to legitimate medical attendants there, assurances were given that future generations' injections would continue if for no other reason that their communion with each other could be an enduring one. Ergo, Pitt Island's aboriginal population remained pretty much as it did from the 23rd century. Self-sustaining Pitt Islanders maintained contact with their so-called civilized brethren to the west and very far to the east, especially in the area of creative arts. Various southeast Pacific communities held art festivals where exchange artists met to exhibit. In order to keep participation costs as low as possible, billeting was common wherever the Art and Athletics Expos were held, which was once every ten years

The always smiling but apprehensive young aboriginal islander was wide-eyed at the paraphernalia of Wellington's centuries-ahead civilization. Marveling at every technical sight, the young Maori descendent was aching to understand what it all meant, not to mention how it all worked – and yet, he knew he *never would* be able to rationalize it all. However, hosts Don and Yvette were faced with the same old dilemma facing everyone when providing board for visiting foreigners. Even if oral audibility *were possible*, it would be a formidable task to explain everything. What's more, Teddy was one of the remote village people who somehow missed a TransPinder injection for voice translation! Using the medium that Sculptor Teddy *did* understand, Yvette, an artist herself, sketched out the sources of water in ground or stream to explain how water came streaming from household tap instead of a pumping it up a community well. So to try to explain to Teddy what made a SAR vehicle operate and why, would have had to be a subject for a ten part lecture series with visual aides and an extended volume of Webster's image reference directory! Even with time and lots of hand waving, Gubor 'Teddy' Bassett would *never* have grasped the operation of any of man's modern day technical toys. For instance, it would have been virtually impossible to explain to him that in this day and age manufacturers of various models of fold-up SARs, (traveling suits of light chain mail metal) were the product of two totally different industrial products – long established garment *fashion* and mobility transportation vehicles. Such motor companies were Honda of Japan who had merged with ready to wear, Guiyang *Styling* of China; GM (Global Magnetic of Sweden) produced wares in tandem with Armani Apparel; Ford Industrial, co-producing Peugeot Travel Conveyors with Fashion Outfitters Ltee. of Euro Franco. Meanwhile the Euro Benz Company merged with makers of Air Bus Travel Engineering to produce an exclusive sales leader in Stratospheric Magnipods.

The concept of fashionable travel was a stretch for most people of the day in so-called more primitive regions. People in those locales thought the logic of mechanical travel 'suit' vehicles and fashion producing creations together were totally incompatible – like jungle cats and wild boar! Notwithstanding, every year – just as they always had, both collaborating parties of each corporation created new models and produced suit-vehicle SARs for a world consumer market. To Teddy, these human advances were not the natural way of bird and animal kingdoms. His people would always carry on life in *their* way – the way of Pitt Island for many thousands of years!

Not to empathize with Gubor Bassett's backward standing, there *were* people, even in *today's* updated society, who still could not grasp the unlikely by understandably practical *difference* between fashion plated SARS suits and long distance Magnipod conveyances for stratosphere travel. However, as long as he didn't ever have to sculpt one for his island-art series, Teddy probably wouldn't gave a damn one way or the other.

* * *

Meanwhile, on the floor of world's largest area warehouse and laboratory at Reykjavik, many skull protected personnel, armed with acetylene equipment, were crawling all over the scaffolding.

Doctor Elio Bochelli, Chief Engineer for Space Vehicular Recovery Projects, turned to face his tour group of about thirty of those who would, themselves, soon be involved in sphere dissection study.

"Folks, we've already put UCLA's Penetray RI Scopes to work on the sphere hull's unusual skin to determine structural joints, layer conformation and content, The seams are precision joined, probably with interlocking edges. Exterior bolts and brackets holding the sections together are barely discernable. Bolts have been inset and ground to surface level so you can't see them with the naked eye, let alone turn them in or out. By the way, they *are left* threaded – that's trouble, even *if* we figured a way to *get at* them to unscrew them! Why? Because Penetray images show, these bolts are splayed inward but threaded toward the *outside.* How the hell they managed that, I can't begin to calculate. Those pins won't come out even with industrial pressure vacuum or reverse-screw equipment"

Bochelli, the vintner, professor, space vehicle investigator cum engineer had reached up to try to indicate a bolt depression to illustrate the object of his aggravation but could not find one. All he got was dirt up his sleeve. Trying to shake it out, he kept up his tour spiel.

"Penetray Scopes also shows us that there are at least *three* layers of sphere shell. Each of those has a minimum of a two meter, or more, 'air' space between. *Looks* like they are all made up of composite metals. The outer ball surface is 26.42cm (10.4 inches) thick. As dense and rock tough as that is, you can see from some of the inward dents and scrapes on both sphere *and* cone, this ball has received some severe abuse.

Still, from a weight standpoint, it *is* light enough to have the composite elements of strengthened aluminum - or possibly a derivative, like cyanite. Could be an alloy too – maybe a refined form of platinum...could even be a stainless steel... Frankly, at this juncture, I wouldn't be surprised if there were *silicon crystal* elements in the mix, too. Now here's the 600 billion peso question! The so called 'strands' of color which our Magnipod examining engineers reported, are actually 91.44cm (36") rectangular pipe – of a kind of translucent plastic and quartz. How they ever got those two materials together in a structural way, I'll *never* know. But then, *I* never figured out how the 4 million Egyptians and a camel or two got their pyramids' lavatories up and running either! Anyway, those channel pipes are 80% filled with another unlikely base mixture, vividly *colored*, clear oils and *alcohol* – believe it or not – presumably added to preclude the pipe liquid contents from *freezing*. These transparent, rectangular colored oil tubes – that's what we're calling them – were lock set into the 62 cm wide channels criss-crossing the outer layer's surfaces.

The tubes' luminous 'lighting' appeared only in the top half of the sphere – that is, opposite the cone beneath – so that when the sphere rolls like it would on an ocean wave, the lines would appear to be constantly moving like a whole bunch of black, red, green, yellow and blue ribbons. Sort of like, like solid, old LED Christmas tree lighting – only in fluid motion! Very inventive thinking for a bunch of Neanderthals, living in the darker ages of the 21st century. And by the way, these channels are *not* related to where the seams of the shell are melded. Even Neanderthals wouldn't make it *that* easy.

Now, about the *cone structure, This* is a horse of a different color –or of at least a different metal. It was no add-on. Its design seems to be totally illogical. It's too 'over built' to be just ballast, but ...you just never know what these cats were thinking ..."

One engineer in the group volunteered..."George says the cone material is a harder kind of pig iron. Wouldn't that tell us whether the cone might contain cargo or was simply to keep the sphere faced upwards to stay on an even keel? But there's something else going on in there though.

Bochelli's head snapped up.

"Oh Yeah? What do *you* figure, Marsh?"

Marshall scratched his chin and replied in a 'stuttering' kind of imagery.

"Well it's intermittent... but if you catch it at the right time, there's a humming – more like a very indistinct grinding sound coming from inside that cone – not from the sphere, mind, but only the cone. Fact is, last time I heard anything *like* that was when I took a tour of the nuclear plant just outside of Philly. Same kind of sound but a hell of a lot more volume in the plant."

Bochelli pushed him for more detail.

"Go on Marsh. What do *you* think was the source of the – what was happening there to make that sound?"

"Without any detail the nuke scientist showing us through indicated that the sound was just part of the reactor's function! But it was a continuous noise, not like the sound from inside this cone."

Bochelli and a couple of others in the party put an ear up against cone's outer surface. After a minute or two, Bochelli shook his head to support his thought, "Nothing. Not a peep. Look, Marsh, would you follow up on this? Get our security team to use some of those listening devices they've got lying around doing nothing – the ones that record sounds like mosquitoes breathing!. At this stage we can't be jumping to conclusions or we'll never get out of here. *All* our speculation so far is virtually *guesswork* and to get to the real meat of the matter, we *must* resist *that* temptation to guess...unless your name is Bochelli!"

"So again, until our forensic metallurgists and others get a fix, we can't even get a structural birthday on this critter."

Bochelli took a long slug of now cold coffee from his cup, screwed up his mouth and read from some of the documents from the forensic metals people.

"Here are some Penetray images of the orb's outer wall. You can almost see all three layers. Two layers for sure – Second layer registers is a gas - what we perceive to be an oxygen mix, possibly for flotation. But this one here concerns us...the outer layer – easily 2 meters plus of space. It appears to be stuffed with what looks like crinkly paper like they used to use on house buildings... what was it? Tar paper, I think they called it then – and no, not even Bochelli would dare to *guess* what it really is or what it's there for. Disconcerting to say the least. Now on deeper scanning, the scope hints at the fact that there are hundreds of thousands of compartmented sections in the holds but of course, we won't know until - Oh! – Il Capo, din giorno buono! (Good Day Boss!)

Anson Prentice came up behind them and went directly the cone section, projecting down from the bottom of the sphere.

"I assume you've brought every one here up to speed, Elio. Gang Bang George here tells *me* that his group still is not having much luck figuring out the plate seams on the outer surface of this turkey. He says they're so tight, 'you couldn't get a tick hair between the plate sections! And that is even if we knew where all the seams are. Quite naturally, we're reluctant to go at it hammer and tong. He's say he's devising an idea that might work for the night shift. So we'll see. The other problem, as if we needed still another, is that from the Penetray images, we get a hint that *all three* layers' surfaces seams actually *overlap* each other. Therefore *when* we get the outer layers open, we've still got to find yet another seam or two inside the *secondary* layers."

At one section of the cone, the boss stopped to peer at a 2 meter long indentation on the metal surface. Here, Prentice stopped and bent over to inspect it, to be able to envision an image for transference.

"This contraption looks to have been bunged about by some omnipotent force like a collapsing sea mountain range kicking it around from island to depression and back again. The three shells could well have been banged out of alignment, complicating our lives further by rolling one layers seam out of alignment with...It's a dog's breakfast"

He left the thought unfinished. He straightened, sighed and carried on.

"I guess it doesn't really matter though, Elio. When we *do* find a passageway in, there's no guarantee there will be a multiple access portals through *all* layers at the *same* place anyway. In any case, it's going to be one bitch of a long time to claw our way through all two or three layers of this stuff. Maybe technical capability in the old days wasn't so damn primitive after all!"

*   *   *

In the very early morning of the following Thursday, a thunderous explosion reverberated through the entire site at Reykjavik. Pictures rattled off the walls in the barracks' apartments. Rattling coffee dispensers disassembled. At the dirigible barn, ceiling arches swayed in unison. Staccato power surges caused flickering of all illumination on station. Some scaffolding surrounding the sphere came loose and clattered its way down the slopes of the construction complex. Parts of a cord network curtained around one part of the work site caught fire. Night guard personnel quickly sprayed that out. The only sounds missing were shouts of panic and fright – only coughing from falling dust particles. Eerie!

A quick on-site conference was held to establish cause and effect. One hour and twenty minutes later, the project's chief engineer came down the scaffold steps to a gathering of scientists and curious project personnel; some in night attire, some *not*, but all, with "pillow-rumpled" hair.

"The bastards. Now we *know* what that crinkly paper was between the first and second skin layer." suggested a robed Doctor Elio Bochelli to his equally night-garbed colleagues.

Gang Bang George climbed down off the remnants of scaffold, with a hunk of black paper in his hand.

"Hey look at this. Guess we were half-right about the possibility of explosives between layers! So we should all be half dead by now! Holy flammable bird shit, Elio! This had to be the booby trap of them all – installed to deter penetration by whomever! Had the other layer of pure oxygen been touched by any of its sparks, this could have made a bigger boom than it did. But looks like some tiny leak soaked some of the paper over a few hundred years. If it *was* a destructive play, it appears that this 'tar paper' idea failed to flash ignite like it was supposed to".

Harold, a member of the oceanography salvage consultants, offered a thought.

"That paper layer insulation Banger dug out of the hole was a little on the moist side, Elio. That could have kept the whole place from burning down. We might all have slept through it – *forever* that is!"

Banger's lady associate piped up.

"Do you always get this morbid in the middle of the night, Gorge? Or are you just mad for having to leave what you were doing"

She smile provocatively and playfully bumped his arm.

Elio Bochelli expressed the shock of the incident for most people in the anteroom.

"As it turns out, short of a few burned faces of some guys on night shift, we got off lucky. Nobody is out of commission. Right?

So, why did it happen just then?? As I am known to do, I can guess - but I'll bet Gang-Bang George here, can do better than guess – right Banger?"

Banger George Woebegone, Project metallurgist and night shift foreman, had just punched out. Now he came over to Bochelli's beckoning finger. He screwed up his brow in concentration to image a reply,

"Morning, Doc – Here's the scoop. One of our night crew had just inserted a probe into what we suspected was the sign of a seam. This probe has a small, built-in orange colored smoke dispenser on the tip of the probe. We were hoping to send only that hot smoke into the first layer. Smoke was supposed to seep out and show us where other vulnerable areas of access were in the outer skin seams. It could have worked too. Except that much of the paper was not as dry as whoever planned this thing wanted it to be. Could have been, the explosion was aided by a gradual leakage of oxygen from the next layer down.

If that was the case, then it *was* a combination of faulty installation on the part of the designers and *our* spark of heat off the probe. Oxygen can be pure murder in that volume. But, thanks to a 'boomer' gone wrong, we've *now* got an accidental '*manhole*' we can work our way into – so, Elio, for more access to this baby, I've got more hot smoking probes, if you want 'em".

* * *

Just after lunch, two days later, parka garbed scientists and technical specialists armed with power light packs, squeezed through a layered portal in all three sphere shells for a quick appraisal of what was to face them deeper into the interior. Libraried in the half sphere top portion of the object were many thousands of two-meter long cylinders, shelved much like bottles in racks of old style wine cellars. On uncapping one sample cylinder, researchers uncovered literally hundreds of 21st century humans' effects; personal, pictorial and certificates; licenses and documented effects in compressed forms. On another catwalk on another floor were millions of compressed health records, X rays, DNA and genome samples of those global inhabitants of long gone generations. Some cylinders were full of intimate messages in every known - and now, unknown language of the years from 2048. Addressed to their 'descendents' of the future, these were recorded on hundreds of thousands of antiquated CDs, DVDs, voice wire magazines, encyclopedic videos and micro chip systems - all electronic mediums, long since outmoded. As though foreseeing their own limitations, 21st century librarians had enclosed magnetically powered equipment, from now derisory MP3 and MPEG players, medical hardware to display records, original wheeled segway mobiles, digital cameras, and LCD and plasma monitors of the times.

To the delight of the engineers and the antique collectors on the exploratory teams, they found an amazing display of twentieth and twenty-first century artifacts. These were securely welded and bolted to two metal floors. In the middle of the sphere was a suspended Lougheed Lightening P 38, Russian prop fighter plane. Below that were an Indy, track-ready Shelby Ford racing car; a classic Rolls Royce Silver Shadow limo; an exhibit of the difference of consumer mobility of that era – production line products of an original first and last made Chevy Impala; a 1928/29 Ford Model T; a US navy dirigible cabin;

one of the first railway passenger carriages to cross the Chunnel into France. On another steel floor were a 15 meter WWII German torpedo E boat – totally refurbished and sea worthy; a collection of Harley and Triumph motor cycles; a massive grain combine towering above the an array of armament from 2000 and 1000 year old wars, such as iron ball firing cannons off a Spanish Armada gun boat; a 1945 V2 rocket; anti-aircraft and artillery cannonry; a thirteen step gallows; an original French made guillotine;, an electric chair; a stuffed version of the world's largest seagoing crocodile. Suspended above all this and anchored to steel struts between floors, a 'floating' Harrier jet with articulating engine pods turned downward as though about to make a 'helicopter-like' landing; mortuary caskets; household appliances from ice boxes to refrigerators, were welded to the sides of the sphere. All implements exhibited represented mankind's life and death creations – mechanical helpers during those early two to five centuries before they closed the hatches on the sphere.

On an "upper" deck, one complete compartment was filled with volumes of materials that could easily have represented the entire printed and electronic word ever produced from the beginning of man's recorded time on earth. Scientific documents and holographs of every war, of rocketry history, of 20th and 21st space travel, recreation, business, education; all stored and in murals along the curved 'walls' of the sphere's 'screening' compartments.

*   *   *

One week later, sanctioned entry into the 'cone' section made the cone accessible from the inside of the sphere. Where the cone joined the gently curved bottom of the sphere, three air tight sealed hatches, one for each of the sphere's outer surface layers were positioned in the center of three layers beginning at the sphere's lowest level deck. With an easy turn of the spin wheels they opened without struggle. Hatch doors flopped downward to hang by their hinges. A ladder descended some four meters onto ceramic tile flooring in the cone's 'stand-erect' anteroom.

What first struck the exploratory party was the intense *frigidity*. That was the most uncomfortable difference from the now almost 'room' temperature of the sphere above the cone.

Fear of the unknown in the cone antechamber was only part of the reason for a chill that went through their deep pile outer attire to what they figured by now would be blue flesh. The five, helmeted visitors to the cone section were hit by a wave of paralyzing trepidation, just as though they would be punished for intruding on a sacred burial ground. Something was very foreboding here.

For one thing, a 'sweet and sour,' yet pungent odor of some chemical barely discernable, somehow permeating their thermal suits and helmets. Some of the party looked at each other through their Plexiglas-faceplates. They wrinkled their noses, and nodded as though the smell was known to them. They all felt they *should* know that aroma but they just couldn't quite place it. The other foreboding thing was the shock of the intense cold in their enclosure. It caused shivers, felt right through their thermal wear.

Then, as they stood there trying to gather their thoughts for the next move, a grinding humming sound came on to echo throughout the entire cone chamber, however spacious that might have been. It persisted for the remainder of their stay.

The centrally located anteroom was 2.13 meters (7 ft) high to the sphere's entry trap door above them. Somebody guesstimated that the hexagonal ceramic tiled floor had to be about three and a half meters across the hexagon sided 'anti chamber.' Built-in extra luminous sun-lights on their helmets, and cautious shuffled steps helped them to avoid any unseen obstacles on the floor. However, the *ceramic tile floor* was clear. This floor design was made up of alternating black and grey hexagon tiles leading to a centerpiece graphic. There was a ceramic design, much like the sculptured steel insignia on the sphere hull. Here too, was a tiled ceramic graphic of a vivid purple starfish with a white or light grey swan's head in its very center.

The six-sided panels of the anteroom were opaque, like a flexible frosted glass but of a cloth-like material. These angled outward from the floor to the top. From these 'walls', there appeared to be no entryway into the rest of the cone from the anteroom. No switches; no buttons; no screws; no ledges; nothing to press, push, pull or pound on. A preset thermostat box set at -196°C, was the only thing in that anteroom. Every loudly breathing person there was mindful that there had to be a *purpose* for the 'breathless' cold. But what? No material could possibly be impervious to this extreme climatic setting. They had been cautioned not to reset anything that altered the temperature setting. Nor could they find any possible anteroom exit, other than the hatches above them. One hour later, with freezing fingers and blue faces like those beset by hypothermia, all five visitors retreated through the hatches above them, seeking the 'warmth' of the sphere's mezzanine floor deck.

* * *

"So where do we go from here? What else of value could there be in the rest of this cone to make further search worthwhile?"

One crewman imaged to the group.

So thought most of the team.

"I'm still convinced that this cone below us is nothing more than ballast like they thought... If *only* to maintain stability and a leveling apparatus for the sphere above it."

"Possibly. But if that were the case…"

Anson Prentice was thinking 'out loud.'

"..*why* on earth would such ballast – an extension to the main body of our sphere, have to be so damn *big*? And if ballast were the only reason for the cone being there, why is the only entry through these trapdoor hatches providing egress *only* though the sphere? Why a ladder into a ballast space – ladders made for two legged humans? And an obviously fully powered lighting and refrigeration system? That was the reason for humming sound, by the way. Automatic industrial refrigeration! Also, *why* is that thermostat reading set at that precise setting -196°C – just to turn our blood blue? Finally, – if it were ballast, why is the whole cone *hollow* at all?"

"And how do you know it *is* hollow, Doctor?.

"Because a 2 meter high by 3 square meter octagonal anteroom, would *not echo* sounds of our movements like it did!"

Another of the crew transferred this thought,

"The key to breaking out of that fish bowl has got to be there.- it is right in front of us, I wager!"

Anson Prentice stood up and imaged further,

"Come now, folks, what did our mathematics-minded Mensa boys figure? 950 cubic meters of wasted space in the bloody cone alone? That leaves more than 55,000 cubic feet – Hell, that's bigger than the biggest three storey business building in my home town. Would they really have to allow for that hunk of steel just for ballast – or some kind of sea anchor? I don't think so. This 'inverted pig iron party hat' is too intricate for having no functionary purpose. No way folks. We have to figure a way to get through to whatever else is in that cone. *And* we've got to do it fast – before that strict, delicate temperature setting is altered by us just being there! We have an army of investigators and forensics people waiting in the wings for the *second* feature – and we're it! So we better get at it."

* * *

As they crawled back down into the cone's anteroom to search every inch of the space, they were all mulling over what they knew. They were asking themselves. Why *was* there an anteroom in this outhouse at all? Was the thermostat's setting to ensure an exact cold extreme level for *whatever* cargo might be in this 'hollow' space? What reason would there be to refrain from turning down the temperature level? Since the only instrumentation in that anteroom was its thermostat, *it* had to be the key access to the rest of the cone.

The chief power engineer of the project and his crew volunteered to go in again to the anteroom to examine the freeze control setting. This time, an electrician specialist in refrigeration went down with the crew to add his expertise. They were of the opinion that by *lowering* the thermostat, being careful not to stay too long under the original setting, this *might* enable the hexagon sides to open upward or downward. When the thermostatic control was moved minutely downward, absolutely nothing happened to enable entrance through the "opaque" cloth walls.. Then, he dropped down to his knees in order to try to locate any other hidden control switch or aperture in the *floor's centerpiece* insignia. When all of these moves failed to enable access to the cone through "frosted" ante room curtains, the electronics specialist unsheathed a 'cutting tool" on his belt. He tried to slice through what he perceived to be a simple polyethylene drapery. The only thing to break was the blade on his 'box' cutter. Once more they all went up through the hatches to discuss brain waves.

It was only when a young power-logic scientist on the project expounded *his* theory that suddenly the logic of the access puzzle started to become apparent. The young man imaged his thought in more detail. He speculated,

"In *that* icebox, it, would be quite *natural* to want to turn the temperature down a 'degree or two'. Since a *warmer* thermal setting wouldn't move the draped wall sides for *us* when we tried, that may be because we would have interrupted a temperature level *needed* to preserve – whatever it is *supposed* to be preserved," the young man, "but maybe just a slight twist to a slightly *cooler* setting would give us access!"

Back they went into the cone's tunnel and anteroom – this time with a bundled up and helmeted Doctor Elio Bochelli as an expectant observer. At the *very minute* the thermostat setting was adjusted slightly downward to an even cooler setting, *all six sides* of the anteroom *came* silently *down* on their runners, gathering into accordion folds on the anteroom floor. Their helmet lights illuminated the floor and themselves – nothing beyond.

Bochelli grunted out an image warning to the others.

"If I were you, I wouldn't wander too far off this tile. Could be a long drop."

They were all huddled on what *had been* a small ante room floor but which in fact was now, a rather small platform accommodating their six shivering bodies in bulky atmospheric suits.

With the 'frosty cloth walls' down, they saw – *Nothing!*

Only pitch black emptiness and cold smelly air. That familiar sweet-n-sour body shop odor – stronger now – wafted upward. That cold air seemed even more paralyzing now than when the sides were up. The now louder hum of a power generator was the only sound coming out of that darkness. Helmet-lanterns still allowed the exploration team no greater vision than the beginnings of a steel ladder leading downwards into darkened nothingness.

Bochelli broke the ice, literally –with this image,

"That odor. I know it from *somewhere*. But again, I just can't... Damn my memory! Crap! Maybe it's *me* that's older than my bathroom mirror tells me."

* * *

On accessing the underside of the massive circular, steel partition, a ceiling for the anteroom, separating sphere proper from cone appendage, there was a master lighting switch box. Once switched on, several banks of cold solar light boxes provided eye-blinking illumination for the entire, gymnasium sized cone space, right down to the very point of the cone. All cone contents were now clearly exposed.

In fully lined, protective regalia, eight helmeted exploration team members looked down from their suspended anteroom platform – agog at what they were *not* certain they were seeing. Sharp intakes of cold air were heard as the explorers recoiled in astonishment and started down the steel rungs of successive ladders leading to the very bottom. Again, an eerie foreboding penetrated the senses of the assembled scientists and researchers. One by one, they advanced with cautious steps down the rungs of steel ladders leading to steel-mesh, gridded walkways. These bridges criss-crossed over top of each deck spanning the diminishing diameter of the cone as it advanced in sixteen levels downward to the pointed bottom of the cone.

The explorers' visions were ones of stunned incredulity.

Attached along the circular walls of the cone, were 286 two meter high, vertically T shaped casket containers, each within a half meter of the other. Like shadows out of a dark mirror, the outline of faces could be seen through transparent portals the full width of the top of each 'flat oval' sarcophagus .They seemed to repose in perpendicular stand up cocoons, fashioned after the ancient mummified peoples of Egyptian exhibits. They appeared be immersed in a fluid which filled the to quarter portion of the encasement. Some had small tubes leading from somewhere on the inside of the cocoon shell direct to the mouth, nose, ear and probably the heart of the human so enclosed.

Names, vital statistics and all relevant medical reports, (all were scripted in four basic languages, Mandarin, English, German and Spanish).

Respectfully displayed as though exhibited in a mausoleum setting, the sarcophagi collection 'descended' in rows and columns into the very depths of the cone. The bottom level was reduced to just five such containers facing each other in limited space at the bottom point.

In the center sections of the cone, several members of the crew warily crossed the steel mesh walk levels to where rows of waist high cabinets – over 300 in all, contained banks of drawers and bins – frozen shut. But already several technicians in the crew carefully but laboriously pried some open.

Contents subjected investigators to their second shock of the day. Two of the exploration team momentarily turned away from this sordid exhibition of perfectly preserved and now bloodless collection of human organs. There were livers, bladders, genitals, lungs, hearts – all precisely labeled, stating disease or injury trauma.

In other separate storage containers, land and aquatic animals and some birds in curiously depleted condition were laid out for careful examination. Such were oil-soaked seals and gull carcasses, most bearing multi-lingual tabs – suggesting that these non-human specimens were from varying geographic parts of a multilingual world. Almost apologetically, those depicted were carefully placed as though expressing concerns for the animal.

Parts of both animal and human remains were presented in an array of varying stages of surgical procedures. Drawers marked "diseased" (again, in the four, now unrecognizable languages) exposed cancerous, obviously smoke blackened, lungs and nodule-ridden female breasts, male prostates, and cancer-ridden lymph gland samples from both genders.

In wide vertical cabinets, two and a half meters high by fifty centimeters, were door after door of un-casketed, frozen cadavers with gaping open mid sections, just as though surgeries had been abandoned at death; naked people with deformities of limbs and facial features. There were explosion-gutted cadavers, presumably soldiers or suicidal terrorists from their martyrdom days on earth. Some others had bullet entry wounds from head to heart and torso below.

Adjacent to these were still more slide-out, but see-through shelves assumedly marked to indicate cancerous organs. In another, were kidneys, intestines and other human parts taken from early transplant operated patients; among them were tubs with miles of human intestines, some with cancerous growths and all of these preserved in boxes of what might have been a semi-clear brine and alcohol paste. In some containers were the wasted and twisted limbs of poliomyelitis victims; others cabinets contained the small limbless bodies of thalidomide babies.

Still other drawers were 'stocked' with human torso sections; white rib bones protruding through blue-white flesh to exemplify some ancient plague; some were apparent virus cases of a flesh eating disease. The gaunt remains of virus-plagued victims, again taken from all races in the world, alluded to the tragedies of population wipeouts. Partly completed lobotomies and lacerated skulls with hair still attached also packed some of the other drawers with further examples of head surgeries. Preserved brain specimens of autistic and retarded children were also included in these organs cabinets.

One curious "human artifact" was a circular, vertical container split down the middle so that half of the upright was transparent. Through that one could see hundreds of variably sized, blue—grey, 'dried figs' puckered inward in their centers. Each trailed a 10 to 30 cm long 'tail'. The only reference to what they might be was a cryptic, felt pen scribbled note on the see-through portion of the tube containing the objects. This would be studied later and interpreted by university antiquities study groups. Their sardonic message read, "In the eyes of some, these might seem to be symbolic of the medical mentality of dedicates who prepared this collection."

The figs with tails were identified as diseased *rectal sections* from persons aged two to 60 plus.

Of the entire macabre find – 'exhibits' was a vertically-split half 'carcass' of a 9 year old southern hemisphere youth. Nauseating as it was for some of the investigating team, they followed this case through to it's conclusion to learn that this exhibit s was an example of the brutal eradication of thousands of Brazilian street orphans who infested the city during the late 1900s. As though to turn tragedy into a scientific discovery, both halves of the boy's cadaver were marked with various colored, coin sized plastic discs "pegged' to various points of his body and epidermis. Medical reports, to be researched later, explained that the colored coded marks were to indicate what was known of the human nervous system in the 21st century.

Colored plastic buttons were also placed on certain organs, such as tongue, top sections of rib cages, points along the spine, esophagus, small intestine, hip joint, and at several internal points along the body. A corresponding, matching colored tag affixed to the outer skin area, soles of hands, feet and so on, indicated which neurological connections were made to affect seemingly unrelated other parts of the body. . While this has long been known from ancient oriental practices, this 'presentation' was included to allow bioscience specialists the opportunity to understand *why*.

Another uncertainty was the discovery of four metal cartons containing the decapitated heads of one young woman and three men of Manchurian descent. Strangely, all were 'wearing' mid 21st century 'sun glasses'. Removing the glasses, even this era's morgue doctors and forensic researchers were left stunned at what they first thought might have been patched up deformities. However, it was soon discovered that none of the four heads had eyes – *nor* eyebrows. Just smooth skin, where eye sockets would have been. Later, on translation of accompanying notes of ancient Chinese characters, it was acknowledged that these cadavers from different extreme high country regions were found in near perfect condition deep within melting glaciers, well above the Arctic Circle. It was speculated that primitive northern tribes spent most of their short lives in darkness searching the ice pack for edible ice ferrets one of the few food forms readily available at that time in that lifeless habitat. For these four, the addition of sun glasses was a poor attempt at the black humor of such antiquities.

Still another section of the cone was comprised of exhibits on stem-cell research, and resulting human cloning. In the 32nd century, this was now an accepted, but strictly monitored treatment for rare diseases, such as ALS, and to aid in neuron-processes to resolve sexual deviation, among other disorders. For example, those who sought medical clarity as to which gender *they* belonged, were considered at one time, as treatment prospects, if not expendable, human discards..

Appended medical cards alluded to crude, exploratory surgery performed in the later 20th and 21st centuries in experiments to alter the genders of misfits who had committed sexual crimes. Specimen samples of such genitalia procedures were included in two separate drawers. There were also charted records that demonstrated the trial effects of chemical or surgical procedures to either establish, reverse or to eradicate the 'bio-causes' of *homo sexual / lesbian* categories.

Invaluable as this whole collection might have been to students of previous cultures, both pathologic and neurological study of 22nd century man, it was a display which most hardened coroners would be adverse to decipher without their own moments of revulsion.

*   *   *

Later in their freezing, walk-around tour of one steel-treaded, bridge crossing after another, the cone section's first eight explorers were about to be astounded beyond their already awe-shattered minds.

The sound of an out-of-breath researcher, who had gone down to the cone's lowest point, was heard, as he frantically scrambled, double time, up the ladder to the seventh level. He stood panting on the walkway, face white with shock, trying to concentrate on the image message he wanted to project.

One of his colleagues went to his frightened colleague who was now doubled over, gasping to get his air back. All TransPinders were centered on the message, emanating from the mind of their stricken companion.

"Hey! Whoa! Whoa – Glenn – what's the problem?"

He imaged.

Another researcher came down the stairs from the level above.

"What's got Glenn so agitated? I've never seen anybody climb seven levels of ladders so fast... "

Glenn looked up at his attending partner. He was still out of breath and shocked out of his mind. He managed to image his concern above his scrambled fright.

"Bud, you – you aren't going to believe this but, (puff) -- here...Sorry...can't think straight to image you."

His friend, trying to pacify him, tapped his TransPinder, focused in on the man's thought image. Then he stepped back wide eyed and thought out,

"Krykee! That's not possible. Are you sure, Glenn? ...that's what you *really* saw?"

Still gulping for air, Glenn nodded.

The image, now emblazoned in all three men's minds was a sarcophagus, like all the rest, except this one was *four times the* size of the others. It contained the great hairy shape of a *perfectly preserved* African gorilla, with open, glistening, brown eyes that would make one believe he was alive. This animal species had become extinct by man's encroachment several centuries ago.

* * *

Meanwhile, other medical examiners, by now ready to surrender themselves to the warmth outside this deep frozen sphere and cone, were studying and laboriously trying to transcribe data tags. These were English language footnotes on many 'specimens' soon to be removed from the sphere's cone.

Some of these notes compelled many of these young future medical scientists to attempt to consider resurrection of the identified eighty five 'humans,' cryogenically treated before death, who might 'show any *signs of life!*'

"*Oh come on!*" a shocked, mouth-contorted medical scientist imaged his incredulity,

"Who are they trying to kid?"

Another remarked in mind expression,

"What in hell were those guys putting in their *coffee*, when they wrote *this* stuff?"

Another surgical researcher thought out his opinion.

"They actually *expected us* to identify and treat – live, *thousand year* old patients?! They really *were* a naïve bunch of wish doctors!"

"You mean *witch* doctors, right? *Naïve!* If all our ancestral practitioners possessed bone fide wall documents, certifying their acquiescence with their version of the Hippocratic oath, they must *never* have understood the meaning of ethics! This just gives all us witch doctors a bad name!" Murmured laughter ensued.

Cyber Prophesy Regenerated

Chapter 1

Global Summit Opts Out of Human Rule

2278/23RD/2309/24TH CENTURY/GIBRALTAR

The Proposition:

'Whereas, the epochs of turmoil and degradation of humanity
by a multitude of successive sectarian governances,
embedded in the ruling bodies' of mankind,
since the advent of civilizations on earth,

And whereas, we the people of this planetary enclave
deem that the human race must no longer endure the
loss of rights to dignity and justice in our time,

Therefore, we hereby propose that
we endow to ourselves a secure world governance under
one of three ruling principals, yet to be resolved.

To this end...

We seek the strength and fortitude
of a council of persons of one created universal faith, or....

*We propose a system of non- partisan, cyber implements
to rule us forever in perpetuity, or....
We draft and convocate, within every generation hereafter,
a collection of wise humanitarians, of the stature of Solomon
to guide us through future ages.*

* * *

Even at the outset, it was apparent that an undercurrent of common man's/ women's discouraging lack of individual advancement. A graduated and growing concern was emerging all over the surface of the earth. It stirred its soul-weary civilizations. "There just had to be something better..."

At first it spread slowly – as just a 'movement'. Less dramatic than a bursting flare but more solidly evident than a ripple of discord and wishful thinking, it might be now. After centuries in the making, now might be the time to render a call for unprejudiced universal change.

The movement came into being in 2113. At one annual conference of financial wizards and social-standards icons, conclaves of influential benefactors for an idea for reformation picked up on the convention's keynote address. It was given by think-tank president, Madame Claudette Bartoc, well known Swiss citizen and pharmaceutical scientist. In and of the tone of things, according to the media, the human race had finally come to the cusp of advancing humanity into an advanced form of governance that must eliminate the inequities of man's political rule. So overdue is the gathering of earth people's symposiums to enact reforms that one day, little green men visiting from Mars, might ask... "What took you so long?"

* * *

It was an inevitability that human administrators of sovereign nations all over the world knew would have to come. It was a subject that was part of humankind's evolution for the last 100 years or more. Existing finance and political entities were cognizant of the long standing groundswell of mooted change to come but were content to ignore the makings of a quiet but firm rebellion. They believed that the citizenry of the earth would see the error of their ways and would participate in the political process as they always had. This time, however, they wouldn't.

The movement to end existing means of rule heralded the finality of existing political and monetary interests. In her usual impassioned off-the-cuff demeanor, Madame Claudette Bartoc delivered her conversational style address without hiding behind the customary dais. With a remote broadcast mike affixed to suit lapel, she actually *sauntered* among thousands of delegates at a world conference of humanitarians and 'earth movers'.

As casually as though she delivered a heart-to-heart talk with her friends and family in her living room, she did the same to a much larger group. This time, expressing herself by waving her hands, Madame Bartoc cried, cajoled and exerted her very intellectual charm to challenge the Status Quo with alternative propositions to over 40,000 stadium guests in Paris. Many influential notables of government and industry were attending the worldwide Conference of Governance For All Peoples. She talked to them of *their* roles on the status of kingdoms, colonies, empires, protectorates, political and military dictatorships, and semi-democratic baronial entities. Her message was simple enough. It repeatedly reemphasized *two key questions* that had been on every world citizen's mind facing concern of the discrimination of one-sided governance for over many thousands of years.

She had stood in the middle of after dinner tables and asked,

"One. Why are *you* truly satisfied to allow incompetence and prejudicial politics to continue the high human costs of misrule and mistreatment of *your families and loved ones?*"

Two. How much longer should *you* trust incompetent, inadequate human rule, too much in favor of their own exclusive benefits with utter disregard for the real needs of *our families and loved ones?*

Monaco ruler, Madame Claudette Bartoc stood at the highest point in the stadium to conclude high point of the evening.

Three. And here is the critical proof of your answers to the previous two questions. 'Are *you* prepared to commit to attend and support the first of many Global Symposiums to program a world wide movement for the purpose of affecting the futures lives of *your descendent families and loved ones?*'

She stopped for a sobering silence. The eyes of the room remained on her. Hypnotically, she intoned to her great audience,

"Answer that *without* qualification. Answer that with words of one syllable. Answer that as though your best friend and partner were at your shoulder.

Please know, my brethren, *eventually the old ways must end* and know that because you want it to happen, it will happen. – and soon. The process to that end begins Tuesday January 21st in Brasilia's Mount Zenith Park. Be there. Your neighbors from around the world *will be.*"

* * *

From that day forward and for 35 years onward, 70 global symposiums were staged. They were multi-day assemblies, dedicated to determine an cover-all system of administration. Attendee volumes grew bigger with each Symposium event, continually seeking solutions for more *central*, more tolerable, more stable, more relevant, and more efficient kinds of fair governance. An administration of man-presence and/or non-political cyber impartiality has been envisioned.

For the seventy first and final Symposium, the sole objective was to draft ways to adapt simplistic applications to prevailing governing complexities.

* * *

Following 34 years of multi-generational debate, the choice for a planetary system of people governance was down to one final Symposium. Delegation arguments and conclusions of the three acknowledged and workable positions [previous sentence needs a verb]

1. A technologically generated Cybernetic central administration.

2. A one-dimensional structure of universal faith in government.

3. A draft of worldly wise persons, interwoven on singular decisions to govern all peoples on earth. The latter alternative was reasoned to be a preferred choice owing to the fact that persons of the caliber of Solomon and Socrates, did in fact, justly rule, albeit a smaller and different kind of world at one time.

Some might argue that any of the three 'cures' to our existing malaise could be worse than the disease for power, currently in place. So far, with rare exceptions, one common opinion has already been made. The days of entrenched tyrannies, monarchies and republics, which have long been out of touch with reality, fairness and the welfare of common persons in the next thousand years – must be replaced!

Gibraltar's silver, purple and black peak on a radiantly sun-washed Mediterranean day in June 2305, seemed to have dressed itself up especially for next most grand entrance in the evolution of humanity.

Poetically magnificent as is, it just seemed apropos that this place was again to be the site for a gathering of human beings. What was to be the full momentous evaluation of all mankind, would be a seventy-fifth and hopefully, final Symposium to determine an outcome. It would be dedicated to a new kind of planetary unity

Of everyone on the rock on this auspicious day, two thirds were combining organized tours as part of conference activities. As on most days in the summer months, business and tourist holiday excursions base themselves out of guest villas in Spain. They cross the narrow isthmus and the two hour, border 'traffic jam' to the Gibraltar Symposium site. Two corridors of pavement encircle the Rock's peninsula carrying buses, taxis and cyclists to tourist attractions. One such route leads up the rock to the cavorting and impudent Barbary apes, beggaring for their families. All are born and live their lives half way up the mountain, with occasional forays into town to perch on tourist ship transoms.

* * *

The great St Michael's Caverns of Gibraltar are being readied to seat the expected 25,000 person maximum in and outside of the immediate conference

155

area. Individual audio/video speaker daises had been strategically positioned to allow for delegate speakers' contributions. Dias speakers would be visible to many and heard by all in attendance. On the inside and outside perimeters network broadcasting systems had powered up so that they could broadcast to the world to record the profundity of the Symposium

Already protesters and advocates on cushioned seats atop vehicle roofs, hillside rocks, bus and wagon decks, are noisily trying to gather support for one or another of their proposals or grievances. Spectators turned demonstrators – many just seeking the limelight of media attention – were rallying with their "visual aids" and hand-held speakers.

"The world is not ready for big brother machines!"

So bellowed portly British House of Commons MP, Bryce Scott-Sang, the 3rd, to an inattentive crowd. His megaphone squawked as he yelled.

"Let's hold on to our world of *human* governments. Cyber Systems nuts, bolts, wire, buttons and bells are no solution to that which ails us. We want decisions by live flesh and blood *people!*"

Across the sea of chairs and rock benches, hastily being filled with Symposium delegates, Luton foundry owner-operator, Barnaby Twillinger urged his followers to shout back at the bigger, Scott-Sang mob,

"*Now* is the time! The time is ripe - to elect our rulers with *no party* stripe! *Hey! Hey!* wha'd'y'say?"

Still other individuals and costumed partygoers carrying Spanish language placards and shouting Espanola and Françoise slogans, joined in the noisy melee. Similar factions from Middle Eastern, Asian and African countries extol their partisan messages, proclaiming *their* preferences and hoping to influence others in attendance.

Now the moment had arrived. Cave lights in the 'house' were dimmed. Halogen spots zeroed in on a 15 person panel on an elevated rock stage shared with the Symposium moderator's French broadcast executive, Phillip De l'Casse.

The echoes of the audience's squeaking, scraping chairs on rock floors subsided. The 71st Summit Symposium of Commoner was underway.

"Mes Amis... Madames et messieurs, Senors, Senoras, Milne Damen und Herron, Ladies and Gentlemen. My name is Philippe De l'Casse. As Chairman and moderator for this 71st Conference of the World Summit Governance Symposium, I welcome you all!

May I humbly beg your forgiveness for again having to conduct this conference in one language, owing only to time constraints? English is the chosen language due to its precision; its expression able capability, its brevity and its universality.

However, as in meetings past, you are probably aware that with your registration, accommodation passes were issued for your on-site presence here today. Accordingly, you specified for and were issued temporary ear discs that will provide you an *instant*, vocal interpretation in your stipulated tongue. These have been set to virtually all earth's other interpretive languages. I should inform you and all the media here today that global networks are present and hooked up to the same translators so that the opinions expressed will be the same, all over the world."

De l'Casse explained further that the only rule to be followed was respect, courtesy and consideration for others, in voicing a point of view. He provided the agenda.

"From most of the earth's region's delegates requesting formal audience will sit as varying panel members. They will lead the views from the floor, in representing or countering any of the three optional resolutions introduced. Speakers' daises in and outside our St Michael's caverns are live and ready for speakers.

Let me remind all that of the 70 Symposiums held heretofore, from a slate of over 200 concepts for future world governance, three strategies have been selected and concluded desirous by most as being deemed humanly possible. They are..."

The images on all monitors listed all three graphic concepts to which Phillip De l'Casse referred as he read...

"1. A legislative assembly of today's Solomons, Solons, and Socrateses, would expedite the words of ancient wise men's writings - rewritten into law for all people and all regions of the earth for all time, setting a standard for all the world's governments and councils and every individual circumstance.

2. The Anti Illuminati Conspiracy concept for the establishment of one universal faith governance. For purposes of definition in its application here, elitism is defined as elevated lifestyle for all who choose it for the purpose of directing common individuals to one kind of equality, thereby diminishing the major cause of government corruption against the brotherhood of mankind.

3. A computer generated central cyber system of law is advocated. This is to be known as the 'Selectronic Committee' through which every earthly creature and circumstance is recorded and evaluated. All cyber judgments are to be rendered on fact-based only configurations by which to conclude unprejudiced decisions to meet every circumstance and every person in every environ."

* * *

Moderator De l'Casse adjusted his microphone, opened his 'compu-pak', readying himself for the conversation ahead. The moderator turned to the panel speakers' dais beside him.

"Now then, our mandate here today, as it was in previous Symposium sessions, is to explore and ultimately arrange for the resolve and adoption of a singular means of governance on a world wide scale. It is a virtual certainty that one of these eventualities will occur. Although, I might add, maybe not in your time or mine or even our children's time, as existing political powers would have to be negotiated away even before partial institution of a governance for implementation into one world application. Moreover, for better or for worse, there will be little or no likelihood of recourse of the selected system in the hundreds of years that follow. So with those realities ahead, let us now begin a *new* beginning.

At this time the chair invites a panel member, Italian representative of the South European regions, to expound on the 'Wisdom Collection' philosophy and the 'in practice-theory' to which it ascribes.

The Italian member of the panel stood to acknowledge the introduction and to give interpreters a preparatory moment to prepare. In slow, deliberate Italian, he opened his remarks.

"Ringraziaer Signore. The application of sage governance is not only a tried and true experience in world administration but *is* in fact, proven invaluable in the administering of justice and law down through many earlier centuries. That the Wisdom of Solomon's decisions brought self-inflicted punishment to the perpetrators of dishonest, cruel, unjust and corrupt administration is widely recognized. Such impartiality has helped to quell international and domestic issues for all kind of cultures and for settlements that negated wars between disagreeing countries"

The Italian panel member went on to expand his contention, by citing specific incidents of wisdom notable in every administration from the ancient cities of Phoenicia-founded, Carthage to Petra, the Edessa city of Mesopotamia. He related anecdotes of judicious resolve from the southern mountain regions of what is now Jordan on the Tigris to other established empires in this, the region of 'the cradle of mankind'. "May I just add that it would be ludicrous to believe that we simply ran out of wise administrators? But it can only be that wise persons' non-partisan, judgment was *deemed* not beneficial to the aspirations of the politically inclined that followed those times of infinite integrity. Con molti ringraziamenti per la sua attenzione."

Just as soon as he finished his seven minutes opening statement, the floor was opened up to contesting speakers already lining up at the audience daises. A distinguished grey haired woman spoke in Arabic. Her message too, was translated in all other pertinent languages. She addressed the Italian delegate and panel member in his own language.

"Signore. Rispettosamente. With respect, I wish to point a misconception. Simply because an honorable person is intellectually astute, does not make that one impervious to an inherent, humanistic lust for power or riches"

She paused, permitting that observation to sink in before going on.

"And if it were not so, who is to say that even those so eminently wise are really what they are reputed to be? It should also be remembered that wise men such as Solomon, son of David, Athenian statesman Solon and philosopher Socrates are rarities among us but not infallibly. Today earthly subjects are in such great number, wise jurisdiction may be only an impossible fantasy.

20th century's exalted wise woman, Indira Gandhi and the 23rd century's savior of Cuban law, Jose' Zapata are just two such cases. In any society, no matter how large, there are hundreds of millions of intricate matters having to be dealt with every minute of every day. Now, because there are too *few* *ethically* wise people on earth at any one time, it is my humble opinion that, the wise person concept condemns this concept as a *non-option*. 'Graziarla.'"

Another person rose from the panelists table.

"My respects, dear lady," he countered. The accent tabbed him as British.

"Wise men and women of honor, ethics and consciousness, are born *every day* in *all* parts of our world. In every era, even primitive people living in the deepest jungles have had their community-minded chiefs who administer tribal business in a traditional but compassionate, or sometimes, even in a cruel fashion. In the so-called more civilized sectors, there are always many such persons in every social stratum. And *they* can be designated, and appointed, not by the electorate, who are too often brainwashed by insidious propaganda to elect a pretty face or a persuasive speaker. You see, no matter how controlled, outdated voting systems by multitudes of 'sheep' on a voters list, or worse, partisan 'party hacks' who couldn't care less, tend to make electoral decisions based the pre-packaged character of party-backed candidates. It seems to me that if a *cyber* technique is advocated as capable to govern, why not a *computerized appointment* system to *select* such persons to govern? The selection could be made after evaluation of every iota of data on every man, woman and child on earth so that ..."

"Oh Yeah – Right!" A queue jumping, American skeptic suddenly appeared at a floor microphone.

"...And since you tell us that dummies like us can't recognize an *honest* wise guy from *a mobster* wise guy, how and where the hell do you propose to dig up your wise geniuses – out of the Gobi desert sand? Furthermore, what if the computer selected most of your wise guys from *one* area? Imagine the cries of 'favoritism' for some of *their* future decisions! "

The same British panel member, who had just spoken, rose again.

"Supplementary, Monsieur De l'Casse? Does the 'what if' speaker not understand more of what it takes to reason? Sir! I have just explained *how* we can *avoid* the huge selection of miscues for governance – which humans have been making since the invention of the notched stick or ballot box? Please follow my points, Sir.   1. In *every* civilization, basic, *unfiltered, computerized data*, can readily identify with people within *their jurisdiction*. The calibration of a master computer could easily be set to consider the profile of *every* earthly person - noting their age, intellect, marital status, race, gender, wealth, health, criminality, etc Via computer research, so-called *Mensa club wisdom* yet undetermined, can be easily determined by establishing intelligence levels. Given the latitude to do so, this 'supreme court concept' would deal with solutions. Fortunately for us sir, our findings are that there *are* now both technically efficient means and intellectually knowledgeable persons to achieve these objectives.

Turning away from the audience amplifier, the skeptical man threw up his hands in disgust. muttering, as he left,

"Idealistic assholes!"

And so it went...

By mid morning, all three governance subjects had taken their initial hits; both credits and lumps. Now as the Anti Illuminati theory was being described, an *evangelist* at an outside dais shouted out his religious fervor in support of one of the Anti Illuminati panel members. It was the panelist representing this holy cause, who stated,

"When the Lord Jesus Christ went into the counting houses of Jerusalem to raise hell with the money men..." he yelled into a microphone, "He was setting

161

the stage for a rebel movement of Christian adherents. In turn, his disciples were to teach us all that, to smite the elitist Midas's where they lived, was the *only* way to lead and live by his example - to show us all his resistance to the evils of illuminati mythology!"

Another panel member rose to speak, started, but was interrupted by Moderator De l'Casse.

"One moment sir – Hold that thought... Now entitled to rebuttal... the chair recognizes the speaker at dais twelve.

"Mr. De l'Casse. Mine is an accord, *not* a rebuttal..."

A sixty plus lady scanned the audience looking for where Dr Harari had last spoken, and announced.

"If the Jewish gentleman – the doctor who spoke earlier, could lend further credence to our *holy* crusade to rid the world of unholy, moneyed elitists, I relinquish my time to his comments."

Doctor Haim Harari, formerly one of the last "chief" rabbi (Vaad ha'eer) of the New York Rabbinate and now President of Global Institute of Social Sciences, presented his name and credentials. He replied.

"In relating a bit of my earlier bio, I wish to apologize, Madame, if I misled you in any way."

The esteemed professor of anthropology then addressed himself to the symposium audience.

"I believe the lady is hopeful that my religious background would compel me to support the cause of faith, thereby *weakening* my firm belief in the Cybernation concept of world governance. I thank Madame for relinquishing her speaking time but I must inform her that any comment I may make here will *not* necessarily be an endorsement of any *holy* or unholy communion. I cannot support the invocation of a governing body who dedicates themselves to an administration structured on their fantasy of the glory of *their* god over any *logical* process.

We have tried that already – many, many times – for far too long after the biblical lessons of this courageous, humanitarian, the gentle and fabled Jesus Christ. Same thing with Muslims, the Eastern world's Buddha, the enlightened one, the wisdoms and ideals of the Torah and Chief Rabbis of Jewish and/or /Hebrew cultures, likewise, the preaching of Hindu Swamis – all have singularly, but have never collectively, brought human sensibilities to advance the realities of one world governance. Regrettably, neither religion nor the wisdom of these faiths have made any real difference to a humanity with one basic need.

Unhappily, no logical *evidence* exists of the worth of *prayer* to any of mans' *invisible gods*, to help eradicate the pitifully warped injustices of incompetent men and women who govern.

Please prove me wrong here. Tell me. Name one region – Arab, Irish, Chinese, Aboriginal, Slavic – on this once *'good* earth', which has *not* been sadly effected by a *clash* of conflicting faiths – initiated by the modest to the fanatically religious. Mankind is admittedly worse off for having an assortment of unrealistic, man-conceived idols and gods – each with man-created theologies promising after life rewards like Martyrdoms Virginal Paradise, Heaven, Valhalla. It does not seem to matter which good book or prayer or sacrifice or what earthy riches are offered as penance, the holier than thou solutions have not made our world a better place.. To exemplify; as late as the last century but self centered but misguided Pope *actually sanctioned*, albeit by inaction and tradeoffs, one dictator's evil empire and the annihilation of an entire multi-million population of another faith. So much then, for genuine governance by a holy or sacred *church-inspired* state under man. Artificial and short term bolstering of *spirit* – plus tranquilization of mindless people is not sustainable when lies are fabricated, such as espousing concocted epistles of divinity and god-inspired miracles. In fact, they are *deterrents* to programming humankind for life's realities."

* * *

Harari turned slightly at the dais to talk directly to the chair.

"Mr. De l'Casse. Having infringed on this gracious lady's time I beg your further indulgence. It is essential that I *briefly* address the matter of theoretical governance by a *super wise* council.

On the matter of creating a collection of the world's wisest of people to govern, I respectfully suggest that, *even if test tube breeding* experiments were conducted to ensure a *perpetual*, world supply of wise persons, regrettably, it would *fail*. True modern man can be brilliantly innovative. However, for us simple biologically assembled humans, there is no algorithm to restructuring man's brain, which has taken many millions of years to evolve... to produce a *super-logistically, exceedingly* sensitive and, intellectually advanced, human being *completely void* of predetermined biases. Court juries if this singular character have been sought for hundreds of years! Positive results are questionable for any future quest..

Some people are frightened to borderline panic by the prospect of governmental technical devices. In their opinion, it's too new a concept to be able to depend on! Such people, despite all evidence to the contrary, still tend to believe that the wise men's jurisdiction theory is the only option. In actual truth, the wise men rule, in practice is in actuality, little more than what we have now... state control by political ignorance, religion, and singular-minded autocracy. And here is the 'kicker' my friends, Experience of life has shown us all that even the logically wise often can and *do change* 'neuron gears' when given absolute power to rule".

Let me offer this prayer – to my compatriots on this earth..

The reality is so clear. Instead of creating a wish upon a star whereby a wise man and, or faith governs us all with but one accord is too unrealistic to chance. To advocate a digital governing system in the image of man's own likeness to which might be entrusted, a means of instituting *one* and only *one just society*I plead with you, my brethren, is to accept a Cyber enlightened world governance. Because it is only with this *algorithm*, by which we can sustain real human advancement as far forward as our own resources can take it.

My heartfelt thanks for hearing what I sincerely believe to be both an eternal and spiritual answer for my beloved fellow man."

The island audience erupted into cheers. Almost futilely, Chairperson Philippe De l'Casse stood to hold up both hands

"Order please! "

The applause continued and again he stated,

"Please, ladies and gentlemen, Order. Order please. In consideration of the added time allowance and the conclusions of his address, we ask that the speaker give up future speaking time at this 71st session of the Symposium. Thank you, Dr. Harari."

The Moderator pointed to the last panel member to speak, "Again, panel and audience personnel are entitled the right to rebuttal."

This time a white haired Ivory Coast diplomat rose from his panel seat,

"Two points, Doctor Harari. Semi-civilized societies like mine – ones that go quickly from one set of rebel administrators to another – seems like every few years – abide by no other partisan rule, except their own. They rely on changing circumstance to set a changing governance standard. This is no way to build stability, reliability and security for any people'

Frankly, I acknowledge universal implementations of Harari's 'Big Brother' Cyber-machined concept. In my view, rebel law is a law of turmoil

We are, and always have been, dependent on civilly ineffective world bodies, such as League Of Nations, United Nations, Third World Equality Organizations, and the more recently formed Planetary Accord just recently signed in Panama, by all region's leaders on earth. Sooner or later it will prove as ineffective as all other human devised pacifiers. When trade inequality strikes for example look for those familiar signs of discord. By contrast, where there is an investment in trust of constant *trade and commerce between adversaries*, there is usually peace and even degrees of fairness. Not to belabor the point but for many, the very idea of a machine *ruling colossus*, forming laws to meet life's everyday problems is, a scary process. Unlike man Cyber rule can not be threatened, persuaded or bribed. How so? Because facts are what they are – not what some autocrats prefer them to be.

I happen to believe we are truly at the cross roads. Lets take the next *new* step – not those that have faltered so many times before."

The moderator waved his had at a nearby microphone where a smiling woman stood up to the microphone.

"Ladies and Gentlemen. You mustn't be deceived. Your common sense will tell you..."

The woman was an American.

"No main frame in the world will ever be engineered that can out think man. None that will effectively provide cure-all solutions for the billions of mundane and human problems. No technical micro chipped edifice can preclude wars if man is intent on making them. No mechanical system can adapt and react to the many unknown, *unforeseen* events and human anomalies to come. Humans can *at least try* by very innovative means to accommodate solutions but Cyber computers have no such instinct. Why? Because a Cyber System is not subject to human reasoning which is why we all need governing – isn't that so?

Come now, Dr. Harari. Given your steadfast convictions for a Cyber system of governance, are you prepared to discard the thousands of years of proven, positive aspects our *existing* ways of life in favor of untried technical undertakings and replace that with micro chips and electronic magic? As they *used* to say, isn't that a much like throwing the baby out with the bath water?"

Another speaker at a microphone at the far end of the cavern spoke up

"Monsieur De l'Casse, since Dr. Harari must adhere to a speaking time restriction from the chair and is unable to offer rebuttal, I beg to provide my own refutation of remarks just addressed to him by this New York lady. from the insanity of mans gentleman from the Ivory Coast. I might concur with the last speaker, if *I* could be *convinced that* there might be *another* genuine, non-conflicting way for a governance to direct our variable civilizations. So why is it then that the all knowing *human* populations of our planet have *never* unearthed any other universal, 'one *way*' to govern, with equality based on the character on man and his place on this earth? What we are right now is what we have been shaped to be over many thousands of centuries. But from one era to another, our human leaders – wise or otherwise – have ignored and repeated the errors of their ways, time after time, – committing citizens of earth to pay with consequences, often with their very lives?

Yes it is true, Honorable Chairman, it is possible that a Cyber cultured System of Legislative Justice *could seem* threatening. Particularly to those fearful individuals who refuse to understand that computerized drives, can gives us balance and necessary power to live – every day of our existence! If I may, Mr. Moderator, just one more quick point ."

Monsieur De l'Casse waved him to continue...

The Algerian turned to face the massive audience in the cave.

"In the last two hundred and fifty years, we *true* followers of Islam have *had* to defend our teachings and trappings of our faith many times from *our own extremists*. No different than most religions, I suppose. *But now*, as of this time on earth, the opportunity for a new book of life opens to us. Some of us will perish as a price for such a divergent course. Under a Cyber governance system, explosive violence may occur but not in the name of religion. Such protest would be redundant. Why bother with bombs in terminals, airplanes, markets, parks and plazas? Remaining dissident combatants will be eventually compelled to stand before a functioning Selectronics justice maker – not a human court, but an undiscriminating machine. Such instrumentation can be programmed to deal only with the relationships and living matters with *men* and women – not their music, bodily feeling or faiths. Even my Muslim brothers, most of whom firmly believe that Allah and his messenger *comes before all else*...they, like many other factions of the world's diversified people will finally be free of remonstration for such dedication to their god. Praise be – not Allah, not Lord God, not Buddha or any other such icon. But praise only our individual power that we may manage our own lives!"

* * *

Oddly enough and for the first time ever in 71 Symposiums to date, only *one drunk* broke free of conference security forces to slur his own brand of disoriented logic.

He swayed at an unguarded microphone, while he suggested that a conspiracy of Illuminati people had it right by threatening to kill everyone "at the top" of the pile and settle for one god…

Inebriated though he was, he was quick to press his 'point'.

"This conference must encourage …laws for the legalization of prostitution, pornography and free access to grade 'A' opium."

Then he was taken by the elbows and guided from the microphone area. The laughter that followed was one of the few laughing matters of the entire conference.

Philippe De l'Casse smiled wryly, as he thanked the "speaker" for his brevity… then he said,

"The chair recognizes the young man at the end of the panel table – with the hope that the 'local spirits' have not influenced *his* point of view!"

"Thank you, Mr. Chairman." The long haired man wearing a pair of Billy Goat earrings and an imprinted snake's head tee shirt remained seated."

De l'Casse asked him to observe conference protocol by standing to address the gathering.

"Yes sir. Sorry sir. Ah…" he began nervously,

"I'm a third year anthropology student…St Martin State Zoology College in Tallahassee, Florida."

Again, the tall gangly, twenty year old hesitated, ostensibly to gather his wits, his nerves and to stabilize his irregular breathing.

"After much study on the *basis* of one international law for all, I – I am now ready to begin an adult life *under a* universally fair set of laws and decisions. The way I see it now is – a Cyber administered justice, *would* be a definite *deterrent* to those who cause killing, maiming or disabling *any* other person and or animal.. Such sad souls *must* be taken out of the human gene pool... regardless of one's state of mind. *Any* violator, even one consuming a mind-bending substance of any kind causing mental shortage, would still merit the harshest penalty stipulated by law. There must be no exemptions for indiscriminate murder. No one, age notwithstanding, must be permitted to keep on hurting others. Under existing and varying laws, even though having to spend the remainders of lifetimes in penal institutions, these are not deterrents. Owing to the laxity of courts and the holes in present laws and circumstances, long sentenced incarceration is not a preclusion to admonish offenders, either. Considering all the traditions of ethnic groups of people in our world today, existing enforcement and judiciary controls are not likely to keep up with the rate of criminal offenses in any region. Cyber-made edicts could become the only certain alternative.

However, we must concur, there are extreme criminal circumstances involving severe mental deficiencies which are not resolved by *extreme* punishment. In future, such retarded patients would have to be subject to fair but diligent government funded detention in special care facilities.

Therefore, Mr. Chairman, I can foresee that only a finite Cybernation system, however appropriately instituted, will *resolve earth's criminal con*undrums in future. For corrupt militant, political element and/or their political friends in power, only a strong 'black and white' Cyber indictment will suffice to keep them at bay.

Fellow humans, if you give little thought to anything else those of us who favor digital law have uttered here before you, please consider this. In order for our civilization to move forward rather than to regress, consider the ramifications... *an irrefutable and irreversible sentence of permanent exile* for the offence-minded will be *our only hope for our descendents*. We must have a precise definition, structure and enforcement of laws, where *all*, including those benefiting by position, friends and relatives of decision makers are taken out of the equation. Consideration must be given to all circumstances but not of self-caused misfortunes *for any reason*. These cases would have to be afforded the same kind of justice as anyone else. They must be subject to laws they break, that one universal law will prosecute them and commit them to remote exile from past and future victims.

Just as effectively, the *innocent* must be quickly appraised, not by a mechanical law that simply skirts the legal profession but by a detached collection of statistics. This is the justice that leads a Cyber based Selection Committee to a speedy and inexpensive conclusion. By this method, mistakenly accused are left with no stigma attached.

The intention of designing laws by which men and women can abide with each other has always been intended to bring civilized order to humankind. It works *only* when we *all* accept the truth that people, who *physically offend* other people *in any way* give up their rights to society's privileges! *Period.* For the greater good, I believe, only that which will *permanently remove a* perpetrator from the opportunity of committing further crime, intentional or otherwise, will do.

It is now inarguably conclusive, - mandating long-term *exile*, far away from disciplined, lawful communities' lives, will compel the criminally minded to observe man's own civil laws. Mister moderator and assembly of Symposium, Thank you for this time ---"The young man turned from the dais.

As he did so, the entire gathering broke into cheers, whistles and applause in support of his philosophy. Another panel member, a Protestant minister from Johannesburg, Reverend Van Dyk stood to speak. Waiting until the audience response had died down, he embarked.

"Out of the mouths of babes comes ..."

Again, the audience responded with another outburst of applause.

* * *

Moderator De l'Casse spread his hands, palms down, to call for quiet.

"With only a few hours left to conclude the morning portion of the Symposium, the conference's input will proceed with time constraints exacted on contributors' time. Please bear this in mind. Thank you."

Then he pointed to the South African minister to carry on with his comments...

"*If advocates* of Illuminati really believed in genuine religious certification to justify claims of such influence, then they might *have* to consider their kind of simple logic as a worthwhile alternative to rule by micro chip or wise human counsel. But Illuminati power is not simple. Most of their membership preaches their hidden agenda under the robe of religious cover. Their raison d'être is not faith, per se. Even they can understand that faith by any other name is *trust!* It's the same kind of faith that has to be earned – *speaking* it is not enough. Recognize an external force like Illuminati for what it is! It is still a prospect of one global power, – but of theirs no one else's! New Governance Symposiums like this one are ideal opportunities for them to flaunt *their* collective benefits.

Thus, we implore believers in a 'conjured up' *faith*, to disengage themselves from others' umbilical cords. Put your trust in – have *faith* in – and rely on any force that will delete the elites who control you to their own benefit – instead of the other way around. See? I told you this would be brief!"

A young Scot, ignoring the protocol of rational order, inconsiderately grabbed the same wireless microphone out of the previous speaker's hands. Like a gyrating rock singer, he thundered out his message.

"Don't you people realize that since the times of the early beetles – I mean the *bugs*, not the singers – trying to stay alive has been man's singular occupation since we crawled out of the hostile ocean? Well check this out – we are *all still alive*, aren't we? What's so bad about our *present way* of life? Ok, considering the multi billions of earth's population, it's only a *few* cheaters – elitists – evangelists – politicians – whatever – and – oh yes, even the *ominous* Illuminati, if you need more folks to blame, that are the offenders here. OK? So cheaters make a few million undeclared clams off our backs. So Big Deal! In addition, how about those unscrupulous senior elitists, money mongers in existing governments. Yeah right – people actually use corrupt and scandal-laden bureaucrats, congressmen, lobbyists? Gives them something to rile about! And yah sure, we *know* we live with – those sanctimonious, ecumenical, evangelist bastards who con their way into our lives for their own purses and purposes – so what of it? If *they* don't, somebody else *will*.

And y'know something else? Being told what to do, when and where to do it by some, big, impersonal, digital, mainframe in some inaccessible underground bunker is not as great a gig as we might think it to be. Government leeches hanging out on some holiday beach while the rest of us are having to live with the taxes they are holidaying on, is exactly why we are here today. We spend our time, *hoping* like hell that they get their due. It *doesn't* work! Neither does bedside prayer. Yep. It might *seem*, we've got more than our share of unscrupulous political hacks, police commissions, inner councils, bureaucracies and hospital boards to contend with, while we are dying in long waiting room line-ups. Hey look. This is not the end of the world for *all* of us – the real question is, how much longer do we have to spend trying to live with it?

It might sound as if I don't like this any more than most of you but I figure, as civilizations come and go, it is a fact that we've got big problems that *haven't* been handled all that well. But to hear the do-gooders in this place call for a new brand of riskless government is tooth-fairy fantasy! We're not built that way. So why should *we experiment* establishing some new kind of one law while we forget how to look after ourselves? Could be that the cure might be a hell of a lot worse than a big bite of whatever is left to eat around here. Chew on that for awhile!"

The young Scot, wearing a back pack, seemed about to say something else – then turned half away, muttering,

"Hell, we've got it ok…we're all right, Jack…" He passed off the microphone to the next speaker in line and left the dais to the sound of an occasional hiss and boo.

"The chair recognizes the panel member from the Nepal region of Central Asia. He had represented philosophical theory for governance, the Wise Oracle administrative alternative, already before the symposium."

Clothed in orange draped cloaks, a shaven headed Asian priest stood ready to deliver his opinion.

"My country has been globally acknowledged for centuries as a kingdom of wise gurus and of a peaceful and gentle people. Our nation has been regarded by Hollywood as the true 'Lost Horizon' of idealism. Of course, this is a fairy tale. The reality is that for centuries Nepal has experienced turmoil and disenfranchisement under the ravages of powerful Himalayan neighbors in addition to the ongoing conflict of its own rebellious factions. However, like other sovereign nations, we concede that there are still more outside than internal causes. It isn't that we lack the vision, just the initiative to *insist* on changing thousands of years of serenity.

Midway through these *seventy* summit symposiums over the past thirty or forty years, many millions more of us came to realize that there have always been too many inequities and too many injustices in the world. Too many lefts. Too many rights. Too many bigoted, self-aggrandizing, non-action power figures seeking and getting exclusive jurisdiction in every nation in the world. So how are we to rid ourselves of this human pestilence? Assuming this is possible, then by what method or by whom are we to be ruled? And is that not the challenge of these Symposiums?

Let's evaluate the wise men theory of governing. Unlike the times of Solomon, there are statistically too few, if any, strong minded and power-immune human beings that all the world's people could agree to as unbiased leaders for all people over more a generation or two. Not even under the astute guidance of *decent intellectuals* such as were, intellectual pacifists, the Delhi Lama, revered Mahatma Gandhi, Maharesh Yogi, the late Sakarov, Africa's Dr Joseph Mandela, honored humanist, Moshe Dvorkin, the world would still stay divided behind claims of regional bias. That's the mistrustful nature of mankind.

If this reality is so – and it must be – or we would not be gathered here today. A man-fashioned parliament over men is totally untenable. I admit that faith has helped bond many of us together. But religion has *separated* more us. Regrettably, it has not *unified* mankind's spirit with human justice into our everyday existence.

In our small region of Nepal, we are now of the opinion that in order for humankind to survive in a future world community, we *desperately* need the unbiased logic of *digital reasoning* proposed by Doctor Harari's conception of ingenious cybernetics. Furthermore, it is our considered opinion --"

Monsieur De l'Casse, the moderator interjected. "Forgive me, your eminence. You are being heard only intermittently. There is a fault with our microphone facility at your station. While we perform a correction, may we ask you to stand by until that is completed? I shall call up you again – perhaps this afternoon? Thank you, sir.

A group of five dark skinned, young men, gathered at another dais microphone near the moderators. Slung over their shoulders or being worn as uniforms, were lightweight, black silk-like, jackets. Sewn on the long sleeves of each jacket was a multi-colored, Aztec configured design, a crested emblem of South America's country of Columbia.

Looking something like some people would envision an organized street gang, all five young men stood quietly at their assigned microphone. Without introduction or offering identification of the group's representation, one of the young men, their spokesmen, moved forward with a document in his hand.

In Spanish accented English he began in a voice much more adult than his years.

"We have been asked to speak this message to the Symposium. It has been written by one of our country's most distinguished journalists. He was awarded a Peace Prize for his humanitarian literature across the world. He is also a 2852 Pulitzer Prize winner for his published texts. The message reads;

"'In every time period since very early tyrannical chieftains ruled man's earthly tribes, it has been sad testimony to the human species that, he has not been able to effectively rule other earthlings. Moreover, with rare exception, no such chieftain's camp has ever provided for a system of rule designed to lead his fellow human subjects to reach that person's potential. For only such a ruler's reasons of self power, a human sub species was allowed to live through many a dark age, coping with, but not overcoming obstacles that kept one from being excommunicated. Without purpose. Without morals. Without honor. Without a set of ethics! Without just reward.

May I use an example of how an earthling finds himself unable to develop the way he should? A child is born, out of the enfolding fluid of woman's womb. Hundreds of oxygen breathing, child persons have been encouraged to show that they, like some baby mammals, can subsist for long periods of time under water, right from the outset. Thusly, the human's natural capacity for immersion into a water environ as well as air. Therefore, despite the restraints placed on them by parents and peers, baby persons *could* grow up to lead our landlocked species into a duel environ as does the dolphin or the seal.

Similarly, restraining laws of governmental leaders lacking vision and foresight for their people, become progressively worse in terms of advancing the human race. It has been a matter of record that lack of self confidence causes people to go the way they are led to go, instead of being inspired en masse to meaningfully improve their lives on their own terms and on their own initiative.

Can such autocratic controls *ever* be reformed and implemented by some technical revolution to come? Is it not a better thing we do so by recruiting Solomon-like, wise persons with broad precepts over personal favoritisms? Is a universal religious foundation a more unified way to meet the millions of complexities of any worldwide administration. Alternatively, is it not sounder to reform the *manpower* behind governance instead of the building technical manuals for an alternative form of administration, never yet tried? If a change of governance were possible through the combined strength of entire populations to compel elitists to give up their domination, this Symposium's task is done. If not, humanity's last opportunity to live on, blessed by creation of an enduring orderliness, will be forever lost.

These are the writing of *Amigos del mundo, de libre hace y firmeza de la mente* – I am a human being, concerned for other human beings. I am *Jorge Eduardo Luis Torres, El Sol de la Ciudad de Columbia*" '

* * *

The moderator glanced at his timepiece. He added,

"And so, to the entire assembly, may I suggest that this might be a good time to stretch our legs. Take twenty minutes, if you will, and we will continue with a panel assessment of opinion to date. Listen to the buzzer to call you back to on-going discussions. Thank you."

During a leg stretching intermission, lobbying and opinionating that which had made during the first morning session is exercised. Discussion goes on at the urinals, at the cavern's quick coffee counters and even at cliff side perches outside the caverns.

A half kilometer away, one group of NorAmeric young people were about to test their opinions on a gathering of religious British delegates wearing purple arm bands showing an ornate white Cross.

"So what do *you* folk believe should be the chosen outcome of this Symposium?"

"Well lad, speaking for our little group here, we believe in the spirit of the Lord."

"Oh. Yeah? Well, everybody should have a hobby."

"That – me boy, is borderline blasphemy."

"Are you bible punchers still using those long gone, cockamamie, words? Blast famy is it?"

"Keeping the word of the Lord is still the name of the game, my child."

"You mean – word games – like, thou shalt not kill, rape, pillage or buy votes? "

"Not exactly - but for all of that, we still forgive misled cynics like you lads."

British Member of Parliament Christopher Bryce Scott-Sang continued his own high-pitched banter with fellow Brit, Barnaby Twillinger, who had cornered the MP and his followers near the entrance to the cave. In a move to beat him to the opening verbal punch, Twillinger moved forward aggressively.

"Y'know, you politicians have demonstrated that you are *not* part of the solution. In fact you can lay claim to being part of the world's governmental problems. Haven't you figured out yet what you're doing *wrong* – and *why!?*"

As expected the rebuttal was frenetic – like an argument in a Westminster Ale House.

"I can't speak for all my colleagues," Scott-Sang began,

"But I believe it's because we *know* what *won't* work, Mister Twillinger...and *that's* because, from our experience in the house, we *still know more* of the aspirations of our constituents and their *needs*, than your data processor ever will!"

"So you know *what* – you just don't know *how*. So tell us *how* has that worked out for all of *us* so far?"

"Well, for one thing, *you're* still here. Your cyber machines will never know when *not* to push the nuclear button."

"Remember, Mr. Scott-Sang, cyber systems did not create the bomb or push the button in the first place – 'twas the American, Russian and *British politicians* who did that! And by the by, your Cyber machinery won't be creating a means to *our salvation* either!"

He quickly added,

"..and *when* it does, *your* only salvation will be having to take an honest job for a change, Brycie, old boy. There'll be no need for a MP then, will there?"

With that, the tough little Luton foundry boss, turned on this heel to walk back into the cave. When he *did* glance back, he spotted his antagonist gesturing argumentatively to a young man with an Aztec emblem on his jacket sleeve. They were both walking away toward the now empty visitor balcony above the cove.

Meanwhile, delegate identifications and declaration counts were still being collected in preparations for the voting primaries tomorrow. Symposium sessions resumed with a tap of Monsieur's gavel at the moderator's dais.

The buzzers sounded. Most of the now estimated thirty one thousand or so gathered in and around St Michael's Caverns, were already seated in eager anticipation of more frank exchange of views and ideas.

The moderator.

"Friends, it is our hope that delegation leaders with voting privileges take note of well identified registration stations and poll depots throughout the Gibraltar isthmus. Tomorrow, when you are ready to indicate your constituents' choice, you will go to any station with your delegate registration cards in hand. In exchange for your card, you will be at liberty to choose one colored granite "ballot stone." This selection will be known only to you at that station. Your constituencies choice of governance will be chosen by depositing that one colored stone when you are proffered the welded steel receptacle.

Remember the choices. They are – One. Anti Elitism and Ongoing Religious Influence 2, Cyber Digital Management 3, World Rule by Mankind's Wisest Humans. 4. No change or Status Quo. Even if the choices or method of voting is not yet clear to you, your station personnel will advise you of the process in your language."

De l'Casse looked up from his notes.

"Now let us continue the Symposium. There are still many people we must yet hear from. "

The moderator nods in the direction of the panel.

* * *

From just beyond the main cave entrance and beyond the sea wall road, came a wailing, high-pitched scream. Heads swiveled in that direction. Again, what at first sounded like a woman's screech of distress, brought many people to their feet at St Michael's caves. Waiting their turn to speak at the microphone daises, many already standing had bolted and scurried out the door. In what could have only have been five or less minutes, an emergency vehicle whooped its alternating high and low siren squeals in the distance – and getting louder.

Minutes later, yellow suited divers, ambulance paramedics with gurneys and respiratory equipment, Gibraltar police, press and photography personnel were gathered in and around a roadside balcony three meters above the Mediterranean's surface level near the steep cliffs. When divers were aided by ground personnel to lift and receive a human from the water to a street side gurney, onlookers became silent. Even in death, dressed in misshapen summer garments and white shin tuning grey, Britishers among the spectators recognized the form being covered with a tarpaulin. Seems like just less than an hour ago, Bryce Scott–Sang was a very vocal part of the Symposium activity. Now he was dead.

* * *

Gregarious, personable Bryce Scott-Sang had been a fifty-eight year old British Member of Parliament for Willowsby, part of the electoral district of London's Westminster South constituency. According to his constituents, who were charmed by his public relations diatribe, he had missed his calling! He had to have been England's smoothest talker.

His influence went a long way to smoothing whatever way his drug lord friends required of customs and excise in the various trade and commerce departments of countries other than just the UK. To this end, his 'hail fellow, well met' genre was part of the subterfuge covering under the table deals and smoothing out the Food and Drug Departments obstacles for his Columbian suppliers. If that had ever been publicly known, his polls would have been down considerably.

In his support of drug cartel exports, his expertise made him a *trustee* of key people of South American governments supporting the drug trade.

In advance of Bryce Scott-Sang's attendance at the 71st New Order Symposium, he was visited on Gibraltar by an Ecuadorian 'foundation' official presenting him with an offer he wouldn't dare refuse.

* * *

179

On the Friday night before the first day of Symposium '71, Scott-Sang was surprised to learn that one of his paid insiders, working with Columbian cocaine shippers, was in town here in Gibraltar. He thought that odd. Jose Garcia was far off his beaten path. What could be wrong? They arranged for a meeting at 7:30 am, well before the Symposium got underway. They agreed on meeting for coffee at a wharf-side café.

He joked. "Hey! Buenos Dias, Jose. Are we having French roast or Columbian, this morning?"

After the niceties, his Columbian 'acquaintance' and occasional partner leaned over his shoulder and whispered,

"They find out, Senor Bryce"

"How, Jose?"

"My brother in Iquitos –– he say Columbia bosses have talk with spy man in Ecuador about – ah – how you say – double crosses? Portland Oregon container dock, boss. He talk too."

"Did your brother learn what our Columbian friends were told?"

"They no your friends anymore, Senor! They know you make *same* deal with Ecuador big guys for *same* shipments going into Oregon 'Portland' place?! Bosses no like that. There *is* problem! Senor. What do we do now?"

"How long ago did your brother learn of this?"

"'He tell me yesterday morning…so they know since –"

"They'll miss you. You better run …I'll pay you off now, OK? You must get your ass off this rock right *now*. Before you go, call your brother. Tell him to get his babies away to some safe place. You and he should head for Istanbul. Find a German poppy exporter there. Helmut Klinnenbroeker. He'll look after you."

"Si, Senor, but somebody visit for you too – *soon* I think so"

"I think so too, Jose. Looks like I've got a forty-eight hour head start on them. I'll take a charter boat out of here tomorrow and head for Tunisia. No one knows about you and I working together, so you should be OK, Jose, - but right now, lose yourself in Spain, anyway   You should out fast –"

He let the sentence hang – then left the Café.

He knew he would have to spot his cartel partner's 'firing squad' *before* they found him! Then he left for the opening of the Symposium proceedings.

⁕ ⁕ ⁕

After the disturbance outside the conference De l'Casse continued to introduce speakers.

"I believe the lady panelist from Liverpool wishes to speak to the subject. Madame?"

"Mr. Moderator ...Ah – Mr. Chairman "she began.

"Regarding the previous young man speaking to the matter of criminal and civil offences, law enforcement and judiciary in a *computer*-administered system; I am concerned that the pendulum of justice could swing in favor of such harsh punishment, without recourse – rather than the time honored policy of correction through rehabilitation. In my part of the world, criminality continues to accelerate. Local council scandal and nepotism in tandem with corporate manipulation are being dealt with, but around, badly municipally produced laws.

This slows both unjust and unrelated decisions in courts, so increasing lawlessness continues rampant. Very few systems of jurisprudence in *any* country seem to show any indication of effective controls. Maybe – just maybe, that young man's earlier suggestion of permanent exile *is* a solution – even though those years of exile to Devil's Island, Elba and others did not prove to be worthwhile deterrent to others. Long after those brutal periods, we still have an upward crime rate in every country.

In any case, there are those of us who are convinced that, in all instances, elitists' *political influence* has been the *common* cause for perpetuation and escalation of crime - if not the worsening of *moral* justice in our social fabric. Ergo, we must be prepared to render the cause of crime ineffectual and unrewarding."

"I understand your point Madame and I thank you for it".

Moderator De l'Casse checked his watch and turned to the panel once more to seek out the advice of someone who had not yet voiced an opinion. He motioned to the middle-aged, dark complexioned woman, bundled up in sweaters to protect against the cool drafts of the cavern. She stood and read from her notes on the panel table.

"Thank you Mister De l'Casse." In a deep resonant voice with a distinct southern American states accent, she said,

"My name is Angelica Budd. Since my kids have all left home and my husband passed on, I have journeyed to all these forums since my first attendance at the 64th Symposium session held in my home city of Atlanta, Georgia. It keeps occurring to me that in order to make a governmental change for the better in this world, we had better understand what the worst qualities are in all of our existing systems of government."

Mrs. Budd took a deep breath and steadied the notes in her shaking hands before going on.

"First of all, is it safe to assume that those who seek politics as a means to perks, power and recognition are oblivious to the fact that politics is a fatal man made disease? Politics *is* highly infectious. Its symptoms are distrust, deceit, lying, cheating, and corruption. It is a disease which taints the civil service system to the very core. It weakens the stomachs of the politically elite so that they are fearful of any loss of their dominance. Thus, they ignore the real needs and preferences of people they're supposed to represent – common people like me. The very structure of governmental political machinery is an abomination. It is *designed* to foster the spread of its insidious, political virus upon the *next generation* of would-be politicians! It is high time we find *some other way* to keep their mental madness from eventually from killing us all off...as they *have* almost done, without a degree of conscience, in thousands of wars that *they* have started, mismanaged and fought with *others'* lives. Our political masters have done all that without getting their own feet wet in the blood of others. I'm tired of them – you should be too – and I urge all of us to begin the process for change to anything but the politics we have had to endure for thousands of years – and we must start right here – right now."

The Atlanta lady sat.

The silence in the cavern lasted all of ten seconds before the isolated cries of approval started. "Dead on, lady!" "Can't argue with that!" "Just too logical to dispute" "Let's do it" When that ended, the moderator spoke.

"The chair recognizes both speakers, from the floor at dais 26 and then dais 8" said Philippe De l'Casse, waving to one first, then the other.

"That Atlanta lady panelist was sure right on about *one* thing," The speaker at dais 26 was a young man of Middle East Asian descent. An aging gentleman stood at his side. The younger man adjusted his thick horn rimmed glasses.

"I have been living in the United States for the last eleven years and I can tell you that indicted murderers and crooked politicians, unscrupulous bureaucrats, including some police, remain *free* to practice their deceit in the whole of North America – free to steal, kill rape and swindle again. However, *if* you have the right friends, *or* the right lawyer, know the President, *or* have the right amount for bail or pay off money, no criminal has to pay the price – ever! Yet, *if* Joe *Average* over parks his car too long in a hospital zone, having just brought in his injured kid in for emergency service, he's nailed with a hefty, parking fine. The injustice of that is that an exorbitant fine *has* to be paid – or he loses use of his impounded car to his work place – and no reasonable excuse is accepted! There is no recourse. That was my injustice. It was against me.

In a court of law, the fact that I am Iranian didn't help my cause either.

So bring on your wise men or your anti illuminati or your Cybernation systems, because what we got in place right now *is not the answer*".

In his native language, the white haired man beside the young Iranian depended on a nearby Symposium translator to decipher and broadcast as he spoke, slowly and deliberately...

"In my eighty-four years, I have found that there have been too few persons of *absolute moral purity* and fewer still, of pure, *people-first,' wisdom*. For the most part, those that *are* our present day governors are incapable and ignorant of the real issues from which their people suffer. They are not only *not* concerned with countering dark minded infidels but in some cases, to be in league *with* them. Therefore, I have concluded that most of the dismissed injustices of mortal man are inflicted by our present day leaders."

"The chair recognizes the standing panel member at dais 8."

"While we are on the subject of people, lacking morale conscience,"

So spoke up a panelist, who earlier had spoken for the illuminati movement,

"I can testify to the need for focus on a serious global condition made worse by political cowards' disinterest in the worst kind of criminal behavior. I am referring to the matter of internationally spreading *child abuse*.

It too, is an increasing malady in every nation. Unbridled child prostitution is becoming epidemic. Some of the thousands of perpetrators are more often found to be older men of an elite social stratum, *sometimes*, even members of our rectories and courts of law! For years, charter operators in Britain, Japan, the U.S. and other *civilized* countries have been loading tour airplanes and boats bound for the Caribbean islands or the poorer countries of South America, and South East Asian countries, Thailand and others. They go there for a week of satisfying their lusts at the expense of degrading underage girls *and* boys. By the *thousands*, even children orphaned by loss of homes and parents, such as were those in that Indonesian tsunami tragedy less a hundred years ago or so, were targets of these animals, Enforcement of reprisals to eliminate this sick element from committing abhorrent acts like these cannot be left to machines. The sooner we return to God's values and common man government, the sooner we can dispose of these monsters."

* * *

At an open mike, the entire assembly heard the accent of a Scot... "Aye mon, – but *which* God?"

Now he elaborated.

"Mr. Chairman. I may be out of turn here sir, but after listening to an assortment of views on future direction for common world governance, I hasten to point out that of the explanations of any of the three of the options this assembly may choose, so far, we have yet to hear of *any solutions* to a multi-thousand year old problem.

This is one of *greatest* magnitude. We know from sad experience that everywhere in the world, contravention of law and morality has been functionally *unenforceable* and excruciatingly flawed in its legal constitutional makeup and its misapplication.

From the *beginning* of civilization, every judiciary system, in every nation on earth, has been *based* on pecuniary regional law protecting the interests of their cohorts, by fostering a traditional *religious* doctrine designed to keep us in line."

Listening to his Scottish brogue emphasizing his statements, the attentive audience keeps waiting for another shoe to fall.

Then it falls.

"Therefore, what may be compassionate grounds for releasing one offender in one country may well be seen as a blatant capital offense to another, depending on which nation is the one of birth or residence. The latitude of its application of penalty differs in extreme degrees, from region to region. In Arabian and some South East Asian cultures, justice has been traditionally or religiously rendered in the harshest means possible under their law. Loss of limbs to loss of life, even for loss of virginity – not even a minimal offense in most countries – is a crime against Allah in some Middle East and Asian cultures.

Alternatively, in western society's government service a *politically appointed judiciary*, dressed in democratic clothing, exacts light penalties to pedophiles, murderers, and perpetrators of animal cruelty, fraudulent embezzlement and criminal extortions. Lacking the will and law makers' support system, this evil element is sent out, often on probation, to offend over and over, again and again.

185

So whatever of the three world administrative choices we finalize here in the next two days, we must do so with the certainty that fair laws should always be in place for the protection and to the benefit of those who *do not offend!* At this point, I am certain that a cyber software program fed with proven circumstances in every case of non-religious and tribal custom in every region of the world, *might* just resolve some basis for clearly defined laws to ensure consistent jurisprudence across all borders.

As the young anthropology student suggested earlier, bringing a common order of law to justify decisive law enforcement could work by rendering similar degrees of penalties in keeping with jurisdictions everywhere. Concerned over their loss of personal revenue, this option would naturally preclude support of the world's legal fraternity, objecting vehemently, as they would, to this kind of binding law."

"And finally, my own thinking, as a law professor at the Edinburgh Academy of International Law, is this... Even *if* it is decided here at this 71st Symposium in Gibraltar that Cybernation has no place in common governance; Even if digital justice is deemed unconstitutional or too complex in actual practice; Despite being a universally acceptable solution in courts of law, I am one professional that wholeheartedly condones Cyber governance as the only alternative left to those of us who covet a sane and peaceful civilization.

Forgive me, but at this juncture, it seems apropos to revive a famous quote from Dickens 'Tale of Two Cities'... 'Tis a far, far better thing we do than what we have done before.' Cyber law *does* make it possible to bring closure that effects our next generation of criminals or victims. It can be a simple solution to the purging of the irresponsible and twisted mind."

De l'Casse interjected. "Your point has been effectively made, sir, though as you admit, out of turn – if not out of order. Now, may I request that the distinguished panel member from Beijing be heard? Mister Zhao Wei, please."

The Chinese gentleman rose to speak and removed a note from his jacket's breast pocket.

"Please accept apologies for having to express myself in my own language. I do not believe you would prefer such a struggle as trying to understand my attempt to speak in the English language. As westerners express it so well, (in English),"It is not pretty!'

Mr. Wei waited for the outgoing translation and the amused laughter that followed.

"During those earlier forums of the last 13 years, I was at that time a member of an inner circle of the government of China proper. I am unable to explain to this esteemed audience the formidable and immoveable power that it was – and *still* is. This Chinese government, responsible for the welfare of the world's greatest numbers of people, formulated harsh orders to maintain much needed self discipline – stern and cruel for their own people.

Many a government, as benevolent as it may claim to be, is *not receptive to any* alternative proposing to replace the existing power base. No matter what populace improvements it may bring, *any* hostile autocracy will reject replacing themselves by abdication. So the most important question is, what could possibly be the incentive to have that power base, *release their despotic* hold…to have them reconsider the future of their rule?

In China's case, convincing existing generals, marshals and inner circle policy commanders to yield their power base required manipulative confrontations. If increasing personal wealth and other individual monetary benefits came with 'retirement' from the ruling cabinets, so much the better. However, in this land where historic legacy passed from one dynasty to another, there could be another more attractive perk for existing administrators who might trade individual power for a new world order concept. Were present day legislators given the opportunity to achieve everlasting recognition for giving up so much for their people, which would be a family honor too treasured to refuse. China's legendary patriots are honored for eons in the future. In China's case that legacy to nationalism would be enhanced by the option of building additional Trade! That has been that nation's advantage since before the days of March Polo. Trade, Trade and more *Trade*."

Mr. Wei paused to let that sink in and then continued.

"Mr. Moderator, after all this time listening to one proposition after another, it is now apparent that *any and all* proposals would be faced with this one negative reaction attempting to convince many an existing reign to submit to one common global administration. Only the *threat* of diminishing *trade*, its very lifeblood –would signal mass objection from a nation of patriotic Chinese. As in all things, reward or consequence is the natural order of all activity of earth.

For the sake of argument, as the western expression goes, let's say that *only one* country out of five *agrees* to accept the rewards of an intensifying one world, free trade – no tariffs, no restrictions, and no sanctions on any commodity. Then, let us say that there are *two* of the three countries, that for other reasons of their own, *reject* – say, cyber national rule, if that were the choice of this symposium. So, these two countries opt to retain their traditional governing system. Since they know that now, military might is of little value in this one government mentality, would it not make sense to those *not* benefiting from free trade, that siding *with*, is more profitably advantageous than siding *against?* Would it not be safe to believe that isolationism is more likely to compel a governing power to yield to half a loaf of *personal* perks rather than forsake several loaves in a brisk economy? Or would the absence of amenities and a comparable *standard of living* as enjoyed by other neighboring countries be an incentive for hold out governments in a one order world administered countries, compel their populations to overwhelm their 'hold out' government leaders?

It is my sincere hope that by imparting these real scenarios to you – as confusing as I have made it, I might lead this gathering here today to see more clearly resolutions to join the world's most enduring governmental alternative. My apologies for exceeding my speaking time"

After receiving his translation, Moderator De l'Casse nodded to Mr. Wei and said...

"No matter which *improved* form of world governance is preferred by the majority at this symposium, Mr. Wei, we shall always be grateful for such thoughtful direction... Now, before we listen to further comments may I remind the assembly, that as we approach the lunch hour, we must remind you that that the afternoon session of this Symposium will begin *promptly at two PM* in this very cavern."

With this, the moderator again looked upward towards the panelists on stage.

"Meanwhile may I invite the Italian *panel* speaker this time, representing the Wise ones collection as a means of world Governance, to take the floor?"

"Signore De l'Casse... I must agree with comments made by the second last speaker. It *is* understandable and well known that *political* legislative bodies and judiciaries' decisions, rendered in the name of fairness and equality are often perceived very differently from hemisphere to hemisphere; tradition to tradition; economy to economy; and in both corporate and public entities. All can be very different in the way they are formed to be functional. For example, people in the tropics have lesser need for hydro and fossil fuel power to keep climatically comfortable than do inhabitants of the North. Hence, there is minimal need for trade and barter in energy requirements. Similarly, legislation governing the conduct of sea fisheries are of little consequence to rural prairie or desert people. *Their* main concerns are *weather and water related,* with irrigation being their priority for the supply and their demand of that utility. It just seems to many of us, distrustful of both the evangelical and the Cyber system of rule, that *only* a concert of wise and respected persons *from those regions;* from those walks of life; can be sufficiently flexible to render effective, ethical and informed rules of law, very pertinent wisdom imposed world administration system."

The moderator nodded to the panelist and said.

"May we hear from one last speaker before our break for lunch? Dais 12 please?"

"My name is Dianna Louise Finlayson. When I was a very small girl being raised in England, my father was apolitical but as a working person with a feeling of responsibility for his fellow man, he did belong to a political advocacy movement called *Technocracy.* In those cays, it couldn't be labeled as following a left *or* right doctrine. It called for a government in which all economic resources – and hence an entire social system would be the responsibility of technical scientists and engineers. To my father and many millions of technocrats, very few of whom were even remotely connected to educated science or engineering people, it all sounded Utopian *but* feasible and right for the times.

I know that this movement is not on the list of governmental alternatives being proposed here today. Still, for purposes of comparison I wish to explain the mandate of Technocracy Inc. It was established in 1933 as a non-political, non-profit volunteer membership organization to politically educate and inform – strangely enough, it was conspired – would you believe – for a *new world order* ahead. I will also be forever dumbstruck that the constitution of Technocracy has many of the same *philosophic policies* of the last few centuries' political parties, autocracies, presidents, tyrants and self-appointed chancellorships. Still, old and outdated as it is, Technocracy deserves to be evaluated -----

Then she was interrupted!

A trim six foot (2 meter tall) a middle-aged man with a salt and pepper crew cut, bellowed into the microphone.

"Mister De l'Casse, "he shouted.

"My name is – No matter. Who cares? And where I'm from is of no consequence either! The truth of the matter is I am declaring myself as the Symposium's *grinch*. Moreover, what I am about to share with you may well *spoil this party*. . .

After what I've heard this morning, I 'm beginning to think, I must be one of the few *sane* people on this pile of rock.

Mr. Moderator, all your speakers have all left me dizzy with their freethinking. I've gone from bandy assed boredom to pure skepticism. When I'm not astonished at some folks blathering impractical and abstract concepts, I am embarrassed by another bunch of dreamers espousing a Peter Pan like, pie in the sky, diatribe to a world wide audience. We just can't break past this droning sound barrier. If I had to listen to one more philosophical academic, spouting flowery phrases, and impossible schemes just to forever rid ourselves of the stuff we don't like on this big ball of dirt, I'd put in a call to the nearest mental institution, to reserve space for everybody in here!"

The 'grinch' shook his finger at varying speakers in the audience.

"This is turning out to be a bitch 'n fantasize session complete with Cybermares added. We should *all* be pissed off with these repetitious complaints and kooky, imaginary doctrines! Is this what we traveled all this distance for – to listen to sad sacks and losers whining about the state of our union here on earth – and how we should fix it? What are you all *smoking* these days??

One more thing. Are we actually supposed to accept this wild and woolly theory that Micro-robotic Cyborgs are the latest versions in governments? Let's get real!

Folks – do *not* swallow all this new governance stuff! It is a diet of wishful thinking – about as nourishing as bag of popcorn and twice as noisy!

Faith, you say!? Faith in what? Religion? Hah! What's your flavor? Orange or Green? Muslim or Infidel? Sun Gods? Black Magic? Witch doctors? Mayan sacrificial rites? Whatever turns your crank is acceptable – but remember, fanatics usually speak only for *themselves*, don't they?

Ok then. As the salesman once said, 'How about this model'? *Faith in ourselves*, they call it. What has that done for us masses lately? Ask those poor sods who 'gave' away their earthly possessions and followed their faith in religious icons, on the road to Auschwitz Camps in Poland, the Dravidian Compound in Waco Texas and Jimmy's Cool Aid Café in Jonestown in Venezuela – plus many more recent others?

Hey. Tell me! What is all this crap about *wise guys* who will keep us from being eaten by the bad guys? Ah – like *who*, you say? Are the Genghis Khan, Mau Tse Tung and Bin Laden families still hanging out together after all these years? As for the idea of wise guys, hired to make a supposedly, more orderly world work for us... forget it! This old globe isn't whirling around the same way like it did, when wise old Solomon lived here. First of all. There's a few billion more of us here now. *And* we're surrounded by a hell of a lot more technical complications than when old Sol was giving out advice to the peacenik crowds. Frankly, I really don't care *what* you've all *heard*, here, but the bottom line is – god-like Solomons and their understudies just don't exist any more! What there *are*, have changed too – to fit the mold we *all* have – stupid and unhappy with our lot!"

Now the self professed grinch turned away from an open mouthed audience to end his harangue.

"So, folks. Having heard the promises of a *new* reform for a *new* dawn, where do you or I apply for *new* strength to go on living for some semblance of humanity in centuries ahead? Don't ask *me*! Unlike these other cats here, I'm all out of wishful thinking... Anyway, why change for a devil we *don't* know?

Don't despair. Face it. It's not all about *how* we live now. *How* we'll live *later* is really a matter for which most of us can't *do* any thing about, even if we wanted to. N'est pas? Hey look. All this had to be said and I regret having to be the one to say it. ..But, what the hell – good day to you anyway!"

With that, the grey headed athlete turned and quickly walked out into a cavern passageway.

Still recovering from the latest discourse, De l'Casse announced,

"After lunch, at exactly two o'clock we shall reconvene. In the light of what you have just heard, I have to believe that the *real* emotional comments are yet to come in the afternoon's *reawakening* sessions. Enjoy your lunch."

* * *

Coming back to the cavern after lunch, Luton's leading foundry owner Barney Twilliger was seen talking to the local constabulary. He was gesturing to the sidewalk balcony overhanging the water, where only a couple of hours previously the politician MP Bryce Scott-Sang had been pulled out of the Mediterranean. He had had a heavy iron bar rock tied around his ankles. A crowd gathered as two other policemen came out of the cave with five handcuffed young men in black sateen jackets. From pieces of the ensuing conversation, Twillinger repeated his testimony that he had seen the five young men from Columbia encircling a cowering and very frightened Scott-Sang when most of the crowd had gone to their seats after the morning break. No one knew then that the Cartel had very quickly solved their public relations problem.

Back at the cave, at 2 PM precisely, Philippe De l'Casse announced that we would continue to hear from the English woman who grew up under Technocracy.

She walked back to the microphone from her seat. She began her second attempt at her address by thanking De l'Casse for recalling her to finish her speech.

"It seems, and always has, that the real bounty of the earth is in the hands of elite *capitalists and social democrats*. Like all other forms of government imposing its rule on humanity over the last ten or twenty thousand years, they all have one common failing. It's that to survive in today's expanding world, every form of government today still requires *management*, administered by human beings under countless regional flags. Ignoring their justification of false patriotism, it is clear that they were in it principally for their own good.

Their senior bureaucrats were usually a collection of non-professional amateurs, ordering around a government ministry, for which they were never trained, for purposes they never understood. We all knew them and their underlings. They stood behind wickets and desks at every licensing office in the governmental administration. They inspected every structure we ever built. They were the meter maids and patrol cops who decided who gets a ticket for parking a bicycle next to a fire hydrant – and who does not. They were the four or five year elected wonders in their parliamentary suits who pretended to represent us when they were really paying homage to a party line, while partaking of over generous salaries, perks and pensions they had often set for themselves. Even today, *they* don't think that we law abiding citizens recognized them for what they were – but we did and still do – for reasons they wish we didn't. While on the job, in expectation of retirement pensions well above those who worked more than 4 years for a living, government representatives and 'servants' as they call themselves, were deliberately avoiding people's concerns. They demonstrated little, if any compassion for individual cases and virtually *no* interest in justifiable exceptions to the rules. The greater public good was just a quaint response to avoid dealing with people's specific issues.

As Dr Harari has often said right here, these people make decisions *that* do not, have not, and never will *represent* the greater number of average citizenry of earth.

We really need a system where the whole world is marching to the same drummer —led by neither commissars, nor capitalists. It is eerily odd, but if what *I* am *interpreting* from what I am *hearing* here in Gibraltar, it is that the technocrats' philosophy, for almost 400 years, has some astonishingly similar convictions much like what Dr. Harari has proposed. Both call for the role of a digitally *technical professional form of world governance* for all mankind".

As the woman turned from her microphone back to her seat, De l'Casse nodded his head toward her, in respect for her contribution.

"Thank you Mademoiselle. This promises to be an afternoon of constructive reaction to the naysayers in our presence. I am confident that from all positions on the floors of these caverns and verandas, we will be reaffirmed of the necessity to reform world governance. I'm told by our staffs who count bodies around here that our on-location attendance has increased by half again, for the afternoon sessions. If fresh registrants are *that* interested, they too *must* believe in our determination – our

serious intent to commit to a diligent global administration. May we now hear from two more panel members regarding any of the three presentations we have before us?"

* * *

By the conclusion of Day 1, the moderator ended that day's conference with these words.

"Concerned for the welfare of their descendants in a future world, the Symposium's voices of reason have been heard, rebutted, repeated and revaluated. In that regard, we trust that *serious points* of view expressed here today – and that will be reinforced again first thing tomorrow morning, are valued by those millions of earth's peoples who have attended this and previous Symposiums.

To world media, we thank you for spreading the objectives of a new world organization. Please know, as well, that humankind is aware of, is better off for and very grateful for your commitments to factual reporting. Sincerest thanks. Be assured that we are aware of the media's dedication and contributions to the welfare of all populated regions on earth."

De l'Casse spread his hands to imply all in attendance.

"On behalf of all peoples in all regions between the earth's poles, my sincere thanks for your patience all attending *today's* Symposium. Tomorrow, Sunday sessions will commence at eight AM. Good night."

* * *

One and one half days and 64 points of view later...

At the conclusion of hearings, Philippe De l'Casse addressed a final word to the now lesser audience in St. Michael's Cavern. Many had already left for the polling stations.

"It was appropriate that the very neutrality of Gibraltar, perpetual gateway to and from man's birthplace in Europe, Africa, and Asia, turned out to be such an ideal location for such a momentous occasion. The freedom of expression has been a wondrous exercise for men and women, unshackled from fear of expression. Our concepts of destinies for humanity are more than just symbolic. Such an honorable task fills our forum participants with the pride of knowing their contribution has more meaning than any and all efforts before now. That is because we appreciate even more than most of the world what it takes and what it means.

So now, where do we go from here?"

The moderator paused to choose his words carefully.

"We're now ready to make a choice for our hope in a new order of globular governance for all people. As in the previous 70 Symposiums, the abiding condition is that only *one* ballot – in this case, *one* colored oval stone, may be cast *per registered delegate.* Two of those earlier Symposiums declared that the preferred choice of governance must be made up of no less than 51% of the total ballots cast. Committees will be struck to carry out the will of 38 years and 31 days of study, research and dialogue to an inevitable conclusion. However, taking care not to rush any part of the greater population of the world into a lawful reform, by which it could not abide, no imposed deadlines for delivery and installation of that system have ever been mandated. Whatever time is takes to achieve the stated preference of people of the world is the time allotted.

Now go to the voting stations and do the one thing you know is right for the earthly existence of your children, theirs and their children's children. To them, we will not be forgotten. May the names of every registered delegate attending this and previous Symposiums, be eternally blessed for the thoughtful consideration and concern of our descendents' welfare."

* * *

At the ballot depots, the process was secure and simple. In exchange for their Symposium registry card, every person who had attended this World Conference would be issued a choice of one of four, oval shaped, *colored crystal stones*. In the course of twelve voting hours, one large all steel box with it's recessed steel chute box, stood in the centre of the bare voting room. The box would receive all stones regardless of color. Frosted glass side panels would make any outside visual count virtually impossible.

Seventy still sealed boxes from previous Symposium sessions were brought in to this final World meeting. They had been shipped in under tight security from vaults of the Zurich International Banque. All stones would now be counted.

Red granite stones would represent an *illuminati/religion governance*, RED.

Emerald green soapstone would signify a *Cyber governance*, GREEN.

Yellow silica stones indicate support of *Wise Persons* governance, YELLOW.

A totally clear stone would be a choice for the status quo – a no change governance.

On a Sunday evening, the sixteenth of February, at 21:17 hours (Greenwich Mean Time), in the year 2288AD, formal counting of all 71 boxes of stones *was conducted and certified* under the direct supervision of senior directors of the World Court of The Hague, as follows:

5325 were clear stones

63474 were red stones.

271,222 were yellow stones.

2,315,277 were Green stones

All 2,655,298 eligible stone ballots were cast. (except that of Bryce Scott-Sang- deceased)

Over the thirty-five year period of conducted Global Symposiums, total attendees exceeded twenty-nine million, seven hundred and sixteen, allowing for duplicated registrants. When tallied, organizers were quoted as being 'certain that the regional preferences for each of the three plans were proportionately similar per occasion as those totals of registered votes for all seventy one Symposiums.'

"My name is Philippe Del'Casse, I have been appointed by World Administrative Council at The Hague to be your Chairman and Chief Legal Counsel at these Symposiums. The purpose is to receive representative population input for the future governance of the human race and creation of a New World Order on Earth. I have the pleasure to be your dedicated servant, in conducting this voicing of global population convictions for world governance in future. May you have a safe journey home satisfied that your participation will make a difference for all following generations? Bon Chance!

Chapter 2

Ousting Existing World States;
Cyber Governance Begins

2288, 2324/23RD/24TH CENTURIES / SUDAN, JAPAN,

BY THE START of the 24th century, almost 100 years had elapsed since Gibraltar's 71st and final Symposium for reformed new governance. Those forums had concluded with the decision to move towards *one Cybernetics-run, global government* to assimilate every member-country's population into one planetary government. Fifty to eighty years and a generational change of attitude were expected to attract all previous countries to abide.

In that time period, other events were occurring. Worldwide pressures were assailing the long standing, international monetary gold standard. Speculation was that the U.S. dollar was gradually losing its measurement position against the expanding trading strength of Asia's never ending population increases and their resulting gross national production. Adding to these gargantuan changes was the difficulty of implementing a singular global system of governance. Then, in 2360AD, earthly matters were dealt a tragic blow, when in its orbit around the Sun, the earth went through a poisonous galactic gas affecting the voice boxes of all animals on earth. It also cast doubt on the potency of hundreds of thousands of human males on the planet. In simple but deadly terms, the impact of all this was one of non-endurance, bringing even more hundreds of thousands of very exasperated victims to the portals of suicide.

In the matter of movement towards a one-world governance; less than half a century was spent on the complexities and 'infighting' of ridding the world of the hangers-on to the patchwork quilt of status quo, regional governments. Under the auspices and interim governance of The Hague's International Cyber Authority, still another 30 years was used to program and install the system. Integrating the combination of people and systems to operate the technical aspects of such a massively detailed Cyber system was tediously demanding. To construct and interconnect four great mainframe components deep in the earth's crust was equally challenging and time consuming. At that point, consistent, equitable and decisive regulation of international and local regional law for all humankind was a fait d'complet.

*   *   *

Up until then, there were some regionalized militant, and often bloody, squabbles to be overcome. The period of 'persuading' the exit of man-run administrations in some countries was still an ongoing process of conversion in many countries. Cyber governance leaders, along with each county's citizens had extreme '*difficulties*' trying to rid themselves of traditional political insiders, tyrants and despots of all shapes and sizes. Admittedly, not all *transferences* turned out as bloodless.

This was especially the case in the Upper Nile, Central Equatorial regions and neighboring Bahr el Ghazal regions in the early 2320s of the 24th century. In the most recent revolutionary cause, insurgents were threatening to bring down a Cybernation-resisting dictatorship. The entrenched military-Islamic parliament at the old city of Khartoum North, was not about to surrender its power of this second largest in area of all African states.

Since before the 20th century, continuing conflict in this region of the continent was seen to be a shortfall in the theory of rationalization. It was becoming an even increasingly agitated SPLM, (Sudan People's Liberation Movement.) against a five centuries old, unjust, uncaring legislative elitism.

From time to time, staccato laser fire from almost *lethargic,* local flare-ups, made it seem almost as though Sudan's 'common' people were staging scattered, noisy shows of discontent due to a corrupt Khartoum parliamentary farce. Every day in most areas – southern anyway – there were isolated acts of rebellion against cruel rule and illicit taxation. Above all else, it was the eternal Sudanese government's indolence and indifference to pitiable rural conditions, still unchanged from the times of the fourteenth millennium. Yet, whenever rebels *did* rebel against government-imposed injustices, it was *always* with *barbaric* consequences for those taking up arms.

For decades past, the uneducated populations of certain provinces, particularly those in the Sudan's lower provinces, were of the mind that the state of deprivation and poverty was a global standard. How could they *know* any better? But, they reasoned, militant confrontation, as scattered and ineffective as it had been, was the only course left by which to demonstrate frustration and antagonism against a never ending corrupt government.

Then, over a plodding period of time, just after Africa's great inland flood in the late spring of 2321, that rural unrest became accentuated. Every day they faced situations that exemplified that the comparably more 'affluent' people living in Sudan's *upper* provinces were enjoying increasingly better standards of living than was prevalent in the southern regions. Khartoum was beneficiary of excessive revenues from increasing tourist excursions to Sudan. In the eyes of southerners, such receipts generated by Southern regional 'national park' attractions, required long maintenance hours by local Southerners toiling for pittances.

* * *

Originally, Untela Zambagali was Ugandan. For over 27 years, she had been married to a Sudanese farmer and part time SPLM rebel in the small village town of Pibor, situated on a tributary river leading to the White Nile. They maintained a poor farm carved out of the jungle, raising groundnuts (peanuts) and sorghum. Unlike many in the region, it provided them with at least daily fare in their bellies and some hope for a future. Prior to marrying a Sudanese man, Untela had taken part of a post secondary education in her home country of Uganda.

The indoctrination of living with an honest hard working Sudanese husband – dissatisfied and infuriated as he was, added to her own inborn fiery and rebellious character. He had made a willing activist out of her.

Now, thirty one years later, her husband, now long since dead, her grown-up children scattered to the winds of African change, she finds herself at a street barricade outside the presidential palace in Khartoum. She has a brand new, Chinese made Autofau, ray-repeating weapon crooked over her arm.

Up ahead are experienced fellow 'liberators'. They were rebel 'commando' units, wiping up the remnants of last resistance of an oppressive governmental army, *inside* the Khartoum palace walls. When that was completed, she would zigzag for the palace gate, along with a thousands of other 'southern' vigilantes, all in the non-descript, tattered garments of farm people; they with the gnarled hands and swollen stomachs.

Crouched behind the barricade, Untela felt a nudge at her arm. Two Sudanese women, one older, the other not yet 13 years old, had come up unnoticed, behind the overturned and burned out taxis. The older woman pointed her finger to her open mouth and extended her other hand cupped outwards. They were either nearby residents or part of the throngs of street people. Neither female carried arms. But then, other than machetes, nor did many of Untela's rebel friends. It was obvious that the two, probably mother and daughter, were less concerned for any sudden end to their lives from random fire than for the pain of hunger.

A mother herself, the woman Zambagali recognized those bulging eyes of despair and desperation. She felt around in her coat pocket for her own rations. She pulled out a handful of dry corn and reached out. The younger girl, half bent forward to receive the gift of corn kernels as did the older woman. They each had Untela's corn spilled into their hands. In their excited relief at having their first food in many days, they stood up and turned to leave. The snipers bullets were one right after the other. Their souls had left their bodies before they crumpled to the hard road stone. With unseeing glassy eyes still open, they lay bodies contorted where they fell, dry corn dribbling out from between their outstretched fingers into the cracks of pavement. Untela wept.

Now, a whistling horn – like the ones used on ocean ships – sounds from inside the palace walls. Streams of rebel men and women spill out from barricades that had sheltered them, all running for the wall's arched entrances. They attracted only snipers' light fire. Untela cautiously slides herself behind an overturned palace bus just inside the gate. Federally uniformed bodies lie in grotesque shapes around her. On the full length balconies of the three-storied building in front of her, she witnesses figures without uniforms – her people – pushing open outer doors; firing their lasers into whatever or whoever might be in that space, before going to the next door.

Soon, there was no more battle to be done in the courtyards. It had been done while the main rebel force waited at the barricades. Now there was bloody evidence of that earlier battle. All over the palace yard laser-burned and torn bodies lay in twisted shapes like run over duffle bags.

After an hour of helping to tend to her own rag tag "army" wounded, Untela joins other SPLM fighters emerging out of one of the palace offices, handing out hastily printed leaflets to their fellow rebels. She reads the tersely worded statement before handing it on to her compatriots.

"The President of Sudan is dead. His inner cabinet members are also dead. They can hurt us no more. Now we must meet our obligations to ourselves. Within hours, we are meeting with members of Earth's International Cyber Authority to request that they take over the job of governing all Sudanese people. Apart from medical care, expect no immediate relief from them for the next while, regarding internal or personal problems. They will take command of organization of cyber governance first. Our own care will come after that."

On the reverse side of the document was printed...

"We were as brave as we had to be. Now we must be braver. We must go about solving our individual problems ourselves. As true brothers and sisters, let us thank each other for this victory and for survival of all Sudan's children. May the heavens bless you and those for whom you fought. Your SPLM leaders."

Untela Zambagali left her Autofau ray-rifle leaning up against the Palace wall as she started the long barefoot walk, back to Pibor.

*   *   *

Twenty five years after the Sudan regional uprisings, a Japanese parliamentary secretary walked into the Tokyo office of Yasuo Matsui, Prime Minister of the Empire of Japan.

Although by now the effects of the dusty gas, which had long since impeded humanity's capability to converse orally, changed with the innovation of the Image TransPinder. This remarkable implantation brought a single communications culture to all the world's inhabitants. No further need for characters and sounds of a regional language interfered with the pictured image- thought, projected processes. This in turn initiated the art of creating and comprehending the art of imaging. Starting at the child level, educational outlets right up to vocational schools and universities provided the elements of transferring and receiving through the mind's-eye messaging. Just as the rest of the world learned to think differently, schooling and persistency would prevail in a surprising short period of application in Japan.

This day, years later, the Premier had convened his inner cabinet members in his conference room for one primary matter of state. They were in one of their many conversations of the prospect of acquiescence of powers to the Cyber International Authority. Today, they were gathered to hear the complete and summary presentation of the Authority's request for a takeover date of governance of the land of the rising sun.

His secretary placed an electronic document before the honorable Yasuo Matsui. He stood to express his opening statement to his colleagues. He adjusted his TransPinder, as did many of his colleagues for the address to come.

"My countrymen," he imaged,

"Before me is a formal presentation; a formal request by the secretary-general of the Cyber International Authority, for an agreed time and agenda for takeover of our governing responsibilities, much as we have been discussing for the last eight years. Notwithstanding our government's leadership role within the merger of economic affairs between China and Japan, we here have all endorsed the basis of the agreement and the reasons for it. China is facing its future role with due diligence for the industrial preservation of a massive population in a far-flung nation."

Pausing long enough to relieve his busy mind of the tedium of transmitting his address, he took some water and continued.

"To resume, we elected members of our people and their political parties agree to leave our out-dated political system behind. As compensation, all cabinet personnel with high administrative responsibilities, are to receive a specified sum of individual payment for governing services rendered to date. We acknowledge that these payments amount to sums, which; One. None of us could ever attain in any other way, and Two. Every one of us and immediate family members will be relieved of financial obligations for the rest of our lives and those of six generations thereafter."

The prime minister smiled. He bowed his head to cabinet.

"Understandably, a universal cybernetics governance system, soon to rule all peoples in all regions of the world, with true applications of computed laws and solutions – our roles as legislators will have become redundant. Still, a huge army of government support staff will remain to administer the will of the Cyber Selection Committee.

Let us respond now to the Secretary General's message to the rest of the world, that after millenniums of Empire of Japan civilizations, we are ready for a just society under a secure cybernation administration. If we hesitate at all in our acquiescence to move forward with the rest of the world at this time, it is because of our concern for the honor of our commitments in an economic alliance with China.

Matsui's Foreign Affairs minister, Iku Asamura stood bowing in the direction of the PM.

He addressed the ministers of 27 key portfolios.

"Honorable Prime Minister. I believe I speak now for every member of your government. We too, welcome what is intended here, not only for Japanese people's equity in their own beloved homelands, but also for the rest of the world population. However, esteemed sir, we must be assured of the preservation of Japanese tradition of non-rule through the continued exaltation of our beloved emperor, master of our rising sun. To others, this must not be perceived as a religious matter. It is instead, a living symbol of our heritage. It must continue to be respected".

He paused. The foreign minister looked upward as though searching for the thoughts that would convey his next comment.

"Prime Minister, of yet another concern, regarding any cybernetics proposal, we must be assured as much as possible, that this cyber governance system is beyond reproach. To discover later that it shows any malfunction – such as we have come to expect from human governance, we're are much farther back than from where we started. I need not remind this revered cabinet, of the turbulent history of our island homes. Quakes, typhoons, violent militancy, volcanoes, conquering hordes, nuclear disasters… Japan's very existence has been challenged many, many times. Therefore, your eminence, we trust we will be privy to Cybernetic Governance with yet unrevealed architectural detail, proof of perpetuity, and intended everlasting provisions, by and from a complexity of centralized main-frame computers?"

"You will be so apprised," nodded Prime Minister Matsui.

"The security and integrity of rule by cybernation, Minister Asamura, has been trepidation for all of us, just as is your particular apprehension for the continued establishment of positions of their exalted royal highnesses.

Still, with what we know now, I am convinced, as will be you and every person on this earth, of the impregnability of such a structure. This is also true of the methodology for programming perpetual technical competence under any circumstance."

Prime Minister Matsui slowly turned his chair, from the foreign minister beside him, back to his cabinet.

"So, to this end, gentlemen, may I ask that you give your undivided attention to an electronic image simulation of the narration accompanying a visual holograph presentation. As you would assume, there are diagrammatical statistics and information given herewith of work achieved to date and that to come, already in progress."

The cabinet conference room lighting is dimmed and the holograph begins in an flickering light of the dome. Structured for just this kind of showing with the image self correcting in the centre of the low conference table. Over top of 'background sounds' the visual holographic host appears and begins the imaging of his narration.

"Honored Ministers of the Japanese Governmental Inner Council... At this very moment, assembly and installation of World Cybernation systems is underway. As you know, it is by cybernation that we join the rest of earth's countries and regions to achieve a revolutionary change to one system of governance. For almost one hundred years, we have been seeking answers. Now, we are in the final stages of assembling a technical "central governor" to provide all the world's inhabitants with a utopian-fair government, such as never before believed possible.

Under the charter given down by the Symposium's regents, the Cyber's "Selectronics Committee" is within its authority and capability to rule on all integral issues involving man.

Gentlemen and Gentle women. In simple image graphics, please know that the Cyber system can be counted on for timeless and inexorably just management for our world and everyone in it – eternally.

Complex in detail, but simple in concept, a comprehensive mainframe computer is or will be filled with every known factor of the genealogy of every living person, every region and every creature on earth.

In meticulous detail, the Selectronic Committee will maintain data banks on every known public and personal issue and result, which has ever occurred in the known history of man. To these will be added updated pictorial encyclopedia data updating newly discovered and newly proven data, since the inception of Cyber World governance systems. In some cases, even details of ancient barbarian cultures will be depicted if ever needed. Storage and automatic filing is provisional, made for the future inclusion of every person and known creature, every varying circumstance affecting common rule for every man, woman and child in every region on earth. All common and corporate laws will emanate from this Cybernetics decision maker – no matter how complex, no matter how inconsequential or earth shaking the issue may be.

For example, the icepack breakup, seen here, represents an ongoing issue and becomes a little known capability of Cyber Selectronic Committee, world citizenry guardianship. In the matter of global warming, one of world scientists' greatest concerns, the matter is to be classified as priority to be imminently dealt with. It will do what man would not do! The committee will enable a prevailing economic benefit for all mankind's endeavors. This will be balanced with a policy of enforcing strict effluence laws for industry to preserve the pure air and water environments

Every judiciary law for every regional jurisdiction it will ever face will be encrypted and part of the cyber structure. No one will ever be able to alter data for their own personal devices for as long as this planet exists. In that regard, here is a graphic concept of the housing of this digital miracle."

At this point in the presentation, the in-motion holograph depicts an upside down, Swiss chalet style roof. In the shape of a V, its reversely pointed gable 'roofline,' is out-sizably thick. According to mental image narration over the action of construction personal, the downward point is to enable any magma flow moving upward from below the structure's deep-earth position to be deflected. This helps to preserve the integrity of the impervious-to-heat structure. Judging from the relative size of people at work on the Cyber edifice, the entire structure is more the size of an Egyptian Pyramid.

While holographs zero in to on-site locations and surrounding terrain, image narration goes on.

"'To ensure that this manner of governance is without end, there will be four such Cyber Centers built and interred deep inside our planet!

Right this minute, such a network of mainframe processors is being assembled for installation in four different locations on the planet. They are being constructed in such a way that, once in position, they will be forever sealed with absolutely no access by anyone at anytime thereafter. So invulnerable and resistant are they to nature's most violent incursions, excluding planetary explosion, nuclear explosions of any magnitude would fail to alter the operation of these structures. Cyber monoliths are encased in a poured molten, composite steel encasement, that even an earthquake of 14 Richter points could not disable or disrupt cyber function – by transmission to and from any such installation. If the earth falls in on any of them to a depth of 32 kilometers (20 miles) below the surface of the earth's crust, they will still continue to operate, dependent of course on an absence of extended molten lava temperatures and equivalent densities. Geophysicists today are convinced that at 12 or more Richter points, there would be little human need left for any kind of governing body, let alone sufficient remnants of populations to respond to Cybernetics proclamations."

Against a background of moving graphic design of protons and neutrons, image narration informs its TransPinder equipped audiences.

"While on the subject of interferences by man or nature, we should advise you that three of the four carefully selected locations are not within 20,000 kilometers of any Tectonic fault or ridge, subduction zone, plate, or volcanic hot spots. The one exception, a deliberate placement at the geological point of Atlantic and Mediterranean tidewater system, will be near a relatively inactive fault because a unit has to be there for proximity reasons. However, the system can and would run efficiently with just two emplacements where some unearthly disruptions occur to any two stations.

As long as a sun centers our galaxy, resident nuclear power will be their independent and eternal source of strength in all four units. Also built into adjacent quarters will be simple, non-maintenance, air-conditioning systems for the edification of a staff of technologists on or about any site and preservation of mainframe components thereto. Right now, as you can see from our visual footage that secluded highways to sites are being constructed;

power stations, crew housing, medium airfield and heliport facilities are being built; all in readiness for installing mega projects like no other before them.

What you see now are actual on-site holographs of current action on these stations. They depict depots where technical staffs both feed new data in and translate the decisions of the Selection Committee out, relayed to a central communication center at The Hague. These holography images of waving cyber depot staffs show only the limited number of earthlings needed to operate and to be 'in touch' with main frames that will run the lives of millions of earth's humans."

Graphics in motion pictures show the mountains and tunnels of the four locations of underground mainframes.

Narration image transmissions continue over top of the site graphics.

"It should be noted that technical input can only be performed with the acceptance of the Cyber system itself, which has been set to receive and respond to updating, new technical input and changing circumstances of the times. For example, were a world wide virus to threaten man's very existence, given all factors, the Selectronics Committee would provide special dispensation to prepare for any indicated eventuality. Please understand that the Cyber main frame will not respond, nor react in any way to any outside non-contingency order on any matter.

In other words, there is no concern for what a potential hacker with exceptional, insightful knowledge of Cybermatics within our cyber giants. An attempt to access for the purpose of redirecting any pre-set data process is just not possible. Human decision making emanating from anywhere but the main terminal is also impossible. It can truly be said that as of this century, intercontinental law and ensuing justice on this planet will be entrenched and known by citizens in all four corners of the Earth."

The holographs continue to move images in sequence with the narrative 'dialogue'...switching then to a flattened, oval depiction of a slowly revolving earth. Wherever the locations are discussed, the motion image stops to graphically zero in on the locale of "Selection Committee Unit Installations.'"

The image transmission 'describes' where those locations will be...

1. Former quarters of Colorado Springs NORAD base under a mountain in the Cheyenne range in the U.S.

2. Entrance through Glen Rock Cavern on Gibraltar Rock on the most western mouth of the Mediterranean Sea leading north to deep relay installations under southern Spain.

3. Western Mongolia, built under a 1220 meter (4000 ft) peak near the city of Uliastay Jauhiant in the Hangay Nauru range, Dzayhan province.

4. 100 km (62 miles) from the Australian capital, Canberra. Built underneath 2229 meter (7310 ft) Mount Kosciusko, Snowy Mountain Range (Alps) in New South Wales.

The holograph ends with the host narrator bowing and thanking the distinguished audience. The Japanese caucus meeting concludes shortly thereafter with a meditative Shinto prayer...(Live eternally, Samurai spirit.)

* * *

Circa 1938, Winston Churchill, England's Lord of the Admiralty at the time, referring to one war-mongering dictator, suggested to close friends, 'Assassination if necessary, but necessarily!'

So by what other means can a countries' resisting leaders, determined to hold on to power, be compelled to abdicate? By persuasion? Bribery? Threats?

One British ex-MI6 agent assigned to the diplomatic corps was advising some of those countries now preparing for Cyber governance when the four buried computers come on line, said it best.

"For any non-revolutionary transition in governance in any country, it is usually an exercise in extreme patience. Governmental overlords do not take kindly to those who call for abdication. They are the kinds of 'leaders' who *laud* the cause for the *greater* good but who steadfastly rail against any claim on their chosen command, *especially* for the obvious *good* of their constituents.

So there are only two fall back positions to be taken when programming for a change of government. Number One is to take *whatever* time is needed to program and institute a change. It may take fifty years or more and any number of elections or declarations of government dictatorships, judicial appointments, retirements, and resignations for *whatever* reason – these are ripe take-over opportunities. And they come along frequently. Rare occurrences of impeachment and rebellious take-overs are *not* opportune times. To the country's electorate, the promise of improvement is all too often a very negative time to try to win favor for any long lasting replacement. Number Two is when the incumbent government's massive public support groups and the private financiers – those big-spending, self-benefiting band of hangers-on who bought and got the leaders into power in the first place, are pissed off with each other. Those are the only occasions that can be used to implement new leadership to use these occasions to 'campaign' for legitimate turnover of almost any government. Right this minute, I believe that deep-rooted powers in USA, Russia, China, India, including Arab caliphs and a buddy system of colonial autocrats as well will be extraordinarily hard to move. In some smaller countries like Iran, Cambodia, Honduras and Indonesian, governments are considered by many to be as 'dug in as an anchor in a rock pile'. It is sorry testimony to man's intellect that it may take half of the world's gold reserves to move the world to Cyber Governance."

The agent's countenance changes from positive to cynical as he explains further.

"To leaders facing ousting by their own subjects there is always the realization that a bagful of rupees, rubles or doubloons is better than a stressful revolution. They could take refuge in the old adage that 'half a loaf or less' is preferable to a forced early retirement. Ultimately, however, it will have to be the weight of a populace. It always is. How do subject citizens perceive an opportunity to move an out-of-favor leader to the sidelines? As the crowd of serfs once chanted in front of the Bastille's carnival of guillotines… "Our will, will be."

* * *

212

Now, in this 24th century, younger generations in almost every society have finally learned from the young followers of 'martyrdoms' of earlier centuries. To them, violence and wars are out! From the harsh lessons of previous generations, they are aware of the risk of destruction to themselves and fellow humans in armed regalia. Nowadays, young people are likely to renege on the 'extermination' of an entire people for the sake of their mentor's franchises.

Without the usual show of facetious leadership by parading majordomos wrapped up in the flag and oratory of promoted patriotism, the new young take exception to the risk of militant exhibition. These fresh-minded, new bloods have developed their own diabolical plan for non-violent alternatives of 'persuasion'. They can – they would and they will, 'manipulate' concession from unyielding groups of governors and chancellors who refuse to step down from a political power pedestal.

Recent history records that products of this day and age, are adept at selectively excommunicating anyone from office – and even from the face of this earth. Over the centuries, many hundreds of strong, well-protected individuals have been 'expunged' from power in ways different than by the ballot box or an assassin's bullet. Their 'targets' simply disappear or mysteriously, disappear into the world's faceless human fabric. It's been done before. Hoffa. Shaw Mohammed Reza Pahlavi. Fernando Marcos. Jamal "Butcher" Bokungo. Yasser Arafat. Mugabi. Nehru. Juan Peron. Julius Caesar. Qaddafi. Aristotle Trichinous. – to name a few.

As to continuance of entrenched dictatorial power, one politically astute American senator once analogized, "What's the use of being the school bully anymore if there's no one left in school to bully?"

* * *

As it turned out, the promise of a 'just Cyber society' for an entire planetary population began to ring true from its first year of implementation. Admittedly, there were some stumbling blocks. Negotiating contracts with unyielding unions threatening work stoppages and boycotts was still the stickler to implementing fair and common law decisions concerning labor.

But now, compulsory Cyber employee/union contracts were agreed upon much quicker than in times past. That was because when all the indisputable facts and statistics were presented to the 'Selectronics Committee', the unions' irrational propaganda of the past was discounted by the Cyber systems because micro chips and ports don't recognize favoritism. In cases of dispute between management and organized unions seeking justification for building membership and big steward's salaries, judgment for both sides was now based on equality of issue. Of course, there will always be dissenting sides, perceiving themselves to be losers in a cyber decision. At first, they would find themselves in the same position as thousands of American air traffic controllers back in the 20th century. Unwilling to accept the obvious, this skilled army of technocrats were fired en masse. Replacements – a miraculously well-schooled generation of controllers were brought in to restore a commonsense work ethic aimed at organized union domination. Out of the threat of chaos came sensible resolve. And not a commercial plane was lost!

Inevitably, as one country after another climbed aboard the Cyber wagon, each region's judiciary, officers of their court, and their police enforcement agencies were on the firing line. Each was compelled to recognize the reality of intent and enforcement of Cyber Selectronics Committee's straight arrow laws and penalties. For that reason, when all the legal smoke had cleared, there were fewer and fewer legal court actions per se. It was as though a specific region's peoples accepted the reasonability of Selectronic Committees judgments. Cyber-rendered decisions were predicated on submitted evidence from discovery examinations and later from in court legal hearings. The court of law was a hearing formality, conducted to ensure that all facts were laid out for both prosecution and defensive purposes. They laid out the sentence advocated by the law of each region. Argumentative, glib dialogue was not a factor, for or against. Sentence was rendered, impassionedly, impersonally and accordingly. Case closed.

Chapter 3

3. Cryology Suspends One Lifetime For Another

<u>1900/2050AD</u> – EUROPE, ASIA, AFRICA, NORTH AMERICA

THE PRACTICE OF Cryogenics in North America had been active sometime before the mid 20th century. Almost immediately, the originators had to solve a major method of acquiring and sustaining effective storage of regenerative frozen human beings. Human body ' warehousing' had to be easily accessible, close to treatment facilities within Cryology laboratories. It also had to be; *Expansive* to accommodate many thousands of 'patients'; Perpetually *refrigerated* to ensure a precision comatose state for those still living; *Self energize-able* to replenish chemicals, in absentia; Constant power maintenance would always be in a fail-safe condition; *Centrally located* to operative and treatment refrigeration so that human 'subjects' were instantly storable while awaiting treatment; *Inaccessible* to all, except Cryo-member practitioners and staff; *Operated undercover* to isolate the practice from public sensitivity and governmental intervention.

To such unsavory purpose, storage of humans and Cryology procedures were never, ever to be mentioned, written or even implicated in any form by any member involved.

With the paid and/or commemorative cooperation of 'inside' parties, most humans, even barely functioning bodies, were either 'officially' declared deceased or released to relatives for ultimate treatment and/or funeral services. They were almost always surreptitiously taken from morgues, private care hospices, hospital beds, ambulances, operating tables, rescue vehicles, accident sites and even the homes of care givers. Clandestine processes were in place to negotiate and transport such bodies in total secrecy and concealment. Agreements with survivor relatives were that no public announcements were ever to be issued or discussed concerning the passing of a loved one.

When a living person was contracted for Cryogenic treatment, cadaver substitutions came from mortuaries, universities and hospital disposal facilities. In every case these were substituted for the purpose of closed casket ceremonies and cremations by specially appointed crematoriums.

Without exception, all this was performed with no questions asked of well-rewarded palliative care personnel. All that relatives really wanted was the knowledge that their loved one would live on – at any cost. Indeed, it often cost minimums of mid six figure fees for cryogenic processes, storage and treatment for one person, no matter how it might end, in life or death. After treatment patient storage and cadaver substitution was covered by the Cryology preservation fees. The costs of squeezing profit out of Cryogenics practices after the exorbitant costs of such storage care had to be made clear to the moneyed 'mourners'.

Aside from the recruitment of potential patients, the most critical problem for cryogenic laboratories was the method and costs of "storing" them for *genuine, future* treatment. Of course this care was not yet known to present day medical and pharmaceutical researchers, nor to medical practitioners themselves. It wasn't intended to be an underground business, but that is what it turned out to be – in the fullest meaning of the phrase!

Dedicated cryogenics surgeons were sometimes referred to as the hyenas of the relatives of the dying. It was as much for what Cryo people referred to as 'necessary back-room tactics in the face of *politically unacceptable* Cryogenic practices.

Here's another reason why the term 'underground' business had such a literal meaning given to Cryobiology.

By 1990, storage of 'viable' future patients had been going on for almost 100 years. For instance, many a 1960's farmer would put in his crop, year after year, without realizing that a mere 20 meters (65.5 ft) *below* where he was doing his harrowing, much of his "field" there, was actually a double story, concrete structure, covering five to ten acres. It was equipped with power generating dynamos, continually operating beneath the farmer's combines.

For that reason, expanding city sites out of rural areas were also restrictively zoned. As metro growth replaced rural growth, some engineering departments and city councils were persuaded" to set ordinances restricting excavating below 60 ft, owing to certain ground conditions, porous rock, moisture content, etc. etc.

In metropolitan regions, more *new* Cryo storage facilities with the same geographic requirements were also structured in accordance within civic specifications. They often doubled as legitimate, commodity warehousing which accommodated large volumes of heavy vehicular traffic, night and day, to a depth of 85 ft beneath the basement of the building on the property. Exact locations were also chosen. For example, proximity to swift and voluminous underground rivers, by which what little power was needed, could be harnessed to control and to provide essential and almost perpetual refrigeration. Other power alternatives were employed, such as windmills and solar panels; enough to generate sufficient energy to power storage warehousing without have to attend to the maintenance required to operate in such undercover ways. When farmers' properties eventually became covered by urban settlement, the same kind of traffic was carried to several different underground entrances by private refrigerated vans and well-identified public service vehicles under legitimate, illusionary institutions.

One day, in a thousand years or so, this kind of subterfuge, enabling everyone an opportunity to their complete life, will be – laughable".

Chapter 4

Souls Readying For Cryogenics…And Longevity

2003/21ST CENTURY – GERMANY

FOR HUMAN BEINGS, part of life's strange yet wonderful concealments is that conscious living does not entitle one to forecast, even remotely, one's own destiny – not the where, not the when, and never, never, with the whom. Speculation, not calculation. Yet, destiny of one's existence is often perceived to be the harvesting of one's human soul, alive or gone from life. If one ever *does* define a resolve before their time, one might discover it has nothing to do with either life *or* death – not a beginning, nor an end, but more pointedly – why and to *what* possible purpose?

When and if one's mind finally realizes that one has rarely ever been *truly* conscious, *many* humans, either now or later, will then come to a clear perception of *why* a strange and wonderful destiny unfolds itself to them. Perhaps then the foregoing unintelligible rambling will explain the mystery of two separate episodes of two separate people, 1014 years apart who will share a common destiny.

* * *

It was two years after her son was born (1995) that Frau Nina Kratz and the rest of her family admitted to what they had noticed, but not really acknowledged, when Erich was one year old. His seemingly thickening fingers and burgeoning – but not chubby – frame was beginning to take on an adult-like, muscular appearance. Shoulders were *extended*. Thighs and calves were *bulging sinew*.

Growing up in a tiny village near the city of Unterhaching, in the Bavarian region of Southern Europe, tow-headed, Erich Kratz was as energetic as any other five year old; walking at 11 months, babbling at 16 months, eating everything his mother put on his high chair tray. He was normal in every way *except* his *expanding* "body-builder" physique.

It was at his *fifth* birthday party in a park near his home that he fell off the park's whirling swing rings at its highest point. He should have suffered a bundle of *bruises*. Somewhat miraculously, he did not have an even slight blue mark anywhere on him – not even skinned knees. In such incidents, parental concern favors caution over dismissal of injury from just one of many such childhood tumbles.

From Frau Kratz' home just two km northwest of Unterhaching, the downtown walk-in clinic to the Munchen (Munich) Medical Klinic was a thirty-five minute intercity rail ride via Schnellzugstraßenbahn. Their family physician maintained fourth floor offices on Sonnestrasse. (Sun Street).

"Guten morgen mein junge"

The doctor greeted his five-year-old patient. He welcomed the Kratz family and gathered details of the playground accident before he commenced his examination of the patient.

"From what I hear, you remind me of my little girl's rubber doll!"

As he continued his examination, the physician teased the boy,.

"I can see you took a bad bump – but you *must* have *bounced* when you hit the ground" he chided.

Now he addressed the mother. "There's no indication of any bruising or swelling anywhere on him, Frau Kratz. Naturally, we will do an internal check-over. On the surface, no injury is evident – but something *does* concern me… Erich's unusually enlarged physique."

The doctor continued to feel prominent tendons on the small patient.

"It is very curious to me – that for a small boy, his *muscular* stature is so – so extraordinarily advanced. Most curious!"

The medical man's eyebrows took on a worried twist as he lifted the youngster's leg and pressed his fingers into the groin area.

"Frau Kratz," he began.

"You must have noticed Erich's exaggerated muscle formation long before now."

"Oh ja. He was *born* a chunky baby." She answered. "Two or three weeks after his birth, we first noticed his shape but thought nothing more of it. After all, he was an exuberant, bubbly baby. Frankly, we were delighted, because after some anxious days during my pregnancy, we regarded his healthy frame with relief. He *is* healthy, ja?

The physician seemed not hear the question as he spoke quietly, almost to himself, still feeling the boy's muscle tone in both calf muscles.

"Hmm…Normal tissue density. Doesn't seen to be any less pliable – For the moment, I think we have to dismiss this, ah – overall swelling of ligaments as just a mutated form of some kind. Perhaps a kind of glandular edema."

He speculated to himself in medical terminology as he probed and thumbed the child's muscle formation.

"I just can not think of any natural biochemical in the body system that might cause such solid tissue build up in a five year old. It's extremely unusual and certainly puzzling".

The doctor turned away to make notes before turning back to talk to the parents.

"By the way, is there anyone else in the family with this unusual muscle mass?"

Erich's mother laughed lightly and said, "No. not really... Aberrr..(but). His uncle – my brother – is always working on his body conditioning to impress his female friends in the gymnasium. Erich here loves Schwarzenegger TV movies. He often pretends that it is himself in those tough scenes. But nein – no one else in the family has ever experienced this – to *my* knowledge."

The physician nodded.

"Well, while I'm not too surprised with young bodily formations these days. I must tell you, I know of no other record of any child in Deutschland, at least, that has ever experienced this kind of sinew growth. It *might* be mentioned in some of the world's medical journals. I *will* scan some back issues to see if this condition has come up elsewhere. There *is* the possibility that the boy's condition might be some kind of latent mutation. Nevertheless, from what I can discern right now, I see is nothing *abnormally* wrong here. If anything – it is abnormally *right*! Meanwhile, I hope you will permit me to arrange examination appointments for Erich with consulting specialists. This should to help us to arrive at a more accurate and comprehensive diagnosis. That would ease your concerns too."

The doctor realizing the *mutant* remark might have unsettled Erich's parents. So, as they were about to leave, he hastened to add,

"I don't mean to suggest that Erich is turning into some kind of malformed monster that one might see in on of those bad Rumanian horror films. *Nein. Nein.* Nothing like that. In any case, do not let this accentuated muscle *growth* distress you. It *is* entirely possible that, at puberty, he will even grow out of excessive sinew development. However, to be on the safe side, I believe Erich should be seen by specialists such as those practicing in athletic and astral medicine - definitely a pediatrician, a circulatory specialist, urologist and internal organ doctor would also be in order. They will want to run their own tests; blood work, analysis, possibly scans, ultrasound examinations – that sort of thing... And yes, I know. It probably *will* be very inconvenient and time consuming for you – traveling back and forth to different appointments in various medical offices. I must repeat – based on our initial check, I see nothing about Erich that would indicate poor muscle tone – quite the opposite. However, let's find out what is causing this accelerated muscular growth at such a young age. If you agree, my receptionist will set up those appointments and let you know."

Several weeks later when Erich, his mother, father and grandmother returned to the Sonnestrasse Klinic, The doctor brought them up to date as he did a final check out examination on the youngest Kratz member's muscle growth.

"From the diagnoses I have received from the specialists who have seen Erich, it is basically the same conclusions from all five practitioners. According to the reports on record, they have thoroughly examined the boy with in-depth tests, studied DNA reports and have recorded all other laboratory specimens – that sort of thing."

He rose from his desk chair and moved to his exam table motioning Erich to sit on its edge as wound the gauge cuff on the boy's arm to take his blood pressure.

"All specialists seem to agree. Your son's body is not producing, - in *normal volume* at least, a form of protein called *Myostatin*. To our knowledge, this shortcoming, though rare, is neither life threatening, nor is it inhibiting to future growth. From what we know now, there is no reason why he should not enjoy a full and normal life – muscles and all."

Now, washing his hands at the examination room sink while the Kratz family entertained young Erich, the physician thought to himself....

'Mein godt! In actual fact, this child may be the first and only person on earth to bring the medical community to the first real physical character change since we all lost our bushy eyebrows! All because of some weird mutation. Just imagine – it was *my* initial case study that may lead to validating the purpose and function of Myostatin in the human system. Such an anomaly could be a positive first in recorded medical history. Hell, fellowships have been awarded for less. Eventually, that wouldn't hurt *my* reputation any - or my Klinic for that matter. Truth is, this whole thing could be a super application for those requiring ample *deposits of healthy flesh* – like in space travelers, where lack of normal activity tends to waste body tissue...ah well, we'll see.'

Now he addresses the Kratz family.

"Anyway, go home now and resume living just as you have. Nevertheless, check with me every six months or so. I want to monitor the boy on a regular basis. And please let me know the minute Erich's muscular condition becomes accentuated or changed in any way... and until then, don't worry about it."

* * *

When the forensics scientists at the world's largest particle physics lab CERN, Geneva, finished their own diagnosis and study of the little German boy's condition, they instructed their media people to issue a press statement. It fearlessly owns up to speculations that if another stage of Darwinist development is proven, it *might* now be added to the archives of humanity's physical evolution. From this singular example of muscle enlargement in a pre-pubescent subject, the CERN organization now seems to acknowledge the possibility of a first sign of a mutated alteration that, if medically advanced, could herald a much shorter term, evolutionary change within the structure of the human anatomy. Not at all typical, but it could launch a new worth of the structure of man. The World Health Authority issues this press release.

'Only millenniums from now will this singular case in the Kratz patient become solid evidence of true genetic growth. Theoretically, this could launch a means by which humans could structure a new highly developed physical level for all the worlds' peoples.

At the same time, some obscure world media, prepared to dismiss the subject as pie in the sky rhetoric, carried this kind of semi-jocular comment on a non-humorous subject.

"*Myostatin 'May' End Muscular Dysfunction, Sclerosis, Dystrophy*".

From the article beneath the headline, it taunted,

'In terms of medical development, in a time recognized for its daring work in stem-cell research, organ transplants, flesh-eating disease, Legionnaires disease, HIV infection, Hepatitis C, petri dish conception, oral contraception, treatments for morning after, night before and even *during* baby making, such medicinal controls seem to confidently predict less health concerns than ever before. Now for that uncommon cold – good old aspirin will still relieve your mind if not your ailment, acting so efficiently fast you will not even have to bother swallowing it!" This was brainless ridicule on a subject many such authors and editors knew nothing about. Nor were they prepared to learn and inform as was this general news story in the Times of London..

'Every so often, a *health* condition appears to create fresh opportunities for which the medical profession dutifully studies and prepares techniques to provide a new kind of care. The Kratz Myostatin case is one such creation.

What is so ironic in the analysis of normal amounts of Myostatin in healthy young specimens was that the shortage appears to have become a coincidental *advance* for the *overall health* of a human species readying for both adventures and tribulations to come.

A child is born without the normal balance of a protein derivative, Myostatin, which controls normal muscular growth. From this diagnosis, there appears to be a growing conclusion and acceptance by the medical research community that by limiting Myostatin protein production and its assimilation in livings humans, many a disease, pestilence and deterioration of bodily functions could be rendered archaic.

Medical sciences divisional heads at the newly formed, ITSC (Interplanetary Transport Safety Commission) are contemplating the actual *treatment* of muscle tissue to make it more impervious to the deterioration of all bodily tissue, particularly of those subjects being prepared for decade-long space journeys in future. Any biologist specializing in skeletal development for weightless flight has foreseen eventual opportunities for any healthy earthlings to lengthy travel without the wasting of human flesh and bone.'

On an inside page continuance, the article read,

'On learning of the prognosis of one of their junior citizens, some members of the Medical Sciences, Krankenhaus Administration in Frankfurt, advanced an inconclusive but fundamentally sound theory. They speculate that, should an entire group of people with a genetic history of muscular Multiple Sclerosis – and possibly Dystrophy too – were to be administered a glutethiamide antidote to enable healthy muscular growth, this could introduce an overall advancement as a result of the lack of Myostatin in the human system.'

Another International morning journal headlined *'Myostatin Control May Sustain Future Astral Travelers'* It was certain in this particular area of study, young Erich's condition drew the global attention of both governmental and academic agencies to take special interest in Myostatin deficiencies. Whether administering controlled Myostatin emulation in space travelers were to be ethically possible or not, some leading forensic students of space flight were quoted as 'optimistic'.

Sanctimoniously, the Dansk Medicinsk Forsknings Institut Reistrerings Arkiver, the Official Medical Rekord of Denmark stated, "The very real prospect of deliberately diminishing disabilities in earth's citizenry, by controlling the volume of Myostatin in the human system, is almost too incomprehensible to conjure."

Further biological speculations stimulated editorial comment on possible medical advances in other related applications.

For example, The Human Health section of the Sunday Times lead with this human health copy *"Time Capsule Planners Consider Cryogenic cargos"*. Whenever a medical advance is announced, fly-by-night, time capsule schemes take on added significance as though to suggest that human body development is directly related to storing live people in time capsules. But then, why not? These oddballs get their publicity in unworthy coverage with every news story that even *hints* of another reason to tout the same old time capsule idea. Setting the stage for television shows was this column quote from the Frankfurt Express weekly.

"Contemplated as timely for creators and promoters of speculated cosmic capsule projects is the advantage of tissue enhancement. This relates to recent rationale concerning Myostatin as a favorable human *endurance* factor. Now some radicals envisioned stocking a container not only with documentary and electronically recorded diaries and artifacts, but now also bearing a *cryogenic human* whose body could *contain* minimal Myostatin".

Some space journals suggested that time travel organizers, aided by updated bio- and nano-technological evidence, now foresaw a concept that could help to extend the lives of human beings *in deep sleep*. Certified news records cite comatose victims of drowning from very cold rivers or lakes, having been revived from their *hibernation*, days after restorative treatment.

Not to be outdone, Fox Network Syndicated affiliates conducted some cursory research to justify 'Allan Gaelic's' Feature Series, "A Break for Cryogenics." They broke this concept following Massachusetts medical sciences white paper, *denouncing* the clandestine practice of 'freezing' the terminally ill, who hoped to return for treatment in a future where advanced medicine could bring cures. They critiqued the claims of cryosurgeons and supported the 'established' fact that straight liquid nitrogen can *not* perpetuate flesh, 'Myostatinless or not', but conceded that the chemical does indeed purge some tissue of some unestablished diseases!'

As this kind of reporting demonstrates, breaking news is all too frequently, purposefully blurry. If this preceding news account were typical of integral reporting, a story might be broadcast this way ... "Renegade Ice Planet Swings Erratically Through Galaxy Towards Earth! Evacuation recommended! Details At Eleven".

Equally disjointed is another 'off the wire' statistic:

'Cryobiology (the unrecognized practice of extreme freezing of humans to preserve them for a future time, when their ailment becomes treatable) Makes Another Surprise 'Advance'.

'Fresh evidence of the "rediscovery" of a chemical, not yet publicly identified, that can be unequivocally proven to extend life of the dying by controlled freezing procedures to an entire human system, without incurring cellular breakdown in the body. This compound is a chemical that neutralizes matter between tissue cells to preclude negative effects on healthy tissue as well as neuron assembly. It just so happens that these discoveries coincide with the announcements of positive effects of restraints on the body's normal Myostatin productivity. The result of both revelations elicits promises of strengthening muscular cells *before* a cryogenic procedure, assuring greater prospects for success of intended resurrection."

Another soul for Cryology?

2016/21ST Century – Connecticut

One of the bank of nurses' video monitors blinks out its alarm. A flurry of activity at the nurses' station sends cardiovascular staff flying in the direction of heart patient Ellen Furbisher's glassed-in cubicle. This was the Intensive Care Ward at Yale, New Haven's Hospital and Heart Center in the downtown core of New Haven, Connecticut.

When the first dose of nitro is sprayed under her tongue, her clutching hand on her own neck and jaw, relaxes. This time, the pain was lighter. It always passes more quickly when the team on the floor is so fast with treatment. Her mother had been sitting, sniffling in the corner of the room. She rushed back to her daughter's bedside the minute after the monitor attachments had been replaced and checked out.

"Nevertheless," said resident specialist Dr. James Harvey to the gathering of medical personnel while he scanned the Frobisher chart at the nurses' station.

"We have to start admitting to some cold, hard conclusions, regarding Mrs. Frobisher's stay with us. This is the fourth angina attack since – when did you say she was admitted?"

A nurse monitoring the registry scanner replied,

"Fifty two hours and ...16 minutes ago."

Head night nurse, Elsa Danzig, stood at the station counter. Head down, she was leaning forward with both arms stiff in front of her with her hands flat out against the desk below the counter. Right now, she was so bushed; the only things she could feel with any certainty were the aching arches in her feet. Beyond that, little else was getting through to her. She was sore as hell. Throughout a 12-hour day, feet get that way when they have to respond to over 31 ICU beds, seemingly all buzzing their heart-rate alerts at the nurses' ICU station at the same time.

With her discomfort, Elsa was not regretting any missed dates to go dancing with hubby, Matt!

Elsa's body might yield to stress in her pre-middle years but her deductive powers continued to work well into overtime, considering she was working on her second straight shift. Completing a chart note on a patient pharmacy requisition in front of her, she looked up to face Dr. Harvey. He was writing notes to nurses regarding two other patients he had in ICU. He felt her look and said,

"Ok, Elsa, what are you mulling over now? Lemme guess. Right now, your mind is working overtime on the Frobisher case, right?

"Yeah", she sighed,

"I just think that whatever we can do to keep Ellen Frobisher on board, has to be done – *should* be done – *post haste*, before she becomes *post mortem* – *Jim*, shouldn't this case be prioritized for a medical board meeting – first thing in the morning"?

The resident specialist was still working on his prescription pad, wishing he were somewhere else. He breathed out a long exasperated sigh and said, dejectedly,"

"Maybe - *If* she could hang on that long." he commented almost to himself.. Then he said out loud,

"I don't know, Elsa... Nothing much would come of it, I'm afraid. Nothing that *I* can see, anyway. Meanwhile, I called her physician, a couple hours ago. We both concur that her heart's blockages are – well, with five stents in it already – she may not withstand another angina attack, even small vessel closure. Worse, she's got at least three more pending small vessel plugs that we *know* about, on both sides... In all, her pump could be said to be inoperable *and* irreparable".

Resigned to the sad prospect, he plunked down in one of the nurses' swivel chairs. . .

"Thing is ... the whole organ could go – massive attack at any minute – and..."

He trailed off ...mused' resignedly, staring straight ahead as though in a trance,

"Even if a donated heart *were* available, I know damn well none of the cardio chiefs would approve *any* surgical procedure at *this* point – let alone recommend it. At best, until and when she gets a regular beat back, or until she shows a reversal – improvement instead of continuing deterioration..."

Cardio resident specialist, Dr. James Harvey shrugged and sighed.

"As of now," he said "she's too weak to improve, even for more extensive angioplasty. I know of only one surgeon in the whole New England states, with one in a few thousand *chances* of conducting a *partially* successful bypass *or* an implant procedure in Frobisher's condition. Lucky for him, he's out of the country."

The only sound for thirty seconds was an elevator bell sounding down the hall...

Harvey picked up where he left off.

"Huh – as *if* the right organ were *about* to become available. Would the committee approve a transplant, which in all likelihood could be deemed wasted on a patient too short term to be approved? No cotton pickin' way!"

The nurse looked at him with just a hint of moisture in her eyes.

"I feel so helpless, Jim. God damn it. You know, we professionals are *supposed* to be dedicated to the *preservation* of life, no matter how unlikely that may seem at times. And yet we're caught between the politics of the medical community and the commitments made at the alter of Hippocrates...I just feel so – guilty!"

"Don't beat yourself up, Elsa. You're no more responsible for Ellen's prospects than you are for her measles when she was a kid! What else do you *think* you're supposed to do for this patient's condition except observing that old saw about keeping her comfortable? Dying is *not* all that comfortable!"

He put an elbow on the service counter and turned up a palm, to pillow his chin.

After a moment of silence Harvey said, "She's a mother herself, isn't she?"

"Um hm – boy seven and four year old girl. Nice Lady." Head night nurse Elsa Danzig was checking the early morning pharmaceutical distribution sheet.

"Her parents alive?" asked Harvey.

"Apparently. Her father is a shipping czar out of Seattle... well fixed but a business-first type...he's on the ocean most of the time. Ha may not even know how critically his daughter's case had turned for the worse."

"Husband?"

"Sash and door manufacturers' rep...never home. Always on the road. Had a strange first name..."

The nurse dipped her thumb in the wet sponge dish, picked up the open Frobisher file and spun a few pages.

"Yep - here it is – "Dacron – Dacron Frobisher. He brought her in..."

Elsa turned a sheet or two more and shook her head. "Hasn't been back since – who knows? Doesn't say here... Frankly, most of the girls on day shift duty got the impression, when his wife was admitted; he didn't act like he cared all that much one way or the other. The scuttlebutt is, he rides around his route with a teen-aged Italian squeeze."

Glumly, the doctor did his best Mel Blanc impression of Bugs Bunny. "Dacron?! *Dacron??*! What's a Dacron? Was his mother a frustrated seamstress or what...? Isn't there a fabric called – Dac-?

"Yes doctor there is."

The nurse retorted in a sardonic tone of voice. She was obviously irritated at the medical man's attempt at humor. At a time like this, too. Mindlessly, she monotoned a reply to his puzzled look..

"Dacron *is* a clothing material, sort of like a woman's second skin - and funnily enough, some Dacron *fabrics* in drapery and furniture upholstery departments!"

"Not all that funny, considering..."

Elsa abruptly dropped an aluminum clip-held chart on station counter, dumped down on her own swivel chair and turned to face James Harvey.

"...Jim...There's something..." Danzig hesitated. She almost didn't go on.

Finally, forehead wrinkled, she whispered,

"...Just a thought. I know it's far out. Probably very, *very* unprofessional of me – but ... at times like these, I tend to clutch at straws when there's nothing left but air to clutch... I know I'm out of line here... but wouldn't it be worth checking out that Cryobiologic research group over in East Haven. Near the airport? You know their offices? Just off Brighton Street? Maybe they'd give us the straight goods on what they would propose – like their freezing procedures... usually sought by close family members of dying people - for the later prospect of treatment.. Things we can't do now - but in future...Maybe they can..."

Her thinking out loud petered out.

Doctor Harvey's whole body shuddered. He leaned forward to the woman and cut in.

"You *must* be over tired, Elsa. Otherwise, why would an intelligent professional like you venture out on such a slim *limb* as that – I'm no psychiatrist, but, one would have to be out of one's *mind*, even to *suggest* such an unproven procedure... the freezing of a dying person's failing body? – for what? A million to one shot for a *few* more years of breath? – And even *that* has to be more optimistic than realistic!! Good god, my dear woman! Get a grip"

Elsa hit back. Angrily, she exploded in loud whispers.

"Well it's better than doing fuck all, isn't it? Like you said, Ellen's situation is *past* grave. And she's only twenty six years old, for God's sake.

She resumed her normal low monotone.

"Seems to me, it was some pope – Pious the second I think. Anyway, Pope *whoever* – once described death 'the complete and irreversible cessation' of brain activity. As I understand it, Cryobiology is a practice that when provided at just *that* time, just before the brain signs off, they can actually – "

"Oh yeah...really?' said Dr Harvey sardonically,

"Medically speaking, of course",

"Frankly, we're *still* not absolutely certain just *when* that exact moment is – couldn't be the same for *everybody* though, could it?, Ellie. Ellie! You've been misinformed. According to blurbs by these Cryogenics people, they *profess* to be capable of staving off the inevitable until new treatments *might* be available! But who's to know? What can they say if and when it doesn't work? Then what? Is future society going to be stuck with a bunch of unfrozen, retarded mutants on their hands? Fantasy! Hucksterism!"

The desk phone cheeped!

"Station Eight." Elsa answered the caller.

"No. Not over-crowded here at all. So we wouldn't need your extra staff mistakenly called in to - "

She paused to listen, looking up at the ceiling, while the other end spoke further.

"Tell you what. Send your spares over to pediatrics – they're *always* in demand over there. No. Not at this time of night. An admin shift planner and an RN from Detox were up here half an hour ago, looking for hard asses with fresh legs to work those wards. Yeah, sure. Try 'em."

After she hung up, she faced the cardiologist who had come over to her side of the desk.

"Jim, I'm not saying Cryo procedures are another chance at life. That implies choice. There is no choice here and we all know it! But frankly, this far out possibility is just as close to a last chance as she's going to get – slim though it may be!"

"Yeah. That's about the size of it...Chances! Maybes! Couldbe's!"

The night security officer came by, nodded and walked on. Harvey resumed his rant.

"All questions! No sure answers! Whatever credits these Cryo researchers claim, it's really all *academic* to the real point – that being – *no body* really *knows if* this left field approach really works – they maintain they've had recent successes – but in what? Chimpanzees? Frogs? Lab rats? Goldfish? Hell! Just the *claims* of successfully thawing out diseased bodies for advanced nanotechnology in the years ahead, is still just so much guess *work!*"

The resident cardio blew out a long sigh – then carried on.

"Elsa, I can't believe I'm listening to a dear friend and professional colleague talk about – Good Lord, I shouldn't even be *discussing* this." He whispered, "How could you ever think *I* could abet such an unethical, unprincipled exercise?"

She retorted.

'cause you're my' --

"Sure I am – and because I *am* your friend, I would! But *then* – *then...*"

The doctor was silent for a moment as though considering his options. But then he turned sardonic. He threw up his hands and growled...

"I know. I know. It's as much about me as it is about Ellen Frobisher...fact is, were I to be perceived as being in any way involved, my practice would be in the tank. Kaput! Null and void... Over and done with! In the dumpster!! Better I should reserve a Cryo-freezer container for *myself!* And you are inviting me to have a dying patient supposedly under *my care*, undergo this kind of hokey treatment? No cotton pickin' way lady!"

Nurse Danzig opened her mouth to speak but got cut off before she could get a word in edgewise, by the medical man's rant.

"Moreover...and you should understand this, *Nurse Nightingale!*"

Doctor Jim Harvey pointed his thumb over his shoulder.

"This state's best associate cardiac-care clinic in over in Hartford wants me in their line up as a *partner* – next spring *already*, and I'm going to *be* there! As for you – I hear *your* prospects for a senior *executive* position around here are very good. So honestly Elsa, I don't recommend that *you* bring up this Cryogenic idiocy ever again, either."

Her face was in her hands. With reddened eyes, the nurse looked down at him between her fingers.

Dr. Harvey looked quizzically back up at the head nurse and spread his out hands, palms up to imply they were clean. He finally caught on. Nurse Danzig and this Frobisher patient had commiserated together and had become special friends.

He now realized that his assault on her frantic pleas and sympathy for Ellen were as things would be if they had been sisters. Now he felt remorse. He *had* come on pretty strong. For her sake, he had been condemning. He had been hurtful. He regretted that. Just the same, he just could not condone her off the wall attempts to save the Frobisher woman, even at the end of the nurse's frantic sixteen hour day.

"You're one good lady yourself, Elsa Danzig." he admitted, "I don't mean to poop on your compassion for Ellen Frobisher, but..."

As if she wasn't listening, the nurse went on quietly.

"Jim. This is about the *life* of a super fine young woman. I've come to know her and she's much, much too fine a human being to have to leave us. I just can't give up on her without going all the way to give her a chance to live a full earthly existence."

She paused. Then, she brightened a little and spoke to him in a low voice..

"Y'know. Matthew – my husband belongs to the local chapter of Loyal Order of Otters. It's the same Lodge that has a member – one of those guys from the Cryobiology laboratory over there in East Haven. Oh damn - What *was* his name?!? Anyway, if I were to persuade Matt to get his freez'em friend over here to talk to Ellen Frobisher, maybe they could swing a deal between them and her rich old man of the sea... Then we might – "

The resident physician couldn't help it. He was fighting his own feelings now; He rolled eyes and blew out an impatient breath of rebuke.

"There you go again. What d'you means 'we' Elsa?"

The surgeon tried tact.

Now softly he said,

"The thing is – you, coming from a family of medical people...your Austrian ancestors would do back flips in their graves if they knew what you were thinking... Imagine! Throwing yourself on that kind of grenade!"

Harvey stood up again, put his two hands up before him in resignation.

"Aw hell – I give up!" Look - it's *your* conscience and – and it's sure as hell *your* career to do with as you see fit! So ... Go ahead. Give Matt's Cryogenic friend a subject for their 'freeze now – cure later' program. But please, – *please* don't even *breathe* my name – *unless* you get tangled and mangled in inevitable, medical red tape – and even then...."

Harvey stopped. A full minute elapsed before he moved a little closer to Elsa, putting his hand around her shoulder. Then, he said quietly, "Yes. Of course – you call me if you find yourself boxed in – but for god's sake – and mine, *don't count* on me to promote Ellen Frobisher's ice box treatment."

He bent to hold her and gently kiss the back of her neck, then whispered in her ear,

"...unless there's no other last resort!"

As far as Doctor James Harvey would ever know, there wouldn't *be* a last resort. Three days later, head nurse Elsa Danzig and her very good doctor friend, attended a memorial service for her *other* very good friend, the late Ellen Joan Frobisher. Her cremated remains were to be sealed in the New Haven Cemetery Vault. Apparently, that's somewhere in East Haven – in Connecticut.

Chapter 5

Multi Marriages Makes Many Moms and Dads

2370-2390/24ᵀᴴ Century – Brazil, Mexico, Ireland, New York

IN THE MATTER of residual effects of the galactic gas invasion on our solar system and its chemical cause, mankind must now deal with the startling effect on humanity's *diminishing birth rates.*

Heretofore, before the atmospheric infiltration of Dusty Gas, the species of man had only to deal with loss of young reproducible lives through wars and disease ending in mass death counts. That and climatic and geophysical devastation throughout the centuries had failed to quell *over-population* rates of the planet's upright creatures. Until this inconceivable galactic invasion, planetary population continued to rise. But *now* humanity was faced with the very real threat that the genus of the human could become extinct – just as certain as would humans should an asteroid collide with earth.

In the face of uncertainty, speculation runs rampant. There are those groups of medical scientists, who speculate that an ion of the mysterious gas composite in the blood stream could cause negative functions of those organs. One anthropological/biological research clinic (a breed that often combines hard research with soft theory) had a paper published in the medical news publication, Lancet. It concerned a study of the sample residual astral gas compound showing traces of *Endocrine* in the space cloud of yellow tinted gas. It was thought that Endocrine, indexed for its disruption of hormones, could impose *gender-bending* faults in the process of human reproduction.

Therefore, the presence of this element had to be considered too, in the equation.

Adding to the prospective likelihood of a virtually extinct human communication system, are the discouraging revelations of some scientific bodies, many direct from ongoing world conferences. Cases of impaired and deteriorating human speech are one thing, but *now*, deceleration of human *propagation* rates was a whole other set of unsolvable problems!

Some shocking conclusions were implied, clearly revealing another depressing fact. Apparently, in the testicular 'apparatus' of the human being, there exist, a *tissue elasticity* similar to that within in the human voice box. Again, this tissue is the 'culprit' that, in the euphoria stimulated, activates the ejaculation of spermatozoa when a male ejaculates in his orgasmic convulsion. Thus, it is reasoned that these Dusty Gas effects *could* affect *the virility* of potential progeny for expected generations, well into the future. Only a severely declining birth rate the world over would give credence to the warnings.

Even to a few remaining optimists, this appeared to be a final nail in the coffin of restitution.

* * *

Historically, the earth's natural cataclysms, such as those that plagued and reformed the Greek Islands; Krakatoa and Mount Etna eruptions and more recently, the Panama quakes; Sumatra tsunamis, where more than a quarter million people perished; The Kobe eruption which drowned and buried much of quake-riddled Japan to its man survival limits.

Then there was the South American tragedy when one million square kilometers, comprising mainland and islands on the southern tip of Argentina the island Tierra del Fuego and hundreds of mountain tips (islands) belonging to the formations of Chile's Archipelago, all collapsed into the sea. This latter catastrophe was due to one plate grinding over top of another, but it was the rarely recorded, two for one catastrophe – a subduction zone beneath the shift uplifted carbonated rock formations within the Peru/Chili Trench in the year 2244, resulting in an unaccountably huge loss of life. Repetitive and intermittent tsunamis alone took 120,000 souls. Another ten or twenty thousand persons were unaccounted-for, lost in the boiling waters of the continent's southern-most archipelagos, now strewn with urban structural wreckage.

Notwithstanding the world's cooling off disruptions, mass disasters of this magnitude had *failed* to markedly *reduce* existing populations and to arrest the *rate of human reproduction*.

In fact, without a drastic extremism like another ice age, the human head count in the late 24th century had reached twenty one billion souls – up seven billion from the year 2150AD. Under 'normal' TFR (total fertility rate) circumstances, world population to the 25th century, was estimated to be no less than 35% greater than the it was two centuries earlier. The limits of earth's sustainable resources to 2400AD was reached – *and passed!*

Only a demented mind would have dared to conjure up a galactic gas infestation from out of nowhere, which could actually curtail the life of man's habitation on earth. A more logical but more heinous theory was that the upward population spiral could only be mercifully alleviated by a mass induced genocide to those left-to- fight for the sustenance of those who might be left on earth.

Short of interplanetary collision, or a full scale, world wide, nuclear war, mankind continued to wring its collective hands, over an imminent future or lack of it.

Paradoxically, a less painful solution appeared to be at hand. A bane to humankind, galactic Dusty Gas would *slow* down propagation of earth's teeming billions. In his panic, man and his Cyber mind added to the malaise. Polyandry, one woman receiving multi-men, followed.

* * *

The sexual revolution was about to begin anew. All that could be expected was that, for the sake of perpetuating the species, (if for no other reason) both man and woman would accede to a stringent law of sexual sharing to achieve an ultimate purpose – continuing evolution.

The law as enacted by the Cyber Selection Committee called for a three male, one female household. Medically known viral males and men of undetermined potency were to cohabitate with one fertile woman. This was believed to establish potential for a rate of human reproduction that would sustain pre-Dusty Gas levels. At that time, every medical lab on the face of the earth reported studies that clearly inferred not only the waning volume of sperm but the lessening of its potency.

In basic terms, the law called for revamped personal profiles and a new set of multi-adult household responsibilities for every participating adult.

If the plan had a hole in it, it was not the mandate itself, but man and woman's emotional adaptability. Could they handle the strains, jealousy, guilt, loving preferences, unwanted habits and traits? In the broad spectrum of things, none of that really mattered. Regional matrimonial certification would be necessary to legitimize and to record cohabitation with *no less than three* men in one household. All peoples would be compelled to comply. This would impact on *every healthy woman* of childbearing age in every region of the world.

Sustain progeny futures. That was the Selectronics Committee's universal law.

Church and state was neither the issue, nor the pretension.

This was not polygamy! The actual terminology was *polyandry*. An artificial mismatching of male and female to achieve a scientific end. On the basis of hard numerical evidence, the 'Repeoplizing Charter' was struck and activated if for no other reason than to ensure the continuation of the species.

Under the edict, all three – or more men would lawfully join a household wherein one brood female would be expected to conduct regular marital relations with each male. The female was obligated to report to medical and civil department recorders each conjunctive occasion to establish an operational procedure.

In order to meet the economic requisites of a growing household, each male resident would assume one-third financial cost of all household costs. In addition, taxation collection gratuities would be guaranteed and issued to women applicants meeting specified regulations.

It was logical to *assume* that human reproduction would gradually increase over generations, driven by the instinctive hormonal lust of participating males. The women were permitted to officially reject and eject abusive certified partners but to officially accept other or additional lovers under the same conditions. So long as the reproductive objectives of the edict resulted in an assembly line of healthy fetuses – 'family' discord, moral conflict, woman's existing marital status, emotional ties and preferences' – were of little concern and irrelevant under the newly declared law.

And so it was, many residents in the so-called civilized parts of the world compared the new statute to promoting *state*-fostered, breeding-farm conditions within the human community. But in view of the crisis – the real possibility of less than half dozen persons would occupy 100,000 thousand square kilometers of land surface – objections were few.

From a moral standpoint, it was reasoned; it wasn't as though the practice of multiple partners wasn't a fact of recorded human cohabitation, over the evolution time of semi-civilized humans. More recently, in the 1800s, 1900s and most of the 20th century, German, Dutch, Russian and other émigrés to North America had lived communally. In most of those cases, multi-wife families had only the threats of a disciplined religious "paste" to hold such unions together.

At what point in time and under what conditions the Repeoplizing Charter *might be deactivated* was neither forecast nor stated by any source. Some oversexed male prospects rejoiced – as they gleefully conjured up a never-ending copulation banquet!

* * *

On his semi-recorded media show intro, the usually over-excited, 'happy mouthed" announcer yelled above the prompted clapping of a studio audience. This time-worn show opening was supposed to stroke the ego and pump up the stardom status of the host, Martin Lancer, world's greatest newscaster and interviewer since Edward R. Morrow, Lord Hee Haw and Deacon 'Out to lunch' Morgan. That kind of bluster went along with the usual network hype; two octaves higher shouting and crowing like... "Tonight. From the community of "Bountiful" in the state of Utah, we present *Open Secrets!!* Presented by the *World's* most sought- after news network, brought to you as it happens ...*This* is...the ALW – the all live and all worldwide – Holograph Empire.

On and on it went the diatribe with hyped up credits and program content and lead in commercials. Off camera, the show's warm-up staff was giving Lancer's studio guests the usual cautions to be direct, brief and to say what they honestly believed without fear or favor, Blah. Blah.

"...and *now*, your host, *star* of the ALW Network's, Dramatic Events of the Day" – *tonight* from Central NorAmeric here in Utah, Here's Martinnnnnnnnn *Lancerrrrr!*" Audience cue applause...Up, hold and fade out clapping.

"Good Sunday evening to you all - in both NorAmeric and SouAmeric regions, and *welcome* to audiences joining us in the Middle East, Southeast Asia and Southern Europe."

Lancer paused and then continued...

Four elderly folk about to appear on the walls of households everywhere, via their holograph projectors, were nervously concerned. Some had long since lost the lung capacity necessary to pressure their vocal cords into more than guttural squawks in order to be understood. The network's audio technicians had set up an automatic translator system to make sense of breaking voices. They would also spill enough text-over graphics and visual effects to be able to let his aging guests to go for the gusto with their responses to the interviewer's pre-programmed questions.

For this week's show, the network feed was enlarged to include an additional 280 network outlets, on and offshore. For that reason, interviewer Lancer was going to be at his best. God knows he'd had enough experience. He'd broadcast many put-'em-down features like this before, where he had to struggle to make sense out of the cough and cackle crowd they put in front of him.

'Screw these inarticulate, pensioned, old freaks', the on air celebrity mused to himself, "So what if I *do* have to ride roughshod on these el *blanko* memories in this phlegm-factory set? Who really gives a sympathetic fart for opinions of these wheezing old geezers?"

The idea that geriatrics are *invisible* even when they're right in front of you was also the view of most Network Executives. So now, armed with network vice presidential approval, Martin Lancer went to work with his attack.

"This polyandry issue, in the form of a kind of perverted law, laughingly called the Repeoplizing Charter, has really been a bogus issue to begin with. Nothing will be resolved or satisfied with the possible exception of *ménage a quatre* – *good* times between four consulting adults! My contacts tell me that suspicions abound, the Charter was being introduced to promote moral decay; to satisfy a gullible appetite for titillation. It would certainly promote additional personal liaisons by most lecherous, peasant-citizens."

To himself, he mused, 'that way, we members of the broadcasting intelligentsia could continue the daily brainwashing of the herd mentality of these sheep-like minds – wherever such folds were gathered!'

Out loud, Lancer's insensitive observations went on.

"Looking back, our present century has tested the mettle of the human spirit ever since the year turned 2300, almost 90 years ago. Indeed, a scant forty *years* back, when our planet *whirled* its way through that solar cloud of Dusty Gas, the destiny of the human race was never more than a disguised question of survival. Now, as a result of this street side opinion, we are not only faced with the prospect of *relearning* to communicate, but our very reproductive organs are under question. It is well known to all, within days a Cyber proclamation will declare a human relations program that purports to encourage fetus production to guarantee a human species! Everybody knows the polyandry law will actually *promote* cohabitation. Hey...is that not heavy mambo we'd all like - or what?"

An ECU (extreme close up) on Lance, was called for by the video director. With his lips almost kissing the camera lens, Lancer opened up. In dramatic newscaster fashion, he intoned,

"World Administrators at the Hague are anxious to convince us that increasing male impotency in our species makes it essential to introduce a form of backwards polygamy. Soon, that law or Charter will be globally legislated and enforced. Bet on this! Homo sapiens will be faced with the prospect of *sharing* sexual intimacies with what most ignorant but faithful men *already* had...one deemed to be his *exclusive* female partner."

Now Lancer seems to be working himself up into a frenzy. He began to sweat. His tonal pitch increased even more.

"So what is the hope behind the premise of the "Repeoplizing" law? It is the hope that, despite a loss of universal male potency, increases in pregnancies can be achieved through the *sharing* of a variation of male partners to alleviate the diminishing production of viable sperm. If this – correction – *when* this mandate becomes enforceable legislation on an international scale, it will, sure as hell – come to us all, creating a shambles of the status quo – you know, established social/sexual life styles around the world. I foresee conflicts of macho *envy*, raging jealousy, abuse of unprecedented brutality, decimated family units and many other kinds of ensuing discord. I ask you. Will all this be worth the preservation of animalistic males as they joust for the sexual priority of just one household female?"

Rising from his moderator's chair, Marty began a slow shuffle to an appointed mark on the studio floor.

"But," he went on, "Who can predict an outcome?"

"Isn't it just possible that an accepted state of "in house" sexual permissiveness *might* evolve into a new era of family *unity?*' Anything is possible. Believe it or not – *I'm serious*. Could tomorrow's family unity become founded on the need for sexual and meaningful loving? It's possible – right?"

Now having sauntered to the panel of elderly people in the studio, Lancer elaborated.

"There *are* those who will pooh-pooh this unity possibility. Tonight, let me introduce you to a group of people who *do* know something of both the positives and negatives of 'multi marital unions'".

Like a curving fluorescent tube, surround-around, holographic cams encircle the four elderly show guests seated on podium loungers.

Martin Lancer stepped to the front of them.

"Let me introduce you to Martha, Betty, Fiona and Ernie Halliburton - now all past 70 years of age. They were part-sibling descendents of one of many communal religious sects, wherein the practice of polygamy was symbolic of the rights of man and his rightful dominance over women; where generation after generation sought preservation of *their* way of life by producing children – and lots of them."

Lancer squatted down beside a sitting Ernie Halliburton.

"Ernie, let's get your opinion first. How would the sects' elders communicate this concept of one male with many women, to the commune's young boys - as you were at *that* time? How young were you when you were sexually introduced to your first woman in the commune? – *And* was she already a member of your family?"

Ernie appeared somewhat thunderstruck by the speed and directness of the question. Lancer figured to himself, he'd have to fight this guy's lack of fire with real fire. Finally Ernie responded

"I don't know *who* she was. Remember, I was just a seven-year-old tad then. When I was put to the pussy of an adult woman I wasn't even sure what the exercise was suppos't to be all about."

"But Ernie you were *so* young - not yet at puberty - how do you think now that they believed this act was to prepare a young male – in this case, *you*, - to meet the obligations of the sect's polygamous customs?"

247

"Who knows? I sure as hell didn't have the foggiest notion – but I guess this stuff makes good entertainment to *somebody* – *else why would you be askin*'?"

"Is it possible that such a crude sexual encounter was supposed to provide you with some kind of lesson for future?"

"Yeh...could be... But nobody ever told *me* what that lesson was suppos't to be."

For a fractional, frustrating moment, Ernie's vague answers threw broadcast host Martin Lancer off his train of thought.

"What about the lady you were supposed to –"

Lancer interrupted himself, then exasperated, he exhaled loudly, "I'm confused... Think Ernie! *Think* now. How come you were - as you say, brought to the – ah, vagina, of an adult woman?"

"Because she took me from my bed in the middle of the night to have me screw her, I guess. – But I fooled *her*. I came off before she could stuff me all the way into her. Boy! Was she mad – Heh,Heh."

"Are you suggesting, sir - she might have been the female version of a communal pedophile?" asked Lancer.

"No sir. Don't really think so. Mainly 'cuz, I really had no idea what a pedo–file *was*. Still not sure even *now*, either... Isn't that one of those gals who does your toe nails?"

After five minutes of this going-nowhere nonsense, Martin Lancer decided on a new tact *and* a new target.

"Betty Halliburton, as a child, did you know that you'd be destined to become one of the wives of some old man with a lust for sexual variety in his household - just as it was in your own father's household?"

"Well first of all, Mr. Landlord, my married name is not Halliburton anymore. Halliburton was my father's name."

Sheepishly, the moderator replied, "Of course. Sorry Betty. What *is* your married name then?"

"Well Mr. Landlord, I been married three times since - so really it takes too long to give you all my married names so -"

"OK. OK. By the way, *my* name *is* Martin... Martin *Lansord* – *ooh gawd* – I mean, *Martin* - Martin Lan*cer*!"

The show host was flustered. He was actually sweating underneath his hairpiece.

"OK? Now look... Let's get to the meat of the matter here."

As host of a fast moving news/data show, Lancer was supposed to be *used* to disjointed and irrelevant responses to his probing, but *never* like this. He was aware that he wasn't performing like the pro his promotion posters say he really is. He had to recover – and quick!

He circled the panel and stopped in front of one of the other women.

"In order to repopulate our world in the coming years, we are faced with changing the face of family units, where there is to be three possible fathers and one mom. When *you* four were growing up, it was more like three mothers and one father... How about *you*, Fiona Hallibur – sorry. Sorry... Fiona, Can you tell us what it was like, as children of a polygamous relationship - what kind of emotions were effected by commune intimacies? Sadness? Grief? Disappointment?"

Fiona looked up at Lancer for a clue.

"Does *hate* count?"

"Yes Fiona. Hate is certainly a *different* emotion - but it counts. What was it you hated so much with *your* role in the sect?"

"*The Sect!* I hated *the* Sect! From the time we kids learned to walk, we were assigned work – and it was work, work, work from then on - from milking cows at four AM, to baling hay in blazing hot sun 'til suppertime - to heating jars over a hot stove in the middle of summer for putting down preserves for winter,- to hours of butter churning 'til your arms drop off! As my grandma used to say, 'That sucks!'"

The other women on the 'panel' were nodding heads up and down. One muttered,

"Sect children didn't learn to play like other kids do today."

Fiona ranted on.

"I *hated* the elders who set the rules - and the *roles* too - for all sect members. I hated fathers who administered punishment for work undone, tardiness and all that... and I hated sect mothers who turned the other cheek while their 12 and 14 year old daughters were given like playthings to already married, old men – supposedly to keep up the sect's population of workers. That's crap. The old guys just wanted to get off reg'lar on those kids. And all this was being done for entire lifetimes, – all in the name of a merciful Lord Jesus Christ who - we kept hearin', had once said, 'Suffer little children to come onto me.' Yeah! Right! That had to be a load of Old Testament bullshit if I ever heard it..."!"

This diminutive little old lady was just getting warmed up.

"Lemme tell you, Mr. Linseed. If any form of polygamy is to be set up under any kind of government law just in order 'to *peopilize* the world' – as they tell us it is, they better get a bunch of things settled first. Things like household costs to raising a pack of kids – let alone the ethical questions... For example, who's gonna foot the bill for raising and schooling hundreds of millions of kids nobody – including some mothers, really knows who parents 'em? I figure this big computer we got to govern things now, has made its first big, sizeable mistake!"

Martin Lancer smiled. Thank God for Fiona, he thought. Ole Marty was beginning to regain his best sheep herding form!

"Thank you Fiona. Now – let's talk to the one of these three women who remained in a commune during most of her adult, child bearing life. Martha, since you stayed with the sect, I don't suppose you agree with Fiona's evaluation of a polygamous relationship...."

"The hell, I don't!" croaked Martha. "She's *dead* on!"

MC Lancer waited for her to go on. When she didn't, he said,

"Is it not so that most women look for compatible male companionship along with *meaningful* doses of intimacy when they commit themselves to their husbands? I wouldn't think a wife-sharing, *sisterhood* would be any kind of substitute for a normal, loving relationship?"

Martha snarled her reply, "That's sure as hell true! But remember! Polygamous marriages are *neither happy, nor* healthy relationships and mine sure as hell *was not* a happy kind of a marriage!"

"When you married, Martha, were you troubled by the directness of sexual involvement? And were you at all put out with the fact you had to share his embraces with other wives? In other words, did you adjust to a *schedule* for night time activity?"

Martin thought...That ought to do it. She'll blast off on the sect, burst into tears or blurt out confidentiality or two.

She spoke sadly.

"The answers to all those is *yes!* And *No!* – And Yes! I adjusted to my fate because I had to, Marty, just to keep me half-assed sane. Hey. Lemme tell you why I stayed with the sect for so long. Like other women there, I was, frankly, *scared sick* of leaving. I just didn't have the courage to venture into an outside world that didn't promise me anything better than what I thought I had – like three squares and my own kids...

Now as for night-time activity, as you call it, my growing up was quick and dirty. Jacob was 45 year old when he took me sexually - he was *supposed* to be teaching me arithmetic in the loft of the barn. I was 13 at the time. Afterward, he said, 'that was fun worth marrying for,' so we did. I married him a day after my 14th birthday. Was I jealous of his other five wives? Hell *no!* Usually, I was never so damn grateful as the times, when *our* husband called one of *them* to his room to service him, 'stead of it being me. Yeah I adjusted all right. At least I got to preserve my dignity – and I s'pose most of us will never have anything better than that. No sir. Quilting and making canvas clothes is not my idea of a satisfying, worthwhile kind of life – in *or* out of a commune."

Martha dabbed her eyes with a Kleenex from the coffee table.

"That's why, had I stayed to now, I guess I would have had to admit that the only goodness of life for women within the stockade of communal living, will only be found in creating some kind of joy for their children. Seems to me it's their only chance to reconcile either their personal worth or a broken hearted existence in the self imposed prison they were born into."

"So how did you get away and stay free, Martha?"

"When some of my kids grew up and left the commune, they persuaded me to join them in their homes. I did eventually, but I actually had to hide out for a couple years because the sect elders actually *do* come after you."

She wanted to change the subject and tried cheering up.

"But I'm better off now. My life is better now. For one thing, I'm older. Even if I had stuck around, no need to worry about having to serve the sect's males anymore either in body or spirit...Old men who never *did* give a god damn then whether I enjoyed any part of life in the beds of the commune. Today, my *real* joy is my children and *their* children's children."

Martha stopped, used two fingers to wipe tears from both eyes and regained her composure.

"If human beings are to become extinct because of loveless *or* same sex relationships, well, Ok. In my opinion, that's a lot better than having to face the crushing existence of polygamy – or polyandry - or whatever fancy name they got for it now.."

"Thank you Martha, Betty, Fiona, Ernie. May I personally wish *you* overdue joy for whatever family companionship you do achieve, for the remainder of *your* life? - This is Martin Lancer. Next on the ALW Network – the investigation of 'ESP – mental magic or mystic rite? Advocates cite its value in such instances as controlling the central nervous system for tranquility after brain surgery! Featuring an exclusive interview with the man who is claims to be the world's foremost ESP analyst, direct from the Amsterdam Institute for Advanced Telepathy. Be right back."

For some geophysical reason or other, some parts of Ireland's very rural regions in the north end of the northern hemisphere were one of the last regions on earth to be affected by larynx deterioration. Speech was still possible. While Colm Garrity and his young wife might noticeably be losing voice capability to the ravages of Dusty Gas, there was enough modulation level yet left, to be clearly understood? Especially when one raised ones voice in anger. As Colm was doing again here tonight. And as far as Garrity was concerned, it was an Irish male's responsibility to propagate and to protect his own marital possessions.

He said so, one 'foine noight' as he sat at their kitchen table, banging his forefinger down on a magazine article that pronounced the prevailing Cyber legislative edict, instituting a universal edict of "3 men, one-woman' family units.

"Great t'underin' Chezzus, Mo!"

Young Garrity riled against it to his young wife.

"I'm not at all sure dat I could look on another'n mountin' your body – takin' his pleasure while I'm farced t'lettin' me wife get pranged, jest t'produce anoder fellar's kid," grunted out 26 year old Colm, "And doan...*doan*, I'm expected t'end up halping t'support da lil baastard! An – *and* what's t'stop m'wife from preferrin' his cluster over mine and spreading out for him three noights out of foive! Hell woman I got t'ya farst.."

Colm stood up and pressed his finger to the kitchen table – obviously to emphasize his point as if his decibel level were not emphatic enough,

"I tell ya, Mo, - S'not *natural*! And the bible says so, d'nt it?" He turned and sat again – this time on the other side of the table.

"To be shoure, I don't tink I'm man enough t'take dat koind of sharin' - lyin' dawn...'cuz I'm *not*!" Maureen hid the start of what would have been a unintended but delightful play on Colm's words He was no mood to share in any humorous side to his loud sermon.

"But then wot's a mun t'do?"

Colm sighed.

"Well *Mister* Garrity," His wife spoke up. "Yaw may think *yaw* got it rough in that koind of situation but yaw might give some t'aught to wonderin' how revoltin' the whole thin' could be for every garel like me in County Armagh"

On her wedding day last year, Maureen passed seventeen, going on eighteen, she promised to love, honor and fuck Colm's brains out, whenever he felt up to it. So far, it was a parfect arrangement.

"An' now," the northern Ireland born colleen went on, "Depandin' on how dey propose dees tree-on-one match ups, I could end up gettin' plunked some old codger like Orangeman Daug Farrell, one noight and den his father, da fish monger, da next...and wouldn't that be a great turn-on for an innocent lass like me? 'Sides, what koinds of mutated kids would *dat* produce?"

"And what do yaw *call* dam kids? Farrell? Gavan? Marphy? Or jest, Nomber foive!"

Colm Garrity waited for his wife to finish – then shouted.

"Naw, yaw's roight, Mo. Yaw is bleedin' roight! I'll tell yaw sumpin' – roight naw. First shariff pokes his nose in here wit' a couple jacks in tow - and a court order to let da fuckin' begin, will get dar asses full of shingle nails and flamin' magnesium. I figger d'ats gotta discourage 'em from enforcin' dar "share da wife law makin'"! I don't really give a sweet tard why dey – "

"Colm! Colm. Listen naw."

Maureen had joined him to sit at the table.

"Colm, Dare's anoddur side to all this. Does it occur to yaw... by da *same* law, yea – *yaw* and others could be recruited – dat reg'lar couplin' with my little sister Paddy – or – or maybe d' post masters wife? Oh yeah...and ain't it so

- yau've *fancied* his Mary since da last pot luck social in da chorch basement? Now Colm, m'boyee. Does that change yur tinking' atal, atal? Hmmm?"

* * *

It seemed ironic to lieutenant de Ejército, Juan, Alberto, Luiz, Rodriguez, that as late as the last twenty years, the very army to which he now belonged, had been part of a judicial order to help police hunt down and literally kill the thousands of surplus street kids of Rio de Janeiro. Thousand of rampaging parentless kids infested every quarter of the city with crime and misdeeds of these unwanted adolescents. Yet now, the universal Repeoplizing Charter was intent on *producing more children?* Crazy!

Juan gave *his* participation in this incongruity some deep thought as he rode his bike home. Under the terms of the new Repeoplizing Charter, home was a "temporary" billet in a base officer's residence section of the army base, with a couple, Major Ernesto Demerara and his Mexican teen wife, Melina Rosita.

Following the "all clear" of the dusty gas some 20 years ago, it was still possible to voice-communicate in raspy, sometimes whispering tones. Still, most people could *still* communicate by a collection of speech and vocal sounds.

In the compound mess, a young Capitan from Army HQ explained to Juan, that within 28 days, he would have to assess domicile compatibility with Major and Senora Demerara. He must gather and ratify health report documents of all parties in the billeting home. He is then encouraged to file for *marriage to Melina* Demerara or find an alternative household to join, with a view to the same kind of objective. But in the first seven days of living with the couple, the *unexpected* occurred. The Lieutenant had fallen deeply in love with big brown eyed and dimpled Senora Melina Rosita 'Demerara'.

Every day, the 24 year old Brazilian Army lieutenant, went to work on the base now as a supply clerk for the Recon Corp. And every night, returned "home' to a supper, prepared by Melina for he and the Major. There was no question that Melina was attracted to Juan. Her eyes said so. After curfew, he'd retire to the living room, pull out his cot and listen to the sounds in the annexing bedroom where the Major was pounding out his passion for – and *on* Melina on a squeaky spring bed. Heart sick, confused and enraged with jealousy, he eventually gets four hours sleep before reporting again to the Supply Depot in station, at 5:30 am.

At headquarters, his social affairs officer kept asking him about his experience to date. As a result, Juan always felt goaded to initiate action that would include him in matrimonial action with Senora Demerara. An action that would get him involved in the male seeding process with Melina.

One night at the billet home, the Major went to bed early in their curtained off bedroom. Juan and Melina sat up drinking sweet coffee.

"Melina, All three of us know why I am billeted here."

The young man approached the subject as directly as he dared,

"Are you not *curious* as to why, after six days, I have not proposed to you and your husband for permission to be with you? That I take my turn in having sex with you – as ordered by the new populating law?"

"Not really, Juan. I have come to know something about the nature of men like you and my Major. I am experienced with man's desires and their need to have sexual love with a woman. As early as 11 years of age, a brother, a family friend and from time to time – a neighbor, who enticed me with his a big furry pet cat, used me. He used to lure me over to his place to play with the animal while *he* played with me."

"Well then, what is it about me? Why am I not invited me to your bed?" he asked.

"Well. If you really want to know, please believe me – I have *never* invited *anyone* to have sex with me. They just tried and if I liked them – I *let* them.

The Major, came to Guadalajara on Army business. I worked in the commissioned officers mess there. Eventually, I lay with him – several times. Then he paid my family much money. We were married in what was then a secretive convent. That was two years ago and now I am over sixteen years." Melina hastened to add, "I like you. The Major likes you. You *are* so shy, but you never really let us know that you would have liked to share my body. Therefore we thought...."

"Sí entiendo. But, Melina..." He hurried to reply, "I just don't understand how it is *supposed* to happen. Do *you?*"

She laughed softly. "It just happens, like – like right here – and right *now*, if you want."

Without any embarrassment or immodesty, she removed her flower printed top and stepped out of her long yellow skirt. She stood like a sumptuous statue; one he had seen on a trip he'd made to the Baja red light district near Brasilia. Black hair tumbled deep over her shoulders. She walked to him as he sat, bringing her martini-glass-shaped breasts, with their small pebble-hard nipples, close to his face. She started to undo his uniform blouse. Meanwhile his arms encircled her naked hips and he thrilled to her pelvic forward thrust toward his open mouth. With the rest of his uniform off and now as naked as she, he shut off the lamplight and pulled out the cot. Juan was so enraptured with her animal display of affection; his own love lust for Melina; the heat emanating from her delicious body; the lifting of her labia to meet his prodding penis; that self control was no longer his to command. When he finally slipped into her, it happened almost without his knowing. As he did, the young senorita thrust back up at him. She uttered a slight whimper and an ecstatic but muffled groan, such as he had never heard from her times with the Major. Suddenly his every muscle went taut as he experienced an eye fluttering euphoria – several paradisiacal moments of orgasmic rapture that caused him to convulse and splatter himself deep into her body.

Just as he was *supposed* to – in accordance with the Charter, of course.

As they breathed heavily in the after glow of breathless ecstasy, Juan's eye caught the glow of a cigarillo on the other side of the bedroom curtain. The Major had been watching them.

Next day, the Lieutenant would report to the Capitaine that Melina Rosita and Juan Alberto Luiz would want to plan for a ceremony for the first available Sunday, signifying a consummated and "compatible" union in accordance with the Charter.

The young lover now had only one concern. How could he ever tolerate the inevitable addition of yet *another* male, a third, besides him and the Major, into sexual embrace with *his* beloved Melina? "

Screw the objective of babies, especially other people's babies out of his woman's womb! That was *not* Juan's law!

Chapter 6

Excommunicate! Exempt! Exile!

2670/27CENTURY – 'PRISONER' ISLAND, BRITISH COLUMBIA

'AS THE MEDIA forecaster would say, "Don't look *up* today — unless you'd like another 32 centimeters of rain in your face... Same today as it was yesterday and the days before that. It's miserable grey skies and despondent moods again. Ideal for a good game of crocinole by the fireplace...In a moment, our lead story, but first..."

The man in the Italian cut weather-proofed suede coat was the CEO of Cyclops Hydro Inc. Umbrella bumping into umbrella, he was waiting in an outside line of about fifty very wet footed guests. They too were there to act as witnesses. To that end, they would pass in through to the prison's observation area of the exile holding depot.

He thought to himself

'I'm about to see for myself – the way of the wayward'

He continued his contemplation of an almost unreal event about to happen in front of him...the departure flight of global society's worst criminal element would departing this world into permanent exile. He was here to witness the boarding of two former Cyclops Hydro accounting executives who had embezzled millions from the employee pension fund and took the life of a younger junior accountant who threatened to blow the proverbial whistle on them. *That* indiscretion was the straw that finally tripped them up.

'It must have looked to be so easy to these guys,' he thought. 'I guess these two guys figured they knew how easy it was to swindle an overgrown and seemingly disjointed corporate giant – while nobody was looking!'

This hydro company boss, Chief Executive Officer Hugh Cameron, turned to his lawyer friend in the line and offered a thought through his TransPinder.

"In the old days, Tuk, prior to 2500AD getting convictions and indictments was so damned involved... a clutter of red tape and costly legalese, left over from times past. And, as if that wasn't enough, industrial thievery was one hell of a lot tougher to uncover and to nail these pricks, than it is today."

Cameron's associate nodded his head and responded,

"That's a fact. Think of all the trouble, our society could have saved if it had always been this way." he imaged.

The line was moving ahead now as the Observation platforms doors were opened. They stowed their visitor-issue umbrellas and shuffled to the observers' seating area, tiered directly in front of a wall of floor-to-ceiling windows.

Outside, in front of them, a chain link fence and with a razor blade barbed roll atop, leading to the ramp up to the launch pad The giant 400 meter long ship (a city block long structure – longer and deeper than many an ocean liners) lay in a horizontal attitude, ready for the impending loading of close to 280,000 passengers onto four levels of it's amphitheater—like hull...a 'cabin' unit, over 30 meters in diameter.

"What you're about to see, sir, is the implementation of Cyber justice. I think you'll agree it is as swift as it is appropriate."

This had been expressed by one of Hugh Cameron's executive officers on this day of his impending flight to Port McNeill.

Now he tapped his TransPinder and alert cell, to receive the mind-sent comment of Clifford 'Tuk' George, a corporate lawyer and a full blooded descendant of the BC/Alaska, Haida/Tllngit First Nations bands.

"You know Hugh, there's an interesting analogy to all this. Those Hydro execs who tried picking your employee's pockets are getting the same treatment *now that* my very ancient forefathers *used* to dish out to tribal miscreants, many centuries ago. Today as then, its 'Go to discovery. Enter all the data, circumstance and background. No plea bargaining. No deals. Judgment finds – Not guilty *or* guilty. Set free or sentenced to banishment from the band. Case dismissed'. All within a couple of days."

Clifford George dusted his gloved hands together to emphasis that this was 'all there was to it'. Now, he added,

"Only difference now is that it all happens a tetch slower than it should. Thank goodness for that. Or we lawyers would have to fold our teepees – if you'll pardon an indigenous metaphor. But really, it's good that trials and sentencing happen so much faster and more precisely. I know you won't believe this but according to our tribal ancestors, that's how it *used* to happen in those days."

Cameron raised his eyebrows, looking up querulously,

"Oh yeah? In those *good* old days, huh?"

With a grin, the lawyer mouthed his image in reply,

"Well pardon my prejudice – but they had to deal with those problems *quickly* in those *good old days!* See – their very plains existences then depended on braves being there ahead of the moment of the caribou run and the buffalo herds when they came through – and they were *always* on time! Great, great, great old grandfather and his boys had no time to waste on listening to the excuses of *maverick* Indians!"

The Cyclops CEO faced the lawyer,

"I see what you mean. Simpler times, right? Things were clearer. Sorting mushrooms from the toad stools were easier to figure. But then, that was before lawyers, plea bargaining – and daylight saving time!"

"Pretty far out, even for you boss – but yeah. I admire the no-bullshit way in which justice is meted out today. All I'm saying is that some things never did *have* to change! For all kinds of political reasons over the centuries, man-made idiots fussed over right and wrong, taking so god damned long to deal with what they saw as profitably long range and complicated final judgment. Ah! But *now* we're back to square one efficiency. Things move so fast under the same system as tribal wise men used *then*, it has forced us legal leaches of today into quicker action. Less time in which to pad our hours!"

Hugh Cameron chuckled not so much at the self depreciating humor of the comparison but for the semi truths of what was meant.

He looked out over the water of the Charlotte Strait, all around them. He imaged,

"Tough place to escape from. And just to *get* to as well, in case anyone had a mind to rescue their exiled friends from their trip to no where." he thought, as he recalled the details on the institution's stat sheet, handed them while in the entrance gate. 'On a tiny uninhabited, 75 hectare rock islet, one of the Hope group, twenty kilometers, northeast of Port McNeill on Vancouver Island in Canada's British Columbia, a massive, prisoners holding complex had been built, mostly underground and below sea level. It's a rabbit warren type of accommodation...over 300 thousand cells filled with filled with persons up to three times a year. They are all bound for *exile* to our Galaxy's planet-moons, Europa of Jupiter and Sabrinza, a speck of planet whirling in the rings around Saturn'

Along with assorted RCMP members, other representatives of other countries justice administration system, waited in the unnatural silence of the observers' room.

In the morning fog, the mat black, hull of the interplanetary seat shuttle ship with its eight thousand tonne lift-off capacity of supply-holds and fuel load, sat slightly angled in its holding carriage. When ready the whole carriage would lift hydraulically like a child's teeter totter taking the ship to a 45 degree attitude. In so doing, start up engine blasts would be confined downward into their deep bed rock pits. 300,000 semi stool

In the grey cast morning chill, molecular fueled engines, idled; rattled, and rumbled as they readied for a high velocity ejection into astral nothingness.

Hugh Cameron was as grateful for his TransPinder-aided image dialogue now as he was during the mental banter of board meetings. Here, thought transference overcame such much earlier communicative impedances as having to make oneself understood over the roar of the massive ship's power compartments.

Hugh had contemplated their respective views of the so called justice system. Now he responded to the previous comparison comment that Clifford George had conveyed.

"Y'know, I have got to credit you Tuk! You've got a way of sorting out the honey from the bull shit. Comparing the similarity of ancient tribal justice to the Cyber administered system of today is dead on.– and you know what else? Think of all the hoops that law enforcement had to jump through after that, just to meet out courts stance for 'offender's *rights*'! *Rights*, my ass! Ninety percent of these mindless buggers forfeited their *rights* at the precise moment *they* *decided* to impose their unjustified 'take' on *other* people's *rights!* Not mention their *lives!* When you think about it. . . *under the* guise of a kind of unreal rationalism, courts in those days were nothing more than judicial circuses, playing time games with penalties, fines and incarceration sentences. Second time offence reprimands! Time off for this! Probation for that! Good behavior for this! Conditional sentences for that! It pisses me off just to think about really was for so many centuries. How the hell could it have lasted for so long?"

"I know where you're coming from, Boss."

Tuk' George was one of many hundreds of lawyers retained by Cyclops Hydro. He had worked with the prosecuting attorneys on the case of the Hydro company embezzlers cum murderers. In that capacity, he was here to witness the carrying out of the exile sentence for the people now departing for their lifetime junket into isolation.

He imaged, "And I also share your venom for man's condescending sympathy for offender's arrogance brought on by weak willed law makers. And before *that,* not too many centuries ago, it was biblically minded Barrabas who didn't get any breaks for his misdemeanors under Caesar's Roman Empire justice. A couple of centuries following *that,* everyday starving peasants in France caught stealing bread, would be invited to check into the Devils Island Hotel for an unpleasant stay for the rest of their lives. Around King Henry's time unfaithful wives also got it in the neck; an infamous time when many an English beggar was fitted with a garrote flavored 'neck tie' for *their* blue collar transgressions. At the risk of over stating the whole mess, it was not that long ago, that we went soft *and boy – did we pay for it!* Until now, seems like it has gone from one extreme to another. Yeah. I share your venom alright, for our past – but now – don't know about you, but *I'm at* peace with the present."

This waiting gives you time to reflect, thought Hugh. He turned to face his attorney friend. He imaged his opinion once more.

"Exactly! I can see why you're satisfied with what we're watching now/ After twenty-five centuries of judicial insanity – as you say, from one over reaction to another – we've finally got a judicial system that is no longer in danger of imploding due to past misjudged and misspent priorities. Every business and every citizen seeking redress *should* be satisfied with that aspect."

"No argument there," imaged the lawyer.

"At last, we've got the kind of crime retribution that is *finally just!* That's one of those bigger steps for mankind."

Cameron overlapped George's with his own thought.

"And here's the *best* part, Tuk! Law enforcement and offender maintenance is negligible, compared to what it was – even with the expense of having to send these, paddy-wagons off into space every so often."

"There's *another* best part to this way of expunging the distress caused by these kinds of misaligned humans."

Cameron raised his eyebrows and looked into Clifford's face.

"Really? What's that?"

"It's that the procreation of thousands of evil spirited, low life will ultimately end – right here! *Both* offending genders are headed to two different exile locations. *Cohabitation* will ever again be possible to any of them! How clean is that?"

* * *

The Queen Charlotte Strait was under gale warnings – wind whipped seas of white caps, even though, *on shore*, winds were lighter. A March mist of rain clouds hovered over the snow topped mountains and deep green island groups, just off shore. Dancing rain drops spattered down onto the large stretches of cemented areas, leading to the 6 acre launch pad ramp. On the positive side of this dreary scenario, early spring's purple crocuses and daffodils amidst year-long, green grass were leaning with the wind, along the side of the chain link fence leading to the underground prison exit.

Hugh and Cliff were joined in the prison terminal's vestibule by defendants' lawyers and assorted court officers plus a dozen blue uniformed station guards. Each of these had a 'side arm'. These were hand held laser remotes, that when electronically activated, would severely restrict the movement of any prisoner who 'stepped out of line'.

The underground holding gates opened up. Donned in copper colored, metallic foil coveralls, prisoners, four abreast, were led up tiled steps to the ground level heavy plated doors and brought into loading formation.

Seen through observation windows, a parade of over 222,688 prisoners, each carrying their own parkas, shuffled into position. First, the woman's contingent to one deck – then men, filed past, four abreast to board the massive shuttle D deck, accessed through three portals in the three story thick, space conveyance. Each inmate was neck-harnessed with wide banded nylon-twine, to three other prisoners in the row.

Cyber mandated international law directed that legal representation and officers of the SC court for *all* parties were to *witness* and record the departure of their clients to exile. Hugh Cameron mused,

'One can understand why relatives are not present at these things. I suppose it's in order to avoid emotionally distraught *occurrences* between them and their imprisoned relatives."

There was a strange and sinister calm in the annexing waiting room. It was eerily akin to the watching those who walked up the pirates boarding ramps or to those who once shuffled their last thirteen steps to the gallows of their own hanging. All observers had to be feeling ill at ease watching their fellow man leave this world for all time.

Imaged Hugh Cameron to no one in particular,.

Its really is an ominous and menacing picture but very *necessary* parade ritual."

At the boarding point the collection of earth's assembled criminals and murderers had been assigned shuttle 'seating' in rows of one hundred across for a total of 300,000 semi stool/lounges.

Once loaded – that took little more than I hour and 35 minutes – shuttle hatches were closed.

Moments later, when observers had been guided back behind the sound proofed, blast shields, the crew of the massive shuttle ignited their 36 nuclear-powered ground rockets. They thundered up for a ground shuddering lift off to the new Elba. Once through earth's braking atmosphere, hydrogen fuel cells together with the harnessing of galactic magnetism, booted the craft on its predestined course.

The men-offender's *subsurface* exile camp was under translucent shelter on Jupiter's Icy moon, Europa. From earth, the 'space run' to that village on Europa, 629,700,000 kilometers from earth would take 15.5 days. Six hundred and fifty million km and another 8 days further on, the female contingent would debark on Saturn's most recently discovered moon, Sabrinza, 1,280,000,000 kilometers from earth. Twenty three earth days from departure the shuttles crew saw its remaining cargo of women exiles exiting to settle on its surface. Both moons were also chosen for the same alignment direction, away from this galaxy's sun. Raw Nitro/Hydrogen fuel cell supply *was* always available in raw form under Europe's deep ice shelf and in Sabrina's rock and lava—lake-like, mud formations.

Supplies and male prisoners unloaded first on Europa. Then the same prisoner 'platform' took a course for Sabrinza to unload women and supplies there. After that, the crew rocketed back to the now more sane tranquility of an earthly civilization.

After the shuttle had deposited their human cargos on both moons, it was left to earth's criminal offenders to administer for and to themselves. The bottom line was that, shown how, they would have to provide for each other if they were all to survive in an unruly world of their own making. An electronic means of contact with earth was enabled for any certain situation such as depleting medical supplies. In such cases, supplies could be dispatched via small unmanned vehicles direct to the settlements.

Further, no other unauthorized earth people, except refueling crews, were 'permitted' ever to set foot on either "Elba" site.

With no designated leader per se and no laws to answer to; no arms to deal with, only the rule of the strong, prevailed in these unlawful communities. Certainly, no opposite gender would ever be assigned to the comfort, enjoyment or torture perpetrated by the inmates The only guarantee of human regeneration on either Europa or Sabrinza would be the 'next trip' flights, bearing thousands of 'replacements' also committed to exile.

Conceivably, these wayward communities could well herald the beginnings of expansion of human settlement on these planetary outposts. Not that this kind of unruly citizen would be a welcome addition to any space community.

Commensurate with the impact of their offense, underage and *juvenile offenders were incarcerated* on earth for a minimum one year after the offense. At that time, they would *again* be 'Cyber Selectronically' judged on updated behavioral status and updated data on the effects of their offence not mention the inmates attitudinal outlook.

In addition to supplies aboard the prisoner transporters, once per year, unmanned supply barges were launched to both moon-planets of Europa and

Sabrinza. They carried earthly supplies of food, emergency oxygen tanks, emergency water, medicines, clothing, shelter components, mechanized equipment, tools, and power generators along with required fuel. Dispensable, non reusable and therefore minimally low cost, unpressurized *space barges* were left, unfit for further space travel and used by moon inhabitants as part of whatever additional shelter construction projects they deemed fit.

* * * .

On this particular day of prisoner dispatch, a post send-off gathering of 60 to 70 agents and officials on hand for both sides, held a breakfast coffee session in the Shuttle Launch Station Cafeteria.

As the visitors filed in to wait at the lunch counter, two station staffers were already in imaging-discussion on a comparison of humans' and animals' motivations.

"Well sure, early *people* started the trend! In fact from day one in the world versus 'humans erectus', they ignored the benefits of peaceful co existence with others – folks who were weaker maybe, better off maybe, and maybe even more clever!"

"That's right, Broph! Some primitive guys were *better* mammoth hunters. Other guys knew how to start and *keep a fire* going. So these university- level, cave guys made good targets for attacks by those dull witted, slope heads of other, neighboring primitive tribes. This hairy bunch of knuckle draggers, existed on bug bellies and saber toothed, pussy cats, despising those smart asses who lived better in nice warm caves and feasted on *barbequed* mastodon."

Broph gulped his coffee and retorted by picturing *his* thought to his fellow worker.

"Sure! But compare that behavior with the Shark, Python or Gator. They didn't resort to killing their own kind for such stupid reasons as taking over their possessions and women –*Their only* reason for physical with other animals was a *hunger* for 'prey' – a natural, unemotional quest for food – the need for sustenance to stay alive! And man refers to animals as *dumb*".

Clifford and Tuk took their coffees to a table occupied by a few other legal people they knew.

One defense attorney, Marjorie Johnson, image-expressed her own self regrets at her inability to convince the Cyber Committee what she wanted so badly to prove...that her client was indeed not the unremorseful, vehicular-killing, drunk he was judged to be.

"Still, exile *is* like a death sentence, you know."

Clifford "Tuk" George adjusted his TransPinder and retorted an image message.,

"Sure but a lot less permanent. Better in many cases than the choices given to their victims. I know you'd agree that mature, sane, human beings are free to make the right choice *prior* to their unlawful act. Regardless of the circumstances, Marjorie, for whatever reason, they and they alone *chose* to take the *wrong* initiative for whatever reason – likely as not, because they truly believed they could get away with it."

Given the indication that Marjorie would deliver an imaged objection to that thought, "Tuk" hurried to add..

"It isn't as if they *don't know* the consequences of violations against others in a civilized society. It's as if they don't *give* a sweet damn."

"Yes. Yes. I *know* all that, Clifford, but it *is* a *woman's* prerogative and *her* instinctive nature – mine included – to consider *all* people, as just emerging from the womb. *If* it is not the blame of our environment or unhappy circumstances or the condition into which we're born. That admittedly can turn many of our young into non-caring persons – disregarding their evil influences on the lives of others – so then *whose or what's* to blame for it? Maybe mental deficiencies are by an inherited *gene*. Maybe it *is* because of the baby who was 'bumped on a door jamb at eight months syndrome' –

Hugh Cameron interrupted her imaging.

"Sometimes Marjorie, I am certain that we *all* were "dropped on our head' at one time or another. But if you think about it, autistic, slow, retarded, and all mentally disadvantaged, really *do* know right from wrong and live their entire lives that way. What are the odds? The percentages have got to be a hell of a lot lower than that the percentage of ordinary individuals that neuron-deficient persons end up charged in a court action. You legal folk would know better than I, but I'd bet a few hundred shares of our own stock that it's a fraction of the norm."

The station master – they *used* to call them wardens – was still fighting with a mental imaging technique but with the aid of his TransPinder, he was able to imply one basic thought.

"In all my years of serving penal incarceration on hundreds of people, I can not *ever* recall even *one* person with a retarded shortcoming *ever* being locked up. They went on to our psychiatric care programs. As I recall, they more often, emerged to live peaceably among us"

Defending legal counsel, Marjorie Johnson beamed and turned to the older man to express her response.. "

"Thank goodness for that, warden," she responded

"I'm afraid I couldn't live with the thought of a convicted, autistic person being dumped in with that lot of men and women we've just seen off to exile isolation. Thank goodness our Cybernetics governing system provides for first-time offending and disabled kids, *one* last chance to avoid that kind of penal-colony education."

"Absolutely" observed Clifford, always conscious of his 'first nations' responsibilities,

"And while we're at it, let's credit our parents and ancestors for showing us the errors of our ways and for the justice we now have now. We now have a system in our time, which means what it says about keeping all the good eggs in one basket and leaving prison-pallor to those who deserve it – in *exile*".

Chapter 7

32nd Century Hear First Ever Human Voice

31380/ 32ᴺᴰ Century Reykjavik

Back at her post in the ICU, where twenty seven, one- thousand year old hearts were still barely beating, Chief Medical Officer, Dr Mona Randall and her staff of 13 specialists assigned to the medic-scientific investigating team, were discovering their own twenty seven 'surprise' packages. Surprising, in that their now, *un-cocooned* patients were still taking in oxygen on their own. They were also surprised that that bone structure was still intact. Sinew and flesh deterioration in the twenty seven patients had been miraculously little following ten centuries of immobility. So much for the true value of exercise, she thought – to herself of course.

Speculation was that this unexpected condition was creditable to cryobiology's use of liquid nitrogen in their preservation techniques. Further study would *confirm* that hair, nails and 'unused" teeth continued to grow but only marginally even in a comatose state. Still, deprived of ingestion of common nourishment and that intake which promotes normal physical growth, further development of these human components ceased any signs of growth given an unspecified number of years in subjects' encasements or cocoons..

In fact, one "live 'n bulky" prospect, fifty five year old *Erich Kratz* of Euro Germanic extraction was something of an exception. He had an overgrown "garden" of grey hair and curved down finger and toe nails. Despite the lack Myostatin in his system and resulting in virtually *no* loss of a somewhat 'extra' muscular build, it seemed somewhat ironic that he would have been susceptible to ALS, Amyotrophic Lateral Sclerosis – principally a *neurological* disease. Now, thanks chiefly to medically practiced, embryonic stem cell insertion, ALS was considered a virtually dormant disease after the 2900's.

Pulse-active while still in a frozen state in their cone sarcophagi, twenty seven living bodies had been scheduled for immediate surgical or chemo therapy when the strength of their pounding hearts justified it.

One particular case was occupying the minds of medical researchers. It was akin to translating ancient hieroglyphics from Egyptian tombs but by securing using old reference dictionaries, German language documents were *arduously* translated. *It took* five specialists to reproduce , early 2003 documents from the sphere into a means of understandable image transference. Indeed the Germanic text did confirm the link between sub normal Myostatin and the mutation that formed in Erich Kratz at birth. Moreover, the physical volume of Kratz's remarkable tissue formation had quite obviously endowed him with extraordinary strength to endure *any* long, involved 'recovery' process – then and now. If there was a genuine optimistic outlook for the extended life of any of their patients, Kratz was one. Just as soon as his system responded significantly to revival measures he was the most qualified for immediate stem cell implementation and surgical treatment of his ALS condition. At the time of Erich Kratz 21st century life, there never had been any chance for curative therapy, since stem cell research too restrictive by most 'civilized' countries.

Another surprise to both medical and technical staff, was that in the 'marginally living' victims out of the cone section, open wounds and scarred flesh from burns, which had contributed to cause of near death, had not seemed to worsen *after* cryogenic freezing. This was also true of flesh deterioration by disease. Cancer cells, for example, did not seem to continue to advance further under cryogenically treated individual humans. Starting in 3133, this would be the subject of laboratory study for many years to come.

Therefore, it was deduced that known cures for similar life-threatening illness *could* in fact, now be effectively treated, 1000 years later, confident of their predictions for curing the original ailment. Less positive were prognostications for therapy and treatments of 1000 year old complexities of advanced illness and irreparable injuries. Such was the case of the still cocooned body of John Kennedy Junior. This young man had incurred severe internal organ injury in a light airplane crash off east coast US. In fact he was scheduled for interment in Arlington's cemetery. He never got there, either in body or in spirit..

Meanwhile, the team's medical scientists were scouring their own archives and endeavoring to find interpretation of the contents of the sphere's records to determine 21st century diagnoses and treatment of illnesses. Many of those diseases and other maladies were no longer considered serious conditions in a world where human populations now average *one hundred and fifty to one hundred seventy five years of life!* In their own 32nd century medical records more than a few held birthday celebrations for a few *two hundred years* old pensioners.

For whatever reason, there had been uncovered many, *unidentified* cadavers. Notwithstanding, all retrieved cocoons had been sent to an improvised cold locker in the hanger morgue.

First fourteen of those with name tags to be eased out of their cryogenically state were these "frozen-alive-" people.

* * *

Two days after twenty-seven humans were hospitalized, eight were still alive. While four were struggling and heartbeats in two others was so erratically irregular that the only obvious diagnosis was a brain dead condition. Three were back to acceptable heart beat rates; Two had even regained color and were breathing almost normally according to hospital electronic readers.

It was Erich Kratz whose *eyes flicked open* first.

Dr Randall was signaled to report to Intensive Care Unit.

With image transference, her head nurse image-informed her,

"Mr. Kratz seems to have come back to a conscious state ten minutes ago. He's gone back into unconsciousness now. *No* eye movement but his pupils dilated slightly to an exam light."

"OK. Lorraine. I'm going across the hall to check on the other seven. I'll be back in a minute or two"

Just as Mona reached the IC ward room door to leave, she heard something she had *never heard before.*

A live person, *actually spoke* out loud!

"*Enschuldigen Sie, Bitte.*" ("*excuse me, please*")

Both medical women hesitated, not certain that what they heard was an actual human voice. They looked back at the patient who was laying still with eyes closed - but just then his hand moved up off the Danish dyne (down filled duvet) covering his chest.

Doctor Mona Randall put her finger tip blood pressure instrument to Erich Kratz's neck. The other doctor took his hand in hers just to let him know that he was not alone in the voiceless space of the unit.

The reality of it all was beyond comprehension, in *two* ways. The only human *voice* to be heard in *500 years* just came from a *man over 1000 years of age*!

While not out of imminent danger, Mr. Kratz condition was the only bit of good news in many days.

* * *

Chief of Recovery and revival operations at Reykjavik commiserated over patient reports with his very tired Medical Chief, Mona Randall late one night, in the hanger-dome coffee shop.

His image message was a discouraging one.

"Has it really be four days that we've been toiling in this in this tomb/ Seems more like four years already - And what have we got to show for it? Besides a big ball full of antiques, one hundred nineteen dead snow men and..."

Mona turned to Anson, looked him in eyes and interjected..

"Make that one hundred and twenty *four* semi *refrozen* snow men. We lost four others - last night...one this morning. Even if we had been able to keep them alive after their Cryologic state, we would have lost them in any case – diseases too far advanced and no acceptable blood match for one injury case. Up until yesterday we thought we had a chance to save this one young subject when we found a match in the Ukraine. But she was in hospital herself and was unable to fly here until Sunday. So we lost Kennedy. His head injuries from an at sea air craft crash were just too severe. We couldn't do much about most of those in their late stages of disease. Maybe our 32nd century medicine too is still really *the* primeval science; we all thought we had advanced from!"

The project's chief administrator leaned forward to look into her eyes while he 'image conversed with her.

"You're devaluating your profession, Mona! Think about it! You now have *three, living, one thousand year old bodies* in your care – one actually *spoke* to you! Hell – lumbering logic tells us *none* of them should have come to us as more than piles of skeletal dust let alone *survived* a trip of that duration. It's not over dramatic to believe that it is *your* science, Mona that has upped the odds of mankind coming back from the dead! Regardless of what happens from here on in, Doctor Randall, think about *that* when you have any doubts of that kind again,

*   *   *

In late evening of the next day, debriefing with senior medical people and the PR group for the project, Investigative chief of staff, Doctor Anson Prentice, gave a telepathic summary of latest hospital and morgue reports.

"Of the eight short listed survivors, as little as forty eight hours ago, three remain alive. That's the bad news. *But* you know what? Those survivors from a long time ago, can do something that *none of us can.* They can actually *speak together,* using their mouths! According to Mona Randall, they will be taken off their preservative aids in as short a time can be safely predicted, to institute immediate additional curative procedures dealing with their original illness. There are still many discrepancies. Understandably, our transfusions of blood hemoglobin, though prevalent in all three patients, we are struggling to find an extra sensitive, curative compromise in differentiating blood types – thousand year old blood at that! In all three cases, I'm ecstatic to advise that all three are improving by the hour. By name they are...and here you'll have to adjust your TransPinders to grasp the imagery of my explanations. . .

1. Fifty Five year old at Cryo treatment - Erich Kratz. Munich, Euro Deutch, ALS / Amyotrophic Lateral Sclerosis. Prognosis; 70-30 recovery, owing to treatment to restore muscular tissue to its former minimal Myostatin level status. Sclerosis deterioration terminated. Defective neuron motor functions reversed.

2. Thirty Eight year old at Cryo treatment – Harold Harris, Regina , Sask. NorAmeria. Early stages of terminal Cancer of Prostate; Prognosis; Well conditioned physic of typical working rancher. Non invasive Surgery of chloroform and radium injections to eradicate diseased cells. Still uncertain at this time that residual preservatives in the system can be overcome with intended injection effects. Prognosis; 50-50 recovery.

3. Twenty Six year old at Cryo treatment -- Ellen Frobisher, New Haven, Conn. NorAmeria, Acute Angina. Prognosis; Considered and discarded ICD option (Implanted Cardiovascular Defibrillator), since patient's own heart, too plaque-congested and containing eight steel stents; Therefore, original organ immediately replaced with a Llama ewe's heart This organ was "vacuumed" and patched into existing primary pulmonary vessels and surrounding capillary network before replacement into cavity; transfusion of patient's now radium infused blood and IV'd. New heart organ generating pronounced pulse activity; 40-60 recovery.

* * *

Three patients were wheeled into a totally sanitized and sterile hospital room to engage in dialogue in their oral way, should they wished to do so.

All three wished to – but only two could. Language differences precluded Erich Kratz from expressing himself and being understood by his fellow survivors.

"Gentlemen," spoke Ellen Frobisher. "I must say...I really can't believe – or really understand. I have been informed of the date... that I am now living in another world!"

"Same here, Mrs. Frobisher," croaked Harry Harris, "I still haven't got my regular voice back yet, but I can tell you, I'm finally getting the tractor grease out of my 'system."

"I'm so glad for you, Mister Harris.. And I'm just as excited for – Mister – Kratz, isn't it?

At the sound of his name, Erich Kratz, moved his head off the pillow and smiled. In a gentle voice, he said, "Das hat Recht, Frau *Frobisher*. Bitte,

Ist das namen deutsch?"

Ellen Frobisher turned her head first to Harold Harris, then back to Kratz, then back to Harris. "I know it's German language but I just don't.." her voice tailed off.

"It's ok, ma'am. I've got a German foreman on my farm. Helmut's been with me for years – so I had to learn a few words just to get anything done around there. Anyway, let *me* try.."

Harris turned to Erich Kratz. In halting German, he apologized, "Erbärmlich, Erich, Ich -- wir nicht verstehen deutsche Sprache.."

Kratz replied. "Ich verstehe Herr Harris. Vielleicht später"

"Well, I *think* he got the message." the Regina farmer was speaking to his English speaking partner. "I told him we were sorry, but we didn't speak German – he said he understood and -if I heard right, he figured maybe later, for some reason or other. I gather he's already had his treatment for advance of Alzheimer's and apparently it's been reversed. I'm glad. He's seems like a good guy, Mrs. Frobisher."

"Mr. Harris.' she said, "My name is Ellen. I would so like to hear my name – again and again – without hearing it like it would be for the last time ever".

She started to laugh lightly, coughed with the strain but continued to speak through her own disruption.

"It just occurred to me, Mister –   Harry, that we are the first ones *ever* to actually *talk* to someone in here. As you know, no one in this 'hospital ever says anything *because they can't!* Just goes to show you, it takes a woman to break the ice!"

At that point, both began to laugh at the inside joke – and so did Erich Kratz – but all mostly for the comfort of oral companionship and the sheer joy of being alive. It was the beginning of many such meetings to come.

* * *

Uncommon Species Among Us

Chapter 1

Yuan/Yen Replaces Dollar As World Exchange Standard

2500/26ᵀᴴ Century – China, Australia, Japan, USA

News announcements around the world came as a surprise to no one. As early as the 24th century, industries and financial houses from New York's Wall Street to the Shanghai Stock Exchange and as well as "The City' and 'Docklands' in London's financial districts business was being done as if the prospective news was fait de complis.

> *'Regional wealth moves. Unusual alliances'.*
> *'Monetary Standard based on new Yuan/Yen unit value'.*
> *'Corporate world scrambles to adjust and recover without loss'.*

Classic inflation and ensuing depression had all but *sterilized* America's industrial community and as a result, the economic export markets of the USA. As a world monetary power, it had been a *dynasty* that had lasted almost 700 years, discounting Britain's overlapping economic strength up to the 19ᵗʰ century..

In all major events, altering the lives of human beings and their countries, *timing* was a factor for change in any status quo. In North American terms, it was probably ruination not unlike the cause of the fall of the Roman Empire.

As predicted by many, and planned for by others, the root cause of the decline of national economic power originated from policies originating *as a result of* the country's own economic and its foreign policies.

It was mitigated by those corporate power brokers, who tried with suicidal fervor, to counter the 'restrictive' cybernetics system. To their chagrin, the immovable and non-compromising Cyber 'Selection Committee'. It was not programmed to simply cave in to meet most of the 'traditional' ways and means of meeting American business objectives. The saving grace for the United States of America, if there *was* any, was that the Cybernation system still continued to work the way it was intended; Without fear. Without favor, neither exclusively for the weak nor for the powerful.

Even with the prospect of a change in the international monetary guard, non corporate America could find no fault with the embedded mandate of Cyber governance fairness. Multi-Nationals' manipulators and their public 'servants' on the inside, many of them who contributed to the decimation of American export markets and finances in '29, were now again condemned by their own kind for their ill-advised transgressions. But then, as in 1929, as a result of circumstances, so were 'innocents' who had always held a share in the wealth of a prodigious nation. They were once again reduced to financial disaster by another - but for them, *final* great depression.

Control of the earth's two most precious commodities had helped keep United States of America as an industrial monolith of power for endless millennia prior. One of these is directed associated with easily accessible *Potable water* and lots of it! The other is world perception of the USA powers as being untrustworthy in trade and failed allegiances to commitments made in good faith. No matter what, if the agreement turns sour for political money men... if the deal doesn't taste as sweet as it should have – spit it out!

If an powerful country in control of the worlds purse strings has accessible sweet water, within itself or with friendly neighboring countries, it almost guaranteed sustainable power either to beat off contenders or to sustain it's dominance. Just as if a country had access to most energy forms, either within its boundaries or available through bargained 'gratuities' or by *occupation* of other countries 'liquid' assets, it could forever prime its own industry, keeping the country economically sound. That meant that such an entity could still maintain its world currency standard with impunity from monetary challenge.

But now, in 2480's, China had all that. Just as her overwhelming armies over centuries past had marched into others lands, without impedance, nor question of purpose, so too did Chinese loyalties hold true with the forecast of wealth within this mighty Land. In China, there was there was no major runaway inflation and no monetary depression on the horizon thanks to it's vast trading edge and surplus population. China had the potable water. China had the technology and most of all, China always had a massive volume of human beings in their labor reserves. In this century and foreseeable centuries ahead, China is the embodment with the same kind of unbending diligence that prevailed during the Chen dynasty – of Great Walls, more than just Terra Cotta armies and advanced weaponry to suppress discontent..

In the twilight of America's diminishing energy and as a result it's less imposing economic power its adversity to environmental pressure it became vulnerable. The strength of American national sovereignty along with the advance of alternative energy and ingenuitive implements to advance themselves was not their exclusive conditioning club anymore. India turns out to be the mother of invention. Considering the advantages of USA achievements in space experience, this should have prepared them for the harnessing the earths magnetic energy canopy, but Euro alliances beat them to it. Granted, atmospheric Magnipod and SARs transportation became identified with the US industrial complex because they had the monetary resource ready and waiting to develop the advance the concept before anyone else. While the US was busy rearranging it's fossil fuels future, that energy form was on its way out practically and environmentally. Inefficient but still used as a resource, owing to unsold reserves and lowest ever, oil and gas costs are but a shadow of what it was a century ago. Oil and gas had now become the unthinkable - a virtual glut on the world market. In addition to the Middle east's still inexhaustible oil and gas, Alberta's Athabasca tar sands, off shore Hibernia fields, Scotland's and Scandinavia's North Sea holdings, Indonesia's Purdemena, Russia's expanse of northern oil fields and it's Kara Sea reserves all available for a song. The downside was still the high cost of pollution.

* * *

Meanwhile, China's and Russia's Hydro, dominating electric generating stations dominate the hydro market, notwithstanding wind mill, power, tidal power and still costly nuclear energy.

Then as if to ice the cake, China's running-to-capacity factories continue to turn out engines for hybrid engines and every other to propel transportation systems and industrial applications.

Ample energy was common to most global countries. So abundant was energy in general, that it was no longer the domain of anyone, or any conglomerate of over-endowed countries. So inter-tradable was energy that the universal cybernetic administration, (the 'Selection Committee') had few energy matters and/or disputes to deal with.

Of all the factors that contributed to the downfall of inflationary America's monetary world, its productive and trade superiority, there was one that exceeded all others. Besides China, certain *other* technically advancing, far east nations' with *a steady volume of people* and endless technical solutions to the need for labor had begun to make its 'move' toward regional prosperity.

These were the collective differences that superseded the once indisputable American industrial and trading strengths. As if that weren't enough to out weigh the Oriental side of the world with economic dominance, China and Japan's combined strengths enabled astounding amalgamation of the human and industrial resources of two former, multi-centuries-old enemies. With Cybernetics governing world matters, there were fewer reasons to mistrust each others intentions. They were merging land areas, technology and massive labor forces into one overpowering dynasty, creating a new trading power front unmatched in history. Strangely, these two regions actually became dependent on each other to sustain that economic power. By their very long traditional tenures on earth, they were of one common Oriental mindset. They were now geared to acquiring control in trade, finance and deliberately planned improvements for *improved standards* of living for their populations. Aspiring nations usually tend to populate themselves with aspiring countrymen.

After amalgamating their enterprising 'brothers' on the island of Formosa, China had production power but they found themselves short of a big league capitalistic mentality. Japan had that. So, on that basis alone, their regional merger of people power should have surprised no one as together, they took over world economic dominance. For almost four centuries now, China had been forecast by economists to be a singular world-dominant power one day. All they needed was external impetus. And they got that with the Japanese alliance. The merger was a 'natural'. There were so many *material* reasons for the two nations to join into one trading alliance, bound more by a combined long cultivated oriental attitude—more so than any European Common market could ever be. As always, Japan needed space and a rejuvenation of its productivity. China valued Japans intrinsic strength of never ending, proven superiority in technical advancement and its understanding of world trade, acquired from every historic trading period since the first sale of oriental 'snake' oil.

This unlikely, unexpected but almost inevitable union had occurred largely because of the *mindset* of Chinese and Japanese cultures to *accept and comprehend* the 'mechanics' of Cybernation. This lessened the second guessing of corporate decision making. Better than any population on earth, the long term oriental mentality more readily understood the absolute rule Cybernation. They conducted their economics and investments accordingly to that persuasion. The very character of their century's old self disciplines made it simple to allow them to more quickly institute *real* monetary change. They were born with intrinsic characteristics of honor and integrity . On that premise, they built powerful commercial empires.

In the occidental community of finance the slang term for a new unit of exchange became the *Chinapan dollar*. In trading houses from, pole to pole, it was respectfully registered on every world exchange, as the now revalued Yuan Yen. Monetary trading began, surprisingly at just slightly over unit cost, against the US dollar in the early stages of the merger. From that time on, all other global countries and unions measured the value of their own currency directly to the strength of the Yuan-Yen in *world* trade and supported by its monumental gold reserve. The bulk of other regions' volume of trade was mostly with oriental regions.

And rightfully – for after all, was it not Marco Polo who discovered that the orient created the most practical tradable commodities at the most attractive cost? Then, as if to account for its own accounting process, the inventive oriental had begat the world's first calculator – the abacus.

* * *

'Some things *never* change.'

So though Frenchman Bernard Simard No matter how governance changes or how technology alters the circumstances of human beings, the age old greed, guilt, lust, jealousy, hate, temptations and scheming mentalities never really evaporate. Just because the cornerstone of civilization changes; just because the over riding rule of free men and women changes, there are still many millions of people who cannot shake the injustices of centuries old hang ups.

Forty five year old dental specialist, Bernard Simard, was just such a person. This man was not caught up in monetary exchanges, worldly energy resources and big time finances. His concerns were much closer to home.

Today, he had his assistant cancel, what were left of today's late Friday afternoon appointments. Then he left his Paris office – maybe for the last time. On Monday, tax accountants would show up for their a audit and review. He lifted off his Hover/air vehicle, out of the Dental Clinic storage lot and headed south west...though for his mind being elsewhere, all he knew was, it could have been straight up. For a morbid moment or two, as he swooshed over a high river bridge, he thought of sharply turning the hover's mini control stick, letting his vehicle take him spinning to his death over one of these high level bridges. While that might jeopardize the proceeds of his life insurance policy benefiting 'his imaginary widow', Joanne, he thought, *who* cares? That kind of an 'accident' would certainly negate his guilt and his concerns for incrimination, if not incarceration.. All he really knew was that he couldn't face the legal implications and ensuing court action that would follow. He could see it now. Next week, after speculating his absence from the office, the air in the dental clinic would be *blue* as his 'partners' discover and chastise Simard for his scurrilous bookwork over the past year...."*Vous êtes un embezzeler!*"

Over the last few months, the building pressure on the normally garrulous dentist had been like a weighty yoke over the back of his neck. He needed a place, if not a someone, to isolate him from his fate. Before the big bang on Tuesday or Wednesday, when the auditors traced a suspicious bank entry or two, his impetuous, desperate need for bigger money would be discovered. He had to put big kilometers between him and that discovery.

Sorrowfully, he admitted that his wife Joanne would not turn out to be that someone he could confide in. In fact her *irresponsibility* with a Euro franc was one of the motivating factors for his creation of cash accounts for imaginary patients. He had once adored Joanne. His greatest fear had been the prospect of losing her, for lack of funds. So in the course of his agony, he might have soiled the good names of his *confreres*, not mention taking their share of revenue from them.

As it turned out, it was all for naught, as the Brits say. Joanne had been spreading her beauty – and her long lovely legs around a moneyed family friend. Secretly, Bernard had given him a name he could despise him with. 'Phancy Philippe' from Versailles. As Bernard drove near that city, he decided not to stop and call on Phancy Phil for a 'chat'. Though he thought about it momentarily, he knew any encounter of retribution with Philippe would be only a degrading dissatisfaction. Anyway his wife's lover was the last Frenchman he wanted to see right now.

He needed distance between the nation's capitol and where chance would take him like somewhere on the island of Sardinia, – or perhaps on a beach south of Naples – dead or alive before Tuesday.

Within the hour Bernard Simard found himself on the outskirts of Chartres on the banks of the Eure River. Finally he could see the twin steeples of Chartres Cathedral. No longer a house of prayer, it remains a museum for meditation. The pyramiding stone fascia at the base of the building exuded a peaceful invitation to all. Inside, it is known around the world for its antique 'stained glass' murals.

It beckoned him from miles ahead of the hovercraft thoroughfare. He argued with himself.

'So why would I want stop there? Cathedrals are no longer a comforting factor anymore. To whom would I pray. And for what? For sympathy and guidance?"

As the kilometers passed under him, it had begun to rain. As his power blowers rhythmically blew rain off his Hover's plexicab roof and sides, he mused.

Wasn't it less than 100 years ago, most churches, temples, synagogues, mosques – were converted to historic monuments? All over the world, these houses of prayer, sacrifice and religious ceremony, once rich, vibrant and active, were now silent memorials to unseen gods and spirits. The houses of Allah, God, His son, Jesus, the Buddha, Ra and the other icons of past religions, once offering coveted retreat and protection for flocks of sinners looking for cleansing. Though they still have meditation conclaves for those that need a place of peace and reverence, now they were really museums of solitude and halls by which to study the works of old masters in arts and literature. So, they really *were* retreats – space where one could go to get in touch with oneself.'

In the 'enlightenment' of his own analysis and a desire for a divergence that might calm his troubled mind, the Bernard Simard swung his hover hopper vehicle past the great front doors to a position just around the corner of the Cathedral. Suddenly, it just seemed appropriate that he should visit this world famous house of peace to atone *for* his guilt and disillusionment with himself....

"Pardon Moi, messier, M'excuser, Je—"

Long, wavy, brown/black hair burst out of a toque-capped head as she leaned down to his open Hover-cabin window, to come nose to nose with Bernard. The girl was eighteen or in her early twenties. Bernard slid his plexi window to a side position. She apologized for disturbing him as she proffered a rain spattered tourist map of the cathedral towards him. In his best attempt to image pictures to her, he questioned,

"May I be of assistance, mademoiselle?"

Furthering her inquiry, she projected,

"Oui! I wanted to go in to visit but I'm not sure whether I should use that entrance over there – it does not look like a it is a public entry – "

"Non. That is correct. If I read the sign on the door correctly, I believe, at one time, that entrance would have been used for the Church priory and now for it serves as a gateway to civic occasions only. The other entrance is right ahead, the one with the arching canopies above the doors. But wait – I'm going in myself. Let us both get in out of this rain. You *are* using TransPinder communication, non?"

He left his Hover seat, locked the slide-away entry and looked down at the little girl with the perfect teeth.

"Merci beaucoup, Monsieur"

"Vous êtes American, oui?" queried Bernard as they hurried along the tree lined walk, avoiding small puddles in the hollows of the cement tiles.

She wondered how to image the difference between American and Canadian. So she conjured a mental map picture of Quebec in Canada.

"French Canadian actually. I am using my upcoming spring break from University to go 'one on one' with the old masters – being held captive in the archives of this old church."

She laughed lightly at her own description of the museums attributes.

As they mounted the low steps of Chartres Cathedral, he faced her to transfer his thought.

"Umhmmm." Simard countered. "I *thought* I detected a very *unparisian* way of forming your images. Ah. Would you prefer that we project our messages in any easier way? My mind is a mess anyway so it should matter much either way for me.!"

Titling her toque back, she looked up at him with a twinkling eye and breathed another light laugh.

"Merci. Ah.. Thank you. I understand you, perfectly.!"

She's flirting with *this* old man, thought Bernard, to himself.

She detected his curiosity and pictured her next thought.

"I *know* you think I'm being forward. Alores, non. I just wanted to talk with you. You seemed serious and – and kind of low down in spirit – if you know what I mean."

Bernard joked as he motioned to his right and imaged,

"I'm going to have to stop thinking out loud,"

He walked a head a few steps, then pointed to his right.

"Ah. I see there's a quiet cappuccino café just off the vestibule. Unusual for a late Friday evening and no tourists. But it's just the thing. An elixir to warm the insides against a cold rain. Would you care to join me before you begin your tour and study?"

She hesitated.

He hurried to correct himself by hurriedly interrupting his own thoughts...

"Oh-Oh. What am I thinking? Here I am making presumptions – certainly *not* proposals. But then, how would *you* know that? I *am* sorry!"

"Not at all – and of course. I'd love some coffee and the chance to exchange more thoughts with you. And *my* name is Chantal – what's yours?"

* * *

Nine hours later, towards noon on Saturday, Bernard Simard was looking into Chantal's fluorescent-like green eyes looking up at him from the pillows of a cozy room in an Orleans hotel. He looked into her eyes, very close now. He imaged his thought to her.

"It is almost bizarre. Had I not met you, I think I would have been well on my way to the Italian border by now...not back to Paris as you have suggested... I might have been on my way to ending my life – should I not have been the coward I think I am!'

Chantal rolled her naked body towards him and propped herself up on her elbow thinking....control

"It seems to me that you might be wallowing in guilt over your misdemeanor, Bernard. Is it possible...that if you were to be back in Paris on Tuesday,.. Call a meeting of your partners, confess and apologize for your folly and lack of strength. And then if you offered to work there for half of your shared income until you repaid what you took – with interest. It seems to me that owners of any respectable medical clinic would prefer that kind of arrangement to one of embarrassing exposure. Would that not help you to *face the music*, so to speak?"

"How old did you transmit that you really were?" queried Simard. "You're much too wise for being so young."

The girl lay back, gazed at the ceiling and added to her previous observation

"I didn't even think about it – but as you *now* know – I *am* old enough! "

She laughed her tinker-bell sound again.

"And as for Joanne, you're in the control seat, especially if your wife doesn't know what you and I both know now. She might decide she can do without you, even if you were to forgive her for her cheating...You'd have to accept that as another cost of your naïve misdemeanor."

"It's *too* simple," thought Simard, 'but it might just work..."

He lay back and spoke again.

"This is so strange for me. I came this way to escape. If the Cathedral had been a real church as it used to be, I probably would have confessed to a priest to relieve my soul. But instead, all I needed was *a someone* to listen.

He pause for a few moments, kissed her nose and lay back.

"But now – what about *you*, petit Chantal?"

The girl sat up in the bed, letting the duvet fall below her small ivory breasts, and looked down at him.

"When I return to Quebec City and resume my studies at Laval, I'll be thinking of you, Bernard. You are a kind and moral man. You deserve better than you got for the trap you let yourself fall into. And I too have learned a meaningful lesson as a result of this meeting in Chartres – *and* here in Orlean. I believe our meeting has prepared me in some way to learn something of myself before going on to my sociology degree…"

Chantal paused.

"That is to mean – I now really believe that our best possibility for a heavy dose of inner strength is in what we think of our own character – and *maybe* too, it is *in the love of* others that really matters. That really *does* replace any self improvement lectures we might have followed *before* our liaison. Don't you think? I do. I think we have already shown ourselves that much, have we not, Mon amie?"

* * *

Normally, on a Summer Sunday, you would have to call in a marker from a prominent golf club board member to be able to jump queues for an acceptable tee off time. 10AM was a decent hour on the Great White Shark course – originally designed by and named after 'Auzzyland's' revered 21st century, golfing notable, Greg Norman. The golf resort was architected and sculpted on and between sand dunes and rock just off the Great Ocean Road, located midway between Brisbane and the community of Gold Coast.

On this day, four distinguished, middle aged 'businessmen' stood on the first tee of the Resort club, overlooking a surf hurtling itself on the rock promontories of shore rocks on the left of the first fairway. Lush and manicured jungle grass fairways on the right were bordered by Queensland's native Moolah shrubbery, native to that area.

Strangely, there were neither line ups behind them nor golfers ahead, to have to play through. Where had they all gone? The foursome all had the same thought. Had an uncertain, economic, world-wide downturn curtailed even the numbers of duffers on the links of the world?

On the other hand, the reason for lack of other players on the course that day and every other day could have been that the absence of oral dialogue detracted from the sociality of the game. In the previous days ambience of pleasure golf, kibitzing, chatter and side conversations made a golf date the fun it was supposed to be. Not so now. Now there was no need to 'shushed' by galactic gas, golf had been a game where side conversation carried on, without the necessity of having to face your fellow golfers to talk to them. Now, in order to be understood by image reading even with the blessing of TransPinders, one had to direct ones eyes and face to a fellow conversationalist.

Not so long ago, dialogue between foursomes was always possible as long as each was within hollering distance of the other. Now, in the game of 'non-verbalized' golf, image dialogue was hard to get started unless *all* participants agreed to activate their Jones TransPinders. Not all image creating devices were activated in today's foursome. Superseding all else, the singular objective for most *avid* golfers now, was to concentrate on beating one's handicaps. Trying to concentrate on image dialogue with others for the sake of mannerly conversation was taxing for those in a competitive but traditionally fun and relaxing recreational environment.

Unlike earlier times, verbal exchange on other matters – like business – was almost secondary. So without the obligations of forced banter, one often 'chatted' to another player, *only* while planning a strategy with his turn for a next shot or putt. That's why, on one of the later holes of the first nine they leaned on their clubs waiting for the only other foursome on the course to play the seventh green.

CEO and managing director of Australia's Treasure Beach Resort chain, Charles P. Turkevey turned to face American Air force General, Mitchell Patrick, in the expectation of opening a brief remark or two with the amiable general.

"Another two birdies like you had out of the first six holes, Mitch - and the rest of us are going to have to concede you the winner of the free lunch today."

"Umm, well. I'm afraid that's not atypical of my game. Those putts were as surprising to me as they were to you guys, Charlie."

293

The General snickered at what he considered was an 'understatement' of his *own* lack of expertise, before he selected a wood driver for the next tee.

"I'm not as flushed with skill as I am with luck right now. So – hold on to your lunch money!"

Turkevey, the resort CEO spread his arms towards the seemingly empty fairways.

"You know Mitch, with so *few* people out here on the course today, I'm hard pressed to believe that there are insufficient paupers left with enough gambling money to play a simple round of golf. Mind you, I can see it in our own business. Our second quarter was the proverbial disaster. I suppose I'm still trying to reconcile the events of the last couple of six months. Most of the world, including your country, has had to recoup their resources to go forward from here...And if anyone had ever predicted to me that *Japan* would merge an economic trade pact with *China*, of all countries, just to strengthen their *joint* claim to resetting world monetary standards, – oops – I'm up."

Turkevey strode to the tee. He checked the wind direction and mumbled unintelligibly, to himself.

'Humph! Par 4, Two hundred and twenty five yards straight away. Time to work out my big trusty ole' wood. This may be the break I need...'

After his shot, the resort entrepreneur came back to continue his telepathic tete et' tete with Mitchell Patrick.

"Stayed out of the right side rough, that's the good news – 65, 60 yards to the green... that's the bad, – but that drive shouldn't hurt my handicap. Maybe."

When the General went to play his second shot on the edge of the green, ex-politician John Benson-Reynar, once a Queensland Councilman sidled up to Turkevey.

"Hey Charlie..."

Motioning by tapping the back of his own neck with one hand, touching Charles Turkevey's shoulder with the other, he caught the resort owner's attention. He looked back at Benson-Reynar, while returning his wood to his bag. He put this forefinger to the back of his neck to adjust his injected TransPinder. Then nodded.

"If you're tuned in now Charlie, I've got some news that you'll want to receive. Only take a couple of minutes. It's new and it comes with the most credibility you can *ever* get out of an External Affairs bureaucracy."

When he did so, the ex-politician continued.

"Your corporate offices. They're still in the Henley Beach Towers property, aren't they Charlie? I've going to be up that way next week. If you had some time, I've got some interesting *inside* speculation out of the Beijing Tourist Conglomerate. You've probably heard the rumors via the grape vine. But it can now be confirmed.

John looked around quickly to determine how much he could relate before either of the other two golfers came up to them. He went on.

"Apparently the Beijing bunch are putting in a string of resort towers into every holiday corner of AusZealand opening within the next three years. They've got the inside track to sign the big wholesale travel agency shooters. Expecting an avalanche of Asian tourists

And, as you'd figure, there's more than a smidgen of Nipponese funding in that project. Be back in a minute."

At the green, he was being beckoned by Norio Sokoyama. John was the away shot to putt. Generally 'speaking,' it should have been the general's away ball next but like Mitch thought as he walked over to stroke... "Who's counting?"

After Benson-Reynar putted out, he switched on his TransPinder and came over to Charles again, who had transmitted his reply to John's earlier newsy information. Now Charlie and John walked over to pick up their golf bags. They busied themselves readying their carts for the walk to the eighth tee. But Charlie turned to face Benson-Reynar, adjusted his TransPinder and directed the image directly to him only...

"Better get your secretary to call mine for a time that fits *my* schedule and *your* visit to Henley Beach. I should be there all week. John, if *we're* going to play 'who's got Park Place?' along side that Asian crowd, and *still* try to beat their brains out before they slit *our* throats on expanding resort developments, we better have our Peking ducks in order. In other words, we're going to have to use all the espionage data we can get, including yours. Without it – to misuse a metaphor - we'll get our pin feathers burned. Trust it'll be ok with you to have a few, very trustworthy Hong Kong ringers in for tea on that day as well... and speaking of that..."

They passed by Mitch and Norio as the two stood at the next tee's ball washer. Mitch was frantically turning the handle on a ball in the meter like machine.

John cranked his arm in a pantomimed way and transmitted a cheery,

"You honestly think a cleaner ball will make that big a difference on this next whole, General?"

Through his TransPinder, the general came back with,

"Can't hurt. But it's cheaper than opening up a new Birdseye number 2."

Not to be outdone in jocularity, Charles addressed his thought to the Japanese Market Broker.

"And you... *Mister* Norio Sokoyama."

Turkevey put on his usual teasing but most disarming smile. He conveyed...

"From the looks of that eagle, on that 5th, you're the *real* competition on the course today... Mind you, one would have to discount that double bogie you blew – the par 4 sixth, wasn't it?,"

Yokoyama sauntered over to them, smiled, bowed slightly, then shrugged, nodded to his two friends and imaged his retort.

"Thank you, Charles. Remember the humble have their *off* days too - just like their peers."

As they all walked in single file over the creek bridge to the 8th tee, John Benson-Reynar again moved up behind his resort-CEO friend and messaged,

"Charlie, I *can't* compromise my associate's departmental standing at our meeting next week, So *please* – no regional administrators in on this right now – or later. Ok? It's the only way I can be of *any* value to *my best client* – you! Dig?"

Turkevey nodded, and then touched his neck to turn off his TransPinder, until the 19th hole...if not longer!

* * *

Chapter 2

Sea Sphere As Seen From Stratosphere

3129/32ND CENTURY / SKAGERRAK SEA

As IT HAD, every day since creation, today's sun poured forth its glorious radiance over half our green and blue earth...but even in such brilliance while aboard an outbound space vehicle, the naked eye is virtually useless to anyone hoping to pick out supposedly recognizable landmarks from the upper reaches of mesospheric and thermosphere layers. However, earth's familiar shaped peninsulas and islands from stratosphere and upper troposphere altitudes could easily be identified from as far up as 48 km above the North Atlantic. Such was the challenge to Magnipod passengers to recognize landscape configurations as they arched the globe in intercontinental trajectories at 8.2 thousand km per hour.

NorAmeric resident, 54 year old Anna Wyzacowski was one of those travelers. She lay back, in her Magnipod's individual lounge chair. It articulated with in the shell of her individual magnipod. The low trajectory space pod was shaped very much like a donut with a disproportionately larger hole in the middle and a clear bubble canopy over that. As she sipped her automated fruit juice serving, she reveled in climatic comfort; an air-conditioned space nest.

Magnipod passenger Anna studied the pocket's picture literature. All about the very craft in which she rode. This 'inner' space vehicle, a *Magnipod*, was so called for the energy by which it was powered. Electromagnetic waves of charged 'particles' a part of the plasmic content of the ionosphere was the unseen force, 50 to 100 km above. Pictures of the 'Pod were shown being sanitized and cleaned after each use,. It showed the central control center and graphic s of the method by which the craft operated on it's magnetic route. It extolled it's own air-conditioned comfort. It's protection from suns rays, the compartments below it's seating for luggage and animals, it's graphicized directions for waste disposal and the simple control in which the craft is made safe and comfortable by it's riders.

Thanks to the work she was in, she understood some of what was explained in the pamphlet. Candidly, she admitted to herself, ' I really didn't care much one way or the other, as long as the magnetism of the science carries me on the shortest distance between-two-points in a safe and silent, comfortable conveyance in any climatic condition' Her 70-minute Magnipod glide-ride originated right from her street address home in Denver. Destination – a visit with former neighbors, now living in the bountiful Krakow region of southern Poland. She was transported along a layer of the stratosphere by a magnetism known as 'rainbow arching'. According to the company's pictorial promotion, automated ground control stations around the world, commanded and monitored both flight and ground movement of hundreds of thousands of magnipod arcing around the planet, every minute of every day.

Wyzacowski's travel agent was used to reassuring her *new* high fliers in Magnipods that just because there is no visible engine doesn't mean a lack of power.

"In fact," she imaged, "Your Magnipod is powered by the greatest natural force on earth. Sort of like the polar magnetism that runs vertically, north-south. Back a century or two ago, when new energy was hard to come by, man harnessed that magnetism from an invisible layer, high up above our atmosphere. Result? You arch over the earth, direct to Krakow in luxury and in something less than three hours. Not bad, right Mrs. Wyzacowski?"

So formidable is the transport system that it defies an most humans understanding of its very dimension. By way of introduction to novice Magnipod controllers, recruits are shown a holograph model of a huge ball representing the earth. It sits on the middle of the playing field of a football stadium People are shown standing on a scaffold, over top of the ball. They are then instructed to toss handfuls of provided clear-plastic dust-like particles at the earth painted ball. At the same time, lights dim. Controlled jets of air are turned on, surrounding the model. Each spec of plastic dust is shown as millions of layered lights speed around the lobe,. This demonstration shows the volume of vehicle traffic all over the earth at any given time. This suggests that literally billions of Magnipods are like clouds of *darting fire-flies* on their way to somewhere else.

Frightening Magnipod passengers is no way to run a business so they're not told about a *non-event*. Collision with even a speck of space debris traveling at thousands of miles per hour would drive right through any craft like a NASA Shuttle, a space station, research, GPS or broadcast satellite or a traveling magnetic-powered vehicle. However such falling debris is burned up many miles before the rainbow arc is reached. Magnipods also possesses a radar-like component to detect incoming any and every misdirected objects in the path of a Magnipod. The craft *automatically speeds up or slows* to enables a Magnipod to avoid *any* such collision of *any* kind.

* * *

When Anna was diagnosed with a regressive visional impairment two year earlier, restricting the middle aged woman to only minimal sight, at best, this kind of journey, from a scenic standpoint would have been a wasted trip.

As it was, she had been faced with having to temporarily give up her precision lab work in Denver. In order to carry on the work, corrective surgery of one kind or another would have had to be performed. As far as she was concerned, the whole issue related to her job assignments. She enjoyed her role in the company's microbiology division. Such work satisfied her inherent curiosity; her ongoing quest to explore and succeed at whatever life put in front of her. And besides, with no offspring on whom she could rely on for financial support, she needed the income that her position provided. But healthy eyes were mandatory. The alternative – forced retirement. The other alternative was telescopic eyecam implantation. Notoriously cost prohibitive.

She reasoned that a telescopic implantation procedure, more readily accessible to a well-heeled citizen, would never have been affordable, even out of *her* above average earnings.

At 54 years of age, it was obvious that no disability peon-pension was going keep her clear of a welfare existence. And since she not was part of the bureaucratic establishment, she would be initially categorized as non eligible to specialized surgery under the state-paid plan/ Eye cam surgery is a treatment, traditionally provided to essential federal security personnel, laboratory specialists, or law enforcement investigatory personnel. Such governmental largesse is denied the common, so called working class Americans in the private sector.

But as Wyzacowski was to learn, there *was* always a way.

At a coffee break in the office cafeteria, she expressed her disappointment to a workplace colleague in her company's legal department. On his direction, she had sought special concession through their employer's general health insurance plan for surgical solution for her diminishing sight. They in turn made an official National Securities application, based on Anna Wyzacowski long employment tenure and very detailed work experience on the corporation's behalf. They determined that Anna's physical vision disease had advanced past the point of normal corrective lens procedures.

However, her company's invaluable work experience *was* shown to be directly related to high precision, *governmental* projects. Therefore, according to legal interpretation, this performance value *did* in fact; qualify her for a mini-chip, eye camera implantation. The company's claims application to medical and insurance authorities was approved. Within eleven days of the approved surgical installation, Anna Wyzacowski returned to her workstation with a new outlook on life, carrying on her microscopic lab work.

Now here she was, relaxing in the comfort of her Magnipod's deep cushioned, loungette, a full year after the eyecam implantation procedure. As though to reassure herself of her good fortune, she reached a hand toward the eyecam control just inside her hairline at the temple to enjoy the scenic earth below. With finger pressure, she focused and adjusted the eyecam magnification to whatever degree of depth she preferred.

She remembered that while in the brief rehab period that followed optical surgery; her home care attendant had informed her that only one out of two hundred *thousand* people in the nation qualified for telescopic eyecam. Anna had been told that out of necessity to function at their job, most had opted for such implants.

She mused…

'By law, every one of us antiques over fifty *should* be entitled to this gift of renewed vision.' Thus, it was from the meditating confines of her Magnipod, riding a sub orbital polar route to Krakow, Anna gazed with wonder at the deep, almost black and deep purple of the North Atlantic. She spotted only a few bugs (actually sea going liners) trailing stands of white wakes, moving among an iceberg-strewn ocean.

'Ah yes. And that must be Iceland.'

Now, Anna thought about Vladimir, her husband. Had he lived to travel with her, he too would have marveled at the experience. Had she possessed a functioning vocal chords, she would have said aloud excitedly, 'How I wish you could see this side of the icy earth", now she throated affectionately. "I don't care what the Selectronics Committee says…God is still with us…I still believe *you* can see from wherever *you* are, Ljubljana. And look upward, Vlado! How black the sky – not even a star!"

Minute detail like the north coasts of the Scottish counties of BriScotIre slid by. And beyond, more, almost transparent ice.

Then she spotted changing color down there where it seemed so out of place. Suddenly it occurred to her, 'Wait…My! That's odd.'

Her eyecam was still functioning. She magnified its power and continued her self muse . . .

Down there... just below that upcoming, bottom landmass – Norway? A beacon of changing, flashing multi colors. It seemed to be coming from what could be an orb of some kind. It was so strange. Red. Orange. Then yellow. Crabapple green! Where no such color ought to be – Amid the ice pan?

'Vlado – that tiny circle in the water. See? It's changing colors like a –" ... Again, Anna touched her temple to enlarge the eyecam image. "Bright! Almost translucent... like a child's glass marble..."

Enlarged, she could now see that the object was, in fact, a gleaming, multicolored *ball!* Enlarging her eyecam magnification to its maximum optical strength, Mrs. Wyzacowski, managed to discern the sea borne object in more detail. "Colored streaks of constantly changing lines of color across the face - almost like one of those chameleon lizards..."

At a touch of the finger, the eyecam's identifying graphics super-imposed a text explanation of the sighting. It gave GPS location, charted course, shape, speed, and other estimated particulars, such as distance to target, source material, rate of movement, estimated dimensions – most of which was designated, 'unknown.'

And then the spectacle was gone... passed behind her pod and out of sight.

Anna wondered. So that her Krakow friends could also enjoy the adventure, should she trans-record her eyecam vision of the sea surface phenomenon for her old friends in Krakow? No. She decided that it would serve no purpose. Besides, that might raise questions for which she had no answers. Another old person's hallucination.

* * *

Wyzacowki's was one of hundreds of Magnipods enroute over that locale. In a northwesterly direction from Korea, on a similar stratospheric arc, 21 km over the pole, a four person 'pod' carried three KorAsian athletes, competitors to the EuroSwimRegatta. All three occupied the same magnipod, arc-set to land them at the famous Rotterdam SwimGym for the world swim competitions in NetherEuro. (Formerly Netherlands). Five hundred meter national champion, Jo Hwan Kim of Inch'On, KorAsia, levered his articulated glide lounge chair to acquire a better view the Norwegian seascape below. The pod's arcing descent pattern, now at 13 KM altitude, started just off the tip of Euro Scandia, (formerly three countries of Scandinavia). Centuries ago, that area of tundra and icy mountains to the north east of them was once known as Norway's TeleMarke. Never before had young Jo been so grateful for the eyecam implantation provided for him by his grandfather, industrialist and manufacturer of the famous RockRacer vehicle, winner on most NASWHEEL circuits around the Americas. Kim's distant view of Artic grandeur was more fascinating to him than indulging in the juvenile antics of his two other swim team members aboard the same Magnipod.

Laughing and clowning around in boisterous fashion, the Park brothers teased Jo. With the aid of ID ('image dialogue') and TransPinder, they taunted him with their images – that he would be a *real* KorAsian hero if they were able to somehow ditch him in those icy sea fields in North Sea waters.

"Hey, Jo Kim...If you were down there competing in the hundred meters, you could become the world's first hypothermia champion – posthumously, of course!"

While they breath-chortled with glee at their own humor, Jo Hwan Kim shrugged. Compared to what he was experiencing through the downward viewing portal, his companions' juvenile behavior was easily ignorable. He had trained his eyecam on the shards of ice below the arching pod, now directly over a longitude of E007 degrees, 31 minutes according to his eye cam's superimposed text graphic. Jo Kim touched his temple again. What had at first appeared to be a reddish oil-drilling platform was not. He could now just make out its circular form; a ball-like object. To be sure that the glistening, multi colored orb he saw was neither a strangely shaped ship - nor any such marine vehicle; again, he quickly touched his hand to his temple for a better close up.

Mouth open and eyes agog, he realized he was observing something that was unexplainable. It was not a figment, after all. To be sure, he touched his temple mechanism again to magnify his eyecam on an even tighter view of the object. Almond eyes bright with excitement, he beckoned to his companions. He wanted them to try to see what he had spotted. One Park brother also had an eyecam implant. He too gasped aloud at the amplified sight. The other swim competitor could not spot the object even though the pod was dropping its altitude in preparation for arrival at destination. This object was not to be identified at these elevations for not even the sharpest naked eye would be able to define the object of Jo's attention. Had one been able to do so, the object would have been described as -transparent red, black, green and yellow lines seemed to move, criss-crossing the sphere as it rolled among the bergs and pans of ice floes. Strands of vivid glistening black and colored lines streaked over the object. Those lights were similar to the commercial electronic signage they saw recently in the streets of central Seoul. Both boys would later describe it as a ball with 'moving' color bands. Jo Hwan Kim concluded this was no gigantic buoy, ship or any other known vehicle and certainly no animal known to man. But whatever it was – who could every transmit to others what they were not sure they'd seen? It seemed it would be more than they could ever image. It disappeared as their pod decelerated on it's descent towards their pod-port destination into Rotterdam's AmphiSports Arena.

* * *

How many of the many thousands of pod travelers, had occasion to look down at the western end of the Skagerrak Strait to observe a sphere of glistening ball of 'yarn,' where nothing of it's kind has any reason to be?

'Not many, I'll warrant,' thought D'Arcy Boulder. As Dean of AgriGenetic Research and Biosciences at Alaska's University at Anchorage, he was also invited as a keynote speaker to deliver his published paper on Woodland Moss Derivatives. A Podiatry Treatment; Benefiting Tribal Populations In The Southern Hemisphere. Further recognizing his work in native plant sciences, his presence would be welcomed as a head table guest at the AgriFloraFarmExpo show Opening dinner and convention in Alexandria, AfriGyptia. (Formerly Egypt). And just to make his trip worthwhile, he would serve as an adjudicator of exotic entries in south East Asian fauna. He was, after all, a recognized Global Master of most of the world's native Plants.

Now as his Magnipod crossed the 'Med' on descent into northern Africa's principal region of AfriGyptia, Boulder ceded that, '... many would not think to record a sighting of an unusual sea orb, as he had. Another 'professorly' habit!'

He wondered what action he should take first on landing. Like the end of a midway ride, his single passenger Magnipod would glide onto its destination platform at El Iskandariya, (ancient city of Alexandria) north of El Quhir on the Norwest edge of the Nile Delta. This year's historic site for AfriGyptia's six hundred and twenty second AgriFloraFarmExpo was a beautiful resort and historic seaport on the southern shores of the Mediterranean. On debarking his Magnipod's exit tube in the pod chutes taxi area, positioned beside the convention hall and lodge, Dean Boulder spotted an Expo Greeter, checking plant bins being unloading from freight and baggage pod compartments. Approaching the Porter, D'Arcy smiled, touched his TransPinder while, mouthing and tonguing his question to aid in his mind expression.

"I have an important report of an alien object at sea. I strongly advise that it should be reported immediately to some official here for follow-up investigation. Please direct me to such a person."

The porter lifted his head, touched his TransPinder and imaged his response. "Ah Jahsah - there are others reporting that very same thing. I am instructed to send you to passenger debriefing hall in the Hitachi Port Lodge's electronics gallery."

The porter pointed to an escalator.

"Advise you go there first. Take moving ramp, number G twelve, sah. Step off at main gate. Go through arched entrance to right - then down stairs, left to room, Sub 601"

All in all, 101 separate Magnipod passengers in the electronic lab room of the MagniPodPort Lodge, testified to the existence of some kind of foreign object at the west end of the Skagerrak Strait southwest of Norway's town of Kristiansen. The graphic location was noted as being Lat.N57°58 minute and 07°95 minutes E. longitude. Again, thanks to camera implants, 73 travelers could support their sighting of a colorful, luminous 'glassy', ball-like thing, rolling about in the choppy northern ocean. 28 travelers and crews provided eyecam recordings with data graphics over. All this was electronically catalogued and categorized by eyecam serial number to establish source credence. It was then dispatched to each director of the Interplanetary Transport Safety Commission. Researchers and curators at the Hall Of Sciences precinct at Reykjavik were copied.

Chapter 3

Northern Ice Cap On Fire

2919/30ᵀᴴ Century/ Russia, Manila, Norse Countries.

TECTONIC TRANSFORM FAULTS can cause massive undersurface rock slabs and plates to separate. They yawn open as they grind past each other. Unlike subduction explosions, transform faults are frequently slow to develop. These massive 'zipper' lines are not supposed to create sudden and instant havoc. But *this* one did...mainly because; the ice crusted top part of the world was coming undone!

From the first swaying underfoot to the last bone rattling aftershock – five days, seven and one half terrifying hours later, this quake's opening arpeggio began at 18:20 hours Moscow time. The first bump and rumble was modulated to an escalating roar that was the ominous predecessor for what was to come – *cataclysmic decimation!*

It descended on Northern Euro nations and Asia-Russia proper within 4.16 minutes to 5.52 of the first of the earth's movement. This volatility moved vast sections of sea floor to produce ice and water torrents from the tip of Norway to Svalbard and Franz Josef Island groups along the 80ᵗʰ latitude to the Siberian no-man's-land of eastern Russia.

And though unknown at the time, there was something else more frightening about this plate separation in the earth's crust. Something that cartographers and seismologists could never have guessed existed, let alone predicted. Something else had happened, much deeper down, below the Ridge plates themselves.

A seduction zone between 200 and 500 kilometers *beneath* the ridge was triggering and inducing separation along 4000 km, of Nansen Ridge sub Arctic plates. This unusual two on one upheaval initiated the earth's most violent eruption since planetary cooling. *Two* tectonic monsters woke up. The crevasse opened up. Core lava was flooded in from below and affecting an already sizzling sea from above. The eruptions were about to begin.

Thousands of hectares of land mass as far as 100 kilometers inland from the northern coastlines along the Barents Sea, were ripped apart. Simultaneously, east of Greenland, islands started to disappear.

The first shudders started where the top end of the Knipovitch Ridge turned east to become the Nansen Ridge. It is here that the quake's epicenter was initially recorded to be.

Displacement of hundreds of square kilometers of sea floor caused an immediate and immense tidal pool, some 200 to 500 kilometers across, spreading out from there. It originated with an upwelling of water, creating a heightened ocean surface of almost 200 meters (600+ ft) above mean tide levels. In less than 30 to 40 minutes, an ocean of summer ice and water reached oil and gas sea platforms half way to the shoreline of mainland Russia.

On shore 'villages,' undisturbed for centuries but which had become industrial petroleum centers From there surface petroleum ships had for hundreds of years, been drilling and milking the Kara Sea bottom of its hydro carbon resources to feed the vast oil reserves of the country and the refineries of it's trading partners. Even though oil production had slowed considerably over the last two or three centuries, hundreds of roughnecks and ships crew, aboard producing well head platforms were shaken like dust from a mop, from the torn hulls of their vessels to perish in scant seconds.

Those drilling ships with their four poster hulls, closest to the Nansen Ridge were overwhelmed, crushed by a banshee sounding, velocity of wind and waves and never knew what caused the last few second of their lives. Many additional lives were about to cease, mercifully, without their brains ever knowing what made them obvlivious. Riggers and drill pushes alike died at their job positions; others were pulverized and drowned in their bunks. Many hundreds of others had been in the process of eating supper in the petroleum ship's messes.

Rings of waves lifted off the ocean's surface, rolling out at over 1000 km per hour to engulf everything in an irrevocable inland sea. The screams of wave and wind preceded its arrival on land. Every living creature within its reach were stupefied and petrified them in their tracks. The enormity of ultimate chaos to come was beyond their comprehension... even when it became a reality.

And come it did.

The crash and crush of a terminating shore line became extraneous before the power of natural disaster. A high waved tsunami per se, did not occur but inland for over 100 kilometers in many zones, the surface became quickly inundated by rushing, flooding sea ice 50 meter deep and topped by massive mesa-like ice growlers.

Dumbfounding to those experiencing their last nanoseconds seconds of life, they were brief witnesses to their shelters disappearing around them. Loved ones vanished; entire communities were obliterated. Some felt the momentary but excruciating pain of limbs torn away and human torsos impaled on the shards of their own shattering structures... waiting for the next blink of their astonished eyes before nothingness enfolded them. All man-made habitats in all coastal settlements and some inland communities were ground into a muddy mix of flesh and decimated particles of wreckage.

To the open ground areas, south and east, only remaining sawdust of millions of hectares of pulverized forests gave irrefutable evidence to the horrific sub surface power of an unspeakable quake. In a most unexpected way, a large section of the planet was being ripped apart to be reformed.

A night and a day passed before the turmoil of surging lava flow, underneath the sea had lessoned, only the residual effects of howling wind and 10 meter troughs brought on an eerie calm over its now choppy surface. Later, seismologists would confirm that the unseen, shock waves would have been responsible for more loss of life – multi-thousand times greater than the most explosive nuclear mishap ever. In the wake of assaulting waves and wreckage, the last inhabitants inside 120 kilometers of what once was coastline south of the Kara Sea and beyond had been pounded into new shapes somewhat like what a smithy does when he reshapes his metals.

Only a fraction of the destruction was ever seen by victims who did not perish. Still, they *did* see the annihilation of a cherished land that they had always thought would remain forever unchanged.

* * *

It was early fall and darkening evenings. Just after 15:00 and 16;00 hours, Friday, Sept 12[th,] office workers in offices were on the verge of leaving their counters, desks, warehouse activities. They were eager to get an early Friday night start to the holiday weekend. In the Lapp countries, Norway, Finland and Sweden, as well as the endless northwestern coast of Russia family suppers were already on the table. Preparations for the supper hour had started for many communities in the Pechora River sector to the east.

In the northern eastern reaches of Russia, in the still relatively unpopulated Khredebet Orulgan mountain ranges and tundra terrained, Inderka River basin area, it was late evening. Fishermen there were still readying their fleets of vessels for coming winter storage, though some fisheries boats were gearing their holds for a last seasonal run or two through rapidly accumulating ice pans.

Less than one hundred miles inland of the Pechorskya Guba (Bay) extending into the Pechora River, was the region's city of Nar'yan Mar, one of Russia's long time oil/gas, nerve centers. It was also a warehousing supply depot for the northeast oil port of Varandey and the central Kostrama region's main petroleum equipment supply control, at the easternmost railhead and air cargo depot at the city of Nefteyugansk to the south east. Off shore drilling and exploration companies with drilling platforms and producing wells located mainly in the Kara Sea were dependent on this source for everything from Hot House Cabbages to Oil Well pipe wrap and valve stems.

In the Sibirskaya Oil and Gas office building, three, blue-coveralled custodians, armed with janitorial equipment ambled off the elevator on the third floor. They proceeded to the main executive reception room to begin their nightly cleaning, even though they had had the option of doing their janitorial assignments anytime on the long weekend.

"I almost didn't come in tonight" clicked Leonid to his working partners, Sylva and Yuri. All had TransPinders which allowed them some latitude for interpretation.

"If I ever drink Vodka-Slivovitz shooters again, like I did after our shift last night, you can sign me up for a cell in the nearest asylum. This hangover will one take me at least a month to recover. Look. My hands are shaking... and my head is about to –"

That was the last complaint Leonid ever tried to express and the last image Sylva and Yuri would have had time to translate. The floor beneath them all disappeared. The rumbling roar preceded by only milliseconds, the evaporation of walls that crunched in over them. That cleaning team along with hundreds of other workers in hundreds of other office buildings in Nar'yan Mar, was crushed and buried in mountains of ruin. Then as if to hide the desecration, black sea water and broken ice rolled in. Curiously, no towering tsunami was forthcoming. Just fast running rapids moving up at over half a meter, every two or three minutes. Earlier, initial sideways tremors now turned to violent shaking and loud thunderous detonations. These horrific canon-like blasting and roar of reverberating shock waves were audio backgrounds to an insane abstraction. A great chunk of the world was being destroyed by its own debris. Of the bombarding colophony of sounds, one sound would *not* be heard. To a 21st century citizen it would have been unreal— no human screams – an absence of verbal terror, borne of human trauma. No yelling. Long stifled voice boxes could not add to the frenzied terror of the upheaval's resident victims. Screeching sound waves passed like a wind storm; heard long after they fled distantly far away to the northeast; some living people took this as an indication that the immediate disaster was past.

Wrong.

Next came the deafening sounds of buildings, bridges, marinas, rail yards, roads and structural towers being demolished by rushing waves as a flood of icy water blanketed the remnants of crushed cement and steel. Scored like a crescendo of a tuneless symphony's brass and tympani sections, the skreaking sound of mountainous ice bergs pushing inland by rushing ocean currants; cracking off their towering mirrored slabs, to crash into flooding seawater and snow covered hillsides. Tundra country side turned to mush. A mud sea for as far an eye could see – what eyes there were left to see.

Thereafter, from time to time, deep rumblings and trembling underfoot came with dizzying aftershocks, breaking the otherwise graveyard stillness of a crumpled city or village. Oddly, in retrospect of events past, such vibrations might have been that of gently shifting though stomach wrenching earth movements. In actual fact, some jolting aftershocks had to be in the 4 to 5 point plus range, Richter scale readings, that in themselves, would have been considered major quakes. But there was little else here to crush.

* * *

Over in Noril'sk city, west of the Urals, every bureaucrat in government buildings there – the local 'mini-duma' of the Sredne region was becoming catatonic. In the seismographic, astrological and geophysical sections, staff members' panic was rampant, particularly in the seismic wing where they were privy to more quake information than others in other departments. Even so, they too, scurried from desk to desk, directionless, seeking calmer comfort from senior workers. Posted to monitor emitting graphics of seismic activity, the night duty staff of eleven people would have been screaming their anguish, their fright, their panic. But no thanks to a previous voice box disaster, 600 years ago, genetic changes from "Dusty Gas" left them with only guttural grunts and squawks, emitted from open mouths.

If they and the rest of the complex had had any advance inking or alarm of the devastation to come, they would probably have been more resigned to an impending fate. As it was, this government building has been placed strategically near the top of a foothill hill so that in normal circumstances, sea, land and sky's reactive seismic conditions could be recorded and reports transmitted with clarity and dispatch. So it was that this night staff would weather this first encounter with a quake of never before experienced ferocity.

Gennady, the night supervisor, staggered against the sway of the floor beneath him. At his monitor station, he did a cursory study of seismographs and satellite photo imagery, to acquire a glimpse but incomplete evaluation of what had and was *still* happening. After which, he reached for his communications equipment, to interconnect the Stations broadcast amplifier and translator with the seismologist's online *TransPinder* imaging.

He made contact with his superiors in Moskva using the cell alert so common in all telephone exchanges.

"Sir, this is Gennady Kharlamov, night shift supervisor at Noril'sk!"

"Добрый вечер (Dubro Večer – good evening) Mockba Geographies Section, Director of Operations here"

Night supervisor Kharlmov began his report

"Here's what we read so far. It's the Nansen Ridge plate, sir. Interpreting our data base, it appears that the northern plate gave way. The South side plate shifted up abruptly, sir. As near as we can decipher...for whatever reason it rose upwards of 27 meters (88.5 feet) towards the North plate, seemingly to fill the gap between the two plates *at that particular fracture* zone point. It was met with a massive upward flow of lava that suddenly created a release point in the Mantle. I concede, sir that in our scientific zeal to determine the event as it occurred, we are making some uneducated guesses."

The Moscow director interjected, "Gennady, scientists do not make uneducated guesses. But given the same readings here, we tend to agree with you. What else?"

"One thing we do strongly believe, sir is that we have experienced movement in a transform fault, precipitating an active seduction zone collision underneath the upper plates. I'm not sure if that's possible sir, but – "

Again the Geological director overlaps Gennady's next thought.

Doctor Kharlamov, are you suggesting the existence of *two* cracks in the earths crust at the very same point? We have no data on that!"

"I'm not all that surprised Respected Director."

The Noril'sk seismologist gave some speculative reasons as to why two layers did not show active on any previous research on the Nansen Ridge fault.

He ended his report with an assessment of conditions.

"There were no *prior* indications of *any* tectonic activity sir. And no time to sound warnings. Nothing. You probably have the same readings but from our initial 12.7 Richter readings, taken at northernmost end of the Knipovich Ridge on the northwest edge of Greenland's continental shelf. With such extremely high and unusual reading sir, it now *seems possible* there were *two minor eruptions* creating *two very different* Quakes at almost the same time. But then – again – Twelve minutes, thirty four seconds *after* the Knipovich movement, there was yet another follow-up rupture along the Nansen fault line. *This*, we consider to be the *actual*, but delayed, epicenter, 800 km further along the ridge to the east. If our graph interpretations are correct, this possible *third* epicenter would have occurred almost 2100 kilometers from here (1300 plus miles), further along the eastern end of the ridge going towards the New Siberian Islands. Even now, our graph readings point to severe aftershocks and ice waves, sliding east – and believe it if you can sir, - it appears to have has taken out a huge part of the Severnaya Zemla Ostrov (peninsula islands) directly north of our position. The Laptev Sea, is either much bigger or much smaller, we have no way of knowing which."

Igor paused to listen to 'hear' Moscow's conclusions through his TransPinder. He responded...

"No sir. Up to now, there is no indication that many of our closer Ostrov (islands) even *exist* any more. I have absolutely *no* response to our dispatch signals to previously contactable drilling platforms and vessels. Nor any other evidence to indicate that they are still there. Stations at Franz Josef Lands are not responding. But sir, the strange thing that I'm reading on our seismic tape so far, is that even though the initial *epicenter was northwest*, the critical mass of the Tectonic plate to the *northeast* activity has peak registered on our graphs at 8.8." Still high, That could signal another earth shift to come, possibly from that direction sir."

The reply image came back through his TransPinder image translator.

"I understand, Gennady."

The mental image reply from Mockba Geographic's staff director, read further,

"From your vantage point and considering the darkness at this hour, can you see – in what condition is Noril'sk?"

"Da. As I look North West, I can see what look like specters of *mountains* of white iceberg towers – mirages – like ghosts, in the distance along the Yenisey River connecting to the sea. If it is sea ice, it has taken a two hours to get here.

Kharlamov continued toe scan the horizon to the north. He added this thought..

There *must* be flooding even this far south – and there *must* be severe destruction in the city proper. I can not see it. But I *can* hear it, sir."

Moscow station interceded.

"Nar'yan Mar station advises that it maybe too early to be sure but, so far, there has been *no wall of water* coming up *their* inlet either. Are you certain there is no monster wave coming down the river to Noril'sk?"

"No sir – I am *not* absolutely certain. I *do* know from local observers that a swamping flood tide that goes in and out every fifteen minutes is happening along river frontage. It could be that most of the major water movement at the plate disruption went north towards the ice cap."

Peering through his night telescopes in the down hill direction of Noril'sk. Gennady Kharlemov suddenly became very morose.

"I know I can't image it to you as bad as it really is, but – this was no chimney tumbler, sir. Several nearby office towers here, down the sloped side below us must have collapsed, under the shaking and some are already under sporadic flooding. Now that water is coming up. Oooh мой бог (my God) — I see them now. Families... children - bodies are everywhere – in amongst

floating debris – Ooooohh ужасы! My stomach... I'm sorry Жаль

сэр... (sir)... Плиз Извините меня (please excuse me)"

Then Gennady did two things, He threw up into his waste basket after which he began to sob uncontrollably, without regard for his open TransPinder image line...nothing could intrude in his breakdown.

* * *

By 08:00 hours Saturday Oct 23, Stockholm had had to cope with low land flooding from three moderate tidal waves that had moved through the Baltic narrows and into shallower water of the Baltic and Bothnia Gulf.

The Swedish media led by TV4 Nyheter assignment based news teams in Moscow had done a surprisingly good early evaluation job overnight. They filed accurate reporting of what they knew to be true of monumental devastation and conditions. Early official estimates from Moscow put loss of Russian life – just by drowning and hypothermia – at no less than 800,000 *plus* as many as another *quarter million* people from the west side of Greenland to the Japan Trench. These were taken from known population of military bases posted there, as well as all those inhabitants along *3000 kilometers* of coast, now beneath whatever water location is would be now.. The quake itself had buried most of its victims. No approximate guess, no qualified assessment and no accounting of any kind could measure human loss until months – perhaps years later, if in fact such totals would ever be known.

Norway's Svalbard Island group, 700 miles east of the 'jagged' Knipovitch Ridge plate, were gone. Possibly Franz Josef lands too. Speculation was that

318

these huge island masses had been *depressed;* then overrun by the sea as it filled in the *widening* of the deepening Norwegian Basin.

*   *   *

Philippine Public Communication Network's news field personnel took off from Manila on Luzon at 01.29 hours routed for the Russian city of Noril'sk. A magnetically powered, older version model, freight/passenger copter/craft, ferrying personnel and portable holographic equipment, would land them at that city or whatever might be left of it. From preparation to destination it would be a nine hours after the first 'sea invasion'. Considering the remote wilderness of mid Mother Russia, this news team's on-site arrival was *so fast*, a tortured earth was *still shuddering* when they debarked.

Roiling, flooding, on-land currants were swelling in and out by the half hour, by the time debarking PBCNN *reporter,* Ida Palpuan had speedily set up technical requirements for her first holograph broadcast. Her *eyecam broadcast* was to be patched into the holograph transmitting terminal in Manila.

From her hill-side vantage, a Parka bundled Palpuan set her recording switch and integration buttons to be able to utilize her mind's eye image into four dimensional projection.

With her hand control, she was ready to focus in what was left of the land and the rapid sea swells beyond. Her TeleRelator took over her accompanying report details. Palpuan began to image her broadcast..

"Try if you will, to *imagine...* You've just come home from work and looking forward to a weekend of relaxation with your family. You twist the key to the front door of your seaside home, ready to step across the threshold into the hallway lobby. As you take that step, you turn to close the door. Within a space of a very long 3 seconds, your whole house moves sideways – with *you in it*. The pressuring roar that sends a spear-like pain through your ears is another alarm to tell you that *death is near*. If it were not for neck-high surging water currants that sweeps you like a leaf in an autumn wind – through the house and out a window, so small you could barely crawl through if you forced to – you would never guess that this was to be the *last* five seconds of your life.

319

And in that instant, you know that only explosive disintegration of your home could spare you the *fear of dying*."

Ida paused, as broadcast central in Manila, racked up eye cam video of a Russian lady at a first aid station. The PPCN broadcaster continued her image 'narration' over images of scenes and events.

"As it turns out, the Russian старая леди (old lady) who related this event to me at a rescue station *did* live. Though terribly wounded and mentally *frozen* by the violence of the event, she was able to let me know how strange it was – her life seemed so insignificant and how little it meant when compared to this monstrous assault on her world!"

Now back to her live broadcast, Ida's broadcasting eyecam panned a devastated landscape. She dealt with incoming quake and flood data.

"According to limited seismic reports, the Nansen Ridge plates North West of Norway and Sweden were the sites of the first epicenter, though other originating movements were also been declared in the later subsequent reports. As our studio shows you more of the actual events of disasters from other parts, you must know that ALL countries above the 54th parallel suffered damage of one kind or another. The quakes jarred much of the Canadian north and were felt as far south as mid United States. Again on the Beloya More – more commonly known to the rest of the world as White Sea, the city of Arkhangel'sk or Archangel, was devastated. North of that, on the Barents Sea, I regret to advise you that the famous port city to Murmans'sk, just 50 miles inland along the Tuloma inlet is virtually under sea ice. It was known as one of the world's foremost navel bases and a city of much traditional importance to Russians everywhere."

For about another hour, the Manila broadcast reporter remained on station, to continue reporting the scene at Noril'sk. From some Russian broadcasters, she learned of a 'high-above-water trail' access to a river town to the North East. She was 'told' of a grizzly human interest story going on there not far from Dudinka that could typify the horror of the eruptions.

Despite the risk of being caught by another swell of quickly rising water in from the Kara Sea, Ida Palpuan had 'persuaded' the commander of a sturdy

Russian navy cabin cruiser to take her out up the Yeniseyskiy river inlet to a point where she could direct her vision projectors towards to opposite river banks. There, she could get shots and report on the plight of villages that had faced the quake. When she was set up, Palpuan touched her eyecam control to enable a 'split view' of two other scenic directions for broadcasting. Then she started her report for direct transmission to her Manila office,

"There is no way *anyone beyond* the existing tremors of this *catastrophe* could *ever* imagine the chaos we're witnessing here, now just after 08 hours, the normal breakfast hour here in this part of Russia. Nine hours of night has hidden the terror of destruction. In the first half light of morning, the rampage of an angry earth is more than can be imagined.

"What you are seeing now is an earlier recorded news clip," Ida Palpuan narrated over scene and text citing area name..

"We were positioned on a hill as high as we could get near the town of Dudinka. You can see forward 'copter freighters bearing *International Rescue* markings, hovering as they look for solid landing ground. Wherever that is, they will set up mobile hospitals and warehouses for food and water distribution. We suspect that these aid activities are precursors of what will eventually be millions of other relief efforts from all parts of the world. Now on the left of this projection of this holographic report, you can see the North East side of the Yeniseyskiy Zaliv inlet, a gate to the Kara Sea, about 80 kilometers North West of Noril'sk.

On the *right* of your principal image, we regret we *must* show you the true tragedy of a disaster such as this. It is a disturbing report and one which we recommend that sensitive people viewing this broadcast should look away four the next five minutes..."

Papuan's pause was to gain mental energy for the next part of her report.

"This scene is that of what *was* a fishermen's marina at Ust' Port, an area north across the inlet from our position. In our telescopic view, we move in now on the few large trees nearby, – still standing and upright in a flood of churning ice pan. Notice the huge channel *buoy*, lodged *way up* in the one tree at far left. We have been informed that this now flooded area was a *play park* for children. This is where they customarily waited for their fathers to come in on their fish boats. Friday night would have had many children in the park. Understandably, *many* children are still there..."

Now the live image pulled out for a slow pan across flotsam of the marina play park. Reporter Palpuan held her zoom and focus control to ensure the total view at the speed, she designated to fit the narrative.

"What you see now are literally hundreds of tiny eviscerated bodies caught up by floating tree branches, fences and smashed play park apparatus. Many other little people are not shown and of course; *never will be found* as they were swept up and taken out to sea on the flushing currants of Arctic sea water ....We will close on this sad view for now, but I must let you know that, we will not withhold the actuality of any such tragedy. We will continue to ...to give you images of the rubble...the dismemberment of torn bodies...the debris of a once happy communities and remnants of their land."

Against her wish but helpless to stop it, the telepathic images to her TransPinder continued, so Ida 'code-signaled' the Manila anchor team to cut away – while she redid her face and wiped away her smeared cheeks, tears from reddened eyes. When she came back on, she was seen "on camera" through the plugged in eyecam of a technical colleague on the boat. She resumed communicating her images.

"The aftermath – the reality of total ruin here in Russia; the added death toll and the early stench of human decay will become evident within another twenty four hours. I ask you to forgive me for having had to show you these horrors. For me, these are *is* most despondent moments of my life. At this time, there is no way I know, whereby *any* media could depict the full scope or significance of a severely wounded earth such as we know – and it is *still occurring* . There is little else here to destroy any more than it already is.. Instead we have tried you show you vignettes of life and death here *as it is happening* on this, the most world shaking event in the known and recorded history of this planet. My name is Ida Palpuan, PPC Network reporting from the Russian province of Tyumen. And I *will* be back"

* * *

Months after Ida Palpuan had left Noril'sk for other locations on Russian soil – that soil *still* trying to recover small parts of it's losses.. Sea water on Arctic tundra moss would simply seep into much of the rich but tenuous earth beneath. Delicate Tundra grass *would* grow again – in a generation or two. Farther inland, sea water had so inundated the rich soil and forests of agricultural Russia that it could be declared baron for as much as 20 to 30 years hence. Some agro-scientists, who knew best, the corrosive effects of oxygen with salt water, believed it would be impossible for anyone to expect that productive plant life would ever reproduce again in these hollows and lowlands. Right now, the whole region was a shallow sea and now, even it too had a tidal movement. Whatever fisher persons were left, would have no way of knowing if and when life would again exist in Russian edge of the artic seas.

Ultimately, new seismic surveys and oceanic research would have to rechart the whole northern sea floor to determine how many and where marine surviving marine life might yet be found. In the next few decades, fishermen would have to know where sea life really is now, if they are to recoup and preserve the livelihood of human settlements on Russia's North Sea coast.

Vast areas of Barents sub terrain had been moved and displaced, along with petroleum well heads, sunken ships and *one anchored spherical time capsule*, no longer anchored at the position where it had been planted in the summer of 2053. In fact, where it would end up could be almost anywhere else in the world's oceans.

It later occurred to much of the rest of the world. An almost unthinkable speculation.

Was it possible that the deep, underground global Cyber stations, sensitive to entire earth crust movements and their ultimate result, were *prior warned?* Otherwise how was it so possible that almost instant mobilization of aid and rescue teams were on most Russian sites just two hours or less after the final trembling of the earth surface? In fact, did the "Selectronics Committee" extend its finding to management agencies in northern coastal countries? If so, why were they not advised in advance of this fast occurring and colossal distortion of land, sea and ice? Was it just *possible* that in the mathematic calculations of Cyber systems, no advance warning would have made any difference to the number of victims who died in this 'crack-cooling' of the earth's crust? The only difference would have been, which ones would be

victims and who would not.

Chapter 4

Untold Stories Inside The Reyk's Morgue

3129/32ND / REYKJAVIK ICELAND

FOURTEEN MONTHS AFTER the opening of the 21st century Sphere and forensic examination of cargo contents, the file labeled '21st Century Sphere Find' was officially closed and deposited with the Cyber Selection Committee for future reference only.

It had been intimated that this was consideration for the three Sphere survivors. It was not beneficial to anyone to have these three individuals forever pestered for stories, lectures, and media rights not to mention the savagery of the eternal paparazzi, and news image-hounds. Those selected researchers who attended the Iceland investigations and research were sworn secret witnesses to the distressful unwrapping of human remnants of an earlier species of our kind.

Vitrified in a cool morgue-like setting, within the dirigible compound, a team of research coroners held an executive council meeting. It was attended by Anson Prentice, Dr. Mona Randall and her surgical staff, assorted anthropologists and genealogy personnel with others with relevancy to the Sphere's cargo.

Flown in for his assessment was the world recognized anthropologist, Dr. Gordon McCullough, renowned for delivery of his papers at major European Universities on the study of mummification on the Euro and South American continents. His special field was preservation of diminishing tissue cell *elasticity*. For twenty one years, Dr, McCullough had also served as Chief coroner for the municipality of Edinburgh. Well versed in ID and technique of total image application, utilizing the TransPinder, he began his forensic lecture and demonstration of recently deceased, cone passengers.

"In this room, today," he began, "are *fifty eight deceased persons* who were cryogenically treated, while they were still alive. They are part of the remainder of a total of *eighty five persons* who were confirmed as having *heartbeats* while in hibernating condition when your people entered the cone section. Those twenty-seven survivors were in emergency quarters, where frankly, it is unlikely that *any* of them could have responded to treatment that would have 'brought them back' to full life status. We were hoping that for as long as we can keep them breathing by providing appropriate thawing procedures and remedial surgery, we may learn more of our 1000 year old species. We did *not* succeed in this endeavor.,"

The Scottish coroner stepped forward to one of two, all steel autopsy tables with hydraulic capability. This allowed cadavers put on display to be articulated into an almost standing position.

Under the tables' canvas tarps were the remains of recently deceased cryogenically-treated victims. He uncovered the one table tarp. Here lay a very old, bewhiskered man with a rotund body in *relatively* good shape. McCullough lifted the card beside the specimen and quoted...

"Well. In this first one, is evidence of *royal* fraternization here! This was a *Sir* P. Ustinov. Writer, Actor, Philosopher. Even though aged, this gentleman was – if I may be allowed a play on words here – remarkably well preserved, but his prostate cancer was just so far advanced we really had little time or prevailing opportunity to define a clear diagnosis and recommendation for recovery and treatment."

With a shrug, the doctor covered the body and moved over to the next table imaging a final thought....

"...today's current methods of applied chemo and radiation therapy would have been of little value even in that patient's 21st century setting"

Now he removed the second tarp of the sarcophagus to reveal the one body, still in its plastic shell cocoon. He moved the table upward for the face to become visible through the cocoon transom.

"To that end, this is Senora Xonasil of Uruguay. According to translations from the accompanying copies of her charts from a Montevideo Palliative Care Center, she had been dying of liver cancer when she submitted to cryogenics, with a view to later treatment in a more advanced medical era. We are *not* convinced that after taking her from the cone in living condition, she actually expired of her *disease*. In this case, we concede that it was more than likely that our unpracticed defrosting techniques were too abrupt for her system. It's possible too, that we miscalculated chemical antibodies. Experiments such as these are certainly not normal. Truth is, we were unable to provide for the woman's biological system to respond to the unfreezing process"

Everyone silently applauded Dr Gordon McCullough's candid self critique for his professional failure to 'bring these persons back to a life – *without* more of the suffering they had already endured from such a 'simple' disease as prostate cancer.' He seemed to be apologizing for contemporary medicines' response to have been able to react more adroitly within required time frames to extend 'frozen' life. He also could have excused the faults that they had had to deal with in cryobiology cases they had never had had to face before. But he didn't claim ignorance as an excuse.

He carried on his imaged thoughts.

"Like others here and in the ICU wards right now, at time of cryogenic treatment each patient, "living" *and* dead, had been taken down into a gradual -196°C body temperature. This was to permit a *controlled* cell freezing with much less cellular damage than one would expect of the preservation process. But we have still encountered a major problem with the exact melt down timing when removing each body from its triple layered cocoon, encasement.

327

Frankly, I have to believe this and the lack of data concerning the preservative used precluded chances of recovery of *any* of the twenty-seven beating hearts that remain."

At this point and as though performing on a relay team rotation, still another coronary specialist took over. She took up a bone saw. Standing in front of Senora Xonasil's upright cocoon casket, she cut into one side of the *'shell'* to reveal the outer shell material and the six cm space between that and the second layer. McCullough, the forensic specialist, conveyed an accompanying message.

"Let us demonstrate how and where these elements were kept.

To the human systems of eighty five bodies whose containers were marked in the English language, 'cryogenized while still alive,' it is here, in this first layer of the cocoon shell that a store of a sugar additive from which was 'fed' in one of two tube to the life support systems of oxygen in another tube directed to supply brains and hearts." Just as tubes fed *into* the subjects, similar tubes led *out*, to self contained canisters that received what minute bodily wastes existed. The canisters converted said wastes to compressed gas for later disposal."

The lady with the bone cutting saw, again imaged a request for attention and on the *opposite* side of the cocoon shell, she made *another two* cuts as she had done before only this time between the second and third 2 cm layer. At the moment she did, a pungent chemical odor filled the room. When the whirring saw noise ceased, she pointed out that *this* side of the cocoon shell held the necessary amount of compressed oxygen, connected with infusion *tubing* from the encasement to the nose and heart of what was, at one time, a 'live' human being.

Once again, Dr. Gordon McCullough came front, to the edge of the exhibition platform, close to the staff audience and straining to direct his thoughts to the group in order to make a point.

"That sour aroma emitting from this layer of the cocoon shell was a clue to what those explorers of the cone smelled in the cone section of Sir Jeffrey's Cypsela time capsule. It *is* a part – maybe a *key* part of the formula mix to the *miracle of survival* of eighty five souls over the thousand 1000 years. The odor *is* a refrigerant chemical, a derivative of *Freon.*"*

*FN-Not a chemical element but a trade name of a class of chlorofluorocarbons

The esteemed doctor waved his hand toward him, and invited..

"Come up if you like. Take a sniff of the stuff and see how it was dispersed into the sealed cocoon."

As most medical and human engineering professionals did go in for a closer look, McCullough imaged on..

"And – added, is an as yet unrefined sugar based ingredient. That too was part of the infusion. But make no mistake – this formula from the past, was definitely a mitigating factor in the preservation of our 21st century guests to date"

As he stripped off his disposable gloves, McCullough invited his small group to retake their seats to enable him to finish his demonstration.

"In order to ensure blood circulation in all 'living' subjects, precise amounts of alcohol to preclude total blood freezing was added to variable thinning medications, depending on the patient's individual age and condition. These included one of the three basic anti coagulants of that time, Warfarin, Harparin and Angiomax. They were installed separately on the vital-contents feed system that you all saw. Depending on the patient's diagnosis, this sugar compound was measurably integrated from internal canisters into the 'coffin capsule' to help promote programmed arterial fibrillation. For all of that, 'survival insurance' applications were as much guess work as scientific fact. But what else was there?

"By the way..." He implied casually,

"For the information of those of you who witnessed the arrival of that super-*large* cocoon from out of the cone, you may be interested to know that the Gorilla's name was Samson. Naturally, he was born in what was then the African Congo and was a fixture of the Copenhagen Zoo and Givzoo Park in Denmark, circa 1970's to '90's. Approximate date of Cryogenic treatment given to Samson was just after the turn of the century 2000. Regrettably his system is still more primitive than ours. Therefore, Samson was *not* one of the *eighty four* pulsating heart passengers. But he *will* make an interesting study subject for *some* delighted group of animal bio-archaeologists."

* * *

"Imagine. *Three*, one thousand years old human beings, have a chance to spend their remaining days with us." projected Anson Prentice. "If ever there was a time for the scientific community to stand up, to rejoice in this limited remedial success and to give thanks to people like our medical staff, this is the time to do it. As far as I'm concerned, these people provide us with evidence and new hope that we are finally making worthwhile progress on this old earth."

Prentice resumed his meeting and informed his entire project group on the last unexplained drawers of organs and other body parts.

Marianna Pellegrino, Born: 1993   Disease: Encephalitis Cryrotreated: 2008

James Riddle Hoffa, Born: 1913   Injury: Skull Fracture Deep Frozen: 1975 - Cryrotreated: 1988

Erich Boris Kratz, Born: 1998   Disease: Amyotrophic Lateral Sclerosis - Cryrotreated: 2053

Ellen Frobisher, Born: 1989. Illness: Extreme Angina. Cryrotreated: at 26 yrs - 2015

Harold Harris, Born: 1983.   Illness: Prostate Cancer   Cryrotreated: at 38 yrs - 2021

Evita Peron. Born: 1919.   Illness: Liver Cancer   Cryrotreated: 1958

Maria Xonisil. Born 1936   Illness: Liver Cancer   Cryrotreated: 1988

Natalie Woods, Born: 19??   Injury: Drowning   Cryrotreated: 1981

"Sampson" Born: Unknown (Copenhagen / Givskud Zoo Gorilla) Illness: Respiratory infection/old age Attempted Cryro treatment: 2019m

John Kennedy Jr.   Born: 1960 Injury: Crushed Cranium - Aircraft Disintegration

Cryrotreated: 1999

Jose Fernando Morales,   Born: 1994   Injury: Gunshot wounds Cryrotreated: 2003

Peter Ustinov Born: 1921 Illness: Kidney Failure (Nephritis) Cryrotreated: 2003

"Dr. Lloyd Simon Verinmeyer, Specialist in Forensic and Psychiatric medicine at Mayo Clinic, Rochester, Minnesota, is scheduled to be with us today. His intensive study of our data files to him, has afforded us with valid findings that are both irrevocable and meaningful. In brief, I have here his preliminary brief. He states...

'Persons responsible for the packing and preservation of human and animal body parts, as well some complete cadavers – some in varying states of activity at death – were directed to record the exact physical profile of each 21st century capsulated citizen. This was to be able to precisely diagnose the effects of time in their frozen state. From a purely scientific point of view, such examples are invaluable in determining our own course of action with human beings coming under our care in the era.'

Prentice looked up from the paper and announced in a slow deliberate imaged statement..

"Here's the crux of the matter, folks. Here's *why* we have this dramatic example of *mankind's physics* in a capsule from the past.

"Do you recall the volumes of notes, micro chips and recorded facts we recovered from the sphere in one form or another? Twenty first century medical and anthropologic specialists, are stipulating what we already *knew* – *and* it *should* have set a course for our investigation but it *didn't!* These 22nd century *medical people* are informing us that, *if they* had access to study deep

331

frozen human remains of Cro-Magnon times, many thousands of erroneous *scientific* conclusions, which the practice of medicine and medical research had made up' until then – would have been *redundant!*,"

The Project leader stopped to consider the indictment.

"That's not exactly the best referral our profession has ever had. But then, again in the English language, they wrote in their English language reports that our translators were able to make s out, quote...

'With specimens of that kind herewith in our hands, it is clear to those of us in the 21st century, that had we had such specimens from such millenniums before, our medical advances would have been sufficiently proficient, as to *negate* the real reasons for which you were sent this exhibit. This fact illustrates how little we have come to know since the first leaf wrapped poultice was applied to an ailing member of a primate tribe of the human race. In our opinion, this should be an opportunity for medical scientists of a future world to make *giant* steps in understanding the mystery of man, his mind and his bodily property. The scientific community of these times, very much regrets our lack of such an opportunity in our time.'"

At that point, the noted Doctor Verinmeyer burst into the lecture room and began readying a picture paper for his address. Doctor Anson Prentice paused before returning to his to original *resume quoting* the pathological documents gathered from the vaults of the Sphere. He concludes by waving a tiny electronic disc.

"The eminent Doctor Verinmeyer's entire report will be available to those that can use it".

Prentice looked up for a moment, smiled at what he thought was to come, then returned to transference concentration.

There *is* one more thing. In centuries prior to the great Nansen Ridge Upheaval, there had been many, many cases of preserved remains. Sometimes, they were of prehistoric people recovered from glaciers and ice depths of our planet. Some were even partially restored, less whole from ancient mummification. All of those recovered people were studies unto themselves but in most cases, medically speaking, they were revelations. Doctor Verinmeyer's report on this is quite startling... Doctor?"

From his frequent lecturing, the renowned doctor Verinmeyer of forensic medicine had become very proficient in providing exacting details of medical terminology and circumstance. Thusly, he imaged very clearly,

"'In the world wide search for likely preservation subjects, there was one – no two – found quick frozen, in an unheated mountain hut, in the cordillera ilicabamba region of Cuzco province in Peru, SouAmerica. Wrapped in serapes of the times – assumedly, to keep warm, they were uncovered to discover that they the couple were coupled in 'complete' sexual embrace.

In a perfectly natural way, it was clear and quite natural that they were trying to stave off the high Andes winter storm by stimulating each other's bodies – principally to thaw themselves out, of course. Obviously, it was a losing cause, *medically* speaking, that is'".

Prentice looked up from his document pad, grinning knowingly at the imaged comments of the attending group. He could not help but project the thought,

"I count thirteen men in this room, who is imaging the thought, '*What a way to go!*'"

"Sorry for the interruption, doctor." added Prentice,

At this, Doctor Verinmeyer belied his reputation for humorlessness, retorting very quickly,

"It *is* true Dr. Prentice. Coitus interruptus in freezing conditions *could* be a heart stopping experience... but considering the circumstances..."

What followed was a swell of grunted laughter where some audience members actually bent over with heaving shoulders in reaction to the remark."

Verinmeyer kept his cool, smiled broadly and continued with his subject.

"Considering the matter that was faced here – that being the science of keeping hearts beating, quick frozen specimens coming out of that spherical time capsule, are inexplicably in better condition than any previous attempt at resurrection. All human specimens taken from this 21st century crypt are as real to their living form as preservatives can make them. As a result of ten centuries entombment, none are deformed, withered, shrunken or incomplete.

In this degree of cold, *facetiously* speaking, lack of exercise is not a factor, either way. Nor was it in the case of those romantic Peruvians. *Their* hearts were definitely *active*. Had the 21st century medical community had access to their blood work, mental processes, lung expansion and many other characters of their last frantic movements, this would have been invaluable to our scientists. Still, for all of that, is it any wonder how it is that the human heart is the *most wondrous* living driver ever evolved?'

Prentice leaned back, still smiling from the repartee he and Verinmeyer has exchanged. The latter continued with his thought processes to the audience.

"In summary, this time capsule has proven itself to be an invaluable gift from our fore fathers and mothers. The originators actually *knew* that *only* such an exhibit could help us to better understand where this era's humans have come from and to where and what extent they can take themselves in future. "

"From what we have received from them," Verinmeyer thought out,

"I personally admire their foresight, their dedication, inventiveness and courage. If *that* is the stock of our ancestors, I am confident that the human race in *our* time is genetically *improved* stock for the *next* thousand years of human evolution. I suspect *all* the rewards are yet be revealed to us as we have, in some way, merged one ancient century, 1000 years ago, with today's *civilized* world"

"And on that subject, "

imaged Anson Prentice to his team of university researchers,

"– and in the matter of our Sphere survivors and *their* time with us - *regardless* of what happens from here on in, our adventure in the last few weeks, particularly with the salvation of the *three living*, cryogenically-treated persons from the *21st century*, I must impress upon all of you who bore witness to this truly remarkable and miraculous event. It has given us cause to wonder at how

21st century man had accomplished so much since his very early days as an amphibian. Don't know about you, but after all this; I now have a renewed, if not profound regard for this *living and dying* business."

Prentice's staff audience was still, waiting for his deduction. Anson Prentice looked tired but contented as he concluded,

"Folks, today we live our *centurion lives* in a time where a human's *every* organ – with the *exception* of the largest one, our epidermal covering - *can* be totally replaced. That's why at ninety-four I'm doing great on the *inside* of me but covered with crinkles on the *outside* of me.

Nevertheless, by replacing organs we have been able to prolong our lives to 150 years and more. Our medical sciences today have eradicated serious disease. We have been endowed with permanent immune systems and built-in anti bodies that repel viruses and illness, designed to kill us. As it is now, in this, the 32nd century of humans' stay on earth, we are more likely *to die of boredom* than any other singular cause. Sometimes, I must confess, I *do* wonder, if extended aging is to our credit. For centuries we have been questioning ourselves about the human indignity of growing old. Believe me, it's not the *indignity* of dying that is so offensive. In deaths final stages we couldn't care less *how we look* or what our loved ones will think of the *unhappy* side of our passing. It's the pain of having to be extended palliative care we suffer, from having lived so damn long. That loss of will is the indignity of it all. Now I believe that it is now our job in this millennium to seek a solution to that part of our evolution.

Finally, let me share this thought image with you.

I firmly convinced that, intentionally or not, our great, ever so great and greater, grandfathers and grandmothers have indeed shown us an important fact of life by letting us see that 'fighting uphill' just to *extend* life *can* bring unnecessary heartache and physical discomfort. I also believe that *some of our forefathers back in the 21st century* saw this inequity and let us know, that there is *little real* living to be gained by having the human race clinging to *used up* bodies, when *nature* has already decided what is best for each of us.

If not boredom, then other kinds of torture can face us when we extend our bodily consciousness beyond its *natural* time — whatever that may be. Folks, take it from one who is several less steps from eternal rest than most of the rest of you...

One thousand years ago or so, an American entertainer named Burns is reputed to have said on his hundredth birthday, 'Life's journey is not to arrive at the grave safely in a well preserved body, but rather to skid in sideways, totally worn out, shouting Wowee...what a ride! By the way, Burns lived to a rare old age for the times, 100 years on earth.

In *our* time, we take a take a different view. 'Life's journey is like a Hawaiian feast. Enjoy as much of life's experience as you choose, simply by *resetting* the spirit within you. That way, one can *enjoy* the option of an ever increasing longevity.

Goodnight - and goodbye, my friends."

Chapter 5

5. Sphere's legends Live as 32ⁿᵈ century citizens

3143 – 3192, Reykjavik, Italia, Alberta, Greece, New York, Wyoming,

Two years following transplant surgery of a Llama ewe's heart at the medical facility within the World Interstellar Agency based at Iceland's Reykjavik Medical Center, Sphere Survivor **Ellen Frobisher** was like an excited little girl on her birthday. She had been TransPinder injected, schooled in Image transference and appliance grooming. Her credit pod had been filled with needed credentials and funding. On this October 18 3143 day departure, she was prepared and ready to make her way into a 32ⁿᵈ century civilization. Discounting her time in Cryogenic storage and her recovery time, her true age was now 29 years.

In actual elapsed time since her birth, Ellen was actually one thousand and twenty nine years of age. Given international citizenship privileges, as were two other survivors, she was to take her first Magnipod ride back to her last known living time of earth, New Haven Connecticut. When she put down there at the Magnipod port at the New Haven, Haven Hotel, she was surprised to be met in the lobby by a conductor (counselor) she knew from Reykjavik.

Still bearing the automatic reactions she possessed from the old world, she burst into laughter, gleefully exclaiming in the English language,

"Shirley!! Wow! Am I ever glad to see you!"

They embraced. Then Shirley Bowerman, still broadly smiling herself, transmitted her own message through Ellen's TransPinder

"Look. *You* have an audience!"

Ellen knew even before Shirley had informed her by imaging..

She knew even before turning to see hotel guests, bell boys and hundreds of silent lobby people some grinning, but mostly open mouthed and wide eyed, at hearing a living member of their species actually making an oral sound!

She breathed in sharply – her error caused her a moment of confusion and embarrassment.

Bowerman put her arm around Ellen and imaged,

"Don't worry about it, Ellie. That was bound to happen. In fact, as I told you back on the Reyk, it will probably happen again and again. But don't let it throw you. Now let's check you in here to regain your equilibrium. Let's arrange for a comfortable Kube room for you."

Ellen thought to ask Shirley about a room, but she resisted. She would probably have hundreds of such questions as they went along. It was not crucial that she instantly learn about everything, so, why not just let it happen and learn it that way?

Not a 'Haven Hotel' staff member was in sight. No doorman, luggage porters but no concierge. Only an office door to the side of the lobby, with an icon above it gave Ellen any hint that any humans were involved. It was the only sign of hotel human personnel. Shirley took Ellen's credit pod to a free standing Kiosk in the lobby; then took Ellen's hand and imprinted her thumb print on a green lighted glass panel at the Kiosk's registration 'desk'. Then she slid Ellen's Bank Pod into an adjacent slot, turns and mentally announces to Ellen, "OK babe, you're registered. Here comes your Kube now."

In this case, the Kube meant self contained 'studio suite.' This up-town kind of accommodation was unlike the old fashioned, European Cubi – a closed in, plasticized, windowless, child's playroom, in your choice of colors! The Kube was a full fledged suite of two or more rooms, part of a common hotel hospitality system integrated into thousands of hospitality properties all over the world in the first half of the twenty eight century.

Instead of going up to one's accommodation – the Kube comes up - from under-surface, service quarters into the lobby. This enabled guests to enter directly. Baggage on invisible conveyers sorted the right ownership and put in the Kube.

The Kube was enclosure of two or more rooms, precision positioned on layered towers of floors. Once inserted into position, all water, power, air conditioning, and plumbing fixtures were plugged into their ready to functioning inlets. When Ellen and Shirley entered the suite, the Kube transported itself and the two women onto a hotel layer with a magnificent open view. Visitors would take traditional lifts right to their Kube level. Ellie was to learn that *all* layered Kube suites have a magnificent view! It wasn't until Shirley had taken her lounge seat by the bubbled 'port' window; and Ellen to another lounge chair with many buttons on its arm, that would turn that furniture into a bed, within this very spacious set of rooms.

At that very moment, Ellen Frobisher became terrified – then nauseated. Her little 'ewe' heart raced. At the realization of what was facing her, she cracked. She imaged her fear through a downpour of tears. She half talked and half imaged her despair.

"Oh god, Shirley, What have I let myself into? I feel like an immigrant...One without a country! What made me think I could handle all this... and I haven't even got past day one of your 32nd century! Oh, mommy - what have I done? I must be *retarded*. Maybe, I should *go back* to my room in Reykjavik...this is too much for me...."

Conductor Shirley came over, put her arm around the woman's shaking shoulder and imaged,

"Ellie, I can only guess, the total frustration you're going through – but I assure you, it *will* become clear to you …in *whatever time* it takes *you* to digest it. Your state of overload reminds me of a history lesson in school…where immigrants coming to a new country, back then, experienced the same feeling of being unable to cope… But they not only got used to it…fact is they turned whatever society had to offer into advantage and some became very wealthy. You are no retard, Ellie. You're one smart woman. Yes, there are many things to learn all over again. But listen. Learn just the *basics* to begin with, and you'll be just fine. Things like – for instance, if you are invited to someone's place, the home or place where we live, even a temporary home like this Kube, protocol is that the home is highly respected, seven *exalted*. Take off shoes. Sit on floor cushions. That sort of thing. *We* didn't start *that* custom. The *Japanese* did that, thousands of years ago. So don't try to learn all this in *one* afternoon because no one else could either!'

Shirley felt her charge's body beginning to relax.

"Thanks Shirley. You really are a friend."

Ellen sobbed – remembering to transmit in image form.

She went quiet, wiping eyes of tears and continued,

"Your kindness is so thoughtful. See? That's what I need – a caring *friend* to get me started. How long will *you* be able to stay to comfort me like this?

Shirley responded,

"My directions from the Interstellar Center were, 'for as long as it takes'. And don't worry Ellie; I am remunerated for whatever time *is* needed.

Ellen hugged her friend once again.

"Then I can suffer *whatever* I must – with *you* to guide me. Thanks for being my sister!

* * *

Over the next couple of years, Shirley traveled with Ellen helping her to trace Ellen's long ago ancestors. They found little or nothing of Ellen's son and daughter, seven and six years old respectively, in 2015. When their mother had supposedly 'passed' on in 2016 and relatives inquires were made, federal registries had no information of her unfaithful husband, Dacron Frobisher. Ellen had it figured, he was not above running from the country to another to escape his responsibilities.

Walking through a small garden park in downtown New Haven The women found a worn statue of a long coated medical man. Slightly bigger than his real stature, he stood almost unnoticeable, on a weathered, black streaked, granite pedestal by a little used walkway in the city park. In what once had to be an antiquated version of English, the plaque interpreted, read,

'For having brought international honor to the state of Connecticut, Doctor James Harvey, for his work in soft ceramic vessels for treatment of heart disease. July 23, 2043'.

While in Naples, searching for the Bochelli Vintners Estate, where they had planned to visit, Ellen and Shirley learned some sorrowful news. Renowned Doctor of physics and investigating engineer on Reykjavik's Sphere Project, Elio Bochelli had died in a tragic train wreck, south east of Anzio just a month or two before.

Meanwhile, they had spotted a freighter in Naples harbor, bearing the name FrobiShips on its bow. On checking, they found that Albanian registered, "FrobiShips – All Refrigerated Cargo Line" was indeed a USA corporation with headquarters in Seattle Washington.

At age 35, Ellen found a man who cared for her. They fell in love. She married Guido Gabriella, an Italian Producer of Holograph Images for broadcast and entertainment theatre. On meeting her, as an immigrant, he offered to 'school' Ellen in Italy's 31st Century living - for as long as he could. That turned out to be for a lifetime. Ellen and Guido settled into Gabriella's home in the city of Milano.

It was with much sadness that conductor and counselor Shirley Bowerman declared herself redundant. Ellen embraced and kissed her friend Shirley

Bowerman, orally whispering a loving goodbye in her ear. Shirley shared a Magnipod with another passenger and lifted away back to Interstellar Agency's Medical Center at Reykjavik, to be assigned to other Medical personnel assignments..

Guido was never told of Ellen's *actual* age. And nor did it seem, that it mattered – much except at tax time. Since conversation was by image transference, it matter little, neither did she ever let him know, she could speak English, *orally*. Though she often forgot – snickering controlled laughter at things she found amusing.

Ellen *did* discover that 'FrobiShips' *was founded* by her enterprising father in 2025. As a legitimate heir, several generations removed, she *was* invited to sit on the company's board of directors, in a well paid functionary as well in a proprietary role. Back home in Milan, she also prepared story lines for children and production by Guido's entertainment company. But the highlight of her second life was soon to come. It would be a celebration of her rebirth and the discovery of her other two survivors.

* * *

There was a time, back in the 22 century and well into the 26th century, when advanced prostate cancer patients were given the initials WO by laymen and professional medical people alike. Hard to detect in its entirety; hard to extract because of its devilish placement in the human body; hidden by bones, its own dimensions and effected by other matter in that area. Prostate cancer was treated with everything from non invasive radiation pellets to 'handiwipes." Though never publicly expressed, it was termed a write off by medical specialists of the times!

Short of amputating anyone at the waist, there was no stopping the insidious cancerous growth in the body of Saskatchewan farmer/rancher **Harold Harris.** So in 2021 at aged 38 he allowed himself to be frozen for a one in a billion chance of living the rest of his life – as he stated himself – 'long after prostate cancer becomes as curable as a case of acne."

After being taken and revived from his sarcophagus in 3139 to immediate prostate surgery, with further and extensive treatment, he spent over almost two years in Reykjavik Hospital's rehabilitation ward. He was then TransPinder vaccinated, trained in image projection and educated in the lifestyles of the 3140's. His interviews for reentry into society were conducted by 'imported' physiologists at the Reykjavik. They set a course of action for him to return to agriculture much as he had done in years before Cryology treatment. His counselors informed him that in the 1000 years Harold had been away from grains, livestock and a country way of life, evolution of grain production became a button pushing process. Grain harvesting was done by putting corporate giant combine/hoppers in a field, without the need for human guidance on-vehicle. Agricultural mechanization was all controlled from a farm house or an operator's office. It was universal. Remote controlled robot machines thinned the company's cherry trees and harvested ripe fruit , patrolling the bushes picking berries, product gathering hoppers, row creeping potatoes hoers and diggers, electronic controlled pasture gates allowing herds to move to better grass in another field. Branding irons had long since been antiquated and now used chemical-tracing brands on live beef-cow hides, as bawling animals stuttered through the chutes. With a non stressful brand on it's hip. These mass production methods that he and hundreds of other farm hand and cowboys of his time, worked at and enjoyed during earlier centuries on this same earth were all, but gone.

He questioned the counselor conductor, assigned to him.

"So how is livestock *bred* – by robotic bulls?"

Ignoring his sarcasm, the counselor sat back in his chair and responded...

"Natural breeding is not as necessary it once was, what with cloning and all. He was still smiling at Harry's robot bull analogy. Then he imaged,

"Harry, there is no agro business anymore – not as you remember it. Just as *before your time*, there was no going west by covered wagon anymore, either. Those eras have past. But don't take *my* word for it. Go back to Saskatoon. Go to Texas or Calgary. Go get it all from the horse's mouth. Who knows? It's a place to restart. *Something* might come of it".

Later, Harris took one Magnipod ride into Calgary; he was ready to interview horses if necessary to get the kind of answer he really wanted. As it turned out, the only horses he found were on dude ranches or in the Stampede parades. Finding open range ranches around Calgary's settlement of five million people was almost like looking for Calico fashions on Rodeo Drive. Agro operations were few and far between. Most of Canada's ranch land in Saskatchewan and Alberta was now housing subdivisions, full of tower-high townhouses.

On learning that Harris wanted to hire back on to a working ranch, one bar maid sat down to image communicate with him on a slow night. Beth, a college kid from America, working Summers in a pseudo western bar, advised him to try Wyoming, her home state. She even gave him a note to go see a relative on a spread down in the Big Horn Range and River country…

"Just off highway 20 at Greybull, then west 30 to 50 'klicks' toward the town of Shell"

She continued to image him,

"At one time – several hundred years ago, I guess – what is now my Uncle Paul's "Dry Crick" place, *used to be* a pretty important cow-calf operation in that area.. But today, raising and marketing beef is almost like specializing in gourmet meats, like Kobe beef delicacies in Japan – it's really a veterinarian's show now. So Uncle Paul turned the property into a paying proposition by bedding down party dudes and their families. It's now a profitable guest ranch but they *still* run a few hundred or so Limousine heifers for some special clients markets. But Uncle Paul still breaks most of his own grade horses for his dude string too. In some ways he's something of an antique in the ranching business."

Harry interrupted her picture dialogue with a thought of his own.

"Sounds like he's got enough jobs there to fill his day but what makes you think he would hire on a middle aged gaffer like me around the place?"

"Experience, Harry! Stability! Like *you've* got. It's cheaper for Unc' than training kids who come and go every spring. He *always* did think, he needed *older* guys who know their way around. I know – I spent my summers there.

I've seen your kind – experience at work. Yep. You and Uncle Paul would get along great. How old are you – 45? He'd be about the same age."

So Harry jumps a Wind Train to Sheridan, Wyoming. Then he rents a SAR – a Shuttle Air Rider) sort of mobile flying suit, for the run over to the ranch.

His niece was right. Paul was fine man with a fine family. The two got along well and would, for the rest of Harry's life. Within three and a half years Paul appointed his friend Harry, as foreman of the Bar D. Harry was also appointed to live in original old main house, a five room bungalow by the creek. Paul and wife Effie looked after record keeping work and the business aspects of the Ranch-Resort. Hiring hands and running day to day cattle operations was Harry's responsibility. He ran it like it was his own. He structured and maintained new guest requirements, building up a horse ramuda, putting green feed in the loft, shoeing all the dude stock. He spent day and night camp outs, riding out on the 10 kilometer range, moving herds around to make sure pasture grass was not over eaten. He was busy. But all the time he knew there was still an indefinable something, missing in his life. What he didn't know, was that he was about to get it

* * *

Big and Bulky Bavarian, **Erich Boris Kratz** was enthused. Even while in a hospital ward, in a recovery mode from laser brain surgery that actually reversed his dementia and an ALS illness, this Sphere survivor was planning a joyous return to his home village near Unterhaching.

Thanks to the lack of Myostatin in his body, he faired better than those normally muscled people, who lacked the extra resources of a robust frame. Because of it, Kratz easily withstood the rigors of regaining strength after hospitalization. During that period he felt well enough to begin his image communication lessons. It was grueling at first. There were times when he sought out his consultants to pick up the nuances and use of picture-conversational 'joiners,'– like how to image … 'to, if, it, c an, would, have, out' – frequently used in imagery's sentences. In fact when totally frustrated, he would startle his tutors by launching an oral tirade of self denouncing epitaphs, out loud in deutsch.

"'Verdammen Sie diese Bildnissprache!

Still confined to a hospital recovery ward, he would often walk down the hall to visit Ellen Frobisher, recovering from her heart implant. Since neither Erich and Ellen could converse by voice, since neither understood the others original language, this turned out to be curse yet a blessing, compelling both to practice their kindergarten picture imaging to communicate back and forth.. They would sit for hours, concentrating on thought projections, laughing at each other's mistakes and *correcting* each other with their own images, for the same views and opinions. Though Ellen still tired easily, the time together afforded them both common giggles at each others' struggles with their silly drawings to clarify their meanings. At least they had an escape from feeling alone. Erich wanted so much to explain to his conductor counselors, that being German; he needed extra attention to make his image practice work more understandable. Finally, he knew. Ready or not, he had had image dialogue basics. That and a quick and an open mind for receiving, though transmitting was not as good, it would have to do.

On the day of his departure from Reykjavik, he had called for a single passenger magnipod. When he stepped inside he realized he *should* have ordered a two passenger seat pod since he really *over filled* this one. He punched in buttons for destination Munchen (Munich), waved a thankful good bye to his medical friends and set off on his adventure. Erich Kratz's solo reintroduction to the world occurred on October 17th, 3138. He was fifty three years of age – plus a thousand years or so.

Thanks to tourist demand, a centuries old railway train to Unterhaching still ran. Because he was at a suburban Munchen Bahnhoff, when the train pulled out. He was on it. Four hours later, he came back the same way. His village might as well have part of the Unterhaching suburbs. He recognized nothing in his village except the old church tower. It was a severe disappointment to him. While in Munchen he became a tourist. He headed for it's tent city. *Oktoberfest* was just like he remembered back, when in 2117, as a young single womanizer, he was there for ten days weeks with friends from Unterhaching's college.

This time, he found an *affectionate* new party friend and hid himself and his 40 year old female friend in a nearby pension for two days and two nights. From Munchen they both traveled by Magnipod to Archángelos beach on the Greek Island of Rhodes. There they enjoyed four weeks of fun before sending his *married* companion back to Munchen and himself on to New York. For sociality, he joined Schierechterer Stamm, a group that fosters Bavarian culture. There, Herr Kratz met the manager of a club, Deutsehtreffen, and was hired as its social events coordinator.

Still on the job, two years later, the manager urged Erich to take some vacation time. It was then, that Herr Kratz had an inspiration. He always had an urge to see and *orally* converse with his survivor friend, Harold Harris from Reykjavík. He decided that just as soon as he could trace Harold Harris's whereabouts, he would pay a surprise visit on his vacation time. His timing coincided with Ellen Furbisher's intent to visit her friends Harris and Kratz.

Reunion

Suddenly Reykjavik's Interstellar Agency was receiving telepathically imaged inquiries from both Eric Kratz and Ellen Frobisher as to where they might find their 22nd century friend, Harold Harris. His former counselors advised that Harris last known address was Calgary Alberta, Canada. But they were not certain he was still there.

Even world wide Cyber data was unable to respond to transmitted requests for the location of a Harold Harris, Agriculturalist from the 21st century. There were literally thousands of 50 year old persons with the name Harold Harris around the world – many hundreds of them also categorized at farmers, ranchers and specialists in grain management as *their* Harry used to be.

When Ellen contacted Erich Kratz to communicate with him in his New York home, Erich had learned enough pigeon English to receive an oral call by electronic transmitter. Though while understanding was disjointed, they still had picture imaging to fall back on. Whatever they chose from moment to moment, neither one of them could hide the elation of face to face 'image dialogue' with their reborn 'sister and brother'.

Wyoming. Sunday, December 3^{rd,} 9:10 am, 3148AD.

Since it was Sunday, Rancher Harris had delayed his, normally early morning chores, to enjoy an extra hour's sleep. Now, having just grain-fed the heifers, those late born animals, held back from the auction, to make up the basis of next years herd, Harry was back in his house, stomping the snow off his boots, then using the book jack to remove them in the mud room. Not even taking time to discard his mackinaw, he reached for the carafe of coffee. He had prepared it before facing a frosty, two foot overnight snowfall, to feed Paul's cattle. With a cup of hot coffee in hand, he glanced out his kitchen window.

All of a sudden, the deep snow between the house and the barns and grain bins was swept up in a huge gust of white... like the landing of an aircraft. Harry thought to himself,

"Now what? Who the hell would be dropping in at this *early hour?* Thank the gods that there are no ranch guests right now. He had been gearing up for nine couples booked for arrival in ten days just prior to the Christmas holiday. But this isn't them. So what now?!"

As he reached for his plaid winter cap with the ear flaps and bunny tail on top, he slipped into his fur covered boots, ready to go out to meet the landing Magnipod, he thought it inconsiderate that some folk would have the audacity to come in unannounced. Probably expecting guest services, how could they not know the guest ranch was not yet prepared to receive them? As he stepped off on his porch, he squinted at the two people emerging from the Magnipod.

"What the hell am I going to tell these two – "

Now Harry stood still holding on to his coffee cup, as he recognized his two 'Freon' blooded angels. Shocked into mind numbing silence, he felt creeping moments of joy. He dropped his full cup of coffee. Both of the visitors were grinning ear to ear. As they stumbled through the drifts towards him they were actually shouting out loud – something no one out here had *ever* heard before. So startling was their shrill yells, echoing on the crisp, frozen air, that the corralled heifers snorted with fright, running helter skelter from corner to corner in total confusion.

Harry, Erich and Ellen came together half way between their baggage, left from the now rising Magnipod and Harry's veranda. With city shoed feet plowing up snow ahead of them, Erich and Ellen rushed to Harry, arms spread wide and roaring with laughter. Stumbling forward, each to a reunion they would never forget. Six arms and three heads came together, clutching and grabbing at each other. They frantically sought hugging and tear streaked, cheek rubbing space. Each knew that it was their miracle of survival that was the intense bond of a intensely loving companionship, one for the other. When the three pulled apart from lengthy embraces, they bore freezing tracks of tears all over their faces. Their reunion was unlike any other, anyone had ever experienced…it would *never* happen again – not in a *thousand* years!

Epilogue

The Hall Of Scientists Report"

THURSDAY APRIL 17- 3156 / 36TH CENTURY/
THE HAGUE, NEDERLAND –"

To THE HALL of Scientists to World Council Authority Chairman:In submission of the attached, the last of 22 reports of our findings of the time capsule sphere, herein referred to as Cygnus Cypsela, we hereby certify and summarize craft and personal examinations, discoveries and concerns, found in a 2 year 6 month research study of the aforementioned marine sphere for the edification of future conclusions of earth's future scientific assemblies. In the matter of World Council's assignment to assemble a scientific exploration group for the recovery and exploration of the object, first observed in 3132 at Lat 57°58' and Long 07°95' E, we declare the following to be an accurate report of findings and calculations between the years 3138 to 3151.

Technical data: "Full OD sphere diameter, 91.44 meters (300 ft) and beneath, an "abbreviated: cone projection to a pointed apex of 22.6 meters (74+ ft) deep. Curators and terra researchers at the Hall of Academic Sciences at Reykjavik are scheduling to commence laboratory examination of composition and possible access to contents within next 31 days. Associate metallurgists advise that the sphere's existing alloy composites, while difficult to decipher could include deeply embedded earth minerals. Early core samples of – sodium lithium boron silicate hydroxide, mined, circa 2060 as ekryptonite might even be among components of sphere surface metals. Such open mindedness, led attending metallurgists and structural engineers to conclude, that they must look backward to reconcile an exact finding as to origination. Further study of the object's solid 'steel' tether chain, concluded a 47/100 gauge common design link of ancient metal. This was utilized to anchor the sphere and cone an ocean floor. At its furthermost extension, sphere buoyancy enabled it to float six fathoms from surface at mean tide for the latitude. The tether extends from a fused coupling at the apex of the massive cone, under section, to anchor point. Remnants of one link of the chain was found to be less erosion proof than other links thereby ensuring a calculated release of the sphere, still dragging it's sea anchoring chain and programmed to emerge from the sea when it did. The whole chain assembly measured, 200 marine fathoms, (over 1200 ft.) in length.

As to the composite of metal of the cone, later tests identified the cone-shaped section, possibly a alloy meld of aluminum, platinum and titanium, once thought to be an impossible fusion. Many more years study would be required to speculate as to the sphere's exact structural age within the 22nd century.

Identity; Meaningless to scientific deduction, are the embossed graphics on the shell's outer surface and the same configuration in the anteroom floor of the capsules cone section.

Archival references still exist that might reveal actual meanings; the term "Liguria" rendered in hieroglyphic text and a relief symbolism of a swan's head over the body of a starfish is also a part of the ancient Greek myth that was chosen to symbolize this capsule's conception.

Cargo contents: An inventory with full particulars is attached at the conclusion of this file, detailing contents findings with particular emphasis to the preserved human remains and human organs therein. Of those 185 humans were taken from the Cypsela sphere, three living persons from the 21st century are still with us as at this date. In this regard and in the matter of sterility of the project quarters as it affects the rest of the world's population in this century, individual file folder reports are attached herewith. An independent investigation was conducted to resolve what was collectively believed to be the 'big picture' message derived from sphere's cargo exhibits. Simpler than first surmised, it became clear that their caveat dealt primarily with the matter of the preserving life and delaying human demise. Inventories with full particulars are attached.

From the nature of the Sphere's cargo exhibits, medical and engineering investigating groups were in agreement that the intent of the 21st century conceivers was clear. They provided a graphic display of not only the biophysical structure of humankind at and prior to that time, but a glimpse into the whys and wherefores of the life and death experience of the human species. In the matter of sterility of the sphere's interior; though a -68°C in sphere property and -196°C in the cone section it is hereby stipulated that a complete and thorough radiation sweep was performed of all surfaces, lockers, walls, floors, and cargo contents to be certain of non existence of bacteria of any description.

To culminate findings to date, we, the undersigned and over 240 assistant professional researchers and technical staff, created and conducted a series of think tanks that obligated attendees to:

1. Assess the physiology of mankind's aspirations to longevity;

2. Assign personnel to determine if there is a common belief that there is no all applicable rationale for every individual, as to what evolutionary or biogenetical purpose is served in response to the century's old question, "why are we here?

3. Determine a psychological study as to why death should be as distressing and painful to the mind as birth?"

4. Assess from the Sphere project the advisability of compassionate supplication of any medicinal formula to render the dying to a comatose state to provide a comfort environ for pre-death and palliative care patients?

FINDINGS ASSOCIATED WITH 'SPHERE PROJECT'

A gentler means of passing away despite the instinctive revulsion of departing human life can be less stressful. Animal kingdoms and countless historic aboriginal practices of tranquil death are comparable with the methods of freezing or drowning. Such alternatives can help to alleviate the cruelty and distress of an extended death experience. Individually stated preferences for a legal means to departure of life must always be left solely to the discretion of the individual with active participation of other close humans to the dying – professional or otherwise.

We have been given the opportunity to found a new beginning of human medical practice based on discoveries in assorted human remains aboard the time capsule, Cygnus Cypsela.

In the hope that these conclusions will supplement those provided heretofore and that the entire data will be submitted to the Cyber Selectronics Committee as input data for reference and hopefully the formation of future law ensures perpetuation of our species. In a celebration of the life and death experience on this planet,

Your obedient servants, dedicated to service and perpetuation of humankind.

Dr Anson Prentice..

Dr Mona Randall..

Dr Gordon McCullough......................................

Dr. Lloyd Verinmeyer.....................

Dated this day, the twenty eighth day of February, in the year, thirty one hundred and fifty three AD.

30

Printed in the United States
100724LV00003B/58-63/A